: THE COMPANIONS

Also by Sheri S. Tepper in Gollancz

Raising the Stones

A Plague of Angels

Beauty

Grass

Sideshow

Singer from the Sea

The Fresco

The Visitor

THE COMPANIONS

SHERI S. TEPPER

GOLLANCZ

LONDON

First published in Great Britain in 2004 by

Gollancz
An imprint of the Orion Publishing Group
Orion House, 5 Upper St Martin's Lane,
London WC2H 9EA

A CIP catalogue record for this book
is available from the British Library.

ISBN 0 575 07565 1 (cased)
ISBN 0 575 07566 X (trade paperback)

Printed in Great Britain by
Clays Ltd, St Ives plc

IN LOVING MEMORY OF KYBO, SKEETER,
TIBBY, BEANS, TIBESKIBO, SCHMUTZIE,
MOGUL, MELITZA, MUFFY, AND ALL THE
LEGION OF DEPARTED COMPANIONS,
AND WITH JOYOUS APPRECIATION OF
PUPUP AND LULABELLE, THE CURRENT
GLAD REVENANTS OF THE SPECIES

THE LITANY
OF ANIMALS

elemental, monumental, fine phantasmic elephants;
hairless hippopotami, huddled close as spoons;
riotous rhinoceri, roistering on grasslands;
tiny tender tarsiers, eyes like moons;

plump pied pandas, pretty as a picture;
gay, giggling gibbons, gamboling in the trees;
awl-nosed aardvarks, excavating anthills;
glowering gorillas lollygagging at their ease.

light on the leaf mold, feather-footed field mouse,
tiny as a hazelnut, the bloodthirsty shrew
off in the outback, wombat, numbat,
gone to have a meeting with kid kangaroo

bulky-shouldered bison, built like a bastion,
wily alligator, floating like a log
wolf in the wildlands, jackal in the jungle,
dutiful and diligent, man's friend, dog.

horrible hyenas, hairy noses quivering;
wildly running wildebeests, sometimes called the gnu,
laugh-provoking lemurs, loitering on tree limbs,
melancholy mandrill with his bottom painted blue

overbearing ostrich, fluttering his feathers
boulder-bounding ibex, helmed like a knight
curve-backed camel, king of the desert
prickly, stickly porcupine no animal will bite

big brown bruin bear, walking as a man does
toucan with a great tall trumpet for a nose
bald-headed vultures, vittling on vipers
(vultures will eat anything as everybody knows)

mad male orangutan, face like a soup bowl
curious xenopus, peculiarly made
quagga, quail, and quetzal, quaint concatenation.
solitary tiger, strolling in the shade

loudmouthed jackass, braying jeremiads;
bald-faced uakaris, kinky kinkajou;
high hairy travelers, yaks upon the mountain;
bringing up the rear with Zebra and Zebu.

: THE COMPANIONS

: The moss world, so said one XT-ploitation writer who had reviewed first-contact images of it, was a Victorian parlor of a planet, everywhere padded and bolstered, its cliffs hung with garlands, its crevasses softened with cushions, every cranny silk-woven, every surface napped into velvet. Here were peridot parklands where moss piled itself into caverned outcrops of sapphire shade. There were violet valleys, veiled in lavender and wine across a mat of minuscule, multicolored moss beads. In that clearing the morning light shone on infant parasols, ankle high, that by noon had sprung upward to become umbrellas, guyed with hair-thin fibers, ribs flung wide to hold featherlight sails that turned softly, softly through the afternoon, shading the sporelings beneath.

Along the canyons were fragrant forests where every footfall released scents that evoked aching nostalgia, as though racial memory held sensations undetected for centuries: Cedar perhaps? Sandalwood? Maybe piñon or frankincense? Maybe something older than any of those? The riversides were endless alleys cushioned in aquamarine and jade, hung with curtains that moved like the waves of a shifting ocean, hiding, then disclosing—so it was claimed—the flame-formed inhabitants of this place.

If, that is, the Exploration and Survey Corps really saw them. If the people from Planetary Protection Institute really saw them. After each sighting the men sought confirmation from their complicated devices and found no evidence of the beings they had perceived. The machines confirmed small grazing and burrowing creatures, yes; they confirmed tall, gaunt trees that served as scaffolding for the epiphytic fabric of the world, but these others . . . these wonders . . . Everyone described the same shapes, the same behaviors, the same colors. Formed like flames, endlessly dancing, an evanescent blaze in the morning, a shimmering shadow in the dusk. Rarely seen, unmistakable when seen, but never yet recorded . . .

"Along that ridge, shining, a whole line of them . . ."

"Right. I saw them. Like huge candles . . ."

What had they seen? That was undoubtedly the question.

A Garr'ugh shipclan of the Derac, a race nomadic by nature, had found Moss quite by accident when their clan-ship was sucked into an instability at one arm of the galaxy and spewed out in another. Subsequently, the exploration and survey of the three inner planets—the rock world, the jungle world, the moss world—were farmed out on shares to Earthian Enterprises. The Derac were accustomed to farming out work to Earthers. Humans prided themselves on their work— an emotion felt, so far as anyone knew, only by humans, as most other starfaring races considered "work" a sign of serfdom, which among them it invariably was. Earthers felt differently. They had their own Exploration and Survey Corps, ESC, and their own Planetary Protection Institute, PPI, a branch of the Interstellar Planetary Protection Alliance, of which Earth was a member. More importantly, Earthers were a settling type of people who seemed not to mind staying in one place as long as it took to do an adequate job of assessing new planets. Accordingly, Earth Enterprises, on behalf of PPI and ESC, was awarded a contract by the Derac to explore and survey, using, of course, the IPPA guidelines governing such activities on newly discovered worlds.

Accordingly they came. They saw. They were conquered.

Two-thirds of the planet's surface was taken up by the mosslands where the Earthers sought to answer IPPA's primary question: Did a native people exist? Time spun by, a silver web; they felt what they felt and saw what they saw, but they could not prove what they felt or saw was real. They thought, they felt there was a people, peoples upon Moss, but did a people really exist?

Did the men and women of PPI themselves exist? Their days on Moss went by like dreams passed in a chamber of the heart, a systole of morning wind, a throb of noon sun, an anticipatory pulsation of evening cool that was like the onset of apotheosis, a day gone by in a handful of heartbeats as they waited for something marvelous that would happen inevitably, if they were simply patient enough.

Patience wasn't enough. IPPA required specific information about newly discovered worlds. Was the ecology pristine or endangered? Were there intelligent inhabitants, and if there were, were they indigenous, immigrants, or conquerors? Did they occupy the entire planet?

Were they threatened? Did they consider themselves a part of or the owners of the world on which they lived? Were other races of intelligent creatures native to the world, or had any been imported or rendered extinct? If there were various views on these matters among the inhabitants, might they be amenable to referring the matters to IPPA for resolution? These questions had to be answered! These and a thousand more!

Moss could not be opened to habitation, trade, or visitation until it was certified by IPPA. Moss could not be certified by IPPA until the information was received. The information could not be received until the blanks in the forms were filled in, but the blanks in the forms remained exactly that.

How could one determine prior claims from creatures that fled like visions? Were they inhabitants? Possibly, though they were as likely to be events. Often, truly, they seemed to be hallucinogenic happenings, light and motion flung together by wind and imagination. Perhaps they were a new kind of creature: ecological animations! Such suggestions met with incomprehension back on Earth, where the carbon lifeform branch office of IPPA was located.

Where IPPA was all judgment, Earth's own ESC made no judgments at all. The only task of Exploration and Survey was to record everything, to take note of everything, to determine the history of everything and establish not only how one thing related to another, but also whether each thing fit into a category that would be meaningful to intelligent persons of various races. Though Exploration and Survey Corps was a subsidiary of Earth Enterprises, a purely human organization, operated for profit and without any interstellar governing body, the Corps had to interface with IPPA and therefore used IPPA categories and definitions for its reports.

There was no IPPA category for beautiful. Humans had several times suggested such a category to IPPA, but no other race had a similar concept. Beauty was not quantifiable, said IPPA. The Tharst recognized a quality they called Whomset. The Quondan spoke of the quality of M'Corb. Neither race could define these things, though they said they knew it when they encountered it. IPPA did not recognize things that couldn't be defined and measured by proprietary devices, mechanical, electronic, or biotech. For IPPA's purposes, human beings along with most other beings were biological devices that lacked standardization. No race with such sayings as "Beauty is in the eye of the beholder," or "There's no accounting for tastes," could pretend to define beauty in terms the various races would accept.

The lack of Beauty—as well, possibly, as the lack of Whomset or M'Corb—was crippling on Moss. How did one record odors that seemed to be presences? What was the meaning of these rioting colors: these flaming scarlets so joyous as to make the heart leap, these greyed purples so somber as to outmourn black? What was the relationship among these thousand tints and hues, pure, mixed, nacreous, opalescent, ever shifting? What profit was there in this giddy growth and incessant motion?

On Moss, the winds were sculptors, molding the stuff as it grew, weaving tasseled ropes into swaying ladders from high branch to high branch, shredding chiffon tissue into feathered fringes along bare boughs, sometimes puffing beneath a fragile carpet and lifting it to make a glowing gossamer tent between the sky and those who walked beneath. Such constructions were often ephemeral, no sooner seen with breath-caught wonder than they dissolved into a momentary aureole suffused with sun-shattered rays of amber, scarlet, and coral. Strictly speaking, moss did not flower, but on Moss it pretended to do so, in clamorous colors and shapes out of drugged fantasy.

As their separate purposes demanded, ESC and PPI approached their tasks differently. ESC lived behind force screens on a small island in a large lake, an island that had been ringed and roofed with force shields then cleaned down to the bedrock with flame and sterilants to protect the workers from any Mossian scintilla afloat in the atmosphere. On the island, the Earthers walked freely, but when they came ashore, they wore noncons, noncontact suits. They did not breathe the air or drink the water on the mainland, they did not put their skin against the skin of the world. They received reports from PPI, which they remeasured and requantified before filing, or, if measurement was impossible, which they filed under various disreputable categories such as "alleged," "professed," "asserted." With ESC, nothing was sensed directly; everything was measured by devices. It was said of ESC personnel that they were the next thing to hermits, monks, or robots, and it was true that Information Service selected persons who were loners by nature, content with silence.

PPI, on the other hand, had to experience a world to make judgments about it, and its people fell into Moss as into a scented bath, only infrequently coming up for air. Baffled by change, assaulted by sensation, each day confronting a new landscape, PPI people spent days at a time forgetting their purpose. The seasons were marked by shifts of color, by drifts of wind, by smells and shapes and a certain nostalgic tenderness that came and went, like a memory of lost delight. Time, on Moss, was a meaningless measurement of nothing much.

PPI was abetted in its lethargy. Exploration of the world Jungle, in this same system, had ended in a disaster dire enough to demonstrate that impatience might be a mistake. If one hurried things, one might end up as those poor PPI fellows had on Jungle, where both men and reputations had been lost and nothing had been discovered as compensation. PPI could not explain its failure. Back on Earth, those in command, who had no idea what a jungle world was like, or indeed what any primitive world was like, decided that PPI had been overeager, had pressed too far, too quickly. ESC, responsible for housing and protecting the team on Jungle, had allowed too much liberty, too quickly. Do not make this same mistake, they said, on Moss.

Obediently, ESC people on Moss considered, reconsidered, weighed, and reweighed, becoming more eremitic with each day that passed. Gratefully, PPI personnel on Moss added Authorized Dawdle to the snail-creep imposed by the planet itself. Dazedly they wandered and dreamed and fell into intimacy with the sounds and smells and visions of the place. Finally, after years of this, the Moss folk rewarded them all by emerging from the shadows onto the meadows along the shore, and dancing there in patterns of sequined flames. Every off-planet person on Moss saw them. Every recorder turned upon them recorded them. Every person saw the curved bodies of the Mossen, as they were subsequently dubbed, aflutter in a bonfire of motion, gliding and glittering in a constant murmur of musical babble that might have been speech. If they spoke.

Who knew if they spoke? Did they have powers of perception? Did they see their visitors? They showed no sign of it except when one man or another wanted a closer view and attempted to approach. As anyone crossed the invisible line, the Mossen vanished, floating upward in a spasm of light, the carpet of their dancing floor raised beneath them, veiling them from below. Moss itself was a wonder, a marvel beyond comprehension. The Mossen who inhabited it remained a mystery, an enigma that baffled understanding.

The ESC island was just offshore of the meadow where the Mossen danced. The compound of PPI lay on the shore beside that meadow. The compound contained a number of individual houses-cum-workstations gathered around the commissary hall, where meals were prepared and meetings held. The outsides of the buildings had been mossened with green and yellow, red and gray within a day of their erection, though the insides, inexplicably, remained unfestooned. The largest building served as a headquarters, and it was there that Duras Drom, the mission chief, sat at his console, sifting his records, searching for something, anything to help him out of his dilemma.

What he found only complicated it.

"When did this report from ESC come in, the one about the ships?"

His lieutenant gave him a thoughtful look as though from a distance of some miles. "What report?"

"Here," said Drom, pointing. "Earther ships, old ones, up on the nearest plateau."

The other man, Bar Lukha, rose and stumbled across the room and back, pausing briefly to look over Drom's shoulder. "Dunno. Haven't seen it. Sage must've entered it. There, let's see, what's today? Hmm. Looks like fourteen, fifteen days ago."

"They found ships! And nobody mentioned it!"

"As you said, old ones," said the other, dismissively. "Mossed all over. Nobody in them."

"They're *Hargess* ships!"

"Really? Hmmm. I suppose the Hargess Hessings might want to know about it."

"You suppose so, do you? Of course they'll want to know about it. Even families with enough money to send off whole fleets of ships on damned fool errands are interested in what happens to them!"

"Ah." Bar Lukha shook his head as he passed his dreaming gaze across his fellow as though scanning shadows. "They've written them off, long since. They've been lost up on that escarpment too long to be of concern. It's no wonder nobody saw them until recently. You really want to open things up . . ."

Drom cursed, quietly, thoughtfully. Though the persons who had traveled in those ships or had owned those ships, or their heirs, might have a reasonable claim to the planet itself, the process of exploration and categorization, inconclusive though it was, had advanced so far that no one would welcome a suggestion to start over. Such a suggestion would infuriate the Derac. And others.

He had no intention of suggesting it. He would simply forward the report. Let the higher-ups suggest whatever they wanted to. His soul told him this world should be left to the creatures who occupied it, but he could find no hard evidence of intelligent life. He had only one concrete fact to use as a bar against this planet being opened up, visited, utilized, colonized, destroyed, but he did not wish to mention that one thing.

Still, despite all the earlier protestations of patience, Exploration and Survey Corps was growing itchy. Taking time was one thing, they said. Taking forever was another. ESC didn't get paid until something definitive happened. Several days ago Earth Enterprises had demanded a report, a preliminary judgment, a few words to indicate what was going on. Either that, or they'd pull their people out, contract or no contract.

This directive in hand, Drom had gone to his mirror to consult with himself, there being no one else of appropriate status left to consult. His consciousness hovered between two sets of identically accusatory eyes, himself glaring at himself reflected; himself, head of station; accountable to no one but himself; knowing himself to have willingly succumbed to the delirium of Moss, to have repeatedly indulged himself and, yes, others, in behavior that PPI HQ would consider . . . no! That he himself considered improper.

The only remedy for this infraction was to stay out of the forest, to confine himself to quarters. The PPI team could not possibly decide anything sensibly when too many people in it, including Drom himself, were consistently guilty of delight, guilty of spending seasons at a time lying half-buried in mossy softness, frittering away years while smelling joy in the air as though each moment were eternal!

Oh, yes. PPI had disported itself, at least those given to disporting had done so, and when certain puritans among them had questioned this nonchalance toward duty, Drom himself had allowed it to go on. Hadn't he commanded and hadn't they served as the PPI team on Jungle, twelve years ago, when eleven of their fellows had vanished into that overgrown weed patch leaving no sign, no signal, no nothing to mark where they had gone or what had taken them? Hadn't they had nightmares afterward, as though from a lasting poison that affected only the sleeping mind? Hadn't they gone directly from the Jungle to Stone, where they'd been daily dust-dazzled, sun-staggered, half-melted by the heat? On Stone, even PPI personnel could not touch the surface or allow the surface to touch them, but it was a great-grandmother lode of rare ores, the most profitable new world found in a century. Still, living things had been found in stranger environments, and years had spun by in baking chaos and a madness of mining machines, while PPI went through the motions of searching for indigenous life so that no one, no people could accuse them of slacking their duty.

After all that, didn't they have some pleasure coming, some relaxation? He had thought so, said so, though what they had earned and what was appropriate were two different things. The truth was they would not be allowed to remain on Moss no matter what they reported or found or believed. Those who didn't die here would be sent somewhere else quite shortly. Where that place might be and how well or badly they would live there could depend significantly on the overall profit or loss coming from these three planets. Profit or loss, defeat or victory, fines or bonus pay hinged upon what was found here, in this system. Jungle had been a total loss; Stone a bonanza; and Moss was an enigma. Finding an intelligent race on this planet, or, if there was none, being able to say so definitively would make the planet bankable. It would put them on the high plus side, the very high plus side. Everyone knew that, but even now, after all this time on Moss, that basic question remained unanswered. Until it was answered, what was the place good for?

Nothing that made money. Retirement, perhaps. Several of the PPI people originally assigned to Moss had been old-timers. They had communicated with colleagues near retirement, and some of the oldsters had arrived, "assigned to temporary duty," and they had been followed by others yet. The installation had been enlarged, at first, to house additional personnel, though no additions had been needed recently. The PPI contingent roll was three or four times longer than the rolls of those surveying any other known world. Of course, the rolls were only paper. The people, bodily, were seldom to be found.

Was there an intelligent race on Moss?

". . . if the flame folk are intelligent, there's a bonus," he said, dreaming into the silence of the room.

"I know," said the young lieutenant from his seat before a bank of monitors. "That's what the ESC expert said. If they're intelligent, we profit."

"An intelligent race is a market," Drom mused. "And a new market is worth money, once you find out what it wants and needs."

Bar Lukha considered this through long moments of silence, saying at last, "But the Mossen don't need anything."

"How do we know?" Drom asked. "The Mossen don't talk. They don't do anything but dance."

"Right." The word drawled out, spinning itself into something more than mere agreement. Into connivance. Into complicity.

Drom said desperately, "Even if they're people, if they don't talk or interact in some way, we can't establish intelligence. If there's no intelligence, we have to leave and let the real estate guys take over."

Lukha kept his eyes fixed on his monitors, which were dancing for no reason. He had not been able to find out what was happening. For days now, the monitors had been dancing to sounds he couldn't hear, electromagnetic activity he couldn't locate. He had finally decided the dials were doing it because they liked it, because it was more fun than standing still.

"We'd stay if they—you know, them. If they wanted emergence," he remarked, in a preoccupied voice.

"If they wanted emergence, yes." More than anything, Drom wanted to stay here, to do what he had spent years doing before he had sentenced himself to confinement: take off his clothes, wander off into the mosses, eat the sweet bulbs of dew that formed on the stems of the blue, lie deep in the scent of the violet, thrust himself against the velvet of the scarlet, feeling his skin prickle and burn and then flare in ecstasy that went on for a seeming eternity. Maybe ask one of the women if she'd like to do the scarlet with him. Oh, yes, he wanted to stay here.

"Maybe the flame folk want to meet other people," murmured Lukha.

"Prove it," challenged Drom.

"Well, they don't talk to us. Maybe they write." Bar Lukha hummed to himself. "Maybe . . . we've found a message they left us."

Drom looked up in disbelief. The flame people of Moss didn't even acknowledge that men were there! How in heaven's name would they send any kind of... message. "It's a mystery to me how they'd do that!"

"Mystery... is the message," Lukha went on, as though entranced. "I think it was on a piece of that flat, gray moss that wraps around the trees. I think they wrote with some of the red juice of those berry kind of things."

His voice was intent, speaking of something he had obviously thought about, wondered about: the enigmatic Mossen leaving a message.

Drom considered the idea of a message. Would it be in the Earth language?

"In Earth-tongue," Lukha answered the unspoken question, half-singing it. "Oh, yes. They wrote it in our language and left it where I would find it. I read their message. It said, they wanted to meet other people. From beyond the stars."

"How did they learn our language?" Drom whispered, not wanting to break the spell.

"Listening to us, Chief. Listening to us. Reading our bulletin board. Looking at our papers..."

"And they want to meet other people, from beyond the stars."

"That's what the message said. The message I read."

"Where is it, Lieutenant. This message."

Now Lukha was, in fact, crooning the words. "I'll look for it, Chief. I had it. I know I put it somewhere..."

"We'd need a linguist," breathed Drom. "I'll ask them for a linguist." And also, he told himself, he would ask them for a team to look at those abandoned ships. Since they were Hargess ships, they'd have to send someone. And meantime, he really would stay out of the mosses.

THE LINGUIST'S SISTER: JEWEL DELIS

: Eventually, the Planetary Protection Institute mission on Garr'ugh 290 requested a linguist. The matter was referred to someone in Exploration and Survey Corps who attempted to link Paul Delis, my half brother. At the time, Paul was deeply involved in quite another activity: a session of manic and escalating eroticism that had driven me to take refuge behind the locked door of my room, where I sat stewing, my annoyance not at all ameliorated by familial affection. Affection for Paul, familial or otherwise, had been eroding for years.

Prior experience with similar situations suggested that Paul would soon propose to his concs, Poppy, Marigold, Salvia, and Lavender, that it would be fun to get sister Jewel involved in their games. Foreseeing this, I'd done what I could to minimize damage by putting away everything breakable during a temporary lull the night before. I'd packed an overnight bag and readied my street robe and veil by the door. An hour ago, I'd linked Shiela Alred to say that I'd be coming over to the sanctuary as soon as I could escape unnoticed.

Shiela had said a few pointed words about people who made the same mistake a lot more than twice, which I chose to ignore. My boss, not Shiela, my real boss, Gainor Brandt, had asked me to continue living with Paul if I could bear it. Thus far I had found it bearable, barely. When Paul was working, as he usually was, he was civil, if arrogant, and living with him gave me a lot more breathing room than any space I could have afforded on my own. It was only during these libidinous fits of his that he took all four of the concs out of their cases, overdosed them and himself on moodsprays, and mindlessly metamorphosed into an idiot satyr, ecstatically disregarding the wreckage he was causing. Each time it happened, I prayed that someone, somewhere, would be in such desperate need of a linguist they'd overlook Paul's extortionate fees and hire him for a long, long-term project off planet. This time it hadn't happened, but the blind hope had persuaded me to overstay a sensible departure time. Now noises offstage indicated the culminating incident was imminent.

"Jooo-ell," came a happy little voice through the door. "Come out, Jooo-ell." This was followed by a wild giggle, then a crash, then another voice, "Jooo-ell-ee. Pow-ie wans you in on the funzies. Jooo-ell-ee."

Concs were a familiar sight on the podways, but none I had seen elsewhere talked like willful children. Concs had limited vocabularies, true, and their voices were quite high, but they were not prattling and manic in the way Paul's concs inevitably were. I could only suppose that concs, who were said to be infinitely adaptable, had responded to Paul's preference for feral childishness that could in an instant become dangerous. Now, though the wee conc voices were still nonthreatening, I knew the next step would be an assault on my door in which the concs would join wholeheartedly. Not that they had hearts. On several such occasions I'd had to call security to get me out of the apartment intact. Each time Paul had regarded this as an act of "disloyalty," which he wasn't quick to forgive.

"Jooo-ell," Lavender cried again. "Tum tum ow-oot wif us."

Reason would do no good, so I resorted to duplicity. With my robe on and veil over my head, I tapped my link into ready, and spoke the code for Paul's library, his "work" room, at the far end of our apartment. He never let a call to that link go unanswered, even when, as in this case, he had trouble remembering where it was. The summoner screeched insistently over the pattering of androgynous little feet accompanying the arrhythmic thuds of Paul caroming from wall to wall.

When he answered, I would pretend the call was from some VIP and ask him to hold. While he did so, I'd get out through the service door by the food service core.

I put the link to my ear and heard his strangled bellow: "Wha... Paw... Paul Delis here..."

It took a moment to realize I'd heard it through the door, not through the link. Someone else had reached him first. I didn't wait to find out who before grabbing my bag and scooting down the hall in the opposite direction, wondering why I hadn't left two days ago while things were still relatively sane. It was probably mere stubbornness on my part. In a thirteen-mile-square urb with over a billion people in it, one didn't give up one's living space without a fight.

Outside the apartment, I followed the flow arrows of the hallway traffic lane to "Local 53," my transport hub, one of the sixty-four locals on my floor. There I joined a clutch of other anonymous robes and veils in boarding the lift, one at a time, each one of us taking position inside the painted grid that divided the floor into person-sized squares. Though out-planet visitors claim to find our separation conventions strange, all our robes and veils, our painted grids, our flow arrows, and the section marks on moving walkways are what keep us sane in public areas. They are more than mere customs. They're the walls between survival and chaos.

The lift dropped four floors to the 141st floor, which is the mercantile floor of my Tier, a Tier being ten floors: eight residential floors above one park floor and one mercantile floor that also serves as a transport center. From near the lifts, I boarded Intersection-Diagonal NW, which took me to the nearest sector hub, where I switched to a sector-diagonal and got off at NE Quadrant hub. Since my ultimate destination was above the 200th floor, I boarded the quadrant express lift to the NE Quadrant Transport Area on the 200th floor and took the Quadrant-Diagonal NE to the pod lobby at the corner of Tower 29. The sanctuary was in Tower 69, four towers east, and I caught a pod moving in that direction.

Telling it makes it sound complicated, but the trip was habitual and quick. I paid as little attention as possible to my surroundings, seeing only what was necessary, keeping arms and hands close to my body, staying in the middle of my square on the walkways, in the middle of my seat on the pod, my head tilted forward and my veil down so as not to offend by appearing to stare at anyone. In the years before grids were established, before all citizens started wearing robes and veils, staring, bumping, and shoving had been the rule, along with a good deal of retaliatory rage. Back then, the annual death toll from gang assaults and crowd rage had been over a million in this urb alone. After tests in a few urbs proved that anonymity worked, rage had been forestalled by edict. No more affiliation buttons; no more gang colors; no more tower or sector IDs. Good citizens wore veils and robes with no distinguishing marks; they kept their heads down, their hands folded, and pretended they were all alone in the world.

Once in Tower 69, I pulled off the veil in the private express lift to the sanctuary on Floor 259. My putative fund-raising office was there, as was the little suite I used when I was working late or avoiding Paul.

Eventually, he'd exhaust himself, and I would go home again to be greeted with sneers and resentment, as though failing to join in his games was some sort of familial impropriety. I'd learned to ignore that stage of things. It would eventually pass, just as each of his concs eventually passed, to be mysteriously replaced by another. I never knew where he found them, though on occasions I had asked some superficially innocent question such as, "What happened to Vanilla? I haven't seen it . . ."

"Her," he corrected.

". . . her around for some time."

"I got tired of her."

"What did you do with her."

"Got a new one."

Eventually, he always got tired of them, or misused them, or destroyed them. Though concs were reputed to be excellent sensual partners for men or women or any combination of them, Paul was never contented with mere excellence. He always pushed the limits toward meltdown and obliteration. Afterward, his easiest out was to blame the concs or blame me. I often thought Paul valued me more for my role as scapegoat than he did for any reason of kinship.

The lift doors opened on a floating cloud of violet draperies and improbable hair: Shiela Alred in her usual monochromatic flurry. She tilted her lavender coif, grabbed both my hands in hers, and looked up at me as she cried in a panicky voice: "You've heard the news then, Jewel?"

Shiela usually sailed along on a sea of aristocratic aplomb, but today her voice rasped and her hands gripped mine like talons.

"No, Shiela, I've been . . . sort of closeted today."

"Dreadful, my dear, dreadful. Those hateful IGI-HFO people! I've been on the link all morning, helping various of our friends plan what to do next. So stupid, this whole thing. It makes me so furious!"

Red spots burned on her cheeks. The flesh around her eyes was wet and swollen. My mouth went dry. I asked, "What have the iggy-huffos done now, Shiela?"

She had to clear her throat before she could get it out. "The final straw, really. In thirty days, all sanctuaries are to be closed. Cleaned out, is the way they put it. My God, if it weren't for the arkers, we'd have no hope at all!"

"Thirty days?" I felt I was choking. The walls tilted nauseatingly. I managed to gargle, "Only thirty days?"

"That terrible man, you know, the head of IGI-HFO? Evil One Moore!"

It was her usual joke. "Evolun Moore, yes."

"He threatens riots among the down-dwellers unless Worldkeeper puts a final end to all animal life on Earth." She laughed half-hysterically. "According to Moore, animals use too much water and air. Naturally, he says nothing about the billions of concs living wherever they like, using up a lot more of everything than animals do."

I managed to ask, "Who made the announcement?"

"Evil One himself, of course. Though Worldkeeper immediately verified it, speaking for who knows what anonymous bureaucrats! Claiming it's only a temporary measure! Only until the death rate increases, they say. Only until ET colonies stop sending people back here by the millions under the Law of Return . . ."

I snarled, "Only until all the dogs, cats, and canary birds are dead and the down-dwellers find they don't have any more space, air, or water than they have right now."

"It'll be too late then." Shiela took my arm and tugged me toward the security checkpoint at the sanctuary door. "I've already called Gainor Brandt. He says he's negotiating an extension on enforcement of the edict on the grounds that our research is vital to planetary security."

Gainor Brandt's public job was as the general manager of Earth Enterprises, which meant he also controlled the Exploration and Survey Corps. Covertly, he was one of the mainstays of the preservationist movement, the "arkists," small letters, no emphasis, hush, don't mention it.

Shiela babbled on. "I've also spoken with arkist headquarters. They have some arks ready . . . well not totally, but they will support life. Oh, Jewel! Have I ever said what a saint you are to us! Living with Paul must be quite *horrid*, but we would never have had so many arks if you hadn't been with him here and there . . ."

I laughed, not because it was funny. "Well I'm not there, Shiela."

"I presume he's on one of his conc orgies?"

"Oh my, yes."

"Does he know you're gone?"

"I'm the last thing he's thinking of."

"Can I offer you some supper? You look just as hungry as you do tired."

Since I'd had limited access to the food service core for the last couple of days, I told her I'd love some supper.

She babbled on: "When you linked, my dear, I thought you might be coming because you'd heard the bad news. Just as you did the first time we met. It was old Evil One back then, too, wasn't it. Terrible man. His face on the news screens, baying like some great, prehistoric . . . crocodile! Ten years ago?"

I suppressed a grimace. "Nearer twelve, Shiela."

"You're right. Of course! It was 2700, the year we started the sanctuary. You were only, what? Eighteen? Dear Witt brought you. I remember your face was all swollen from crying, you'd gotten to Jon Point just in time to keep him from . . ."

She was headed down a painful road that I refused to travel just then. "I'll just go put these things away, Shiela."

"Oh, of course dear, you do that. Go settle in. I'll let you know when to come down for supper."

Shiela fluttered off toward her private lift to her residence on the floor below. She had cued a painful spasm of reminiscence, though by now the memory was so worn around the edges that it didn't stop my breathing as it used to do. The memories seemed more like a part I'd played, a role I'd put on like a garment rather than an event I'd lived through as a person. Most days it was hard to believe I could ever have been as stupid as I had been at eighteen.

The sanctuary residential suites were in the opposite direction from the one Shiela had gone, and the hallway was as blessedly quiet as the caverns of Mars I remembered from childhood. Even the full quota of staff and visitors never filled it, much less crowded it, and the space made me feel as though I expanded, like a warmed balloon, slowly pressing out into the light and air.

In my suite—a bedroom, bath, and small sitting room—I shelved the few items I'd brought then washed my hands and face. Matty, my mother, had always insisted I wash up whenever I came into private space. "People in masses are poisonous," she used to say, her serious tone belied by the sparkle in her eyes. "Whenever we come into private space, we should wash them off."

"I don't see anything, Mama."

"It's invisible effluvium," Matty told me. "The sorrows and anxieties of too many people."

Back then, I'd been sure I could see the sorrows dissolving in the water, washing down the drain. The sorrows were part of a Mars song Matty used to sing:

"Our coats are thin as mist, our heels are horn,
beneath our eyes old sorrows build their nest . . ."

When she became too weak to hold a mirror, Matty asked me to hold it for her, so she could make sure there were no sorrow nests under her eyes.

"We here kept faith alive, but all the rest,
the wisest and the bravest we have borne,
left faith behind to go out, seeking splendor . . ."

"Who did, Matty?" I asked her. "Who went off seeking splendor? What is splendor?"

"No one knows," she said. "No one knows who stayed and who went, or where. The Zhaar, maybe, but they didn't leave the directions behind . . ."

I didn't know Matty was famous until years after she died. I knew she made pictures and music about the weird stony places on Mars. My father was Victor Delis, the Earthian ambassador to Mars. Paul was his son by his first wife, a very rich, spoiled, willful woman who killed herself doing something that every sane person in the vicinity had told her not to. Paul inherited most of her money because, so my mother said, he was just like her.

After Victor died, Matty got together with a childhood friend, the artist, Joram Bonner III. Paul would never call Joram "Father," of course, any more than he would call Matty "Mother." He called her Matty, so I got in the habit of doing that, too, except when I was alone with her and baby Tad. Tad came along when I was two and Paul was four, Taddeus Joram Bonner, Joram Bonner IV.

Right around my sixth birthday Matty got sick. Nobody on Mars could help her, so Joram brought us all back to Earth. While the doctors tried to cure Matty, Joram found us a place to live on Floor 145, Tower 29 in Northwest Urb 15, the same apartment Paul and I were still "sharing." Joram said it was a prestige location because it had windows, even though there was nothing to see except the tower across the street. It wasn't a street, really. It was more like a chasm, the bottom of it stuffed with roaring stacks of dark, dirty freight tunnels and catacombs where the down-dwellers live.

Earth scared me at first. The towers were huge, each a mile square and more than two hundred stories high. Podways ran along every tenth floor, north on the east side of each tower and south on the west side. Up one level, they went west on the north side and east on the south side. They stopped at the pod lobbies on each corner, so when you were on one, it went *woahmp-clatter, rhmmm, woahmp-clatter, whoosh.* That's a pod-lobby stop, a slow trip across the street, another pod-lobby stop, then a mile long *whoosh,* very fast. The pod-lobbies were full of people, too, and that's the clatter part, the scary part. Taddeus and I saw more people in one pod-lobby than we'd ever seen together anywhere on Mars, and many of them were dressed in fight colors: Tower 59 against Tower 58, Sector 12 against Sector 13, all of them pushing and shoving and tripping over each other. Often they got into fights or screaming fits. It took us a while to figure out how to dodge them and keep out of their way, but when we got good at it, it turned into a kind of game, and we rode the podways for fun. It was a lot safer than it sounds, because there are so many monitors on the pods that people are afraid to do anything really wicked unless they're over the edge. Tad and I thought part of the fun was spotting people that were about to go over the edge. We could almost always tell.

Paul and Taddeus and I started school at the Tower Academy while we were waiting for Matty to get better. Matty would improve, then she'd relapse, then she'd improve. The disease attacked her nerves, so she was in dreadful pain, and finally it got into her muscles so she couldn't move. After that, she didn't improve anymore. She got weaker and weaker and finally just faded away and died. Joram and I were with her. Joram said Taddeus was too young for a deathwatch, and Paul said she was no kin of his, not that it made any difference. If she'd been kin, he'd probably have acted the same way.

After Matty died, things got complicated. Paul was ten, and he refused to go back to Mars, and Paul always did exactly what he wanted to do, no matter what anyone said. Since he had lots of money from his mother, and I had some from my father, we each had what's called an NCC, a noncoparenting certificate, which meant we didn't have to have coparents under Earth law so long as Joram arranged for us to be properly cared for. Taddeus hadn't inherited any money, and Joram was his only living parent, so he needed a coparent.

Joram was a vista preservation artist, and Earth had no vistas left to preserve. Joram's grandfather had scanned the last few: Antarctica before it thawed; Ayers Rock before they broke it up; the pyramids, just before they tore them down for landfill. Joram couldn't do his work if he stayed on Earth to parent us, so he decided to make a liaison contract among himself, us three kids, and a Licensed Child Custodian named Luth Fannett LCC. Both my trust fund and Paul's paid something in every year, and Joram sent money for Taddeus, so while Joram was off God-knows-where, we three kids and Luth lived in the apartment with the prestige windows we couldn't see anything out of.

Even at ten, Paul was very proud. He was proud of his mind and of the way he could learn languages so easily and proud of being a Delis and proud of having his mother's money. When he was twelve, Paul told me that Victor Delis had begotten me on purpose so I could be Paul's assistant when we grew up. "Because you'll be smart enough to help me but not smart enough to do anything significant on your own."

I don't know where Paul got that idea. He was only three when our father was killed, and people don't remember things that far back. Besides, I don't think Victor Delis would have said any such thing. He was an ambassador, and they're supposed to be tactful. Paul certainly wasn't tactful. He was just plain nasty a lot of the time, which is why Tad and I spent a lot of time on the podways.

Podfare was almost nothing. We could ride all week on our allowance of pocket money. We'd go across the urb and back again. Sometimes we'd go up to the 200th floor and take express pods that went outside the urb. We'd watch people and make up stories about them and eat pod-lobby food like sizzlejuice and crunch-a-muncheese. One particular day when I was off school, Paul started the morning making me miserable. Tad wasn't home. I couldn't lock myself in my own room because Luth wouldn't let me have a lock. So I just left and went pod-hopping by myself. I found a corner seat on a multipod and rode it back and forth, watching people. That was before people wore veils, so you could really look at people so long as you didn't stare. After a while, I switched podways and rode the expresses, and finally I depodded at a funny-looking tower I'd already passed half a dozen times, trying to decide whether to cross the street to go north or up one floor to go west, and I noticed the glass doors leading into the park floor of the tower.

Every floor ending in a 0 is a park floor, but these doors didn't look like ordinary park floor doors. They were painted all over with tall red letters: DERELICT. DANGER. DO NOT ENTER. I put my nose against the glass, my hands shadowing my eyes. Nothing out there! Except that nothing was something, so far as I was concerned! Space. Real space. Without people in it!

I edged to the crack in the door, where it was chained almost shut, but not so tight I couldn't squeeze through. Right inside, staring into my face, were a pair of strange eyes. I glanced around to see if anyone was watching me, but everybody had already gone up or down or across to connect with another podway, so I pushed the door as far as it would go and scrunched through. No one bigger than I was could have done it; only someone like me, as Paul said, all bones.

Inside, when my eyes got used to the darkness, I saw the creature of the eyes staring at me, so I went toward it. It backed up, and I followed it. It was moving through the dark toward a faint light at the center of the floor. The walls were all crumbled into piles of trash with hairy bits of wiring sticking out, like disintegrating monsters. Broken pipes were hanging from the collapsing ceiling, and way off at the edges of the floor, daylight leaked in where the outside walls had fallen.

The creature was still ahead of me, a darker shadow against the inside walls where the core services had been. It slipped through an open door and into a lighted space, then turned to look at me. Once I'd seen it in the light, I knew what it was, even though I'd never really seen a live one, because Matty had talked about them, over and over, and she'd found the remains of them on Mars, and she'd had one when she was little and I'd had one, a stuffed one, when I was just a baby. It was a Faithful Dog, just like the pictures she'd shown me only bigger. It stepped into a kind of basket thing and nosed around, and when I got close I saw the basket was full of little ones. Seven squirmy, fat sausages with their eyes shut. When the big dog lay down, the little ones started sucking on her, and I made the connection. Those were her mammaries. Like breasts, so she was kind of my cousin, because I was a mammal, too.

I crouched down by the basket and stroked the puppies while they were eating. It was a feeling . . . I'd never had that feeling before. They were warm and soft. Their mother was watching me, her eyes told me to be careful, but she didn't mind if I touched them. She was a man-friend, and I was trying to remember anything I'd ever heard about man-friends in the "Litany of Animals" that Matty taught me and the pictures I'd seen in baby books with animal alphabets, from aardvarks to zebras. *D* was always Dog. In olden times men had dogs as pets, friends, companions, workers, too, I guess. They pulled wagons and herded sheep and all sorts of things. Oh, yes, they'd been eyes for blind people, too, before we could put artificial or cloned eyes in, but mostly they'd been cures for loneliness. All this was bubbling up in my mind while a feeling was rising up my arm like warm honey: softness, friendliness, someone saying, "Hello, other thing." I was the other thing, and this one needed me . . .

Then, from behind me, I heard a surprised grunt, and someone said, "What the bloomin' oompah're you doin' here?"

He was a big old man with a whitish beard and woolly eyebrows. His face was full of lines, and his hands and fingers were thick and bumpy. I could see them very well because he had hold of me by the arms and was sort of shaking me, not to hurt, just as though he wondered what kind of thing I was. I told him my name.

"Jewel Delis! Now, isn't that somethin'. You any relation to that Ambassador Delis got killed on Mars?"

I said he was my father.

"Poor man. Wrong place at wrong time, so they say. So what's Delis's daughter doing here all alone midst all this ruin an' wreckage, droppin' in on Jon Point and his dogs?"

I said, "I've never seen a real one before."

"Don't have dogs on Mars?"

"No, sir. There's not enough air or water for anything except necessities. 'Hydroponics first, people second, and there is no third.' That's what they say."

He laughed about that, and he offered me some algae crackers, not the good kind but the light green ones that taste funny. I still took one, to be polite. We talked, and he showed me his dogs, and I stayed there most of the day. When I got home, Luth was furious with me until I told her Paul had started in on me, so I'd been pod-hopping. She knew Paul as well as I did, and she didn't blame me. Besides, all sorts of people pod-hopped, and nobody would hurt you because everybody was identichipped, and nobody could get away with really hurting anybody without being stun-gunned by the automatic monitors.

I didn't tell Luth about Jon Point or the dogs. I didn't tell Paul, either. From then on, I had two families. I had Paul and Luth and Tad on the 145th floor of Tower 29 and I had Jon Point and several kinds of dogs on the 10th floor of Tower 91. The first family was the one I lived with, but—except for Tad—the other family was the one I cared most about. The dogs needed me. They really did because Jon Point's wife had died, his son had gone off planet, and Jon claimed to be "A vastly overburdened man." If I wasn't there to help give them food and water, if I didn't come to clean their space . . . they might not be able to live at all.

That happened when I was eight. It seemed like my whole life had been aimed at that minute, like I was an arrow flying straight at it. From that time on, I spent every spare minute at Jon Point's kennel. He'd pirated some water and electric lines in the old tower, hiding them so the weirdos wouldn't find them. He said the weirdos scattered themselves through derelict towers like soy-nuts in breakfast food, mostly in the first three or four floors. The lifts didn't work anymore, and climbing higher than that was work. Jon had friends who bred cats, and some who bred birds. *Breeder* was a word like *down-dweller*, not a nice thing to call anybody. Breeding of animals wasn't allowed in regular towers. That's why breeders camped out in towers that were scheduled for demolition. Out of the hundred towers in each urb, there are usually one or two of the oldest ones waiting to be rebuilt.

Jon sold the bigger dogs to wealthy people who had exempt estates with room for dogs to run and act like dogs. The little furry, cute ones, he sold as pets to people living in towers. It's hard to imagine being lonesome in a tower that has ten million people in it, in an urb that has a billion or more, but lots of the apartments were just two hundred square feet, for one person, and if you couldn't have a little dog . . . well, people have concs now, of course, but back then, nobody had ever seen a conc.

The first one I saw was in a pod lobby. Even though it was sort of human-looking, anyone would know right away it wasn't human. It was pale yellow, with silver hair. It didn't look male or female, sort of in between, but it was curvy and had a pretty face and it was graceful-looking, wearing just enough clothes not to be bare. After that, I saw a few here and there; then, all of a sudden, everywhere, different colors of skin and hair, different ways of smiling or laughing, all sounding much alike, little kids' voices using very few words.

It wasn't long before the information network started to do stories on them. They were "companions," or that's what the news stories said, even though everybody called them concs, for concubines. Only a few weeks later Paul came home from his school with a mop-headed, big-eyed, mostly naked, reddish brown thing. I saw it by the door, smiling and murmuring to itself.

I half wanted to laugh and half wanted to get mad, and I said, "Paul, that's a conc!"

"I know," he said in his way-up-there, superior voice. (Matty said Paul had acquired loftiness with his mother's milk, not that his mother ever nursed him.) "But it's only a little one, and it followed me home. It's name is Cinnamon, and I'm going to keep it."

Taddeus was standing right behind me. He said, "You're not old enough. Jewel, he's only twelve, he's not old enough, is he?"

I saw the flicker in Paul's eyes, like a hot, barely controlled flame, and I thought of Paul being amused by a concubine as compared to Paul getting his amusement elsewhere, usually from bullying Tad or me, so I said, "If he wants it, and he promises to take care of it, I think he should keep it."

When I told Luth, about it, I could tell she was thinking the same things I had. It didn't take her long to say yes, let it stay.

When I was twelve, Jon Point introduced me to a boy named Witt Hessing. Witt was one of *The* Hessings, and he came to buy two shepherd pups, Quick and Busy. He needed to know how to care for them and train them, and by that time I was very good at both those things, so Jon registered a contract between Witt and me so I could get paid for helping him. The Hessing place was outside the urb, a hundred-acre exempt estate with grass and trees and gardens. For a while I went over there every day, and Witt and I got to be friends. When he paid me for helping him train the dogs, he kissed me, just on the cheek, and I was so flustered I missed my stop at home tower.

Nobody had kissed me since Matty died. There isn't supposed to be any kissing except between liaised people, people with a contract. You don't dare be involved with anyone without a contract that says who you are and what your intentions are and what the outcome is to be. That's why Jon recorded a liaison contract between Witt and me.

Anyhow, that was the only time. Witt and I stayed friends, and we spent time in each other's company. Once I was old enough that they couldn't stop me, I told Paul and Tad I was doing volunteer work at an animal shelter. Paul was his usual nasty self about it, but I did it anyway. I had a few friends at the Tower Educational Center, but I spent most of my time at Jon's and with people he knew. I learned a lot, and mostly, I was . . . contented, I guess, until Witt got to be twenty-two and I turned eighteen, and that's when everything started to veer off in strange directions.

Paul broke the news first thing in the morning before I was fully awake. Paul knew it would make me crazy, hearing about it, so he stared at me while he told me, ready to enjoy the show. Somehow, I managed to keep my voice calm and my eyes dry as I said, "When did you hear this, Paul."

"It was on the info-net, this morning, early." He posed, repeating the item for effect: "Evolun Moore announced Worldkeeper's decision forbidding animals or birds in residential towers. They use up too much water, too much air."

I swallowed. "What about exempt estates?"

He sniffed. "Oh, the rich can keep their useless luxuries, of course. But in thirty days, no more furry little rats in the lifts." And he turned away, disappointed because I hadn't screamed or had a tantrum or simply broken down in tears. I did all that, though silently, after I was in my room with the door shut, getting ready to go to the kennel. I knew Jon Point very well: He was a man given to frequent despair and when he despaired, he acted foolishly. I had to get there as fast as possible.

By the time I got to Tower 91, my eyes were swollen half-shut, and I was standing so tight against the pod doors that I almost fell into the pod lobby when they opened. The tower doors were still crisscrossed with warning signs, but I'd long since broken the locks and memorized the trail. I could run the whole way without even noticing the surroundings.

Everyone knew that Moore, as head of IGI-HFO (which means "In

God's Image—Humans First and Only,") had been stirring up the down-dwellers. He had founded the group as a religious order, preaching in pod lobbies that animals had no right to exist anywhere on Earth—or on any other human occupied planet—because all space, air, water was needed for the one creature made in God's image. Moore was handsome, he seemed to have lots of funding from somewhere, and he was a marvelous speaker. Even people who hated him as I did could get caught up in the rhythm and thunder of his speeches, so you can imagine how easily the down-dwellers were stirred into a frenzy. Down-dwellers were always dissatisfied with life, even without an agitator, so having their anger gravel shoved over the edge was guaranteed to start an avalanche.

Despite all that, I hadn't believed anyone could want to kill pets. Now I had to believe it, and all I could think about was getting to the kennel before Jon got there and did something irreparable.

Adults aren't supposed to run. Running isn't acceptable. People can be injured by runners. Never mind all that; I ran anyway, conscious of being dangerously out of control. I felt as though I were falling forward onto air, as if my feet couldn't keep up with the rest of me. I'd always had dreams like that, running like crazy with nothing under my feet while I tried to escape the awful unseen behind me. In each dream, I knew flying was the only way to escape, but I also knew if I flew, I'd fall. The thing behind me got closer, pushing me higher and higher, to a height where the fall would be more certainly fatal, and finally I did fall, then woke, heart pounding and throat closed, so terrified I could hardly breathe.

That's the feeling I had as I ran toward the kennel, that I wasn't going to escape what I was trying to prevent. Jon Point was already there because the lights were on. Whenever he left, he disconnected and hid his pirated lines to save them from tower-strippers.

I heard the howls long before I lurched into the doorless corridor and raced toward the pens. Scarlet was howling, my favorite dog, the one I'd met originally. I saw Jon's brows in the dim cone of light, his cheekbone, nose, his white beard above shadowed eyes, pits of darkness peering down at the glittering knife in his hands. The howls and the shrieking rake of hard claws yammered from behind the closed door of the feed room. Scarlet was slamming against the unyielding surface with her full weight, over and over.

Without losing a stride, I jumped the side of the pen and threw myself over the puppies. What drama! God, yes! Not that I'd been thinking so at the time, but there I was, flattened over those little dogs like a screaming pancake: "No, Jon!"

Jon's face was as tear-stained as mine. He stepped away from me, half hiding the knife behind his back. "Jewel, sweetheart, oh, girl, girl, where did you come from? I don't want to, but they passed the law . . ."

"We have two weeks!" I gargled at him, scarcely able to speak. "They said two weeks!"

He wiped at his rough cheeks with a grimy sleeve. "Why make it harder? In two weeks, their eyes will be open, they'll be moving around. Now . . . they won't even know."

"I'll know," I yelled at him, gathering the five furry lumps into my arms. One of them yawned, pink tongue curling like a leaf in the toothless, milky mouth. "Scarlet knows, even though you have her shut up in there. I want two weeks, Jon. You owe me two weeks."

He turned away from my accusations, running his hands through his white mane, clearing his throat with some effort as he stared through the kennel door at the darkness outside. He wiped his eyes again and struggled with trembling hands to fold the knife, dropping it twice before he managed it.

He sounded so mournful when he said, "If I'd known this was going to happen, I wouldn't have bred the bitches. The pups don't have a chance. Neither do the older dogs!"

"I'm going to talk to Witt Hessing," I said. I was quite firm, quite confident. Oh, yes, I knew Witt would fix things. Witt was my knight-errant, my hero. "Witt will help me figure something out."

Jon drew a deep breath at the mention of the Hessing name, as though I'd said a magic word. Jon knew what I knew, that if anyone had the power to change things, it would be a Hessing or a Hargess.

He said, "Jewel, I'll let it go for the two weeks. I'll even help you, if I can, but there's no way we can find enough exempt estate homes even for dogs old enough to leave their mothers . . ."

He was so willing to concede defeat! It made me angry. I said, "Let Scarlet out, Jon. She's going crazy in there."

Jon unlatched the door. It hit him in the chest with Scarlet's full weight behind it, and he went down. She came across the side of the pen in a scrabbling rush, lips drawn back, fangs glittering, knocking me aside as she thrust her nose among the pups, sniffing to learn whether they were all there, all unhurt before turning her head to regard me with eyes as opaque as metal. Her teeth were still bared, her throat rumbled with a growl that told me to keep back when I put out a tentative hand. Her yellow eyes said, "I know what he was going to do."

She knew Jon had locked her up. She knew I hadn't been here. She had heard my voice arguing with him, and then Jon had let her go. She knew the puppies were all right, and her eyes swiveled across me, almost apologetically. We were friends. Scarlet had saved my life once. I would never have hurt her.

"It's all right, Scarlet," I said, my tears welling up again. "They're all right, Scarlet. Honest. They're all there."

Scarlet nosed the puppies once more. If even one of them had been injured or taken away, the odor picture of the litter would have changed. I didn't know whether the dogs were able to count, but I knew they could tell when something was missing. As Scarlet lay down and nosed the puppies against her belly, her growl faded to a low rumble, but she still glared past me to Jon, who refused to look at her. He wouldn't let himself hope. He was too busy convincing himself that disappointment and death were inevitable, despite anything I might do. I hated that, people giving up, not trying to fight. I just hated it.

I stayed where I was until Scarlet let me stroke the babies. Then I straightened my clothes, left the pen, and repeated my intentions, to be sure Jon understood. "I'm going home, Jon. You let the dogs alone. I'm going to talk to Witt."

Which I did, though I sat by the phone for hours before he returned my link message.

"I know there's very little time . . ." I said.

He said, in his very topstory voice, "That's true, but there are possibilities. You know Shiela Alred?"

"I know who she is. Some kind of philanthropist."

"I know her pretty well. She's quite friendly with Mama the Dame, and she has an exempt estate in Tower 69."

"*In* Tower 69?"

"Her family owned the land the tower's on. It was sold with the proviso the family got the top three floors as an exempt estate into perpetuity, so yes, it's at the top of the tower, two residential floors and

one park floor on the bay, two towers over from Government Center."
He fell silent for a moment. "Have you cleaned up, Jewel, since you left
the kennel?"

I flushed. He knew I hadn't. Who could think of cleaning up with
all this going on. "Of course," I said.

"Then get yourself into something appropriate. Give me twenty
minutes to link Shiela Alred, then I'll pick you up at the west flit lobby
on 200."

That was very much Witt. Thinking about introducing me to his
friends, but making sure I'd be clean and properly dressed before he
did it. I was very fond of Witt, but sometimes little things like that
itched at me. Considering the situation, it shouldn't have mattered if I
smelled like dog, which I did.

Nonetheless, I was neat and clean when Witt picked me up in his
private flit. He cut among a clutter of other traffic and spurted up into
the private lanes before cutting across toward Tower 69. From that
height I could see the whole ten-by-ten grid of the hundred-towered
urb, each mile-square roof black with solar collectors, the chasms
between towers glittering with podways, the depths at their founda-
tions invisible in the dark. Outside the city, the huge cables that
brought power from earthcore-generators snaked away across the
farmlands, on to another urb, tying everything together. Almost every
tower had a huge poster of Evolun Moore grinning at us, his eyes following the flit: "Vote for Moore, for Humanity's sake!" He was running for the legislature or the Urban Council or something, whatever
office was a step higher than one he held.

Trees poked out of the top of Tower 69, and I realized I'd seen
them before when I was pod-hopping, the only roof in the urb with
trees poked through it. From the private flit lobby we were escorted
into a sun-drenched parlor just inside, a room that looked all the way
across the sluggishly shifting surface of the bay to the line of scum
harvesters squatted on the horizon. Shiela Alred came fluttering in—
she was dressed in green that day—and Witt introduced us.

"Witt, my dear! So nice to see you. Sit down, take that chair, my
dear, it's comfortable, and you look in need of comforting!" Shiela
seated herself without pausing in her chatter. "I've been devising, my
dears, since early this morning." She cocked her head as she asked
Witt, "Do you know Gainor Brandt? No? Well, he's an old friend of

mine who happens to be second-in-command at Earth Enterprises, very much in line to take over in a few years when the current general manager retires."

At the time, I didn't know what that was. I asked, hesitatingly, "Earth Enterprises . . . ?"

"Earth Enterprises is the parent agency of Exploration and Survey Corps," Witt said.

Shiela nodded. "The Corps makes great use of technology in its work. But, according to Gainor, some of their technology falls short in unfamiliar situations. Technological devices can do only what they're designed to do; one has to ask a certain question before a device can be designed to obtain an answer. But, if one doesn't know what question to ask . . ." She shrugged, her hands held wide, miming confusion. "Gainor tells me that some of the scientists attached to ESC have felt that some answers to technical questions may be found in the senses of nonhuman creatures, Earthian and ET. Dogs, for example, can smell things we cannot. They can detect a coming earthquake. That's been known for centuries, of course. Though we've developed excellent technology, we still have no idea how dogs themselves process the information. Other animals also have senses we don't know how they use . . . other animals whose senses we might learn to use . . ."

"You mean, experiment on dogs?" I cried, horrified.

Shiela reached out a calming hand. "Not vivisect, dear. Certainly not. Nothing painful or invasive. There's been informal research going on for some time, unlicensed, I regret to say, but heaven knows, if we had to license it, nothing would happen."

"Research?" Now it was Witt's turn to question.

"Attempts at modifying humans to become hyperacute, have hearing like bats, for example, or noses like dogs . . ."

I studied the far wall, letting the words *unlicensed* and *informal* slide over me as Shiela continued.

"None of which is the point! Whether there's anything to it or not, it will serve as an excuse, a justification for saving the dogs!" Shiela patted my knee. "I'm rattling, aren't I, dear? But I was getting to the point, eventually. We'll bring your dogs here. Whether we actually can accomplish anything useful or not, working under the aegis of ESC will make us attack-proof, at least for a while."

"Here?" I said, disbelieving, staring at the costly elegance around me.

Shiela laughed, a pretty, social sound. "Not in this room, no. But my family is small—one son, a couple of elderly cousins, and the servants. We use only a score of rooms on this side of this one floor. You can see that we have what's called a sea-view these days, though I'm not that fond of algae harvesters, and I much prefer my Bonner wall vistas to an expanse of green soup. The inner rooms on this floor are mostly galleries and humidity-controlled storage rooms for artworks that would otherwise be discarded to make space for people. We have sculptures, paintings: Rembrandts, the last Picassos, the last van Goghs and Gaugins, all salvaged from the wreckage after the museum riots. I have the very last Ambruster, too, and all that was left of Oakal's works after the Europa pogrom, and some unedited originals of Lipkin's Mars work . . ."

"My mother," I said, surprised. "Matty Lipkin. And Joram Bonner is my stepfather."

Her expression changed, and she really looked at me for the first time. I was not someone Witt had dragged into her house because he was a do-gooder. I had become a person she already knew something about. She took my hand. "My dear, what a wonderful artist Matty Lipkin was. And Joram Bonner! Well. We would all lose our sanity if it weren't for the Bonners, First through Third. But then, I'm sure you know that! At any rate, people who have these fantastic artworks leave them to me in their wills. I throw charity parties every now and then, and people pay a fortune to see them." She paused, shaking her head, leaning forward to pat my hand. "I'm rambling again . . .

"The next floor up is vacant and windowless. The top floor is a park floor. Though it was roofed with solar collectors, I insisted they leave large sections open so trees could grow up through it. So, the 260th floor will serve as exercise ground, and we can build whatever else we need on Floor 259."

I said, "If Gainor Brandt doesn't get a delay, we have only a little time."

"I know. The dogs you're concerned about should be brought here today, now. Bring them by flit along with the poor man who's been taking care of them. I have dog-owning friends who don't have exempt estates, and they need a place for their animals as well, so an experienced kennelman will be invaluable. If you're interested, Jewel, I should think we could also employ you very profitably!"

"Are you ready for all that?" I cried.

Shiela patted my knee again, this time a fond, almost maternal gesture, as she twinkled at me. "Of course not, my dear. One is seldom ready for disaster, but one just has to cope, any old how."

We settled a few details with Shiela; she added more appreciative words about Matty and Joram while Witt shifted impatiently; and we left.

Witt said, "I'm hungry, and you look starved."

"Food hasn't tasted very good lately."

"Earth food never tastes very good. I'd like something different."

He took me to an expensive little restaurant high up in Tower 50 something, a place that specialized in off-planet foods. He ordered, and I ate what he ordered. It was the first time I'd tasted anything I could call delicious. Though Worldkeeper uses engineered flavors and aromas, all earth food ends up tasting alike, and even that is better than Mars food. That night I learned that cheese from a dairy planet is not in the same category as algae-cheese, even when the algae-cheese is labeled AGED CHEDDAR FLAVOR.

Witt grinned at me, he said, because I was scrunching up my eyes when I was chewing as though I was using my whole face to squeeze out every bit of taste. He also said I was looking nice, half-starved, but nice. Mostly we talked about the food.

"No faux pepper," he remarked.

I took a deep breath and smiled. "And no coffee 10, no pretend-cinnamon, no maybe-ginger."

"No can-this-possibly-be vanilla?"

"I know the answer to that one. It can't. No matter what World-keeper says."

He laughed. "Give Worldkeeper credit for seeing that we're all fed, Jewel."

I made a face. "Worldkeeper doesn't have to eat meat substitute or simulated vegetable flakes. It's always weeks or months between the times we get fresh stuff."

"Special-license places like this always have fresh food."

I was annoyed at the way he said it, offhand, as though I was being absurd. "Always for the wealthy, Witt. You're rich, and other people aren't. You keep forgetting that."

"No," he said, shaking his head, flushing slightly. "I don't forget it. It just . . . gets in the way sometimes."

I put down my fork and frowned. "You can be glad you're rich. Most of the rest of us can't eat like this ever!"

Witt muttered. "Many humans used to eat like this. Many of us could eat this way if we got rid of the Law of Return."

"Why don't we? Everybody on Earth hates it."

He shook his head impatiently. "Unfortunately, that's not quite true. The outer worlds don't hate it. They want to keep high birthrates to have lots of workers available for development. Development is everything. If things aren't getting bigger and faster and higher, people aren't satisfied. The trouble is, high birthrates eventually result in very large numbers of elderly people who have to live somewhere, and even at the price of space travel, it's much less expensive to send them back to Earth than to support them on the outlying planets."

"But why do we let them?" I asked. I really didn't know why, and it had always bothered me.

"The law was pushed through Worldkeeper Council the same way it's kept on the books today: Any councilor who votes for it gets lots and lots of campaign money from the outer worlds, along with the guarantee of a luxury retirement on an uncrowded planet." He frowned, fiddling with his fork. "My family knows a great many of them, the retired ones. They have mansions, and private lakes, and acres of grass and trees . . ."

I felt a sudden pang, nostalgia for some time or place I had never actually been. "I want to go off world," I cried.

I didn't realize my voice had risen until I saw people at nearby tables turning to look at me. I flushed, ducking my head, terribly embarrassed. One simply does not speak loudly in public places.

Witt said, "Really, Jewel. Don't shout about it. If you really want to go off world, you probably can. Find out what professions are being solicited and learn one."

"I've done that. They want sewage system managers and city planners and warehouse operators. They want all kinds of engineers."

"They don't use any salespeople or expediters?"

"Oh, of course, they do. It's just that the jobs they're recruiting for aren't the least bit exciting."

He sat back in his chair, twirling the stem of his wineglass slowly left and right, watching the light gather and spin in the pool of dark liquid. "I want to get away from here. I've wanted nothing else for as long as I can remember, but for the next couple of years, I'll be finishing my business course with all those damned ET contract studies. Dame Cecelia insists on that."

I chased the last bit of something delicious to the edge of my plate and captured it with a bit of chewy bread that was nothing like Worldkeeper bread. "I've never asked you, Witt, but I've always been curious. What're those titles your parents use? The Dame and Sir thing?"

His raised his eyebrows. "Hereditary titles from way, way back. Ten or fifteen generations, at least. Before space exploration. Even before pod transport, or aircars. The family was British . . ."

"British?"

"Some islands off Euro-sector, West. They don't exist as a residential place anymore. All noncrop lands in what used to be Britain and the former Scandinavian countries are covered with algae and desalinization plants because they have long coastlines."

I was still thinking about his parents. "I've met your sister, Myra. How come you've never let me meet Dame and Sir?"

His mouth tightened "Jewel, you wouldn't . . . enjoy meeting my mother. My father is at least polite to people he . . . well, people he doesn't know, but there's no way you can meet him without meeting her. She thinks that Dame stuff sets her above the rest of the world. What actually sets her anywhere is the Hargess-Hessing money. She's from the Hargess side; she and my father are cousins, sort of, and she believes the family is . . . well, aristocratic."

"You mean I'm not their class of people." I was absurdly wounded by this. I had always thought of myself as of quite a good class of people. Certainly his friend Shiela had thought so.

"No, you're not," he replied. "Nobody is. The Hessing-Hargess are . . . completely in a class by themselves, them and their cousins and aunts and uncles and so forth. Anyhow, the Dame expects me to take over the Hargess-Hessing empire eventually, when Sir Dahlish and his brothers are ready to give it up. None of the brothers has any children to inherit. I've told Mother when I do take it over, it'll be from Faroff, but she pretends not to hear me. When it happens, she'll be surprised to learn that I mean it. If you really want to go off world, you should be studying something that will help you do it."

He hit a nerve with that one. My innards went into the familiar spasm that was half embarrassment, half fear. I forced myself not to sound whiny. "I know that, Witt. Paul is only twenty, but he's doing advanced level language studies, specializing in ET lexicology . . ."

"And taking personal credit, no doubt, for having inherited his father's talent for languages," Witt said in his topstory, very superior voice.

"Yes, that's true. He does have the talent, however, so it doesn't really matter where he got it, for I don't have the talent despite having Delis as my father, too. Paul will be a linguist, and linguists are in demand."

He nodded. "Every time we encounter a new race we need squads of new translators."

I went on, "Taddeus is more modest about inherited talent, but he got Matty's artistic skills, and I didn't, even though she was also my mother . . ."

"He could have inherited from Joram . . ."

"He could, yes, or from both of them. Whichever, he's been exhibiting since he was twelve, and his future as Joram IV is all mapped out. By the time they were halfway through general schooling, both of them knew exactly what they wanted to do, and I haven't a clue. I got all the way through general schooling without any idea what to do next. I've worked with Jon at the kennel since I was eight. I've taken vet courses and animal behavior and nutrition courses. I've become more and more able to do things that are needed less and less, things that are either illegal or impossible."

He lowered his voice. "How about the ark planets?"

I whispered, "At the shelters, they say arkists don't take anyone under fifty years old."

"They don't?" He sounded both surprised and pleased, which I couldn't fathom.

I said, still in a whisper, "The iggy-huffo terrorists have sworn to wipe out animals and the people who care for them on any ark world they can find. Since it could possibly happen, the arkists only take mature people who are willing to risk losing their lives . . ." I stopped for a moment as I tried to sort my confusion into sensible words. "So, I ask myself, why go on to school? To learn what? With this sanctuary thing happening, I'm sure I'll have a lot to do, but only for a while. Once it's over, if I want to go off world, I'll have to settle for doing something not very interesting."

"You might settle for joining me in a cohabitation liaison, instead."

It came completely without warning. I thought he was joking. I started to laugh, but stopped when I saw the intent, totally focused expression on his face, as though he had been working toward this remark all evening. I said doubtfully, "You don't mean that, Witt."

He sat back, smiling. "Oh, yes. I do very much mean that. We get on very well together. People our age need . . . companions. Even if I haven't said . . . well, I've thought about it. We could make it work, Jewel. I've already taken a single apartment in the University Tower. With my income from the family trust, we can get along until we're ready to go off world."

"I'll bet your mother had a fit about your moving out."

He shrugged. "Well, yes, but it's customary for students to live there, and Father told her to quit fussing about it. Many of the students are liaised . . ."

That surprised me, and I said so.

"No concs in the University Tower," he said. "As I said, people our age need companionship."

"My inheritance is tied up in the liaison contract for two more years, until Tad's eighteen!"

"It doesn't matter. If we're living there, you can find something you'd like to study, and we can get by on my trust funds."

"Your mother will say you're too young."

"We're both young, sure, but a cohabitation liaison is only a five-year contract." He took my hand, interlacing his fingers with mine. "If you had something you wanted to do, something that didn't include me, I wouldn't have asked . . ."

"No," I said, breathless at the sudden simplicity of it all. Liaising with Witt would get me away from Paul! Perhaps this was simply meant to be. "Of course I don't have other plans!"

It was only at home, later, as I was drifting off to sleep that I remembered what he'd said. No concs in university towers. As though his proposal might have been based on that. No. I set the idea aside. Witt was too . . . well, too mannerly even to think anything like that. At that moment I also realized that he hadn't said he loved me, but then, I hadn't said I loved him, either.

REMEMBERING
MATTY

⦂ I don't think about Mars when I'm awake, but when I'm half-asleep, I often dream about it: caverns and canyons so huge they could swallow the moon, airlocks everywhere, XT suits for people moving between caverns or outside. XT suits are very expensive. I got Paul's old suits when he outgrew them, and Taddeus got the ones I'd outgrown. Sometimes I dream about Tad and Matty and me, but mostly I dream about space. I dream of being alone, with no one else around, just wonderful emptiness going on and on forever.

On Mars, almost everyone lives in caverns cut in the sides of the big canyons, where it's warmer and wetter—well, damper, at least. When I was there, Earth embassy was in one of the smaller caverns that housed only a few hundred people. Our home cave was next to the embassy, fairly large, with a room for each of us and a studio for Matty. When I was little, I thought all mothers had studios and made sensories.

Mars food was imported or hydroponic. During a dust storm, dust got through a filter that had been made on Earthmoon by Earth Enterprises, and all the food died. The people got so hungry they rioted against Earth. My father tried to calm them down, which was a mistake. Someone cut his air hose and he died. That was the Great Mars Riot, when I wasn't even a year old, so I don't remember my father, Victor Delis, at all. Matty told me he was a savant, and he spoke fifty languages including Zhaar, which was either a fib or an exaggeration because nobody spoke Zhaar except the Zhaar themselves, and none of them were left.

Almost everyone knows the name Joram Bonner. If someone wants to see and hear and smell a windblown willow dropping leaves in rippling water, he buys Joram Bonner the Elder's "Brook Series" Vista Replication Wall-view, VRW. If someone wants to see the Grand Canyon, hear the shriek of an eagle, see the waterfalls plunging over the rimrock, it's all there in Joram Bonner II's VRW no. 39, *Canyon Suites*. Vista-reps are partly on-site records and partly reconstructions from other sources including substantive records of similar things on other planets. The VRWs made by our Joram Bonner III, or his father Joram II or his grandfather, Joram the Elder, are the only record we have of old forests, lost rivers, vanished prairies; they're all we have of old Earth and all most of us will ever see of the far-off worlds. Almost everyone on Earth has at least one vista made by a Bonner, to keep them sane.

Matty had known Joram Bonner since they were children, and they'd studied art together. Matty's work was very different from Joram's, less realistic, more interpretive and based on her explorations of the Martian gorges. She recorded changes of light and the sounds of wind, then ran them both through a synthesizer, augmenting the wind sounds with vocals and instrumentals, the views with actors, dancers, and special effects. The final result was a work of art that was greater than the sum of its parts, or so the critics were fond of saying. She loved caverns and was never so happy as when she was wandering into the unexplored, leaving a trail of relay transmitters behind her to bounce every nuance of the experience to the waiting recorders in her desert car above. Her last abyss, the one that kept her busy for almost a year in its honeycombed caverns, turned out to be where the last Martians had died a very long time before.

Of course, Matty had no idea she was going to find remnants of a lost people, their bones, their pictures, their words on the walls. She was just going into the darkness the way she usually did. I always carry my copy of her original recording of that cavern. I watch it whenever I'm lonely for her, from the first transmission in the outer cavern as she fingers the control wand of her light-helmet to make narrow beams, like brushes full of starshine to glisten the dark walls, then hard, sun-amber chisels to shatter the shadows, and at last wide-flung sprays of blood and sunset to blush the cold stone into life. Farther in, she uses waves of baffling, beautiful blues, shading every hollow, caressing tall columns with amethyst wavelets until watery light pours across the arched ceiling and runs down the sides to fill the cavern with opalescent foam. When she wades through it, her feet raise pygmy fountains of gilded dust, every step an iridescent spout of glory, a fire-dotted line that follows her farther in and farther in and farther down and farther down . . .

She passes a series of dead ends, pockets leading nowhere. Then she finds a perplexing passageway along a narrow shelf that towers on one side and plummets on the other, ramifying into side trails dark as pits. The shelf becomes a narrow bridge over a bottomless gulf where the wind comes up moaning, full of lost voices, and I watch her going across it like a glowing spider, weaving a web of tenuous tints as she goes, feeling her way, silent as a wraith over that narrow slab, then along another ledge no wider than her shoulders that leads to a long, horridly twisted way full of spiked stones. The narrow path weaves among them into the final place, the fanged mouth of a bubble with one way in and no other way out, the end of the journey.

Over and over I watch her stop just inside the bubble, a single beam reaching from her helmet, a finger probing the dark. The light touches a wall with a difference, taps it once, veers away in surprise, then snuffles its way back like an animal to an enticing but unfamiliar smell, whiskering it gently, nose wrinkling, before exploding into a radiance that illumines the entire cavern with all its carvings, pictures, people, creatures, words . . . Glory! Wonder! Marvel!

How she moved that day is still as clear and familiar to me as her face. I always carry her original record of the exploration and the album she made from it. They're half the size of the palm of my hand. It's hard to believe such little things can hold all that glory. Touch the button on the side and all the marvels hover in the air: the winding cavern, the awful bridge over darkness, the twisting channel, and, finally, the curving walls of the Room of Witness, as Matty named it, carved all over with words and pictures. The pictures show two sorts of creatures, tall and short, biped and quadruped, both sorts always in company, walking, running, leaping . . .

I was with her that day, oh, not down in the caverns, but I was in the desert car. I liked to sit there, waiting for her, fascinated by the recording screen, seeing what she saw. I was waiting there when she came up from the cavern, and I've never seen such happiness and awe on anyone's face, before or since. I was only six, but I still remember her face as I watch the recording, Matty dancing blissfully from one section of the wall to another, here, there, everywhere, before she finally settled into the methodical, meticulous work that produced the final album.

My original recording includes her voice describing the music she intends to set to each sequence, mentioning the Sono-Visual artist whose augmented vocals should accompany the wind sounds; mentioning the dancers to be costumed as the lost Martians; the creature artist who will animate the other beings.

When we got home, she was still ecstatic. As soon as we were out of our XT suits, she pulled me into her arms and held me, whispering into my ear. "They had dogs, Joosie! Imagine that! They had dogs! Or something like."

"Like my Faithful Doggy, Matty? Like in the Animal Book?"

"Just like in the Animal Book. 'Dutiful and diligent, man-friend, dog.'"

I hadn't seen them on the screen, for their bones were deep in dust. She didn't describe them to me until later. People bones. Dog bones. Not exactly like people now or dogs now, but very similar, lying near the carvings, the people's arms around the dog bones, their heads laid close, the way I slept with my Faithful Dog at night when I needed comforting. The cavern was the only evidence anyone has ever found of the Martians, the last ones, the few thousand of them in the cavern possibly all there were, gathered into that place to die together.

Though it had seemed a short time to both of us, Matty had stayed down there long enough for cavern air to leak through a fault in her XT suit. It carried a virus with it, something unknown, something fatal. Later on it turned out that Matty hadn't actually discovered the caverns, she'd just rediscovered them. When the experts magnified the wall scans they saw faint Zhaar seals on the wall, which meant the Zhaar had been there, long, long ago. Matty just laughed, and said it didn't matter, discover or rediscover. Old things often became new things.

She paid a researcher to do a search of Interstellar Confederation Archives for any records the Zhaar might have left concerning the cavern. The researcher found a pictorial record of the Martian carvings, done some fifty thousand years ago or so, along with a translation into Panqoin, written well before humans were painting horses on cave walls. The Panqoin had been allies of the Tsifis, a people who left our galaxy when we were in the middle Stone Age, and the archives had Panqoin-Tsifis transliterations. The Tsifis had in turn mentored the Gendeber, a race now extinct but contemporary with early Bronze Age man. In the Gendebers' last years they had been visited by the Phain, and the Phain were still alive. So, the researcher translated the Pangoin to Tsifis, the Tisifis to Gendeber, and the Gendeber to Phainic, and from Phainic to Earthian common speech so Matty could get her translation and make songs out of it.

Joram used to tease her: "It started out as roast beef, became hash, then stew, then soup, and God knows how the final broth resembles the original menu."

Matty just laughed at him. "I'm sure the translation is close enough, Joram. I recognize the music."

The song Matty sang when she was dying was the death song of a dying people, Joram said, though he didn't say it in front of Matty. By the time she died, she had most of the visuals and all the music finished, and she left enough notes that Joram could complete the visuals for her. It's known as Lipkin Symphony no. 7, the *Cavern* Symphony, in three movements based on the colors and glories of the great cavern; the wind voices accompanying that long, perilously dark passage; and finally, an ecstatic chorale-ballet that accompanies the final wall. It comes to life and dances its own farewell before remounting the cavern wall and changing back into carvings. At the premiere they called it the artistic event of the century. Matty would have loved that.

She loved those caverns, too, even after she knew they had killed her. Until Matty died, I didn't know that things you love can kill you.

LIAISON

⁝ On Earth, liaison contracts are required for every human interaction that involves rights, responsibilities, and money. Every item in a liaison is enforceable by law. If Jane Somebody conceives a child outside a liaison contract, she has two months to get an ex post facto coparent, or the child becomes the property of the state as soon as it's born and is sold to some off-world settlement where young people are in demand. People can have whatever religious or cultural ceremonies or commitments they like, but only the civil contracts are enforceable.

Our contract was simple. Our identichips knew almost everything about us, and our Worldkeeper files knew whatever the identichips didn't. We were rated R, which meant "Authorized to reproduce." Ours was the usual five-year cohabitation contract with a coparenting option. Once we were liaised, we could have a baby, or we could create embryos to be stored and born later. Many young people did this, because young ova and young sperm are healthier but mature people are better parents. Every liaison contract specifies who owns any resultant embryos or has custody of any resultant children. I guess in the past people got into real wrangles about who had the right to stored embryos.

I took my belongings to the University Tower where Witt had already put both our names in the directory. Paul was off world on some kind of fellowship (thank heaven), but we invited Taddeus to our celebration at the new sanctuary, with Shiela Alred as hostess and a few of our friends as guests. Taddeus used a pocket album to record the festivities, then he gave it to us as a wedding gift. Registering a cohabitation liaison is called simply "recording a contract," but if people are invited to celebrate the event, that celebration is still called a wedding.

Our honeymoon consisted of splurging at ET restaurants and buying one another silly wedding presents in shops I'd never seen before, making up private jokes and experimenting with sex. Most young people experiment with concs, but I never had. They affected me deep down, like snakes affect some people who've never seen a snake before. I knew Witt had had concs, because he'd mentioned them, though we never discussed it. The sexual part of our relationship was agreeable though awkward, as though Witt kept having to remind himself I was there.

We had ten days of cohabitation, and for that little time I was really quite happy, and everything seemed open and new, as though all our dreams could come true. When reality returned, it came like a monster from under the bed! That's how it felt, even though it was only a summons from Witt's mother. He answered the link, said yes, no, right away, got dressed and went. I stayed home and fixed breakfast. Time went by, almost noon, and he came home looking as though he'd been beaten. His face was blotchy and strained, totally unlike himself, and his voice shook.

"Mother the Dame found out we're liaised."

"Hadn't you told her?" I was surprised, a little stunned.

"She went on and on about your being nobody, even after I told her who you were, who your parents were, that Shiela Alred thinks the world of you!"

"Sit down, Witt. Take a deep breath . . ."

"I can't! So then the Dame demanded to know if you were pregnant, and I told her you weren't. She said that meant there'd be no barrier to my going on this expedition."

"Expedition?" I cried, not believing any of this. "What expedition?"

"Just listen. Her cousin is with Planetary Protection Institute, and PPI is certifying a newly discovered planetary system, and the contract provides profit sharing to the members of the certification team . . ."

"You don't know anything about planet certification!"

"That's what I told her, that I knew nothing about it, that I wanted to stay and finish school. And Mother said I would need something to live on, which this expedition would pay me. I said I had enough income, and she dropped the sky on me."

"Oh, Witt. Don't tell me . . ."

"Oh, yes. She told me I *had* an income, but the trust is in her keeping, and because I entered into a cohabitation liaison without her permission, I don't get the income anymore, or the principal until I'm thirty."

"Is that legal?"

He almost screamed. "Of course it's not legal! I'm of age. I could prove she has no right if I had ten years' time and a million Earthcreds to spend in court!" Witt's head dropped into his hands, and he ran his pale, tapered fingers through his dark mane of hair, over and over. "Which she pointed out at some length, just in case I'd thought of trying it! As of this morning, we have no income. We can't even break the liaison contract for five years, so she really can starve us if she likes."

Can't break the contract! I'd been getting angrier by the moment, mostly at his mother, but at the way he was acting, too. I tried to keep that under control, as I said, "Witt, we're well enough educated to hold jobs." We were. Either of us was quite capable of holding down any number of boring but paying jobs. I knew, because I'd been checking what jobs were available just in case the sanctuary thing didn't work out.

"This isn't the twenty-second century, Jewel. People can't take a false name and pretend to be someone else. Identichips make that sort of thing impossible. And there's not a job anywhere on Earth she can't prevent our getting or get us fired from if she finds out about it, and she will. I hoped . . . I hoped she'd let me be! She won't. If we don't split up, she'll see that we end up down-dwellers, with minimum I-chip credit, living in a sublevel hole."

"I don't believe that, but if it's true, we'll sign up for a colony and go off world!"

"You think she couldn't stop us? You think she couldn't block emigration permits?"

I was talking to a crazy stranger, someone I didn't even recognize. I knew we could get off planet without an emigration permit! Whenever Joram came home to visit, he told us stories about his travels, including all the tricks he used to get from this impossible place to that impossible place!

I said, very calmly, "Just because she's punishing you, you don't have to go along with it, Witt. As you said, you're of age. There are other ways . . ."

He shook his head at me, raising his hands as though to fend me off. "If we're going to live, I'll have to go. She'll make an allowance for you to live on while I'm gone, I got her to promise that much . . ."

"While you're gone? When?"

"Tomorrow. Oh, God, don't look at me like that, Jewel. It's only three years. We'll . . . we'll have plenty of time when it's over . . ." He said this last as though he'd been told it, not as though he'd thought it out, his mother's words coming from his mouth.

Stubbornly, I went on trying to discuss alternatives. Every possibility I raised, he said it was impossible, and he got more and more frantic and hysterical the harder I tried. He couldn't even hear me. I knew I could convince him if only I had a little time, but he had no time to consider anything except his own confusion, and my attempts to change his mind were only making it worse.

I stopped arguing. He made a frantic attempt at lovemaking that wasn't about love at all; we had an hour getting things together and a flit ride together to the shuttleport. On the way, Witt used his link to drain his credit account, paying the rent a year in advance and giving me what little was left. I put the wedding photo album that Tad had given us into his pocket as a keepsake and kissed him good-bye, like kissing clammy stone. Total time of our cohabitation liaison: eleven days.

By noon I was sitting in the windowless three-hundred-square-foot cell the university allotted to couples. The bedroom was three paces each way when the bed was pushed into the wall under the closet. The living room was three paces by four. The kitchen extended the living room by another pace and a half, the bathroom was just big enough for the fixtures in it. The storage closet, half as large as the bedroom, was packed with Witt's belongings. He had taken almost nothing with him.

I forced myself to make tea and sit down to drink it slowly while thinking my way through my immediate future. I had a place to sleep; the University Tower was number 27, two down and four over from the new sanctuary in Tower 69, an easy commute. I had the job at the sanctuary, which would pay me enough to live on so long as I didn't have to pay rent. Paul and Taddeus's place had already been reconfigured so I couldn't rejoin them unless contiguous space opened up again, which it might never do. I was still entitled to eat with them, however, so I wouldn't go hungry. So long as I slept in this apartment at least half time to maintain my tenancy, I could spend a lot of time at the sanctuary. Moving around might help me keep the walls from closing in. I already felt smothered, but I could do it. By the time the rent on Witt's place ran out, the sanctuary might be settled enough that I could have a room there as Jon did. Then . . .

I jumped to my feet, my hands over my ears to shut out a deafening shriek, and another, another! In the interval between shrieks, I figured out what it was. The door alarm. No one ever triggers a door alarm. No one ever visits an apartment without linking first, to be sure someone is there, or to get a route clearance! Nobody came unannounced except tower management! Was Witt mistaken about having paid in advance?

I gritted my teeth, smoothed my trousers over my hips, ran my fingers through my hair, tangled, as usual, and went to the door, where I was confronted by an imposing woman made taller by six-inch soles on her boots and a hairdo that went up another foot or two. She was accompanied by a faceless servant, a Quondan. Oh, they have faces, but you can't see them.

"Jewel Delis," the woman said, sneering the name. "I am Dame Cecelia Hessing. I've come to give you the charity my son begged me to provide you during his absence."

My mind was absolutely blank, vacant. All that was in my head were echoes. This was . . . this was Witt's mother, the Dame.

She pushed into the tiny room, leaving the door open as she dipped into her pockets, coming out with handfuls of the little podfare coins that people carry to buy a pod lobby snack or throw to a transit musician, a spill of silver, gold, and blue discs spinning away into corners: twentieths and tenths and quarters of credits, bright constellations in the shadows.

She yelled at me. "You know you are ruining my son's life!" She grabbed me by the shoulder and shook me. "You liaised with him for his money, I know that. Pretended to be pregnant, so you could get him for his money. Well, he's out away from your lies now. He'll be gone for three years. And by the time he gets back, we will have reached an understanding, you and I."

"I don't need charity," I gasped, totally astonished, still unable to admit to myself what was going on. "I don't want it."

"Oh, people like you always want it! And I shall leave you to scramble for it, like the beggar you are. I'll be back, every few days, so get used to getting down on your knees. Looking around here, you're probably already used to it, living like this . . ."

"This is Witt's apartment," I cried, furious. "He took it so he could get away from you!"

". . . and you'd better be here to get your handout, for I won't make it up if you aren't!"

And with that she was out the door and off down the corridor, heavy shoes clomping like hammers, the servant two steps behind. I shut the door and leaned against it. Dame Cecelia. Bizarre! Insane! Even Paul never acted like that! No one acted like that! No wonder Witt hadn't wanted to introduce her. And that ridiculous strewing of podfare coins, the only money that existed outside the identichip system, so I'd have to stoop to pick them up. Her way of punishing the beggar girl who had inveigled the young lord into a liaison? The woman was living in a fairy tale!

I wasn't weeping or grieving, I was just furiously, ragingly angry. Well, I would not be around for a repeat visit. Since the woman could get into the residential floors of the university without a pass, I would become a moving target, just as I had when I was a child, evading Paul's attentions. I'd ride the podways and be constantly elsewhere!

I ate something. Five minutes later I couldn't remember what, not that it mattered. I went to work. Shiela Alred wasn't there, but she had left me a list of things that had to be done. Jon was there, supervising the planning of apartments for trainers, runs for dogs. Shiela had said there was to be a laboratory, a veterinary hospital. When Jon was free, I told him about Dame Cecelia's visit, between laughter and furious tears.

Jon asked, "Whyn't you just let the old bitch come drop money on you?"

"Don't use that word for her, Jon! It insults the dogs! I won't do it because that would convince her she's right! I didn't liaise with Witt because he's wealthy. He's the one who asked me, not me him. I never even thought of it until he asked me." The thought of my recent humiliation bent me double with fury. My head pounded so that I had to sit down for a moment. As a child, whenever I'd been this angry, Matty had washed my face, washed the anger away, along with the sorrows. I got to my feet and into the washroom, where I made firm resolutions behind a steaming towel. It would keep me busy just being evasive.

Six slippery weeks went by after that. I disabled the door alarm, using a method Joram had described. I pod-hopped my way to and from. I went to work. I came home late. She caught me twice, once going in, once out, and both times I just stood there, enduring the shower of coins and the repetitive rage. During the third visit, Dame Cecelia noticed the coins were still on the floor, and that seemed to push her fury up a notch.

Then, suddenly, the visits stopped. I held my breath for several days, gradually relaxing though I wasn't certain enough to let the floorbot suck up the coins.

"She finally got tired of it," I told Shiela Alred, who had had to be told about it, just in case I didn't show up for work on time. Or at all.

"Cecelia Hessing? I'd be surprised if that were true." Shiela furrowed her forehead, looking worried. "I've known Cecelia for years, and she has jaws like one of those ancient turtles. The kind that didn't let go until sundown."

"Well, if she has stopped . . ." I said, ". . . if she has, even with Witt gone, I think I can make it. I'll just have to make plans for when he comes back, and since I'll be living in the University Tower for the better part of a year, it's time I took some courses, some that would be of more value to our effort here. Would you suggest what that might be? I'm reasonably intelligent and did quite well at school so long as I stayed away from higher mathematics."

"I'll ask around, my dear, and I do hope you're right about Cecelia Hessing. When did you see her last?"

"Friday a week ago."

Shiela's face was still troubled. "I don't like the feel of any of this. Perhaps only because I'm not going to be here for a while, and you may need me. I've made plans to visit some old friends in Mid-Europe North, but I'll give you the link where I'll be. Promise to let me know if there's a problem."

Privately, I thought there'd be no more problems. Even Dame Cecelia had to realize eventually how ridiculous her behavior was. So I assured myself.

⋮ I was returning to the apartment a few days later, concentrating on some minor problem at the sanctuary, not noticing the two men outside my door until I was almost on top of them. They saw me coming, stepped back and held out their right hands in a motion so choreographed it almost made me laugh. The next movement should have been a dance step, but the only thing visible was the holographic splendor on their outstretched palms, marching letters that spelled out: INTELLIGENCE DIVISION.

The taller of the two said, "Jewel Delis. Come with us if you please."

"Why?" I asked, baffled.

He took me by the arm, but I shook him off. "Let me at least put the groceries down."

The door opened, and I set my burdens on the table. "Now what is this?"

They stared at the scattered coins, shared puzzled glances with one another before one of them demanded, "Don't make any fuss, ma'am. We've shown you our credentials . . ."

"Intelligence Division of what?" I demanded in return.

"Exploration and Survey, ma'am. We need to question you about the disappearance of your husband . . ."

"Witt?" I cried "Disappeared? When? Where? He was supposed to be on that new planet with PPI, the jungle world. What's happened?"

"You need to come with us."

I thought they were going to show me his body. I almost screamed. It had to be that. Why else would they insist I go with them? If his body was there . . . then he had never left Earth. What had his mother done? What terrible thing had she done to him?

Holding myself in check, I went with them to Government Center, where they ushered me into a room with a table and a chair and left me alone. Hours passed. I counted the patterns in the flooring. I stood at the barred window and counted the leaves on the small tree outside on the terrace. I counted my heartbeats. Anything to keep me from thinking. I put my head down on my arms, trying to be hopeful. Obviously there had been a foul-up of some kind. They had someone else's body. It had all been a mistake.

Eventually, I had to go. The door to the corridor was locked, the other door opened on a toilet and basin, where I splashed cold water on my face and drank from my cupped hands. More hours passed. I fell asleep, head on arms. The taller of the two men came back and wakened me by pulling out the chair opposite me.

"Tell us what you know about your husband's disappearance?"

"He hasn't disappeared," I said through the fog in my mind. "He went away, to that jungle world. You mean from there? When did he disappear? How?"

"A week ago. On the jungle world. How did you plan his disappearance?"

"Don't be ridiculous," I snarled at him. "I've never even been off planet!"

"We know you're responsible. We have a reliable informant. If you've never been off planet, then you're saying you paid someone else to do it?"

"With what?" I screamed. "My podfare money?"

From that point on, the nightmare only got worse. They let me sleep in a cell, questioned me again, let me go, picked me up the next afternoon and started again. When I returned to the apartment I found a strange device in the bathroom. I looked elsewhere and found others. I heard a buzz on my link whenever I used it, so I stopped linking anyone. My apartment was very obviously searched, so I'd know it. Twice my tiny cubby office at the sanctuary was searched, more surreptitiously. They wanted me to know, but they didn't want Shiela Alred to know her privacy was being invaded as well. They wouldn't have dared if Shiela Alred had been home, but Shiela wouldn't return until late the following Tuesday. I resolved to see her first thing Wednesday morning.

By that time the newscasts were full of the story. Twenty-seven men from a PPI installation set out on a trail recently cleared by ESC forces, intending to walk a short distance to an observation point. The sixteen who arrived at the observation point found that the last eleven men in line had disappeared. A search was made. Nothing was found. The people at the base saw a brilliant flash of light, but such flashes were not uncommon on the jungle world and were generally ascribed to some electromagnetic discharge.

The two men from ESC wakened me late Tuesday night to question me again, in my own living room. Had I caused Witt Hessing to vanish in order to inherit his money? Had I conspired to kidnap him for ransom? Had I done this, or that? What did I know about the jungle world, the rock world?

"Eleven men disappeared!" I told them. "Eleven. What possible reason could I have for wanting eleven men to disappear. I didn't even know the other ten of them."

"A cover up," said the shorter man. "To mislead us."

That was too much. As soon as the men left, I put on a heavy jacket and slipped out of the apartment, wedging the door so it wouldn't record my departure. Down the hallway I detoured into the loading cubby for a disposal tube. Joram's stories of travel had made much of the fact there are no past-this-point recorders in areas designed for waste disposal. When Tad and I were just kids, we'd marveled at his stories and copied him, of course, traveling the tubes enough to learn it was both thrilling and dangerous. This time it was merely necessary. Certain times of day, the tubes were almost unused. You can put your ear against the tube and hear if anything is coming. If not, you slide in, put your padded knees against one wall, your padded back against the other, and ease down to the next sorting floor. I did that, taking refuge in side chutes when I heard the chute rattle. On the mercantile floor I got out in a trash-sorting room moments before another load zipped out onto the sorting wheel. Half the cubic space in the towers is taken up by chutes and tubes and ducts and shafts that move people, their supplies, and their waste.

Joram said nobody monitors trash-sorting rooms. They don't monitor the freelink used by staff to advise residents of visitors or deliveries, either. So, I linked the sanctuary on one of the freelinks, then took a freight lift to the top floor, and crawled up the nearest air duct to the roof. It was harder climbing up than going down had been. I had to stop several times to wipe my hands, they were so slick with sweat. At the outlet, I almost panicked before I found the concealed latch to the heavy screen and climbed out only moments before Shiela's flit landed illegally in the maintenance area. No one who hadn't known Joram Bonner could have possibly suspected I might leave from the roof.

I should have been too exhausted to think, but I found myself mentally yelling at Witt: "See! You see! Some things are perfectly possible if you just decide to do them!"

Shiela Alred was waiting for me at the sanctuary.

"Now what is it, dear? I know about Witt. We all do. It's a terrible, terrible thing, but he still may be found, you know dear . . ." She reached out and I took her hands, so grateful that she was there.

"It isn't that. It's that they think I had something to do with his disappearance."

Shiela was astonished. "But, dear child, she can't think that! Witt disappeared from that planet. It's a very long way from here. Weeks of wormhole travel."

"They do think that, Shiela. It's ridiculous, but they do!"

"Who thinks you do?"

"These people from ESC."

"Exploration and Survey Corps?" She urged me to come inside and seated me at a table where a pot of tea was steaming. Shiela used tea on all occasions. Since she got it from off world and it was always delicious, I understood why.

"Jewel, drink this. I fixed it as soon as I heard your voice. Come now, stop shaking, just sit here quietly and have a nice cup of tea, and tell me all about it."

I was barely intelligible, telling it all backward, repeating myself over and over while Shiela nodded and murmured and questioned, remaining quite calm until I said, ". . . and they searched my office here at least twice . . ."

Shiela stood up, her face frozen. "On my property?"

"Up in my office, yes. They didn't toss stuff all over, the way they do when they search my apartment, but yes. I could tell, things had been moved and put into different order, and one of their gadgets is under my desk."

"Stay here," she said, lips pressed into a thin line. "I'll be back presently."

When she returned, she brought a fresh pot of tea and a plate of sandwiches. She poured another cup for both of us and insisted that I eat something. "You look famished. Your cheeks are hollowed. Have you been eating?"

I told her no, I hadn't really. Not since Witt went. Not since Dame Cecelia's first visit.

"No, nor sleeping well, I imagine. The person I called needs a little time to sort things out. Why don't you lie down on the sofa there and have a bit of nap. It will do you a world of good, sharpen your wits, and I want you to make sense when you talk with my friend."

Always after, I suspected that dear Shiela had dosed the tea, for I slept more soundly than at any time since Witt had left. When Shiela wakened me, hours had passed, and I only had time to wash my face before being introduced to a stocky man with a glossy dome of forehead above a thicket of eyebrows, melancholy eyes whose lids drooped slightly at the outside edges, and a firm, jutting jaw with incipient jowls. He had the look of a mournful but amiable hound. This, it turned out, was General Manager Gainor Brandt, now head of Earth Enterprises with direct control of ESC.

"Gainor's only had the job for three days," said Shiela. "His predecessor was just about to retire when he caught some kind of off-world fever that he'll be lucky to survive. Gainor has just been promoted."

Gainor Brandt patted my hand as though I were a small child. His hands were firm and thick, his fingers stubby and strong, very much in keeping with the rest of him.

"Shiela told me what has been happening. It took me a little time to find out who is involved and who is responsible for their involvement. It seems Witt's mother implicated you."

"What is it she has implicated me in?" I cried in outrage.

He chuckled ruefully, "In every crime since the fall of man, according to Botrim Prime, a colleague of mine who heads up the Bureau of Order and happens to be Dame Cecelia's cousin or some such relationship. What is this Dame Cecelia thing he calls her?"

"Hereditary title," I muttered. "Obsolete, according to her son. Her husband has one, too. He's a Sir something."

Brandt gave me a sympathetic look. "According to Prime, the Dame had only one son to continue the dynasty—that would be Witt—and she was totally centered on his life. Her dynastic plans did not include his being liaised to anyone just yet, certainly not you, and seemingly she decided she could ease her grief by persecuting you. She accused you of doing away with Witt for his fortune. That is a ridiculous charge, and anyone with any sense at all would have rejected it, but to some extent Prime holds his job at BuOr through the support of the Hargess-Hessing family.

"Prime has a nephew who was heading up one of our ESC intelligence units. Botrin asked his nephew to make your life miserable, and the nephew seems to have assumed he could do a favor for his uncle without anyone noticing or, perhaps, without anyone caring.

"He was very nearly correct. My predecessor didn't notice, nor did I until Shiela brought it to my attention. As a manager, one must depend upon the good sense of one's subordinates, at least until they prove to have none. The equipment in your apartment, in your office here—my people have removed it—has embedded source tags, and there are registries of such devices and who has custody of them. They could have been used for listening to your conversations, though according to the nephew no one bothered. The equipment was put there solely for harassment. No one seriously considered that you were involved in anything more nefarious than liking dogs. Which, these days may be nefarious enough.

"At any rate, Boaty's nephew is no longer with ESC, and you won't be bothered again by *my* people."

"Does this Botrin Prime person have any idea what his people have been doing to me?" I snarled, furious with frustration.

Brandt's voice was grim. "My dear, Botrin Prime never thought about you at all. Botrin Prime does not usually think about people unless they have something he wants, and the Hessings have many things he wants. His only feelings now are annoyance at the whole thing coming to light and anger because his nephew has been found guilty of abuse of authority, false statements to superiors, and unethical instructions to subordinates, all items that will permanently stain his record. The young man has been dismissed with an unfavorable rating, but Prime will no doubt find him a place in PPI, nonetheless."

"And you don't run PPI," I acknowledged.

"No. PPI is under the Bureau of Order. Originally, Interstellar Planetary Protection was a policing group, under BuOr. Even though PPI's purpose has changed to ecological protection for newly discovered planets, it's still considered an enforcement arm, its members have an enforcement mind-set, by which I mean, tyrannical, and I have no control over them."

"Which means Dame Cecelia can go on doing it even though she knows I had nothing to do with it?"

"I've known Cecelia Hessing for years," Shiela said. "I told you she's tenacious. She's charming and generous to her friends, but she can be wicked to anyone who crosses her. You've told me that she was responsible for sending Witt out there. Now he's gone."

"She has to blame someone." Brandt peered into my face, looking for something. Resolution, perhaps. Fury. I couldn't feel anything at that moment, so he found nothing to help him.

Shiela shook her head. "As I thought before, maybe . . . but maybe that's not it. Jewel, are you by any chance pregnant?"

Then the blood left my face, my head swam, just for a moment, and I was suddenly so angry that everything went red. I put out a hand to balance myself.

Shiela fluttered with consternation. "Forgive me, dear. That's entirely too personal a question for me to have asked. If you were pregnant, however, or if she thought you might be, all this nonsense might be laying the groundwork for a claim to Witt's child on the grounds you're unfit. It's the kind of thing she would do."

I was so tangled in fury I couldn't respond at all.

"Do you have anywhere else to go?" Brandt asked. "Somewhere remote? The Hessings have a lot of friends and influence here in NW, particularly in Urb 15."

"Jewel has been sleeping here every now and then. She could just move in," said Shiela.

Brandt frowned. "You told me they'd searched here. Even with increased security, it would be a strategic mistake to draw Hessing antagonism toward the sanctuary."

"I need to think," I said. My reflection in the window opposite was of a tall, slender, very light-colored person with lots of tightly groomed yellow hair who looked icily controlled, which was a lie. Inside I was a boiling pot of lava, popping with magma and threatening havoc. I made myself say, "Just give me a little time."

"While you're doing that," said Brandt, "consider getting a vial of STOP to carry with you."

This broke through, and I cried, "No, why? I mean, that's dreadful . . ."

Gainor took my hand again. "Dreadful, and expensive, but better than being the victim of harassment turned violent, as it might if she decides to hire some down-dweller to be her agent instead of flunkies at ESC."

"I'll pay for it," Shiela offered. "If you decide to carry it, Jewel. Some of our preservationist friends do so. None of us would use it except as a last resort."

I returned to Witt's place by the same route I had taken to leave it, pausing on the mercantile floor to call Taddeus, asking him to visit me that evening and bring a tota-float.

When he arrived, he heard me out, then asked, "You're really going to do this, Joosie?"

"I don't have a choice, Tad."

"What do you want me to do?"

"Link Aunt Hatty in Baja to tell her I'm coming. Use a public link, not your own. Go see Shiela Alred tomorrow. See her in person. Tell her you know where I am and you're the only one who knows. Also, please tota-float this stuff home with you and store it. It isn't much. I didn't bring much, and can carry very little with me. I thought I'd sort things out later, only there isn't to be any . . ."

He put his arms around me. "Any 'later.' I know. Jewel, I wish I could do something . . ." Tad was a very Joram sort, kind and interesting and always eager to help.

"If you just do what I've asked, that's all the help I should need."

The following morning, well before dawn, I was in the disposal tube again, on my way to Hatsebah Lipkin, Matty's sister. Everything of mine from the apartment, except what Tad had removed the night before, was in my pack. Nothing was left in the apartment to show I'd ever been there except an identichip listing made by the door as I had gone out.

Just as there are no past-this-point monitors in disposal or freight tubes, so there are none inside cross-country freight carriers and only a few in high-security sections of tunnels. Joram had crossed continents and oceans in freight carriers, as Tad and I knew from playing transport pirate throughout long, childhood afternoons. Every carrier has display panels that list the contents, the routing, and the times of departure from and arrival in freight terminals. Only these display panels are picked up by monitors. I slipped inside the first empty carrier with a routing code southward, so eager to get away from the urb that I forgot Joram's warning about avoiding empty carriers. I remembered it with shock when the acceleration slammed me against the locked doors. When the carrier stopped abruptly, I slid the other way, the full length of the carrier, crashing into the other end. The floor was smooth and featureless except for key-shaped holes for the anchor straps. I wrapped my clothes around me for as much protection as possible, but by the time the carrier arrived at the urban hub, I was turning black and green and several other colors over most of my body.

When the carrier was shunted from the track into a loading zone, I waited for the voices outside to go away before struggling painfully to my feet and cracking the airtight door. Across the shunt track I found an empty cubby space behind a tool rack, where I crouched in silent misery, trying to observe the pattern of movement in the cargo bay. All the work was being done by robots; the few supervisory staff members seemed more interested in their gambling game in the small office than in what was going on with the cargo. The supervisors' toilet was nearby, and I used it between shifts, getting a look at the livid splotches blooming on my face and arms. No point grieving over the injuries. They'd heal. Meantime, I had to find the shunt where Mid Coast Urb carriers were being loaded.

After looking in all the wrong places, I found a carrier headed in the right direction and climbed painfully onto the partial load only moments before the doors were closed and sealed. This time Joram's instructions for anchoring were uppermost in my mind, so I tied the arms of my jacket to anchor straps and sealed the jacket around me, arms tight at my sides. I fell asleep and woke much, much later, surprised that I'd slept at all even though Joram had told us it was not only possible but advisable to sleep en route whenever one could.

I was slightly rested, but every bruised place on me had stiffened. Even small movements hurt. The midcoastal transfer station was hectic, with people constantly moving about, and I waited for some time before a lull gave me the chance to clamber out and then up to the top of the carrier. I lay there, numb where I didn't hurt, hoping Joram had been right about no one ever looking on top of carriers. When night came, the activity slowed; incoming and outgoing loads were less frequent, and I was able to use the toilet, wash up, refill my water bottle, and nose about for a carrier headed to Baja Urb I. The first several were fully loaded, with no room for either a passenger or the air a passenger would need to survive. The next one was only half-loaded, but the time of departure was several hours off. I hid nearby, hoping it would remain half-empty, as it did. When the time of departure was just minutes away, I sneaked in and anchored myself as before, this time staying awake during much of the trip, trying to remember Witt's face as I imagined furious arguments with him, me saying "See! See!," while he claimed we couldn't possibly do anything to withstand his mother.

When the carrier finally slowed and came to rest, my link-timer said it was evening of the third day "on the road," which was Joram's phrase. He had a lot of antique words and phrases. On the road. Across the street. In the country. Wedding cake. Witt's and mine had been an earth-cake, without any real taste. The thought of that tastelessness made me cry. It seemed suddenly typical of our relationship. We really had not savored one another as I had imagined cohabiting people should do.

Crying wasted time, however, so I sucked in my cheeks and bit down while disentangling myself. Carriers sometimes stop on a siding in the vacuum tube, but voices outside mean there's air, so I waited to hear voices. I finally heard them, too close. I hid in a niche between crates while the doors were opened and the voices went away. Finally, I climbed out, barely able to stand, and hid myself for a while to assess the situation. Things seemed quiet, so I moved gradually toward the loading section where the up-ramp was swarming with people and bots cleaning up after a loaded surface carrier that had been hit by a flit. It was enough of a mess to draw a crowd of down-dwellers and get all the human workers involved. When I went in the opposite direction, I happened on a labeled freight lift to level. As it turned out, I was under Tower 3.

Aunt Hatty lived in Tower 29, seven to nine miles from where I stood, depending upon which side of Tower 3 I would exit from and which side of Tower 29 I would come to first. It was late evening. Since traffic slightly decreased during hours of darkness, the only light at the lower levels was coming from the lighted podways that crisscrossed the urb towers like a giant gridiron. It was actually a good time to travel inconspicuously. Level Patrol officers are supposed to keep an eye on the down-dwellers, but they don't pay attention to anything short of a full-scale riot. Many of the people around me were wearing robes and masks or veils, which I hadn't seen before. Others wore ordinary clothes, perhaps not as dirty as those I had on, but dirt wasn't remarkable at level. Down-dwellers were dirty by definition. Dust had to be cleaned off solar collectors, dirt had to be washed off the sides of towers, which meant it all ended up in the bottoms of the chasms, coating the podways, building up beneath them, even making mud sometimes, when it rained. Once in a great while, the cleaning machines came through and took all of the muck out to the farms. From the looks of it, they hadn't been in Baja Urb for ages.

According to Joram, some urbs had unlicensed taxis at level, that is taxis without monitors. Perhaps they'd existed when Joram was young, but I didn't spot even one of them. I was too tired and achy to hurry. Besides, I had to locate all the past-this-point monitors before I passed one without realizing it. Often that meant quite lengthy detours. I didn't reach Tower 29 until the sky above the urb canyons was growing light. Joram's rule for covert travel was "Go high or go low," so I took a freight rampway down into the first sublevel garage section. Since we'd never had a flit, I'd never been in a garage section, but it looked much as Joram had described it, emptier than other places, and, except for cross walls separating the four quads and sixteen sectors, more open. The nearest walls had huge numbers at each entry, dark yellow on a lighter yellow field. Yellow is the uniform code for northeast, so I was in the northeast sector of the northeast quad, one of the twelve outer sectors used for deliveries and parking. The core, the four inner sectors, was where all the machinery that kept the tower running could be found.

I found an unmonitored service link along the wall and spoke Hatty's code into it.

She answered. "Where are you, dear?"

"In the garage."

"Which sector, dear?"

"Yellow-yellow."

"You're directly down the wall from me. I can't bring the flit down to you because I'm identichipped for Blue-blue. Can you . . . ?"

"I'll get there."

"Do be careful. I'll meet you in Blue-blue, fifth level down."

"I'll be there. It may take me a while."

I located a convenience unit along the wall and stayed there for a brief rest while I ate my last nutrient bar and washed the exposed parts of my body. The bruises were suspicious enough without the filthy clothes, but I couldn't do anything about that. Wearily, I resolved to be very, very sneaky.

Blue meant northwest, and the most direct route to Blue-blue was along the outside wall, as Hattie had said, which had the added advantage of keeping me well away from the workers who thronged the service core. I had no idea how I'd get through the sector wall, but blue sector of yellow quad would be straight ahead. I shambled wearily in that direction, taking refuge behind parked flits or stacks of supplies whenever freight carriers rumbled by or flits screamed into parking areas.

About halfway along the wall, I came upon a pile of small cartons someone had been working on with a routing labeler. A robe and veil were hung on the wall behind the pile, left there, perhaps, by someone who wasn't used to wearing them yet? Or someone who had gone to the toilet and didn't want to be bothered with them? Thievery is supposed to be impossible, but this was an exception. Without a qualm, I put on the robe and draped the veil over my head, thankful the person they belonged to was about my height. Now, I might be seen by people, but I certainly couldn't be identified by them.

As I approached the wall between sectors, I saw the yellow doors of an empty lift standing open, and, almost miraculously, another set of doors, blue ones, at the back of the lift. The lifts served both sides! I took time to be sure no one was watching, then limped into the lift, took it down five floors, and went out the other doors into Yellow-blue. If the quad walls were also served by two-sided lifts, the cross-tower trip wouldn't take as long as I'd feared.

Another quarter-mile journey along the yellow wall under the blue numbers was interrupted only when a long procession of workers, half of them robed and veiled, emerged from a door in the service core and streamed along the quad cross wall toward the lifts, probably the night shift workers going home to their apartments in the tier above. To minimize podway crowding, most people who work in a tower also live in it. I didn't hide. I just fooled around with the machine next to me until they were gone, then I called down the lift and went through it into blue quad, yellow sector.

The rest of the way along the blue wall was almost totally silent, though I saw a few people leaving or entering the core and half a dozen machine operators noisily inspecting a weird piece of equipment in a far corner. At the final wall, I called down another lift and stepped through it to the far side.

Someone nearby said "Ahem," almost tentatively.

The figure was robed. It could have been anyone. I took a deep breath and risked it. "Hatty?"

Hatty lifted her veil. "My dear. Are they wearing robes in NW Urbs?"

"No." I gasped with relief. "They don't. I found the stuff near where I came into the tower."

She sniffed back a tear. "Take that robe off, put it in the lift, and send the lift all the way up, just in case the robe might be identified somehow. Then put this one on. I bought it for you, so you could get to my level without being seen."

When I took off the robe, she gasped. "My dear, what in the name of serenity has happened to you?"

"I forgot about not getting into an empty carrier."

"Oh, child, child. You look beaten half to death. Your whole face is bruised, and look at your arms!"

"All of me is bruised, Hatty. Don't fuss. It's nothing that won't heal."

Hattie started to hug me, then thought better of it since there was no nonlivid part of me to grasp. I struggled into the new robe, as she said, "I didn't bring the flit because I thought people might be looking for you in the flit or pod lobbies, so we're going to take the passenger lift to the sorting lobby on the fiftieth floor. There's a fixed monitor to the right of the lift door as we go out. I'll move out and put my large self right against it while you walk past me and get at least twenty feet away. It will yammer at me, 'Do not loiter, move on,' but you pay no attention, just move quickly past, so I can move and shut the thing up. We'll do the same thing at each monitor until we get home. I've been scouting for two days. We can avoid all but five, but I know where all the beastly things are!"

According to Joram, all four of the Lipkin sisters had been a bit wild. Seeing Hatty in action, I could believe it. She blocked the monitors all the way to her apartment, including her own door monitor, until I was safely inside. Only after we were inside did she tear up again, dabbing at her wet eyes with her sleeve as she helped me out of the robe.

"Do you really think they're looking for you this soon, dear?"

I thought about it for a moment. "No. Not yet. Since I sometimes spend several days at the sanctuary, they'll assume I'm there, or with Paul and Tad. When I don't show up for six or seven days, that's when they'll start querying the past-this-point recorders."

She shook her head, angrily. "Tad and I had a long talk, on a public link just in case they had his link or mine diverted. He told me about everything. I'm so furious at that dreadful woman! Tad has decided that since you've come down to stay with me, he'd like to come, too. He says he's only stayed this long because of you, and it seems Luth Fannett would love nothing better than to have the liaison contract terminated. Tad says Paul is impossible to please, which doesn't surprise me. Matty despaired of him when he was only a child. Tad is family, however, just as you are, and I'm listed in Matty and Joram's original liaison as an appropriate guardian until he's eighteen. So long as I serve as coparent, there'll be no problem."

"I didn't realize that Luth was eager to . . ."

"According to Tad, she badly wants out. Paul sounds most unpleasant!"

I shook my head. "It's probably not Paul as much as it is Paul and his concs. He and I share a father, so he tolerates me so long as I let him manage me. He doesn't share anything with Taddeus, so he doesn't spend any of his limited supply of congeniality on Tad."

She drew herself up, eyes flashing. "And does he manage you?"

"I let him think so. It makes him feel as though he's in charge, and when he's being in charge, he's reasonably pleasant and sometimes interesting. I admit that Tad and Luth are much happier when Paul's away, which means I am, too. Tad's a lot like Mother, and we're fond of one another."

Hattie shook her head at me. "Well then, it's for the best. Fortuitously, there's available space adjacent to this apartment, and I've already spoken for an allotment for Tad. It will be enough for you to have a little room of your own, Jewel dear, even if no one is to know you're here. How long do you think you'll need to hide?"

She saw from my blank expression that I wasn't up to making predictions, so she hugged me very gently, and we stopped talking about it. In fact, I stayed in Hattie's apartment for months. My little room was hardly more than a closet, but I only used it to sleep in, or to hide when Hatty had visitors. When I needed a doctor, as I did soon after arrival, one of Hattie's medical friends paid a call. When my few bits of clothing wore out, Hattie bought a new supply. So far as Dame Cecelia was concerned, I was dead, though Tad stayed in touch with my arkist friends in the Northwest, who knew differently.

Tad brought word from Shiela Alred that Dame Cecelia was in a rage at my disappearance. No one except the lowliest down-dweller could vanish, but I had done so. Record checks of past-this-point monitors showed nothing. I had not returned to Witt's apartment or to Paul's. I was not at the sanctuary. I hadn't taken space anywhere else. After Taddeus moved to Baja, BuOr spent some time watching his comings and goings, but he didn't lead them anywhere but back and forth to school.

When the better part of a year had gone by, Gainor Brandt met Botrim Prime at a meeting of upper-level bureaucrats, where Boaty confided that Dame Cecelia had stopped looking for me.

When Gainor asked why she had been so determined, Prime said, "She's been watching the birth registry, trying to learn if Jewel had a child by her son."

Gainor repeated this to Shiela, who told Tad, who told me.

Shiela had been right all along about the Dame. Hatty arrived home to find me in tears, though whether of anger, grief, or relief, I couldn't say.

"What happened?"

I told her what I'd heard.

Hatty sniffed. "I imagine you're feeling an ambiguous amalgamation of vengefulness and exhaustion."

"I don't know what to feel," I confessed. "Not about her, or me, or even Witt."

She sniffed. "If Matty had lived, you would never have liaised with Witt."

That stung. "Matty wouldn't have stopped my loving him," I cried. Which was crazy, because that word wasn't one we'd used, not ever, not even when we were in bed together, but recently I'd been preferring to believe I loved him. Everything seemed so pointless, otherwise.

"Not if you really did, Jewel, but you didn't really pick him as a mate, you know. You wanted to get away from Paul. You were at loose ends regarding your own future. It was a way out, and you liked Witt well enough . . ."

Her assessment was entirely too close to my own valuation of the real situation. "I'm very fond of Witt . . ."

"How would you know? Paul has been manipulating your feelings since you were a child, so you've learned to repress them, all of them, not only loud, vehement emotions but the subtle ones you need for day-to-day guidance . . ."

I had no idea what she meant, and said so, angrily.

She looked over my shoulder, her face grim. "We all have little feelings that tell us something isn't quite right, that there's danger lurking, that trouble brews, that a person whom we otherwise like quite well disturbs us in unpleasant ways. When the subtle warnings are stifled, we're handicapped."

"I don't think I ever had any," I said, still miffed.

"All the Lipkin women have them! If Matty had lived, she'd have taught you to pay attention to them. If you'd been more aware, your own sensibilities would have warned you about Witt."

It was true that I was angry about Witt and at him, but that didn't mean I didn't grieve over his loss. He hadn't deserved his fate, whatever it had been! No matter how impossibly he'd behaved during the last day we'd been together, he had not deserved that. Besides, I told myself I had many nice memories of him. I told myself I must have loved him, or I wouldn't remember him so often. I did not, then, analyze the memories for actual content, though I did so eventually, with considerable chagrin.

That was the only time Hatty was anything but loving and supportive, and I simply forgot her analysis, or at least set it aside. I went out into the world again, and we went on with our reasonably comfortable lives in the weeks and months that followed until, on my twentieth birthday, I received a link from Paul.

In a surprisingly affable tone, he said: "Taddeus told me where to reach you because I have something that might interest you . . ."

"Interest me, Paul?"

"If you're interested in seeing some nonterrestrial animals, or visiting some other world. You used to talk about going off planet a good deal. I have a contract on Quondangala to study Quondan linguistics as part of an analysis of Human-Quondan legal terminology for Earth Bureau of Trade."

"I'm not a linguist, Paul."

"Of course you're not, Jewel. But you're a woman, and the Quondan are bisexual, with rather rigid societal expectations. The contract is dependent on my being part of a 'couple.' They tell me a female relative will do."

So I would "do." Though his all-too-typical approach made me seethe, the prospect of off-planet travel was exciting! Something new. Something that didn't remind me constantly of Witt.

The Quondan people are often described as faceless. In truth, their sensory apparatus is merely concealed. They have ears hidden behind smooth webbing, mouths under a flap of skin, eyes that peer from behind a fringe of tendrils. They do not betray their feelings through facial expression, obviously, though one can pick up a good deal from their tone of voice.

In late afternoon the females, the Quondana, entertain one another at "Anglazhee," or "sound-viewing of the trees." On Quondangala, trees unfold at dawn and fold up toward evening with a melodic wooden clucking. Groves are planted that fold themselves harmonically. On one such occasion, when I remarked that I was fond of animals, a particular Quondana invited me to visit a farm, which I did. I had thought that unfamiliar animals would be interesting, but the several varieties I saw were sluggish and unintelligent, which surprised me.

In a later conversation I inquired about wild animals, learning there were none, and I remarked, without thinking, "We had many animals on Earth that were quite intelligent. It surprises me that yours are so . . . lacking in interest."

"Caaa," breathed the Quondana. "There were indeed intelligent creatures, but being pious, we killed them all."

I breathed slowly, willing myself not to flush. Tad has always teased me about turning red when I am upset, and I did not want to give offense. "Indeed," I replied, as casually as possible.

"Caaa. Our scripture teaches that Great He/She Quondanapu made only Quondan pairs in His/Her image in all aspects, as is evident from the fact we bear His/Her name! Therefore, to have any creature except ourselves resembling the great Quondanapu in any aspect is an affront to the holiness. Intelligence is an aspect of the great Quondanapu."

"I see," I murmured, forcing myself to sit quietly.

The Quondana continued, "Unfortunately, we were ignorant at that time of other deities. When we first encountered other intelligent races, we thought they were also an affront to the Holiness! We behaved piously and sought to kill them."

"Really?" I murmured. "Which ones?"

"Oh, several. The Tharstians. The Orskimi. The Derac, who were—are—very strong, very ferocious. They like war very much, and they retaliated against us. Quondanga lost several worlds, many, many people."

"But you are at peace with them now?"

"One cannot be at peace with quishimug, how you say? Those-not-like-oneself. But one can be amgrug, that is, not-at-war. We are amgrug with Earth or its people. We allow you fissimugra, tolerated-vermin-hood. This state of affairs is thanks to our great philosopher,

Quandatis-bor-Bastree. It was Bastree who pointed out that other starfaring races had no doubt been created by other gods to resemble themselves. Thus they would be no affront to Quondanapu who, as scripture makes clear, limited His/Her creation to our home world, and all the people originating on that world. When away from our worlds, we are no doubt equal. When on our world, you are no doubt inferior, as our people are when upon yours, but verminhood is not your permanent state."

"I see," I said again.

"One will take you to observe the Perfection of Appearance. It is a worthy thing to do."

The following day, she did indeed escort me to a large building in the center of the nearest city. In a central room of that place, on a high throne, sat one of the Quondan, quite naked, showing that it had both male and female attributes.

"Such are born from time to time," said the Quondana. "One bearing all the attributes of Quondanapu. They grow up to sit in the heart of our cities, a symbol of our image in truth."

I heard a hissing behind me and turned to see a small crowd of Quondans pointing at me. The Quondana I was with spoke to them harshly, and they went away, not before I had heard the translated conversation.

"Why is this vermin allowed in the holy precinct? Who is she who brings vermin here?"

"This is a being from another planet, with another god, in whose image she is made. She is vermin, true, but she is acceptable vermin!"

When we had gone outside, I asked, "Why am I acceptable vermin?"

"Caaa. We have been gratified in meeting the Earthers, yes, for your own scripture and actions are in accord with ours. You also have a militancy upon your world that is vigilant in destroying other intelligences. A human person called Moore, who has named his militancy, In God's Image . . ."

"Iggy-huffo." I said quietly, swallowing the bile that had risen in my throat.

"Ah, you are familiar with it. Your people, also, are made in your deity's image and you, also, are doing away with all lesser intelligences to preserve the purity of your worship."

"The one, back there, will it sit on that throne all its life?"

"Yes. Which will not be long. Holy images do not eat or drink, of course. They do not excrete as we do. They merely show themselves until they have weakened too much, then they are placed in the sanctuary of likenesses. There they die. Would you like to see the sanctuary?"

I managed to refuse the invitation in a deferential way. The Quondana went on to describe some of the worlds her people had encountered, those they found acceptable and those they did not. Discovery was one of the few topics considered appropriate for discussion during the rigidly ritualized observance of Anglazhee, during which many tiny plates of traditional snacks were served, along with tiny cups of differently named though uniformly unpleasant teas, both hot and cold.

"... so we left the little planet to itself," concluded the Quondana. "We will sell it, if we can."

"You chose not to colonize the little planet," I asked, hoping for some clarification, for I had not followed her talk in my preoccupation with swallowing a particularly revolting fluid.

"Indeed. It partook of both tomooze and flabbitz. Flabbitz we would eschew of our own accord, and tomooze our scripture bids us avoid in any place we settle."

I recognized the word *flabbitz* as one used each time the Quondana had said *vermin*. The other word, I did not recognize.

"Paul," I asked later in the day. "What is *tomooze*."

"Where did you hear that word?" he demanded. "I thought the females spoke Earthian to you. Improving their Earthian was why they asked for a couple."

"They do speak Earthian," I said, surprised. "But they have some words that have no Earthian equivalent."

He frowned, annoyed, finally saying, "I suppose it hasn't. Tomooze means something like 'finally-unwelcoming,' or 'totally adversely affecting.' If a group of Quondan go someplace, and one of them gets sick, the place is said to have tomooze. If they eat something that doesn't agree, the food has tomooze. If they encounter one another and a quarrel breaks out, the people who quarreled are influenced by tomooze."

He explained grudgingly, as though it were none of my business. "Or, the place had it. Or the weather had it that day. Or anything else they can think of."

"And *flabbitz*?" I pursued.

"Flabbitz is an intrinsic quality of outrageousness, atrociousness, or strangeness. As a category, the word includes everything the Quondan don't think, eat, wear, or do habitually. It can be associated with tomooze. Anything that has flabbitz is sure to cause tomooze, though not all tomooze arises from flabbitz."

Which was why the Quondanga had objected to my being in their temple. No doubt vermin had flabbitz.

I didn't pursue the matter, but during the balance of our tour of duty, I made copious notes concerning places, people, and things that had tomooze and how the impression of tomooze might be given in places it did not actually exist.

HOW I
BECAME
A SPY

⋮ When our tour on Quondangala was over, Paul invited me to move back into the apartment in NW Urb 15. Adjacent space had become available, the space allotment for two people was much more comfortable than for one alone and the move, so he said, would let me return to my "hobby" at the sanctuary.

I deferred the decision until I'd had a chance to talk with Gainor Brandt. I went to his office, and after I'd complimented him on his changed appearance (he had a new transgenic scalp, rampageous with hair), I explained my problem.

"Aunt Hatty wants to leave Earth to live with her two sisters on Faroff, Gainor, but she says she'll stay to keep me company if I don't want to live with Paul. If I live with her, it means staying in Baja. I'd rather come back to the sanctuary to work, but that means either a minimum space allotment somewhere or back with Paul. He wasn't this bad while he was still in school, but now it's like living on the edge of a volcano." We still had volcanos, of course. Several urbs had been wiped out by eruptions, and nothing mankind could come up with had stopped that natural force, not even tapping earthcore for energy.

Gainor ran his hands through his newly luxuriant hair and nodded slowly. "I know it's difficult, Jewel, but if you can tolerate living with him, I wish you would."

He saw how astonished I was at that.

He said, "Remember the journal you turned over to Shiela when you got back from Quandangala?"

"Of course. Before I left, she told me to keep my mouth shut, to pretend no more than a polite interest in anything that went on, to learn as much of the language as I could and make notes of any discovered worlds that weren't being colonized. I just followed orders."

"I have experienced agents who could not have done as well."

"You mean the information was useful?"

"Using your information, we managed to pick up at auction three planets supposedly cursed with tomooze, and therefore 'worthless.' We'd never have known about them if not for you. We also relied upon your information concerning flabbitz as a precursor of tomooze, which proved helpful in the purchase of still other planets. It takes only a few allegations of ineradicable flabbitz to make places unattractive to the Quandanga."

"Tomooze and flabbitz are useful? I had no idea." I was weirdly gratified and annoyed, both at once. Glad to have helped, miffed that they hadn't told me sooner. "I wish someone had told me."

"I was going to. When the time was right, which seems to be this evening. If you can bear it, stay with him, Jewel. He's in demand. He travels a lot, often into places accessible only to specialists. Anytime you can use him to go anywhere, let us know. Meantime, if he gets into one of his difficult stages, stay at the sanctuary. Consider the sanctuary your refuge; consider the dogs your avocation; and consider traveling with Paul your real profession. Since he gives you little or nothing, for your trouble, we'll see that you're well paid for it."

"Some money would be very welcome," I admitted. At that point, I was still several years from getting the trust funds left by my father. I had some of Matty's original documents, including the unedited recording of her first exploration and a first edition of Lipkin's Seventh, which could always be sold if need be, but I wouldn't do that unless disaster struck. "The worst part is his escapades with those damned concs. They . . . they offend me."

Gainor grimaced, leaning back in his chair and folding his hands across his expansive belly. "His have no doubt adapted to his own preferences, but in the main, concs seem to have been designed to be inoffensive. They're quite modest. The organs which were obviously designed with humans of either sex in mind only evert or invert during sensual play and only to the extent required. Otherwise, they're as sexless as dolls. They don't show temper or frustration or grief, they express no feelings except for childlike gaiety, curiosity, and a consistent sensuality."

"They can feel pain," I objected, knowing so from firsthand experience. "They'll cry like children—or puppies—when they're hurt . . . or killed." They could be killed. I knew that.

"Oh, of course," agreed Gainor, lifting one nostril in disgust. "And ruined ones are occasionally violent, as they've been conditioned to be. Their creators no doubt considered such conditioning necessary if they were to be sexually attractive to all users."

I said angrily, "How would another race know that?"

"Anyone who knows anything about terran animals knows that, Jewel. Competition is evolution's engine. Aggression is a way of competing, sexual aggression increases hormones, increased hormones increase aggression, which is a broadband drive. It is generally directed toward competitors, but it can slop over onto the target or even onto innocent bystanders. An unwilling female can turn aggression into pure violence. Even willing females can become unwilling out of pain or fear or both, at which point the mating ritual can turn into rape, assault, even murder. Stallions sometimes killed mares. Bulls sometimes killed cows. Male primates sometimes killed female primates. So also, alligators, bears, the larger variety of chimpanzees. Work your way through the animal alphabet."

"Not very romantic," I remarked, making a face.

"On a biological level, reproduction scorns romance. Only a civilized intelligence yokes sexuality to sentiment, a team that was never designed to pull together. Which is one reason concs are so successful."

They were that. They were ubiquitous in public, occasioning no more than a casual glance. And of course, no one knew how many were kept in private.

"Why are they here?" I asked. "No one has ever told us why they're here or where they came from."

Gainor shook his head at me. "Have you ever asked that question before, Jewel?"

I said, in some surprise, "No. I don't think I ever have."

"Doesn't that frighten you?" He ran his hand uneasily across his mouth.

I gaped at him.

He said. "Doesn't it frighten you that the question is infrequently asked? There are half a dozen answers, by the way, none of them guaranteed to be true. And almost no one really cares. Which frightens me, a lot."

⋮   That trip to Quondangala was girlhood's swan song, the last time I was able to live on the surface of my world without knowing—or perhaps, while disregarding—all the potent currents and eddies that went on underneath. Like many Earthers, I'd bobbed along on a little raft of acceptable fiction, not in total safety but not in terror, either. After that conversation with Gainor, things changed. I didn't panic. I didn't start hiding under the bed, but the whole matter of why-the-concs nagged at me. I could figure out for myself why no one cared very much. As Gainor had said, they were inoffensive. They were quite attractive. There was nothing at all threatening about them. One thing I was sure of. Someone, somewhere was making a profit out of them. So far as anyone knew, concs were found only on Earth. I began thinking seriously of going off world permanently. Exploring that possibility became part of my motivation in accompanying Paul on his off-world assignments.

Most of his off-planet trips were quite brief. Sometimes I went as half a "couple," other times as an aide-de-camp, someone to take care of the dull details. Before each one, I spent time with the arkists, learning what they needed to know about my destination and who might have that information. During each journey, I kept quiet, listened with great concentration, and gave no indication of interest beyond the merely polite. The information I garnered went straight to Gainor Brandt, where it was used to spread our arkists onto several more "worthless" planets and moons that either were then or could soon be able to support terran fauna.

The seventh trip after Quondangala was to a Phain settlement planet, Tsaliphor. The Phain are an elder race as measured both by the length of their recorded history and the number of worlds they occupy, worlds that are widely spread throughout our arm of the galaxy and even in, toward the center, where radiation is known to be hostile to many forms of life. Usually, the only non-Phain allowed to visit Phain worlds are the personnel working at the embassies, not that the Phain recognize them as embassies. They are "foreign presences" who are allowed to lease space on the planet for finite, and usually brief, periods of time. The Phain do not maintain embassies on other planets, either. They have an observer or two at IC meetings, but that's the limit of their interest in the "younger" races, which includes just about everyone.

"Foreign presences" was at least preferable to "acceptable vermin," and linguists often go to places others do not. Their experience in those places may be quite restricted, however, as was ours on Tsaliphor. As soon as we arrived, the Earthian ambassador told us we were to live in the embassy and leave it only if invited to do so by one of the Phaina, that is, the female Phain. The males were interested in religion, art, and business, and did not socialize with aliens, but sometimes, rarely, the Phaina did.

Paul had once again been summoned to work on legal syntax for IC Linguistics Board. The ambassador said the reason for my presence was Phainic curiosity. The embassy staff was entirely male, so the Phain had never seen an Earther female. I was, in other words, a zoo exhibit. I was prepared to be outraged about my status at the earliest opportunity, but nothing outrageous happened. Days went by with me cooped up in the embassy without ever seeing a he-Phain or a she-Phain. I was assured, when I asked, that none of them had seen me, though I had gone so far as to envision eyes in my showerbath and over my bed that would allow the Phain to satisfy their curiosity. It seemed odd to have been asked to come to the planet so they could see a female, then have no one interested in looking.

At night, when it turned cooler, I would sit in my window and look out across a scruffy spread of bare soil lying between the embassy and its high boundary wall, which ran along the edge of a road. A pair of tall metal gates, ornamentally contorted to represent growing trees and vines, allowed a blurred view of shapes moving on the road, presumably the Phain, though there was too much foliage in the way to distinguish them from any other, equally lumpy shadows. The embassy had been built in accordance with Earthian security regulations, which meant the only windows in the place were at the back, over this so-called garden, limiting our view of the world to whatever could be seen through the gates.

If I wanted to see out, I needed to be near the gates, which could be achieved if I had something to do there. I therefore asked for and received permission to work in the garden, a move of pure desperation to prevent my being overcome by boredom. My only experience with matters botanical had been during my years with Jon Point. The outer edges of the derelict park floor had received enough light and rain to grow things, and I'd been attracted by the novelty of growing something, anything. As I recall, Jon had found some seeds for me in an import shop, pumpkins and squash and tomatoes. I hadn't cared much for the pumpkins or the squash, but the tomatoes had been a revelation.

The ambassador kindly offered me the use of the tools in the supply room, most of them in new, unopened packages. There was no one on staff responsible for gardening, and no one in the place took any interest in it. How could they? The only places they'd ever lived had been in towers, on Earth, and the average park floor, though there were small trees in most of them, had little in common with a garden.

The view through the gate was of an expanse paved with huge, irregular blocks of stone that were interplanted with low, vividly colored creepers. Across the way was a park, or so I assumed, as it was given over completely to trees, shrubs, brightly colored flowers, and stands of gracefully waving grasses in various colors. The embassy garden was an unpleasant contrast. No effort had been put into making it look like anything, not even around the stone terrace that had been laid against the embassy wall. A few symbolic earth plants had been plopped down here and there, but they were not flourishing. The only things that were flourishing were the native trees that had obviously been there before the embassy was built.

The first few days I spent my time loosening the soil around the trees and peering through the gates. I noticed that the Phaina walking in the roadway took care not to step on the vivid creepers that grew between the stones. I knew they were Phaina because they were only half again as tall as I. I'm tall for a human woman—a throwback, Joram said, referring to both my height and my coloring—but the male Phain are twice my height, and the ones I saw always walked in groups, carefully arranged as to height, their footsteps completely coordinated but by no means regular, each group moving to a different beat. One group took three steps, pause, another step, pause, two steps, pause, then started over. The next group might take two steps, pause, another two steps, pause, then five steps, three of them sideways. As they walked, they chanted, their voices coordinated with the beat of the walk, as though it were poetry, which in fact it may have been.

I saw no vehicles while I was there, but I saw no Phain carrying anything either. Perhaps freight was banned from this particular road, or perhaps they had some other mode of supply.

The creepers between the stones were in shades of green and blue and violet, with vividly yellow, red, or orange stems, and a number of them had crept under our gate from the street. I considered this an invitation to transplant them to the terrace, an easy enough procedure since each stem had roots all along its length, wherever it had touched the ground. I put them between the terrace stones, kept them wet for a day or two, and the planted sections took hold at once, rampaging along the cracks as though they could not grow fast enough to suit themselves. Looking about for other improvements, I found several stunted clumps of grassy stuff along the walls, perhaps native plants that had been deprived of sun when the wall had been built. Similar grasses were growing across the street, though they were large, burgeoning clusters that swayed when touched by the least breeze, their gold and blue and pale green tasseled seed heads moving gracefully in the wind.

Since no one seemed to care about the dead or moribund Earther bushes, I uprooted some of them in favor of bunches of the grasses, judging their ultimate height by those across the street that looked most similar. We had arrived, so we had been told, in the dry season, so I carried water to these new plantings as well, and they responded by doubling in size in a few days.

During all that time, I had not seen a Phain except at a distance through the gate, had not talked with anyone except Paul or the embassy staff, and only chatty inconsequentialities with them. Perhaps it was only that I was bored, but the garden began to assume a place in my life equivalent to the sanctuary at home on Earth. It was a place that needed fixing; it held things that needed preserving and nurturing; and, as Gainor had told me more than once, I seemed to be an inveterate fixer. I staked out a winding pathway from the terrace to the gates and resolved to find some way to create a real garden on either side of it.

The following morning I went out to find a score of branches and twigs lying at random on the dry soil. It was what one might expect to find after a windstorm, if there had been a windstorm, which I was quite sure there had not. Staring at the clutter I noticed that though they were obviously from different plants or trees, every twig or branch bore ripened seed heads, an extremely unlikely coincidence. Somebody was helping out.

I spent the entire day examining what I could see of the park across the road through a pair of power glasses borrowed from the security chief of the embassy, trying to determine which trees or shrubs had grown which twigs. One of them was easy for it stood directly opposite the gate, a very large tree with leaves of glossy turquoise and umbels of small, white flowers that gave off a scent something between vanilla and that odor one detects immediately after rain on dry soil. While there were buds on some branches and flowers on others, still other branches bore fruit and large, shiny triangular seeds, just like the ones I had found. I also identified one of the twigs as coming from a much shorter, rounded, many-trunked shrub that some days earlier had been covered with large-petaled, red blooms, the dried remnants of which still clung to the seed heads. One of my Bonner wall vistas had a flowering hedge in it, and I decided that plant was appropriate for hedging the embassy terrace.

I planted the seeds of the large tree along the inside of the wall, where grown trees would shade both the garden inside and the street outside. Seeds of the smaller shrubs were planted along the edge of the terrace to make a border that would soften its harsh appearance. The other seeds were stowed away in my room until I could find out what kind of growth had produced them.

Paul and I met only at the dinner table, where we practiced diplomacy on the embassy staff and one another. Paul spent his days in a conference room just inside the embassy entrance, with a couple of coworkers and a few Phain. At dinner, he remarked that they were ritualistically polite and completely devoted to the business at hand.

"No conversation?" I asked. "None at all?"

"Except for ritualized greetings and farewells, none at all," he verified, grumpily. "Which makes it much harder to learn the language. I'm about to believe they don't want me to learn it."

The long evenings were cooler than the very warm daylight hours, so I formed the habit of taking afternoon naps and watering the garden at night, interrupting myself occasionally to peer out through the gates like some prisoner in an ancient jail, reaching through the bars. Several weeks went by, and one morning I was told by the ambassador that I had been invited to take a walk with one of the Phaina, who would come to the gate for me, that afternoon.

The Phain are tall, as I've said, and bipedal, but not at all humanoid. The Phaina who came for me was the first Phain I had seen close enough to describe. She had four arms, which were extremely flexible, either multijointed or tentacular. Since she wore long, full sleeves on all four arms, and since the sleeves were tightly fastened at the wrists, if so they could be called, it was difficult to say which. Each of the upper pair of arms was equipped with three fingers and two opposing thumbs, the lower pair had simple two-fingered grippers with suction cups on the inner surfaces of the opposed fingers and retractable claws at the end, wrench and pliers, all in one. Her head was virtually without feature except for one crest and one ridge. Visualize an egg, pointed end up, with a thick belt around its widest girth, scaled or feathered above the belt, and with an erect tuft of colorful feathers on top. The belt around the head was made up of protruding eyes with rectangular eyelids, all the way around. The eyes could and did open in any combination, allowing a full 360-degree view of the world. Both breathing and speech came from vertical apertures on the neck. The ingestion organ should not be mentioned, I had been told privately, as it was somewhere on the body that was always kept modestly covered. The Phaina's feet were mostly hidden beneath her robes, but from what I could glimpse, I would say they were scaled, toeless, and rather elephantine.

I carried one of the embassy's porta-putes clipped to my belt, in order to speak with the Phaina, though I had been cautioned to let her speak first, which she did, in a flow of musical syllables. My linguipute said, "We have seen you working in the garden. Do you have any questions about our plants?"

I replied, "Yes. A wind must have blown in some twigs with seeds, and I can only identify a few of them. May I see what the mature plants look like?"

Whereupon we walked for some distance, she slowly and I at a gallop as her legs were vastly longer than mine, stopping here and there to look at bushes, trees, and shrubs, including many of surpassing beauty and lovely scent. Each one that she showed me happened "coincidentally" to match one of those that had "blown" into the garden, and each one had a medicinal or ecological purpose. Sometimes she picked a flower for me to smell, or cut away a section of bark. Her hands seemed designed for such tasks; the claws had sharp edges, like scalpels, capable of snipping even quite thick branches, as I saw when she cut a particularly lovely plant to half its original size.

Before I thought, I blurted, "Oh, but it's so pretty."

"Yes," she said, giving me what I interpreted to be a stern look. "The charb bush is good for many things. It provides a medicine for diseases of the skin. Its leaves make a delightful tea. The flowers create a perfume valued by many, and they are also lovely to look upon. It is necessary, however, to prune it ruthlessly."

I nodded. "Why?"

"You see how it stands alone? Its roots have spread widely and taken all the nourishment from the area around it. It makes a huge barren about itself if it is not kept in check."

I regarded the shrub with dismay. "It must be hard to cut back something that grows that well."

"It is very difficult," she agreed, "but if one is a good gardener, one does it, nonetheless."

I asked if I might take notes, then did so, making little sketches and comments as we chatted about plants, and about animals. The Phaina asked if I liked "other, perhaps nonspeaking beings." I said I did, that I worked to conserve animal life on Earth. She asked questions about this, and I told her all about the dogs and how much they meant to me. Strangely, though I had always followed the arkists' dictum of keeping animal-related things to myself, I talked quite freely to the Phaina, trying for the first time to explain wholeheartedly how I felt about animals in general and dogs in particular.

It was much more difficult than I would have supposed, possibly because I had to start with Matty, who had started my love affair with dogs. She and her sisters had pets when they were young, and the Lipkin family had supported the arkists for two centuries, maybe more than that. Even though no one could have animals on Mars because there literally wasn't any air or water for them, Matty still gave me pretend pets like the toy Faithful Dog. When the Phaina encouraged me, I even sang a little of the "Litany of Animals" for her.

She asked about my childhood, and I told her all about Mars, the airlocks, the algae farms, the vegetable tanks where fresh things could be grown in relatively small amounts of water. I said it was like living in a spaceship where the only beauty was the terrible grandeur outside, and even though people haɑ to wear uncomfortable XT suits to go outside, almost everyone, down to the smallest child, wanted to spend as much time out there as possible. I remember vividly how my continual feeling of being squashed and smothered eased when I stood under the sky and looked across the desert. I told her about Matty discovering the last Martians, and their dogs, and how she'd died because of it.

"Your people found no life there at all?" she asked.

"They found some very primitive bacteria, deep underground, and after Matty discovered the remains of the last Martians, they did another very intensive survey, because everyone thought if there had been a race living there, two races, actually, something had to be left! A building, or artifacts, or more bones, something, but they found nothing at all."

"What did they look like, these Martians, these dogs?"

I burrowed into my pocket to bring out the Lipkin Seventh album, with the picture of the cavern wall on its cover. The Phaina looked at that for quite some time, then asked me to play some of it. The last movement was my favorite, so I set the album on a flat place between us and let the music and the dancers fill the space.

At the end, the figures returned to their wall and the bones lay down on the floor of the cavern, dogs first, then the bipeds, arms around their friends, as they had been found while the last trembling notes ascended into silence. The Phaina remained silent for a long time. Finally, she asked, "This lovely representation, is it accurate?"

I started to say yes, but then reconsidered. "Matty always stylized things," I admitted. "One can always tell what they represent, but one would never mistake them for the real thing. Not if one has ever seen the real thing."

"But in this work by your parent, it is accurate to say the bones were actually there? The images were there? In that particular cavern? That was not invention."

"She didn't invent them, no! They were really there. I have her original recording if you want to see it. Bones of old people and old dogs. Evidently the young ones had left them there."

"Ah. Where is it supposed the young ones went?"

I shook my head. "Well, Matty thought the carvings were meant to represent human people and Earth-type dogs, so maybe they went to Earth. Even though the carved figures don't show faces or details of the anatomy, the proportions are very human . . ."

"So you think it possible that some men and some dogs went from Mars to Earth, long ago?"

I laughed. "Matty thought that. Our scientists say the idea is ridiculous. Earth-type humans and dogs were barely far enough advanced to tie two logs together to get across a river, they certainly couldn't get to Mars. The experts don't accept Matty's translation of the carvings, either. The professors at the IC archives have been arguing about it ever since she died. They've done over twenty new translations among them, none of them alike! The scientists say if there were men on Mars, then some other race took them there, but there's no evidence of that either, and since humans and dogs evolved on Earth and had no way to get off it, then the bones have to be of some other beings."

"And your geneticists say?"

"They say all Mars's air and water were gone by fifty to a hundred thousand years ago, so the bones are at least that old. They say that's the outside limit to get DNA from, even in perfect situations, which this wasn't. The bones had been colonized by some kind of microbes, and the scientists couldn't get any DNA to analyze. Anatomically, the bones are very human and very doggy, the scientists do admit that."

She mused, as though to herself, "And nothing on the planet but this one . . . entombment."

"It doesn't seem logical, does it?" I shook my head. "Everyone has puzzled over it. Prehistoric human people generally left stuff behind, bones and tools chipped out of flint, and then later on broken pots and pictures on the cave walls, and burials . . ."

"Prehistoric humans? Tell me about them."

I shrugged, apologetically. "I'm no expert. I know only what we all learned in school. There were bipedal primates on Earth as far back as six million years ago, various races of them, some bigger, some smaller, very little smarter than most animals, and they didn't change much over the millennia except that some of the races died off. Then, sometime around a million years ago, one particular race made an evolutionary jump and developed a brain three times bigger. They learned how to use fire and chip flints for knives and weapons. Probably they also developed protolanguage, but there's no way we can verify that. They spread around the contiguous world.

"Then about fifty thousand years ago a race in Africa made another jump, a brain jump of some kind. Possibly they developed a better or more extensive language which let them accumulate knowledge and pass it on. My opinion is that they acquired the ability to imagine, the ability to ask, 'What if?' because their technology improved very rapidly after that. That race of humanoids was the one that spread throughout the world, all the older manlike races died off, and with minor genetic variation, that was our history up until now."

"Fifty thousand of your years. Your people live, on average, about one hundred of those years, do they not, so that would be not even a maraquar, only five hundred lifetimes ago . . ."

I smiled at that "only." Five hundred lifetimes seemed a great many to me.

We strolled a bit, then she asked, "You say your mother had dogs? How does one have a dog?"

"Oh, like having a child or an aunt, a member of the family."

"So, the dog is part of your family. Are you part of the dog's family, also?"

Remembering Scarlet, I said, "If we are not, then we cannot say the dog is ours. We . . . love one another, and sometimes dogs adopt children, as if we were puppies. Or sisters, maybe. Of course, on Mars, I only had pretend dogs . . ."

"And then, in time, you met real dogs."

"Yes. I met real dogs I could help and do things for. It made me feel . . . more . . . complete." I struggled, trying to find the right words, the truthful words. "I loved them because they weren't like people. They were different. We need things to be different. If everyone is alike, it narrows our world down, it makes us narrow, too. It makes us think human things are the only things, human ideas the only ideas . . ."

"But I have heard it said that humans believe each human is uniquely different, is this not true?"

"It's true that it's said," I replied. "But it's actually true only in the way any two leaves on a huge tree are different. Some live high, some low, some are healthy, some aren't, some drop before their time, others linger on the tree, but they're all the same kind of leaf. Difference is more a label than a fact."

"You feel you are all alike?"

She asked the question with a peculiar intentness, so I forced myself to concentrate on an answer. "We have different ideas," I said at last. "There's a man named Evolun Moore who is the head of iggy-huffo—do you know about iggy-huffo?" She nodded, and I went on. "He sees humankind as the God-chosen occupiers of the galaxy. He preaches this to people who have difficult and unpleasant lives, and it makes them feel good, so they follow him. He insists they obey him, and that makes them feel good, since it gives them a . . . a position, a place, a particular status. It means he's paying attention to them. They'll lie down and let him walk on them if he wants to, because he's important and if they follow him, they're important, too . . ."

"But not all of you follow him," she said, insistently.

"No. Not all of us."

"Then you differ."

I considered this. "As I said, in ideas. We struggle with identity. If we aren't worrying about who we are, we are busy telling everyone what we aren't. We fret about our mortality. If we aren't grieving over the fact we're eventually going to die, we're courting death because life doesn't please us. I have heard people say that if it weren't for the afterlife promised by their particular religion, they couldn't bear to go on living."

"That must be confusing," whispered the Phaina. "If they can't bear life, why would they want more of it?"

"It is confusing, yes. Mankind pretends to love nature but destroys it wherever he goes. We claim that life is sacred, but we leave it no room in which to exist. Not long ago, even when we said every human is unique and holy, our children were taught which types of unique and holy humans were the best and which they should hate."

"Not long ago?"

"Before we met outsiders, people not of Earth. Now we don't learn to hate humans anymore."

"Just outsiders, eh?" She laughed, a truly amused sound. "You. How are you different from most?"

"I'm an arkist. We're suspicious of following anyone. We like to figure things out for ourselves. When we look at ourselves in the mirror, we know we aren't the wisest or best creatures in the galaxy; we also know we aren't nothing. When we consider that we will die, we struggle to do something with the time we have. We don't confuse heedless and selfish proliferation of our race with reverence for life. We know that other creatures are sometimes better than we are. We try to learn from them."

She nodded to herself, eyelids flickering. "We find you puzzling, you humans, for we have never seen a race quite like yours. Dogs, now, are a different thing. We do know of a race that much resembles this representation of dogs."

"Really! Where are they? What are they called?"

"They are called the Simusi, and they live a great distance from here, near my Guardian House . . ."

Her voice trailed off, and I actually blurted, without thinking, "What's a Guardian House?"

Her upper arms rippled. "Certain areas of the galaxy are . . . protected by the elder races from incursion by marauders or vandals. Those of us who guarantee the defense of such places—the Phain, the Yizzang, among others—maintain Guardian Houses in the neutral zones between these areas and occupied space. Most Phaina grown past childhood are assigned to spend one time out of ten at a Guardian House."

She hummed again, a very thoughtful, quiet hum, then asked me a whole string of questions. What were my favorite animals next to dogs? What had the arkists done to save elephants? Whales? Foxes? I probably said a good deal more than I needed to, for she kept finding things to ask. When she ran out of questions, which she did, eventually, she asked if I would like to see Phainic animals, and I said yes, I would very much enjoy that. She set a date in five days' time.

I, meantime, went back to the garden, uprooted the rest of the Earth plants that no one ever looked at, and planted the seeds that had been identified for me. They grew with great vigor, breaking the surface of the soil overnight and springing upward over a foot a day thereafter. As I was going into the garden a couple of days later, just to see how much they had grown, I noticed a Phaina standing at the gate, looking in and immediately decided she was "my" Phaina, coming to see how the garden grew. I went to the gate, but by the time I reached it, she had gone.

She did, however, come for me on the appointed day, and I went with her to meet the animals of their world. Since she had no "name" as we think of names, I addressed her as Sannasee, which means honored female, and she called me the same—very much nicer than vermin, acceptable or otherwise. We walked down the street, around a few curves, and entered a park. It may have been the same park as the one across the road from the embassy, or perhaps just a stretch of natural forest, which was what it looked like.

"You spoke of your relationship with dogs," she said. "These coming to meet us are the same friends for us as dogs for you."

Through the woods came a monstrous furry mass, a great fanged and clawed six-legged beast which reared upon its hind legs and extended the other two pair as if in greeting, and whuffed at us. He was much larger than any dog I had ever seen, about the size of a big bear, but he smelled doggish, so I greeted him as I would have one of the sanctuary dogs, using my sparse Phain-ildar vocabulary to say something like, "I greet you and wish you well."

Beside me, the Phaina stirred. I thought perhaps she was going to correct my accent or tell me it was inappropriate to speak to animals, but she didn't. Instead, she also greeted the creature, using almost the same words I had used. The beast, which she told me was a P'narg, purred at her, then at me—a noise like a large engine turning over—turned around and lumbered off in a six-legged waddle, while from another direction a collection of brightly colored scaled, winged creatures descended upon us. These were only the first of many encounters during the afternoon. At first slightly apprehensive, I grew steadily more comfortable with the creatures, who seemed to have no fear of me or of the Phaina, and to be perfectly at home with our two species.

The Phaina, several of whom I saw moving among the animals, were equally at ease. Through the 'pute, I asked my guide if this was a special place or if the animals lived here naturally. She said it was just a part of nature, that all Phain dwelling places (which is how the 'pute translated it) had nature flowing through and around them. I asked how many centuries it had taken to establish this balance, and the Phaina, after a moment's hesitation, said, "On this world, after many maraquar, it is still being established. You are perceptive to realize it is purposeful. We remain uncertain how many Phain may be allowed to be born on this world to live in harmony. It is possible we are already too many, and some of us must make the difficult choice."

"To leave," I said sadly, even then reluctant to leave their world myself. "That would be very difficult."

"Or to die," she said, "which is often less so."

I was shocked, though I hoped I did not show it, and I remembered the remark. On the way home, staring at my feet in order not to step on the creepers, I realized that the street wasn't paved with stones. The stones were of an exposed layer of lava that had cracked over time. They had, so to speak, grown there. When I got back to the embassy, I looked up *maraquar*. It means something like era, or age, anything from a few dozen years to a few hundred thousand.

The Phaina's use of the word *harmony* had inspired me to ask about music, and she invited me to hear some. From that time on, though I continued to work in the embassy garden, I spent a great deal of time with the Sannasee, listening to music, talking with animals, learning about trees, and watching processions and rituals. It was always the Phain who took part in them.

"Would it be impolite to ask what they are doing?" I asked one day while we were watching several groups of Phain make their cadenced and chanted way along a road.

"They are praying," she said.

Without thinking, I asked, "What do they pray for?"

"Since your people were allowed to come here, they pray for you," she said. "For your people."

I could not think of anything to ask at that point that would not have seemed rude, but her words joggled something in my mind, and it occurred to me in that instant that in all our walking about, I had not seen a single wall that shut off one open space from the general space. There were no walled gardens in any place I had gone except the embassy itself. When I returned to the embassy, I went to the ambassador's office and asked to speak to him privately for a few moments. I felt strongly that I must do so, though without any clear idea why. I told him the Phaina who had met with me had showed me their town or city or settlement, that I thought the exhibit was purposeful, not casual. I said she had identified plants for me. I said she had come to the gate to observe what was happening to the garden. I said, "Ambassador, I urge you to get a permanent staff member in here who is interested in plants and animals, and do everything you can to make the space around this embassy bloom. Also, you should tear down the garden wall."

He smiled at me in a condescending way, and with a flash of insight I realized Paul had spoken to him about me, as Paul often did, explaining that I was useful though not very bright.

"Dear Madam Delis," he murmured in a kindly, avuncular voice, "when I was sent here, I was given priorities by Worldkeeper, oh, such a great list of priorities that it would bore you to even look at it! I'm terribly sorry, but gardening is not even on the list. And as for the wall, we have no authority to tear it down. It was built for security reasons."

"I apologize for wasting your time," I said stiffly. "I had assumed you wanted the Phain to look on us with respect."

"Respect," he said. "Respect? Are you saying that they will not respect us unless we become diggers in the soil? Unless we open ourselves to attack?" He laughed, a complacent, avuncular laugh.

Despite his manner, I answered his question. "It seems extremely likely that their respect turns on exactly such a decision." I honestly wasn't sure, though I would have bet my own life on it.

He smiled at me kindly, patted my hand, and bid me have a nice day.

It was a nice day, as were those that followed. I saw the Phaina several times more. On the day before we were to leave, I thanked her for her time and courtesies.

"It is the least we can do," she said. I thought she sounded quite sad about it. "A way of atonement to one with exceptional dalongar."

I didn't know the word, but I let it go by. "You have nothing to atone to me for. You have been kindness itself."

She started to say something, then turned away, leaving me no more confused than I had been most of the time on her planet. That time on Tsaliphor was the best and loveliest time I have ever had, anywhere, and that world is the only planet I had visited that I wept to leave.

Several months later, back on Earth, Paul and his coworkers fin ished their work on the Phain language and issued a report that included, in an appendix at the back, the statement that the Phain language was replete with words and phrases referring to "dalongar" of persons, situations, places. Some of these words and phrases were applied to the names of worlds and people, identifying degrees of "dalongar."

I remembered the Phaina using the word, so I looked it up in the Phain-ildar glossary. The word dalongar was sometimes used as a prefix or word root, signifying places or peoples with whom the Phain would trade. Paul had translated *dalongar* as *protocol* or *custom*, which made no sense to me at all. At a meeting of arkists, after the report was issued, a man associated with the diplomatic corps told me I had been among the last human persons to be allowed on Tsaliphor. The Phain had severed any formal relationships with Earth as well as any Earth-settled planet because of human "discourtesy." After hearing that, I stayed awake night after night, wondering what I'd done wrong while I was there, talked to the wrong animal or planted the wrong thing in the wrong place. It seemed to me that I'd walked on eggs to be polite.

I confessed to Gainor that the whole thing might be my fault. Gainor, however, had recently spoken to his friend, the Tharstian who kept trying to convert him to Mahalusianism. (I should remark here that Tharstians were not quite an old race, but getting there, though they still went about meddling in others' affairs and making gratuitous suggestions as to how we might improve ourselves.) The Tharstian had friends among the Phain and was told by some of them that the Earthian ambassador had been warned about his discourtesy, and the ambassador hadn't paid attention.

I shook my head at Gainor. "He really didn't pay attention to things, Gainor. I tried to tell him about the garden, for example, but he simply wasn't listening at all. Besides, I think Paul's translation of *dalongar* was wrong. It doesn't mean *protocol* at all. I think it must mean *courtesy* or *respect* in the context of equilibrium or symmetry . . ."

"Weren't our people courteous and respectful?" he asked, surprised.

"To the Phain, I'm sure they were, but the Phain are only one part of their world. Being polite only to the Phain is like someone being polite to my face while stepping on my feet. Our people were not respectful of their totality, their world." I described how the Phain city had been shoehorned into the natural one without disturbing it, then I described the embassy garden, so called. "The land we sat on was dead, Gainor. And our people killed it."

He harrumphed. "If you could see the implications of that, the ambassador certainly should have been able to see it!"

"Well, he didn't. I didn't like him. I liked the Phain, though. The Phaina, anyhow. I never met a male one."

"According to my Tharstian friend, the males were assigned to provide us with information because our staff was male. It's the Phaina who really run things."

"Well of course," I said, half to myself. "That was obvious." The Phaina dealt with the world, the Phain dealt with art and religion. The Phain could deal with art and religion only because the Phaina kept the world in balance.

Gainor frowned. "After talking to my Tharstian friend, I read your report again. I'm now wondering if you weren't the one who carried the Phain's warning when you told the ambassador about the garden."

"Me? No one told me to warn him. No one ever told me to say anything."

"Perhaps you were simply unaware of being told. Somehow the Phain knew the message had been delivered, and they knew the ambassador had paid no attention. Your meeting with him is the only possible conversation that could have been it. In future, if you should feel impelled to deliver a manifesto, sweetheart, get a message to me somehow, and I'll see that the fools listen!"

: Gainor's group continued to pay me well, and since I had few expenses, I invested most of it as Shiela Alred advised, along with the money I received when I turned twenty-five. Needless to say, I didn't talk about investments with Paul. By that time I was participating in sanctuary decisions and had been elected to the very private board of directors of the ark movement—always referred to simply in that way, no capital letters, no emphasis, and no publicity if avoidable. We did everything we could to foster the impression that there were only a few active but impotent arkists who had succeeded in preserving half a dozen unimportant species on tiny little worlds that nobody wanted because, as was largely true, they were too far from normal space-lanes to be economical to settle. Whenever we spoke to the public, we were dull. When people attacked us, we did not respond; if we had to respond, we whined that our little sanctuary for the speckled waddling beetle wasn't hurting anyone, then we went on and on about mating habits of the speckled waddling beetle until they gave up in disgust.

By that time, I had become very close to some of the people who really made the ark movement possible, Shiela among them, though she insisted on worrying about me, which made me most uncomfortable.

"Why don't you socialize, Jewel? There's a very pleasant man, one of our people, who's quite taken with you. I'm his emissary. He wonders if you would accompany him to dinner?"

"Thanks, Shiela. But no. I'm just not interested."

It was true. I was not even interested enough to wonder who the pleasant man might be. I still woke every morning with Witt's smell in my nostrils. It annoyed and infuriated me, which made me contrite for being annoyed and infuriated. It quite wore me out. One minute I wished him back, the next I was carrying on an imaginary and very angry conversation with him. I decided to focus on a set of pleasant things I could recall about our relationship, a string of memory beads, the way people used to tell beads in some of the old religions. Five nice things: our times training Quick and Busy; the first time he took me to a wonderful restaurant; the time he helped me at the kennel when Jon Point was sick; the time . . . I gave up on the idea because it took me so long to come up with five things to remember that didn't end up making me furious at him.

And at myself! We had never thought ahead to either of our lives alone. He would finish his schooling. We would go off planet, and he would manage the Hessing empire, if he had to, from somewhere else. I would continue preserving what could be preserved. Perhaps we would have children. Neither of us had thought of being alone, what we would do, what we really wanted. Then he was gone, and I ricocheted around until falling into my current pocket, almost by chance. The fact that it was an interesting pocket, one that was sometimes vital, was a good thing, but it had one great inadequacy. No matter what I did, or where I went, or how successful that might be, I felt no anticipation of delight. The only dream that moved me to joy was the vain and ridiculous fantasy that the Phain would invite me back to Tsaliphor.

Aunt Hatty may have been right when she said my life would have been different if Matty had lived, even though I'd resented her saying so. Matty might have helped me find a better way. I stood before my mirror at the sanctuary and wondered what she would say to me if I could summon her up. She would see shadow nests in my face, though otherwise it was, I suppose, a decent face. Witt had said so.

Shiela often called me "lovely," but anyone young and healthy was lovely to her. I couldn't find any character in the mirror. It was just a face, with rather large gray eyes and quite a lot of eyelashes. The eyebrows had a good, clean shape. I had always felt my mouth was too large, but my nose was reasonable, not fat, not bumpy. My skin was my worst feature, very pale, easily burned, a strange shade of skin in our time. Almost everyone now is light to medium brown, all the human former skin colors mixed and stirred until very few people are very dark or very pale. Still, both Delis and Matty had carried the pale strain from ancient Scandinavian ancestors, and it popped out in me, a thin, pale skin that showed every flick of emotion. At the moment, it was blotchy because I was tired and troubled, but then, since Shiela was wearing the same face, she'd no doubt understand.

When I came out into the hallway, I saw one of the older guards, a man I'd known for years.

"Jewel. Did you know Adam got picked up last night by that plipping Species Control? We just got him back."

"Is he all right?"

"He had a seizure or something. They took him to the medical center. One of our tame doctors checked him out and got him home."

I went past the labs and took the moving walkway to the staff apartments that had been built around an atrium cut through both the park floor above and the roof above that, and I found Adam lying on a chaise in the sunlight, the part of his face not hidden behind his beard looking quite gray.

"Whoever designed those pills ought to have to take one every month for the rest of his life," he grated at me, husky-voiced and obviously in pain.

"They have to simulate a real emergency, Adam. Otherwise, you might get Worldkeeper doctors looking at the wrong parts of you . . ."

"All very nice in theory," he snarled. "I'm sure I'll be fine as soon as my ears stop ringing and I can focus my eyes."

I sat down beside him, troubled both by his appearance and his obvious annoyance.

He said angrily, "Jarl Alred needs his head examined. Either that or he needs to stop dosing. He got me into that mess last night . . ."

If he needed to tell me, then I needed to listen. I sat back, made myself relax, and was careful to make my question as casual as possible. "Shiela's son? What did he do?"

"He buzzed me after midnight, told me he was down at this surface club, one of *those* clubs, and he needed a ride because flit taxies refuse to go down there, and who can blame them? So, since I'm blessed with terminal stupidity, I took a two-seater flit from the sanctuary garage and went to the address he gave me, which he hadn't mentioned was level minus three."

"No flit entry," I said. It sounded like Jarl Alred.

"Of course not. And he wasn't waiting for me at level. At which point I should have returned to quarters and sent an armed party after him, five or six mech-guards at least. Being, as I said, lethally incompetent, however, I parked the flit and went down after him. When I brought him up, a bunch of down-dweller users and half a dozen ruined concs had turned the flit over and were climbing the walls looking for something new to play with.

"Alred had the staggers. I propped him inside the door, slipped into the alley, came around the back, and broke up the party. While the running and screaming went on, I went back the way I'd come to pick up Alred, which took a little time, and by the time I got out the door, somebody in the group had called Species Control. They decided to take me in for questioning, because I was there, and because I wasn't Alred, who was dropping his mother's name like concs drop giggles."

"So you bit the pill."

"So I bit. Yeah. Told them I was subject to seizures, just before I shook out. Also told them I saw something funny leaving the alley. Alred backed up the seizure bit, as much as he could, dosed as he was. He's not a strong shoulder, Jewel. I wouldn't want to have to lean on him."

"Gainor and I have had worries about that," I confessed. We had more than that, if truth be told. "Shiela is solid as a rock and she claims her son is supportive, but he's just . . . feeble. With this new edict, he probably won't be involved much longer."

"What new edict?"

He hadn't heard. I told him.

"And now what?" he breathed, his face turning even grayer.

"We have a little time. There are some arks that are mostly ready. Gainor's getting a delay on enforcement. Don't panic yet."

I left him with that, good advice, though I had trouble following it myself. The panic was there, barely held at bay, ready to take over the moment I let my guard down. In the meantime, a specific something had to be done. Shiela wouldn't think of it. Adam obviously hadn't known about it. The dogs had to be told.

I changed direction, taking a branch hallway toward the gated lift that opened upon forest. Trees, of course, real ones, brought back as seeds or saplings from planets where their species had been planted generations ago, stimulated into rapid growth by current technology. Oak. Ash. Beech. Pine. Smaller growths beneath and around: grasses, forbs, ferns. Rock outcroppings with hollows that could be used for dens. The trickle of water. The smell of moist earth.

I knew that the dogs would have heard the lift arrive. I sat down on a stump—imported, along with the trees—and waited, sensing the subtle tang in the air that denoted the approach of a furred thing, an other creature, a nearing manifested also in the momentary hush among the tiny creatures that kept this mini forest alive with chirpings and chewings. A larger thing was coming, a magisterial presence. It moved on tough-padded feet, its tongue lolled, a flow of saliva coursed its edge to spatter on soil; the deep velvet of coat stroked grasses and twigs soundlessly aside, the plumed tail streamed like a banner, air entered lungs like bellows, eyes rested on me.

"Scramble," I said, not daring to look up.

A murmured growl. An acknowledgment, not a challenge. When I looked up, she was sitting behind a screen of willow, next to a watering pool. After a moment, she got up and came over to thrust her muzzle into my neck, below my ear, moving it down my body and across my back as she took an inventory of where I'd been lately and whom I'd been with. Scramble was Scarlet's granddaughter, eight years old, twice the size of her mother, four times the size of her grandmother, twice as fast, more than twice as smart. If Scarlet had sometimes thought of me as family, Scramble thought of me as a puppy. Her puppy. I adored her. She was a manifestation of every dog I'd ever loved, starting with my stuffed plush puppy on Mars.

Vigilant stepped out of shadow, Dapple behind her. Scramble returned to them and they sat, tails wrapped around their legs, utterly silent, watching me with opaque golden eyes.

"Dapple, Veegee. You're going to hear talk," I said conversationally. "People are going to be jittery. We may be taking you off world soon."

A mutter from the underbrush. I had already sensed them. Behemoth, with Titan and Wolf behind him. These were the six "big dogs," the culmination of the sanctuary's efforts to create the consummate paradigm, the essential, perfected dog, bigger, healthier, smarter . . . no, I couldn't say smarter when I didn't know how smart they'd been before people had fooled with them. Maybe not smarter, but far better able to communicate.

With all six of them there, staring at me, it was hard to speak. Sometimes . . . even though I had held these dogs as puppies, helped feed and bathe them, taught them behaviors, even though they were as close to family as any living things, sometimes they frightened me. I always told myself it wasn't fright. Nonetheless, they stunned me; they were awe-ful.

"I don't know where you'll end up, yet," I said, keeping my voice level with an effort. "Not exactly, but it's bound to be an ark planet."

Nothing. No movement. No eye blinked, no ear twitched, tails didn't move. I sat beneath that timeless regard, waiting, wondering. I could not think as they thought. I could not see as they saw, nor sense as they sensed. I could only wait, hoping they would . . . agree? Concur? What?

When I had given up hope, Behemoth growled, "Awl?"

"All?" I whispered. "Yes. That's all. For now."

Silently, they disappeared, except for Scramble, who put her nose to my cheek and tongued me along the jaw. Affection? Admonition? I didn't know which, if either, but it was one more bit of evidence that Scramble thought of me as her pup.

"Yu sai wen is 'ime," she said, or asked.

"I'll tell you at once," I agreed. "It will be a good place." I prayed I was right, that it would be a good place.

"Ai no. Yu aways magh ghu ha'van."

Alas, I only wished always to make good happen. Sometimes I could not make anything happen at all. I hugged Scramble once more and she sat beside me, leaning against me, sharing warmth. Scramble was the oldest of the big dogs. I had known her longer than any of the others, and I would willingly have sat beside her all day, but there was work to do now that I had told the dogs what I had to tell. They were the only ones who needed to know.

MISSION
TO MOSS

⋮ I had twelve hours much-needed sleep at the sanctuary, followed by a lavish and delicious breakfast with Shiela, during which Paul linked me and asked me to come home. He sounded shaky but sober and, oddly, he was without any of his usual postspasm resentment.

"Are you going back so soon?" asked Shiela, with raised eyebrows.

I temporized. "Not if there's something you need me for here."

"My dear, this isn't a matter of my needs, you know that."

"I'll make a quick visit after work, to see if things are back to normal or not."

My plan didn't satisfy Shiela, but Paul's abrupt break with pattern had me interested. When I let myself into the apartment late in the afternoon it was obvious that tower housekeeping had made an emergency visit. The postorgy mess had been cleaned up and the broken furniture replaced, though usually I was the one who took care of such matters. The only reason I could imagine for this transformation, and for his almost apologetic link call, was that Paul had received an assignment so important that he had pulled himself out of his mania overnight. He hadn't taken the two or three days necessary to sleep it off, so he must have used moodspray antidote, despite its nauseating side effects.

Evidently he had had time to get over the discomfort, for he greeted me cheerfully in a warm, almost brotherly voice.

"Oh, there you are, Jewel. So glad you're back. I've just made coffee . . ."

Aha! He was using his charming and reasonable "managing Jewel" voice. Brother dear wanted something, and he was well into his connivance script. The freshly made coffee, the platter of tiny and very expensive cakes from an import shop on Floor 191, the cleanup of the apartment, all intended to distract, to put me off guard.

"How was the sanctuary?" he asked. "Everything going well?"

Anyone who didn't know him as well as I would have thought he was interested. "It's in an uproar, as one might imagine, Paul. The new law will affect us adversely, of course."

"A pity you're going to be deprived of your work there. Well, I'm glad to have something to tell you that may help make up for the loss! A real challenge, Jewel!"

He poured the coffee. He offered the plate of cakes. I took several. They were only innocent bystanders, no reason not to enjoy them.

"I've been chosen as consultant for a compliance contract! It's for an Earth-like planet, with one large moon in Garr'ugh 290 system . . . What?"

"Sorry," I murmured, pouring sloshed coffee back into the cup from my saucer. The system name had surprised me. "My hand slipped."

He frowned. "As I was saying, it's a . . . marvelous place." He tasted a bit of imported pastry while noting how this was being received. I didn't look at him as I concentrated on the flavor and texture of the first cake. Delicious. Quite marvelous. Unearthly, one might say. When eventually I turned widely innocent eyes his way, he went on. "You'll love it, Jewel. It's felicitous in climate, lovely in aspect. Both PPI and ESC are on planet, so we'll be quite safe. It's a primitive world, of course, but the seas are shallow and clear, the housing is luxurious by Earth standards, there are great trees to sit under and mossy lawns to walk on." He smiled at me, enjoying the sound of his own voice. "It's a maximum three-year contract, and only a fool would turn down a chance like this . . ."

I chewed slowly, and swallowed slowly. This was quintessential Paul. He had reached the end of step one, at which point I was either to agree or disagree. I had already agreed, of course. A split second after I heard the name *Garr'ugh 290*, I had decided to go with him for very good reasons of my own, but I kept that intention to myself while taking another slow sip of coffee-14 (which was no improvement over coffee-13 or indeed, if one thought back a decade, coffee-9 or-10), frustrating his strategy by saying nothing while I stared out the nearest window with a totally blank face.

Paul's usual ready cannonade of counterarguments was spiked by my silence. He followed the direction of my eyes. The only view through that window was of the housing tower opposite, an uninteresting grid of windows, some of them framing potted plants. Aside from the tenants and any wandering microorganisms that made it through the decon locks, potted plants were now the only living things in housing towers. On the several occasions when Paul had bought such expensive greenery, however, I had always managed to kill it. Potted plants were not, in my mind, any kind of substitute for warm friends that welcomed one home with soft fur and eager noses.

He shifted slightly, fidgeting.

I caught the almost imperceptible movement and turned to look at him instead of the window. In Paul's script of this encounter, the words "only a fool" had been purposefully used as words at which I might take umbrage. My doing so now would lead him into the usual "in the overall scheme of things, Paul's jobs are more important than Jewel's jobs" argument, with its infinite avenues of digression and ambush. Inevitably, he would needle me until I lost my temper. Then, as would have been his intention from the beginning, he would retreat into a dungeon of endlessly inventive sulks to lick the traumatic wounds inflicted by his nearest of kin. Being wounded was all the justification he needed for making my life intolerable.

Then, after a lengthy episode of bleak unpleasantness, he would signal me that I might now raise him from the depths by apologizing abjectly and surrendering completely to whatever subordination he was proposing. On occasion I had done so, and in such cases, the clouds had cleared immediately. The moment I agreed, he would be sunny as a summer meadow in a Bonner I wall vista. This pattern had been more or less routine, but this time, and not without a pleasant thrill of malice, I refused the bait and skirted the trap.

"What about my work at the sanctuary, Paul?"

He gaped, thrown only momentarily off stride. "Why . . . I assume this new law will pretty well wipe out any need for sanctuaries, and if not, someone else in your ca-ninny group can substitute for whatever it is you do there. Dogs could always be left in stasis . . ."

Ca-ninny. I ignored the prick of the dagger and stood up, saying, "What do you mean, stasis?"

"We'll only be gone three years, maximum."

"Ten percent brain loss per year . . ."

"My ass, Jewel, they're not Ph.D.'s. They're dogs!"

"You'll be leaving the concs in stasis?" If housing permitted, he sometimes took them with him on these trips.

He was genuinely startled. "Since it's three years, I'm taking the concs. Besides, as you said, 10 percent mental loss . . ."

"Ten percent of zero is zero. There'd be no noticeable difference in any of them except Poppy. Once in a great while, Poppy sounds almost sentient, unlike Marigold, Salvia, or Lavender. Particularly Lavender, who has the brain of a virus."

A curled lip showed I'd hit a nerve, a definite no-no with Paul. He brought out the big guns. "Oh, well, stay on Earth if you like, but you can't go on living here. With your Aunt Hatty gone off world to her sisters, there's no place waiting for you in Baja, and my priority housing rating goes with me, so this place will be sublet. I have no idea what you'd rate by yourself. Whatever it is, it won't cover space for hobbies."

What did one politely call concubines if not a hobby! Or was there, indeed, anything one could politely call concubines? "The dogs aren't a hobby, and I have a species preservation license."

He sneered. "The species in question won't even exist a month from now."

Which was the absolute truth so far as Earth was concerned, and no less infuriating for that. In any case, it had nothing to do with the present conversation except peeving me enough to ready my sword and execute a graceful turn with my cape.

"I would hate living as a down-dweller on the bottom level of nowhere next to an algae conversion plant while you're gone, Paul." I paused to ripple the cape. "However, the same goes for residing on Garr'ugh 290 as your unpaid housekeeper as I have done from time to time elsewhere. We both know that the stakes on new planets are enormous; the budget for a compliance mission is huge. I want a fair share, which means a salary and permission to take some dogs and trainers for my own amusement, just as you're taking the concs for yours. Either that, or I'll stay here to accept a recent liaison proposal."

"Liaison proposal? You?"

The sword had gone home, and he had been wounded. I saw his chagrin at this self-betrayal. "A liaison offer, yes. A fellow preservation enthusiast."

He was honestly surprised. "I didn't know you were seeing anyone . . ."

Trust Paul to think of sex first. "I'm speaking of Margaret Olcot. She and I have been friends for years, and she's recently lost her long-time associate. She has an heir-hold on a protected site, over forty acres of trees, which is quite a temptation. She's asked me to join her for the sake of companionship and affinity."

At this juncture, he could still decide to charge, snorting and bellowing. Better all around if we could skip another of his rages. I continued, "Quite frankly, I think the liaison might be a better move for me, but you know I enjoy travel, and I'm curious about Garr'ugh 290. When you've decided . . ."

He turned quite red, pressed his lips tightly together, controlling himself with obvious (and surprising) effort, then took a deep breath, and said, "The general will have a fit."

The surrender was so abrupt that I hid my face behind my cup, catching up to capitulation. My unfamilial brother was ordinarily willing to risk almost everything to get his way. Either he'd been promised a bonanza for this job, or it was one that could further his career or, more likely, both.

When the pause threatened to become strained, I asked, with careful disinterest, "By *general*, you mean General Manager Brandt of ESC? He gave you the assignment?"

"No, of course not. This kind of thing doesn't require involvement at his level. It's an Earth Enterprises contract, jointly manned by ESC and PPI, and it came through the Enterprises' Contract Division, man named Eigverst. He said hold the requirements down or the general would have a fit."

"And you'll clear the details with him?"

"No," he said with an accustomed sneer. "Not if you're going. In that case, you can fight out the damned dog question with Eigverst.

My requirements list is on my desk—combine it with yours and cover all the details."

Which was, of course, what he needed me for. Paul regarded detail and routine as beneath him. Our rent was double what others paid simply because of the extra services he demanded from tower catering and housekeeping. He could not function unless he had someone else to take care of his day-to-day living.

"I'll take care of it," I said with the slight frown it took to suppress a triumphant grin, for I would indeed take care of it, right at the top with Gainor Brandt himself. He'd be ecstatic!

Paul was staring at me with a dissatisfied expression. I spoke quickly, before he had a chance to start pawing the ground again. "If we're going to be gone up to three years, I have shopping to do. Where will we be living?"

"In the PPI compound," he said grudgingly. "ESC has a screened installation on an island just offshore, but one can't very well do linguistics from inside a screen. If one can do linguistics in this case at all!"

If? Paul never said if. "What makes you doubtful? Are the natives shy?"

He shrugged, forefinger stroking the side of his nose as he did unconsciously when he was uncertain about something. "I asked for everything they have on these creatures, but it's clear no one knows what they are. All the ESC people know is what they see. Here's the cube, take a look for yourself."

The wall screen opened to display a stretch of vaguely green meadow or lawn. Forms moved about on it, flame-shaped, slender, round-bottomed cones that flickered at their tips with frondlike extrusions. The upper half of each cone sparkled with points of light, like sequins. I pointed, questioningly.

"Eyes, maybe," said Paul. "Light reflecting off the lenses."

"A hundred eyes?"

He shrugged. "Nobody knows for sure. There are some striated sections below that could conceal mouths or noses. The flat places could be tympani, maybe ears."

The forms circled the meadow, one at a time, a line of dancers, flailing the fronds at their tops as they went by. They were of different colors, wearing veils of some filmy material that swirled around them.

"Skirts?" I asked, rising to get a closer look.

"Moss. It grows on them. See that belt around their middles? It's a kind of . . . bark, maybe. Or cartilage. Local greenery grows on it and hangs down. They shed bits of it; it's been picked up and analyzed, of course, and it's the same stuff that grows on the trees."

The light grew stronger as we watched.

"Moonrise," said Paul, as the pictured forms, together with their dancing floor, suddenly rose into the air and vanished in an explosion of soft light. He closed the wall. "There are several more dance sessions recorded, all very much alike. We still know almost nothing about them after almost ten years of observation on the moss world . . ."

I cringed and staggered.

He stepped toward me, crying "What's the matter?"

I sagged witlessly into a chair, shivering in sudden cold. "No . . . nothing, Paul. We've been talking about a planet and moon of Gar-r'ugh 290. But you just now said, *moss world.* Is this planet . . . ? Of course. It's in the same system as the jungle planet, isn't it?" I should have known. I really should have known the jungle world was in Gar-r'ugh 290, but I hadn't.

He looked momentarily stricken, angry at himself for not having taken this into account. Even through my giddiness, I saw his annoyance. He never liked to overlook things or be taken by surprise.

He said, "The same system as Jungle, yes. I'm sorry. I'd just . . . forgotten that's where . . . where that was."

I took a deep breath. "No one ever mentioned the system name when it happened. Everyone said *the rock world, the jungle world, the moss world:* descriptions, not names."

"They're names now," he admitted. "Stone, Jungle, and Moss. Moss has a moon called Treasure, but it's been sold off already . . ."

I said, in a reasonably calm voice, "I should have realized the systems were one and the same." To stop my lips trembling, I pressed the almost empty cup against them, telling myself I would not cry. "Do we know anything about the physiology of . . . what are they called?"

"The PPI people call them the Mossen. The Derac, who discovered the system, say they *found* a dead one and dissected it. Knowing the Derac, no one can be sure whether they really found it or more likely hunted and killed it. If they killed it, everyone would love to know how they got close enough. Since we and the Derac don't communicate directly, they gave us a copy of the recorded dissection process with the comments of the butchers . . ."

"Butchers?" I asked.

"My translation." He made a face. "The Derac have no scientists, they certainly have no anatomists. The only Derac who systematically cut things up are the butchers who share out the meat and hides in shipclans. ESC and PPI couldn't get within striking distance of a live Mossen until they started dancing, after which it didn't seem politic to try and catch one. In any case, they've never even seen a dead one, so they're grateful for the information, though it's too crude to be genuinely helpful."

"I wonder why they have so many eyes."

"We don't know they are eyes. The butchery film shows a network under the skin that's connected to all of the lenses, if they're lenses. It's been suggested that different ones perceive different things: color perhaps, or motion, or distance. The creatures have to perceive their surroundings somehow; they don't go bumping into things or one another."

"And they move how?"

"We don't know. Some think they might do it like starfish used to do, or sea urchins. A whole slew of little footsies rippling along under their skirts. We say 'think,' because the Derac tell us the body they examined wasn't complete."

"And the PPI claims they have speech! If they have speech, then they qualify as a protected race." This was really the important point. Any race with speech qualified as a protected race.

Paul frowned. "*If* they have speech. That judgment was made on extremely shaky evidence. They have no history of exploration or trade; they have no possessions, no technology; they don't need dwellings, and their clothing—if that's what it is—grows itself. From what the embassy says, they're a lovely, mostly sweet-smelling population of . . . totally enigmatic creatures that PPI claims desire to emerge from solitude, God knows why."

"Well, if we can't talk to them, how do we know that?" I demanded.

"PPI received a written message crudely and briefly written on bark with colored sap. Supposedly, that is. For some unknown reason, the place has become a favorite posting for PPI staffers on preretirement duty, so the installation has a larger staff than one would expect, a staff that's spent several years talking, posting notices, writing things down. The assumption is that the Mossen have heard human speech and deciphered enough of both speech and writing to create a written message saying something like, 'We desire knowing outside people.'"

"That would indicate a primitive people, at best."

He laughed. "If they're a people at all! Which is why they need me. PPI Central can't make up its mind. The Derac contingent is becoming increasingly belligerent. They want the certification done and over with! And ESC is getting itchy. They want to leave the planet since they finished their survey of the moss part over a year ago."

"There's another part?"

"Two continent-sized, very high plateaus with an ecology totally different from the mossy part. The one unusual, not to say weird, thing the orbital surveyors reported on the plateau was a group of Earther ships dating back some centuries, Hargess-Hessing ships, from the shape of them."

I pricked up my ears. "Didn't that stimulate some interest?"

"It might have, if the ships had been found sooner in the process, or if they'd crashed there more recently, but the certification process is far advanced, and the ships are centuries old. ESC hasn't done any more than peek at the plateaus because the contract specifies a joint survey after certification, and PPI can't move toward certification so long as the question of peoplehood is unanswered."

"Surely there's been enough time to have done more exploration."

He made a face. "What Interstellar Coalition calls 'intrusive' exploration and survey cannot be done until native people have been consulted. Native people can't be consulted until we know if there are any. As a result, the only exploration and survey has been 'nonintrusive,' the kind of survey work that can be done by orbiters and airborne observers."

"So what has PPI done in all this time?"

He threw up his hands. "It's followed orders. It's been nonthreatening and passive while learning whatever can be learned, letting the natives take the lead. So far all the natives have done is dance rather frequently in areas near the PPI compound, which is all very pretty but totally unrevealing as to linguistics. The only hard evidence is the written message that precipitated the request for a linguist."

The door opened, and one of Paul's concubines skipped in, half-naked and in full body paint. "Ouw, Pau-wie, din know y'ad comp'ny."

"Poppy, I told you to get back in your case!" Paul growled impatiently.

I accepted the interruption as a chance to get away. I headed for the door, saying, "It's all right, Poppy. You come in and make Pau-wie happy. I was just leaving." I patted the conc's behind as I passed him-her-or-it, eliciting a chortle that covered three octaves.

In my own space, with the door locked, I sat down to make a list of things I would have to do before leaving on a three-year contract. There was not a doubt in my mind that I would go to Moss, and to its moon, Treasure. The opportunity had come too serendipitously to be refused.

THE ORSKIMI

⁝ While I was making plans for our mission to Moss, something consequential was taking place in quite another direction, on quite another planet: the home world of the Orskimi.

That planet was known as E'Sharmifant, "ancestral home." In the capital city of that world, as in all cities of the Orskimi, dawn was greeted by a mass shrilling that rose above the hives to fill the morning air with a pulsating tremor signifying unity, purpose, and dedication. The clamor stopped as abruptly as it had begun and was succeeded by a profound silence dedicated to remembrance of those who had perished while pursuing the purposes of the people. The silence eased only gradually into the normal clatter of morning: wings buzzing as groups flew from one place to another; feet scraping their way into centers of commerce, religion, warfare, or intelligence. As on every early morning, some few directed their steps toward the mortuary complex, which stood upon a low hill at the center of the city and was surmounted by the Temple of Eternal Memory.

This vast pile, assembled by mercenaries from another world in a time so ancient that it was almost forgotten even by the Orskimi themselves, was furnished mostly with shadows. Each corner held its quota of dust and darkness into which futile, gray light oozed from high, hooded openings, the nostrils of the temple, exhaling incense smoke that never quite masked the odor of death.

Some of the dying lay on pallets in the sacred portico, lax limbed, ashen plated, breath faltering, dimmed eyes focused, if at all, on the top of the processional stairs. The servants of purpose would mount those stairs, and those brought here to die watched for them intently, even impatiently, so long as they had the strength for either intensity or impatience. Even these last longings waned before the end, a little seeping away with each breath, until, when the awaited ones came at last, the dying barely stirred at the sound of the bell, the chanting voices, the horny rustle of scraping footsteps, growing louder as the climbers ascended.

Those who still watched saw first the tall plumes of the High Priest's headdress, followed by the chitinous ridges of his forehead, glowing scarlet above great faceted eyes. The six arms of the upper body angled outward, each bearing one of the ritual implements: the censer, the bandage, the knife, the shears, the saw, and the retractor.

"Oh, ye upon the doorstep of death," shrieked the High Priest, as he set his forefeet within the temple door, "prepare for thy final agony." Left and right triple legs made clicking triplets, whikalap-whikalap, as he came across the portico to the altar, the sound echoed by the footfalls of the ritual surgeons, the fire masters, the litter bearers with their quiet burden. Outside in the tall growths, several species of chitterers fell quiet at the High Priest's cry. In the low growths a family of howlers, their cousins, did likewise. Silence brooded. Smoke wafted.

Some of the Orskimi who lay dying here had been born on this world and lived out their lives here; others were residents of far worlds who had been brought from great distances to die here, for this was the sole place in the Orskim Empire equipped to transfer the memories of the departing into the minds of the young. Orskimi were six-armed, six-legged, armored in chitin, capable of making brief flights, capable of walking forever, eaters of any organic matter—no matter how foul others might find it—even capable of regenerating arms that might be lost. However, what was about to be removed from these dying members of the race had to be preserved, for it would not grow back.

One of the old ones lying in the temple had been there for several days. The somber vault reeked of formic acid and fungus, some from this Orski's body, some from the bodies of the pallid klonzi who squirmed feebly upon the drying carcass. Though klonzi were so long-lived that some families removed them from the dying and used them thereafter as a remembrance, the klonzi on this body were too old to be useful. When the old one died, they would begin a shrill screaming, so high-pitched that few ears could hear it. This screaming would continue alternately with spells of panting until the parasitic creatures fell away from the dead one, curled into shivering rings on the floor, and gave up life.

At the IC, among the diplomats and strategists, it was said that klonzi had once been an independent and intelligent race, now modified by Orskimi to be body scavengers who crawled on Orskim body armor, eating away the dried or injured cells. Their brains were too compressed to hold the idea of escape, much less rebellion. Long ago, it was also said, Orskimi had had only six extremities until they had captured another six-legged race, also independent and intelligent. Now that race served as the hinder part of each Orski, furnishing locomotion. On Earth it was said that each Orski, when hatched, was fixed onto the body of one of the locomotors, the locomotor's brain having been removed. Certain nerve connections were then made and by the time the Orski was ready to walk, it had full control over the creature that helped move it. Such things, it was said, were common among the Orskimi as they had been common to the Zhaar, when that evil race had ruled the galaxy.

No Orski commented on these allegations. Let the other races say what they would, Orskimi knew the truth, and what was said made no difference. Now that the Zhaar had gone, Orskimi intended to take their place of power. So the Orskimi themselves acknowledged.

The priest went to the altar, the fire masters to the pit of burning, the surgeons to the creature nearest death. As the priest laid down the symbolic tools in their ritual positions, the surgeons laid theirs on the worktable near at hand. The priest waved a censer and bowed toward the surgeon. The surgeon poised a knife at the base of the dying one's skull and thrust it down. This severed the connection between the memory node and the balance of the mind. Now the old one remembered nothing, thought nothing. He merely was. When the saw began cutting through his dorsal plate, the old one screamed at the pain.

"Do they always do that?" asked a troubled young assistant.

"Always," said the surgeon, who was manipulating the heavy shears at the bottom of the skull shell while his assistants retracted the stiff dorsal shell to the sides. "Of course it is painful. There are many nerves attached to the dorsal surface. There will be even more pain as we cut into the head shell."

"Can't you give iki some of the drugs we use to ease pain?" asked the same youngster.

"Doing so runs the risk of corrupting the memory," said the priest. "The node is still connected through a nutrient duct. That duct will be influenced by any drug owki might use. In any case, this honored one does not know that iki is in pain. Iki's body shrieks, but it is a mindless shrieking. Since the memory can no longer be affected by what is felt by the body, using anesthetic would gain us nothing."

"The Orskimi do not waste materials," said an assistant surgeon to the students around him. "On the battlefield, if one is beyond repair, the physician makes the same cut we have just made, separating memory from the body. We do not give precious drugs to relieve pain. Only those destined for continuing are given such things in order that their memories not be clouded by trauma when the time comes for them to go. If this one had been injured a year ago, iki would have received pain medication, to prevent a memory of agony. Such memory might adversely influence later decisions."

"I do not understand," said a student, antennae quivering.

The surgeon bobbed his head. "It is much easier to deal objectively with the subject of pain if one has not felt pain oneself. Surgeons, for example, deal with the pain of others. Those destined to be surgeons are carefully protected against pain so they can make decisions without any sense of personal involvement. Now watch as the memory node is removed."

The node lay quivering beneath flap of brain shell. Within moments they had it in their pincers, an oval organ, the size of a large egg. They held it high, still connected by a length of nutrient duct to the body of the old one. Now the litter bearers came forward, carrying between them a young Orski, one already anesthetized, iki's exoskeleton already opened, the site of transplantation already prepared with a length of nutrient duct exposed. Only after connecting the node to the nutrient ducts of the new body was the old nutrient duct severed. The old body quivered with its last breath.

The students heaved a collective sigh, both awed and somewhat dismayed. It was a holy occasion. Anyone might, during iki's lifetime, gain memories that would be precious to the race. Those who did would live on in successive generations. It was almost immortality, and it was not out of reach of the ambitious and venturesome. Though the thought of that final agony was not pleasant, living on, virtually forever, could make up for a good deal of pain. Particularly since one would not remember it.

While the High Priest perfumed the sacred bandages with the censer, the dorsal plate of the anesthetized young one was glued with an organic cement before being bandaged to hold the plates in place while they grew together. The honored ones who bore the memories of earlier generations could easily be recognized by the long ridge of scarred integument down their backs. They were revered wherever they went, though it was said they were not interesting company for ordinary persons.

"Iki will sleep for a few days," said the priest. "When iki wakes, there will be no memories of this. Within twelve days, however, the memories will begin, and all that the old one knew, iki will know. As the old one was laden with the memories of twelve or thirteen generations before, so this new one will have all those plus whatever experiences iki will have from this time on."

"Will he experience adventures?" asked the irrepressible young Orski. "Travel far worlds?"

The priest shook his head. "No. Our repository people may not adventure, for those who carry our memories are too valuable to risk. This young one will sit among the councilors and hear the reports of travelers and adventurers. This one will advise the warlords with rec-ollection of past battles, comment upon the plans of the Great Work, made and remade in perpetuity by each generation in conformity with the plans of generations past."

"What shall this one be called," asked the surgeon, indicating the unconscious youngster.

"This one's name is Gerfna'ors," said the High Priest in hierarchical tones, laying three pairs of hands in blessing upon the young one. "In the lifetime of this one will the eggs of the humans be broken, the eggs of the Derac, the eggs of the Tharst. In this generation the plan comes to fruition, by which those races will be overcome so that the Great Work may be accomplished."

There was a generalized thrill at these words, a vibration of wing cases, a moment's shrill exultation. "Gerfna'ors! Breaker of Eggs." "Great Breaker!" "Mighty Crusher of the Defilers!" "Profound Exalter of the Great Work!"

"Enough," said the High Priest. "Lay the old one's carcass in the fire pit. Put down your klonzi to clean up this mess."

Several among those present detached one or two clinging creatures and set them upon the floor, where they obediently began eating the tissue and fluids that had accumulated during the surgery as well as the bodies of the dead klonzis. Later, when the ashes and scraps were put outside, argni, larger scavengers than klonzi, would consume them. On E'Shampifant, nothing went uneaten.

High above the floor of the temple, on one of the great rafters that supported the heavy roof, an observer lay hidden behind a perforated ornament, an observer who saw and heard all that went on below. It had no involvement in what it saw. It had no feelings concerning what went on. Its presence was unknown, unguessed at. The Orskim on whom it spied were too complacent to believe themselves vulnerable. They would not have thought to look for a small, mostly biological device capable of listening, remembering, reciting; capable of smelling any odor present; capable of seeing and identifying individuals, even touching them occasionally, though usually not until the being in question was quite dead.

The observer, a member clone of a vast set named by its Tharstian masters, "Perceptives Number Eleven," was able, if required, to translate the language spoken here into several other languages. As it heard the word Gerfna'ors, it translated into Tharstian and also into Earthian, "Breaker of Eggs" as it zoomed its eye parts to catalog the attributes of the klonzi: two eyes, one nose, one mouth, two ears. Not unlike the human physiognomy, an ear on each side, short little arms, four of them, for picking and scraping. A strange set of legs that could carry the creature either on the feet or on the knees with the feet latched up behind. The observer looked closely, searching for signs of intelligence, finding none.

As those below busied themselves cleaning their equipment, the observer sent out a tiny probe shaped like the ubiquitous chitterers. It darted to the floor below and returned unobserved, carrying in its sharp little beak tissue samples that would yield the genetic pattern of the klonzi, of the leg section worn by these Orskim. Orski DNA had already been cataloged and its relationships and descent studied, but these other creatures were not of this planet originally.

The observer noted that the younger assistants had gone out, into the sun, while the surgeon and the priest walked down the line of the dying, assessing when the next implants should occur.

"Tomorrow for this one," said the surgeon. "Two or three days for the rest. When will we have the first humans to work on?"

"Within our allotted time. As soon as the humans go to war."

"Will they go to war?"

"Oh, certainly. Very soon, one of their planetary survey groups will be attacked by the Derac! Atrocities will be committed! After that, it will be impossible for them to avoid war. It is all being done as we planned, generations ago. In the fury of war, the disappearances of humans will go unnoticed."

"Has it been decided what they will be used for?"

"The females have a large and capacious organ which will serve to hatch up to twelve of our eggs at a time, thereby freeing Orskim incubators for more rewarding work. The larger males will make good laborers, and we have many other ideas. They are a particularly valuable race to us, inasmuch as they can survive wide variations in climate, adapt to a great variety of tasks, and apply intelligence effectively. Unfortunately, we have not yet learned how to retain the intelligence while removing all independent thought. We are, nonetheless, continuing the effort."

"And the Derac? Will we use them as well?"

"We are using them, to start the great war. When that is finished, those who are left will make good warriors. The young ones are almost brainless, even now, so there will be little adaptation to do . . ."

Reabsorbing its probe, the observer on the roof beam added this bit of conversation to everything else that had been collected during the past several days. The information was scanned to remove duplication while assuring that nothing was lost or understated, then the information, already translated into Tharstian and Earthian, was encoded and compressed. When the observer was fully satisfied, the information was spurted on the first step of its journey, to the hidden amplifier and accelerator here on this world. From there it would be sent out to the Tharstian spy ship, hidden in a crater of a small and unimportant moon, where it would be amplified once more and sent from that ship to Tharstian headquarters and eventually, the observer inferred—for it was capable of inference—it would be relayed to Earth Enterprises and the office of Gainor Brandt.

Gainor Brandt, who would receive it and show it to me, too late, far too late to do any good at all.

THE DAYS BEFORE DEPARTURE

⁞ Though Dame Cecelia's harassment was not resumed after I returned from Baja, other forms of persecution were directed at all sanctuary workers, and we had, therefore, learned to be as unobtrusive as possible. We used different robes and veils to make ourselves unrecognizable; some with pads to give the impression of greater bulk, some with raised crowns to increase apparent height. Whenever I left the apartment, I reminded myself to be alert to possible followers.

The day following my agreement with Paul, I intended to visit both Gainor Brandt and the sanctuary, but I did not go directly to either. First I stopped at my medical center on the mercantile floor for the usual travelers' kit of preventives and treatments, then went on to a few import shops in various towers for supplies I would be unlikely to get through agency supply routines on Moss. Whenever I boarded pods between towers, I noticed who boarded after me. Given that the purpose of robes and veils is to guarantee anonymity, it is difficult to identify individuals, but I had acquired some skill at recognizing details: the way a seam lay on a shoulder; how a person walked and moved; the little nervous movements people make without knowing it.

Each time I depodded, the same two figures depodded after me. Though they wore the sort of masks worn by a great many others, one mask had a frayed place at the corner and the other had the eyeholes widened, allowing me to see a mole beneath the eye. I took covert note of both, thinking they were probably IGI-HFO foot soldiers. Next stop was the storage garage, where I made arrangements for storing Paul's flits while we were away, as his garage space in the tower would be subleased with the apartment. That long-ago journey to Baja had taught me several tricks that had proven useful over the years: accordingly, I left the storage garage by descending to the fifth sublevel and exiting into another sublevel sector from the lift, thereby losing my stalkers.

Backtracking in another pod, I took a flit to Area Government Center, a tower at the urb's edge, surrounded by many-leveled terraces with some plants and trees, the only trees to be found in the urb outside the park floors. I asked for a landing on a fortieth-floor flit lobby, a little-used landing, some distance from Gainor's office. Though the lobby was virtually empty, I still took a circuitous route via lifts and moving walkways to reach the office of the general manager, confident at last that if I'd been followed, it had been by someone invisible.

"General Brandt, please," I said to the young man at the reception desk as I removed my veil.

"Citizen Delis," the general boomed through his open door, sounding forbiddingly formal. "You are very punctual. Do come in." He bowed me into the room, then shut the door and closed it before pressing the lock plate to be sure it stayed that way.

"New person out there," he said softly. "Jeffry somebody. Goes all giddy with authority. Doesn't know when to listen and when to stop listening. Could be a spy, but I don't think he's smart enough. How are you, my dear?"

I gave him my hand, then my cheek. "Gainor, I couldn't wait to tell you. Our *moon* project? Garr'ugh 290? It seems you have an ESC team on the third planet."

"Yes," he said, puzzled. "Both ESC and PPI are on planet. I was talking to Botrin Prime about it just last night."

I felt my nostrils lift at the mention of the name. "How is nasty old Prime? Aging fast, I hope."

Gainor pursed his lips reprovingly. "He hasn't forgotten you, if that's what you mean. He needles me every now and then, asking about you. I always say I haven't seen you, have no idea what you're doing. Boaty has a mean streak, and I wouldn't suggest running afoul of him."

"Don't intend to. Did he tell you his PPI team on Moss has asked for a linguist?"

"He did not!" He stared at me for a moment before it clicked. "You mean Paul?" He lowered his voice. "And Paul wants you to go along?"

"How could he live otherwise? Why, he'd have to arrange for his own laundry! And feed his own concs! I told him I wouldn't go unless he let me take some trainers and dogs, for my amusement."

"Good heavens," he murmured, grinning. "What a stroke of luck. What marvelous timing! We couldn't have planned that if we'd tried."

"I'm sure you could have, Gainor, if you'd thought of it, which I certainly hadn't. I had no idea there was any question of intelligent life anywhere in Garr'ugh 290."

Gainor took a deep breath. "Did he agree to your taking the animals?"

"I think he's counting on my being discouraged by the bureaucracy. He told me to take care of details and said you'd have a fit."

He sat back, beaming. "Well then, I shall. A small but stormy one. Can't have anyone thinking I'm easy on animals! Who's the PPI contract officer?"

"It's a joint contract through your office. Somebody named Eigverst."

He thought a moment. "Not a man I know well. If he follows procedure, he'll kick up about your entourage. I'll give you a note for him advising immediate compliance in the furtherance of the contract. No, no. I won't give it to you. Don't want to give him anything to talk about. I'll send it to him directly, saying I've been advised they want a linguist, linguists are notoriously picky, we're already over contract time, so let the linguist's party have anything they ask for; I want the work expedited and no logjams in acquisition! Now, who are you taking?"

"I've spoken briefly to Adam. The six big dogs and three trainers were intended for the moon, weren't they? I know it isn't quite far enough along, but the job on the planet, Moss, should take up to three years, by which time . . ."

"By which time it should be ready," he mused, eyes fixed on thin air. "Especially if we double up on prey seeding. Oh, my. I'm glad you want Adam. All this iggy-huffo stuff is tearing him apart. He'll want his brother Frank with him. Clare Barkley should be your third; she and Frank work well together. And of course the six big dogs we planned for that moon anyhow. I wish you could take some of the others, the smaller ones, but they aren't nearly so far along, and I'm finding places for smaller animals among the arkists' holdings. Several arks are ready for birds, two are ready for cats. Ark keepers are eager to have small dogs, particularly since we don't allow children on ark planets. Oh, by the Great Mahalus, Jewel! This solves so many problems."

"You're calling on Tharstian gods these days?"

"I have it on good authority, from the Tharstian High Priest himself, that the Great Mahalus listens to humans. I say, as he does, 'Haibo! Any deity who'll help.' "

I surprised us both by hugging him, then sat in a visitor's chair, pulling him into the one beside it. "Paul says we'll be living in the PPI installation, and they mustn't know why I'm really there, that is, any reason beyond my being a silly, animal-loving, nonproductive hobbyist who happens to be taking care of details for Paul. I'll need an intro to your ESC people, Gainor, if there's anyone there you really trust to be sympathetic and close-mouthed. AND, I beg you to keep the ESC people there for a while. Paul says they're pushing to leave."

He frowned, his fingers making a drumroll on the arms of the chair. "They're impatient, yes. Normally they stay as long as PPI does, but absolutely nothing is happening with PPI, and we have other calls on our time. It might raise eyebrows if I delayed them . . ."

"Not if you had a good excuse."

"Such as?"

"There are two huge plateaus that make up about a third of the landmass," I said. "You could always have those explored and surveyed."

"I could probably think up a way of doing that, yes, if I had a reason to . . ."

"Paul says they found old Hessing-Hargess ships on the plateau."

"Did they, by heaven!" He mused doubtfully for a moment. "Abandoned?"

I shook my head. "I don't think anyone knows."

"I suppose one could look for survivors, or bodies . . ."

"Would it help if the Hessing family asked you to?"

He grinned at me. "Wouldn't that fluff Boaty's pillow! But how would that come about?"

"I thought I might speak to Myra, Witt's sister. Moss is in the same system as Jungle, which you may recall was where Witt disappeared."

He frowned at me. "Might be wisest not to attract Dame Cecelia's attention to yourself!"

"She won't know I have anything to do with it."

He stared at the wall for a moment, abruptly shifting subjects. "You want contacts in ESC. Well, you'll be traveling on an ESC ship because we do supply for both teams, and our ships go back and forth fairly regularly. On the ground, however, who's best?" He spoke to the wall: "Bessy!"

The wall replied. "Yes, sir."

"Find me the ESC roster for Garr'ugh 290."

"One moment."

In that moment, the paneling slid aside to reveal a data screen and the roster heading.

"Read," said the general, rapidly scanning the faces that flicked by. "Stop."

"Who is it?" I asked, looking over his shoulder. "He looks like a Himoc priest, all sensitive and repressed."

"Started out wanting to be one," grunted the general. "Good man, though, unflappable and totally sympathetic to our cause. His name is Lethe, Ornel Lethe." Then, to the screen. "Print Lethe, burn-book." He searched further and had two other files printed: Wyatt and Durrow. "Sybil Wyatt, age nine, was the sole survivor of our colony on Holme's World after that inexplicable attack."

"By the so-called Zhaar."

"That's the rumor at IC. One day they tell us the Zhaar are all gone, the next day they tell me the Zhaar wiped out a planetful of people. Could be an attempt to turn our attention in the wrong direction, but the only other IC members known to have that kind of power are the Phain, who pay no attention at all to anything we do or don't do."

"The Phain wouldn't do a thing like that," I said, firmly. "Did you ask them?"

"No. It wouldn't have been tactful to ask. But the subject was discussed in the presence of several Phaina at IC level, and they said they had foreseen the happening but had been unable to avert it."

"Avert it how?"

"That was the point they didn't wish to discuss. We got the impression they'd issued some kind of warning to Holme's World, but no warning was found in the records."

I stared at him for a long moment. "When I was on Phain, you thought I carried a warning to the Earth ambassador. Did you have any record of it besides my memory of it?"

He looked startled. "That was years ago, Jewel!"

"So was Holme's World, years ago. All I'm saying is, perhaps the warning wasn't official. Maybe it didn't go through official channels."

He went on staring at me, his face gone blank, his eyes focused on something I couldn't see. Eventually, he snapped back into the present, saying, almost casually, "Not for the first time, I wish we knew more about the Zhaar."

"My mother obtained a translation of ancient Martian by way of the Zhaar language. It was done by a worker in some special IC archives."

He sighed heavily. "You're speaking of the Archives of the elder races. I happen to believe that the elder races have neither departed nor gone extinct. They simply don't want to be bothered with the politics and maneuvering we younger races seem to find necessary. They've lived long enough to know what works for them, individually and collectively, and they have no interest in wasting their time reinventing systems they know aren't useful."

For some reason, the subject was making me extremely itchy. I said in an irritated tone, "So, if they're not extinct, one of them might have wiped out the people on Holme's World."

"That's possible. All we know is, something vanished every person on it except one little girl of nine and her pet, whatever it was. Sybil was brought back to Earth. When she was twelve, she joined the ESC preparatory corps. She's a twenty-year veteran and a driven woman so far as interspecies relations goes. Abe Durrow's been her partner for most of that time. Except for one another, they're both loners, the kind of people who gravitate to ESC. They tend to be a little odd, but they're perfectly trustworthy . . ."

I gave him a look.

He flushed. "That is, those who aren't a member of Botrin Prime's clan! Tell the people on Moss check your credentials with my office, and don't tell them anything until they've done so. I want them to know that discretion is essential and ordered from this office."

The file-prints popped out of the desk slot, already assembled in a self-disposing burn-book. He handed it to me, saying, "The captains of any ESC ships in the area will be told to offer all possible assistance. As for this, learn and let dispose promptly, particularly if your brother is still going through your belongings."

"Paul hasn't done that since I first came back from Baja, though he used to do it all the time when we were children. As though he thought I knew something he didn't or had something he didn't. I don't think he does it now, which doesn't mean he won't if he feels like it."

"Strange worlds can exacerbate neurosis—if that's what we can call it. Be careful around him. We'll be in touch before you go, and if you need anything, just call me!"

From Gainor's office, I went directly to the sanctuary, where I found Adam looking somewhat better than the last time I'd seen him. "More bad news?" he asked as I approached.

"You tell me. Just listen for a minute." Taking his grudging nod for consent, I went on. "My brother Paul is being sent to Moss as attaché for linguistics to the Chief Emergence Compliance Officer of PPI."

"Who's the CECO?"

"The planetary commander of PPI, a man named Drom. Paul wants me to go along, as usual, hostess duties, catering, laundry . . ." I made a disgusted face.

Adam aped my grimace, lips drawn back from very white teeth. "What does that have to do with . . ."

" 'The dogs'?" I asked, putting the words in quotes. "The big dogs are going along. Housing on Moss is what we'd call luxurious in terms of natural space. Security will be more relaxed than here. I'm also taking three trainers."

He said doubtfully, "Three of us and six dogs is a lot. Have you room for us all?"

"This is strictly confidential, Adam. Don't whisper it to anyone, not even the other trainers. We've been working on a canine econiche on the moon. It's called Treasure."

His eyes widened. "Moss has a moon? How possible is the econiche?"

"Oh, if this mission to Moss lasts a year or so, 90 percent likely."

"Prey animals?"

"They started seeding the moon quite some time ago, as soon as it was bought. One of General Brandt's little projects. It's been in the works for years now."

He gave me a long, weighing look. "You and he are . . . ?"

I smiled, shaking my head. "He and I aren't. Never were. When I met him I was eighteen, and he was well over twice that. He and I are coconspirators and friends, I guess. Which is also not for mentioning, Adam. Paul has no idea I know Gainor Brandt at all, much less that I know him well; it would annoy him immensely if he knew. Paul is frighteningly temperamental and when he's annoyed, he interferes, sometimes destructively. He's also very good at his work, and I'm . . . inured to him. That doesn't mean I'm going to be stupid where he's concerned."

"Well then, assuming I'm one of those you intend to take, I approve. And my brother, Frank. You will take Frank."

I grinned at him. "You, and Frank, and Clare."

Despite himself, he smiled. "A good time for everyone to have a vacation. Does Paul know about . . ."

"What Paul mustn't know," I said warningly, "would fill a black hole."

THE DAYS BEFORE
DEPARTURE:
CONTINUED

⋮ My friend, Margaret Olcot, was the last surviving descendant of Horgan Olcot, 2053–2130, a founder of the ark movement. Horgan had devoted his life and great fortune to preserving earth fauna anywhere he could, his success made possible first by the "discovery" of mankind by starfarers in 2085 and subsequently by Earth's acquisition of gravitic-repulsion, grav-rep, space travel. Olcot purchased small, out-of-the-way planets and moons, listed them in the star registers as "freight transfer sites," and adapted them for selected earthian fauna while protecting the indigenous species, or, if the planets were lifeless, terraformed them for earth fauna and flora alone. Meantime, he convinced Earthers who owned exempt estates to put their acres in perpetual trust for the growth of earthian flora.

As the IGI-HFO people had not yet attacked private arboretums, Mag Olcot still had her forty acres of trees, including two giant redwoods. Her little forest was surrounded on two sides by an algae factory, on the third by a desalinization plant, and on the fourth by the heaving surface of the virtually tideless porridge that had once been the Pacific Ocean, long since rendered incapable of supporting any animal life much larger than a bacterium through its function as sewer and oxygenator to our human race.

Margaret had been my dear friend for years. I couldn't go without replying to her liaison offer or saying good-bye, so I dropped in on her a couple of days before we were to leave.

"So you've decided to go with Paul," Margaret said, when I had explained myself. "I confess, I did hope you'd take me up on my offer."

"You know why I didn't, Mag."

"Of course I know," she said. "You're doing the only possible thing, as I am also. Let's go walk on the beach. It may be our last chance . . ."

We walked on the beach, our usual ritual, eyes fixed on the sand at our feet. Only when some great upheaval took place on the ocean bottom did waves wash up on this tiny strip of sand, painting it green for a while. Just then it was almost clean, and halfway along, Margaret dropped to her knees. "Oh, look, Jewel. A whole one!"

I knelt, regarding the shell in the sand with awed wonder, a tiny spiral of ivory the size of the tip of my little finger, curled and knobbed, rarer than gold. When I reached out for it, Mag's tears fell on my hand.

I whispered, "Don't, Mag."

She tried to smile, unsuccessfully. "I can't help it. I have one of Joram II's ocean vistas in my bedroom. I know the feeling it gives you, the strange smell, the surprise of spray, the unexpected winds and shifting colors . . . When I see one of these, it's almost as though I'm there, that the place is real. Then I pick it up, and I know what's in my hand is all that's left . . ." She turned away hastily, wiping her face on the hem of her shirt.

"I get mournful, too," I said brusquely, swallowing my own tears and willing myself not to jump into her emotional river after her. Easy to drown there. Seductive. One of the things people like us warned ourselves against, wasting time and energy grieving over the irretrievably lost while there were still some that could be saved.

I stood up, brushing the sand from my trousers and blinking against the wind. "Come on, now. Let's make some tea."

"What was that thing your mother quoted about the sea?" she asked. ". . . beneath my eyes the sorrows . . ."

I recited it:

> *"Our coats are as thin as mist, our heels are horn,*
> *Beneath our eyes old sorrows build their nest*
> *and peck at us where we are torn and tender,*
> *reproaching us as shore birds . . ."*

"Like shorebirds," she repeated. "And it was supposedly written by whom?"

"Well, the original was written on Mars fifty thousand or so years ago, and Matty paid some linguistic expert at IC Archives to translate it into common speech. Of course, by the time the thing had been translated five times, whether it was still close in meaning to the original is anybody's guess."

"There were really shore birds on Mars?"

"There are fossil remnants of sea creatures, yes."

She mused, "Fossils. I studied paleontology, did you know that?"

"Yes, Mag, you've told me, but never why you did."

"No reason on Earth, obviously. No place left to discover anything here. I was just interested in us, trying to find out why we do the stupid things we do. According to the experts, we really were stupid for millions of years, all of us habilises and ergasters and Heidlebergenses. I've told you this before!"

"Tell me again. It's interesting."

"Well, our ancestors got to the point they could build fires and make some rather nice chipped flint tools, but basically, they weren't that much smarter than the rest of the fauna. Then, fifty thousand years ago, we . . . bloomed. No one has ever learned why. We started making better tools, painting marvelous animals in caves, dressing ourselves up in beads and ornaments. From that point on, there was no stopping us. I've often wondered if we wouldn't have been happier if we'd just stayed what we were, a slightly brighter animal . . ."

"Come, Mag. You don't mean that."

"I do. Animals aren't mean. They're dumb, sometimes, and they kill, of course, but they aren't mean. When we bloomed, we learned to be mean! We even choose up sides and kill our own kind!" She sniffed, wiping her eyes. "You will go to services with me tonight, won't you? It's Midsummer Roll Call and Memorial . . ."

I stopped dead. "I'd forgotten! Ever since this trip came up, I've been so involved getting things ready that I've forgotten everything else."

Margaret opened the door and ushered me in. "You ought to come. It may be . . . it may be the last time we see one another, Jewel."

I would not be maudlin! "Margaret, you've got a good thirty years ahead of you, probably more."

"But not here." Margaret stopped as a cat emerged from hiding to wind itself between her ankles. As I leaned to pet it, three others came from behind the furniture.

The hair on the back of my neck prickled. "Why? What are you going to do?"

"My quadruped friends are scheduled to go out with a group of others next week. The dispersal committee has a large moon with atmosphere, a little less than Earth gravity, well grown up in vegetation and young forests, including some Earth trees, but it had no fauna at all. It's been populated with over five hundred species of insects, over one hundred species of small rodents and birds, including raptors. They're balancing the ecosystem now, and cats are to be included as predators."

"You'll miss them," I said blankly.

"I'm not willing to live, missing them. I'm going with them."

I gaped at her. "Leaving Earth? Permanently?"

"I turned fifty last month. That made me eligible. With the new law, there's nothing left here for any of us arkers, Jewel. Every friend I've spoken to intends to leave Earth in the near future. It'll be a general exodus of the arkers. Some families I know are unable to afford to go, but they're sending their children. If there aren't enough arker planets to hold us, then we'll have to find some new ones. Shiela's going. Didn't she tell you?"

"No," I said. "We've had little time to talk recently, but how can millions of arkists . . . ?"

"Billions, actually. Enough that their dues have been used to purchase yet a few more 'worthless' planets with no natural resources at all except sunlight and soil and water, and what more do we need than that? There's no life left on this world. Hordes, yes. Hives for swarms. Anthills for ants . . . no, termites. What did the high priestess call us last Memorial? 'Pallid dwellers in a spiritual darkness'? Except for you and a few other friends, I won't miss anything. Earth gravity, maybe. It's the only thing we haven't ruined."

"But, if I'd said yes to your offer . . . ?"

"I'd still have planned to go, but I'd have stayed a while longer to turn over the estate to you."

"The estate!"

"If I die out there, this is yours." She gestured at the surrounding foliage. "The trees are worth preserving for the seeds, even if there are no birds to nest in them. It won't be any trouble. A man lives here and takes care of the place, collects the seeds in the proper season and ships them out. It'll be here, give you something to look forward to. Getting away from Paul . . . Oh, Jewel, please come to temple, tonight! It's our cadre."

I could only nod, overcome.

Our Temple of Remembrance, one of some thousand such temples around the world, was some distance outside the urb on a former chemical dump site so heavily and deeply polluted that it had had to be encapsulated. A couple of centuries back the movement had purchased the buried encapsulation and set the temple on top of it with plenty of room to park flits that came in from hundreds of miles away. No one building could house the millions of arkist members who lived in the nearer urbs, so Midsummer services began weeks before actual midsummer and extended weeks afterward, one service for each cadre of members, with only enough time between services for one cadre to depart before the next one arrived. The identichip detectors were set to reject anyone not of the cadre, and security guards were numerous, as were the shrieking protesters with their incessant "Iggy-huffo, iggy-huffo," and their battery of signs bearing Evolun Moore's fiercely frowning image.

Roll Call was conducted over a chorus of small animal sounds and children's voices, though not, I thought, so many of either as I had heard in the past. Arkists usually brought their children and grandchildren, and many people, including Margaret, brought pets to receive the blessing. The children would go home with their parents. The pets would either leave Earth in the next few days or be compassionately killed by their grieving owners, many of them those same children. During the processional, we cadre members used the datalinks at each seat to enter our own names, the names of absent members, members who had died, and those who had had children born. Names on the Solidarity Wall lighted up in blue as they were reported present, in green if they were reported absent, or were moved to the Memorial Wall for those who had departed.

The dancers danced, the choir sang, both magnificently. It was traditional during Remembrance for the orchestra to play and the choir to sing the rollicking "Litany of Animals" for the children in the audience. I'd loved it as a child when Matty used to bring me to Temple. I still loved it.

"Elemental, monumental, fine phantasmic elephants;
Hairless hippopotami, huddled close as spoons;
Riotous rhinoceri, roistering on grasslands;
Tiny tender tarsiers, eyes like moons!"

As each animal was mentioned, its likeness appeared on the great Wall of Remembrance, and the singing went on through several nonalphabetized alphabets of animals, from the awl-nosed aardvark to the zebra and zebu. The children in the row behind us were singing. Mag and I were singing. For a moment, it was dream childhood again, when we had thought all the creatures were real, not merely memories on wall vistas.

The blessing, a sober one, was delivered by the High Priestess, who, coincidentally, asked a particular blessing on dogs, "for millennia of interspecies friendship." At the end of the service the names of the departed were illuminated with rainbow lights while the choir and congregation sang "Unto Grass," which always made me cry, as much for the loss of grass itself as for the many who had died trying to keep things growing. No one on Earth would ever again go into grass, and the thought of being broken down into constituent elements in a recycling plant did not evoke the quiet acceptance many of us had felt when we planned to achieve the same end through natural means. It was all in the hows, I thought. The whats are inevitable, but we should be able to choose our hows.

As the congregation was leaving, I heard my name called and turned to see my former sister in-law, Myra, working her way through the departing flow.

"Jewel, I saw your name go blue at Roll Call, so I've been looking for you. I got a message you were trying to reach me." She smiled and nodded at Mag. "Hello, Margaret, how are you?"

We moved out of the aisle, as Myra said, "I was so surprised to get your link message about Paul's going to Moss day after tomorrow. You've decided to go with him?"

I said carefully, "It looks like it, yes."

"You could do me a tremendous favor. Would you have a little time tomorrow to get up to Hargess. I need to talk to you privately before you go."

"What is it . . . news of . . . ?"

"No. No news of Witt. Are you still . . . ? I can see you are. Oh, I wish . . . I wish you didn't think about it anymore."

"That's not likely, Myra," I said firmly, wishing fervently it were!

Myra patted my hand. "Let's not try to talk here. Come tomorrow, for lunch? Margaret, it was good to see you, you're looking well . . ." and she was away after the scattered remnants of the crowd.

Even though I liked Myra, being reminded of Witt always angered as much as saddened me, and by the time Margaret and I had reached the flit, I had worked myself into a fume. The commotion at the nearby pod stop did nothing to soothe me. There, from a hundred handheld signs, Evolun Moore's face scowled and his finger jabbed accusingly at all of us while his followers chanted his slogans:

"PEOPLE NOT PUPPIES!"

"EARTH FOR SPEAKING PEOPLE."

"BAN THE BEAST LOVERS!"

"IN GOD'S IMAGE: HUMANITY FIRST AND ONLY! IGGY-HUFFO! IGGY-HUFFO!"

It took some time to get through the departing arkists to Margaret's flit, where she stowed the cat carrier and told me she would take me home. We had already said good-bye, and I didn't think I could bear doing it again. I glanced toward the pod stop, now almost free of protesters as our service had been the last one of the day. "It's a long way out of your way, Mag, and there's a pod waiting. I'll take that." I hugged her. "Please, let me hear from you."

Margaret said, "Garr'ugh 290. Care of the PPI installation. And you let me hear from you, too. Through headquarters."

I turned away, hiding my face. I would never know where Margaret was. Only the ship that took her to her cat-haven would know precisely where it was going, and it would go there on autopilot in response to coded orders that no human pilot ever saw.

"Hug the dogs for me," Margaret called, as I walked away toward the tag end of the crowd. I waved without turning. It wasn't a smart thing for Margaret to have said, not that loudly, at any rate, but then Margaret hadn't been in the daily thick of it as I had. We arkers had learned, sadly, the need for security. Recently a private aviary in US North had been invaded by terrorists who had killed the last wood ducks and sandhill cranes alive on Earth. That incident had followed hard on an invasion of the panda sanctuary in China, where the ten remaining animals had been first slowly vivisected then slaughtered, the whole process sight-and-sound recorded for public viewing.

The message had been clear. If arkists didn't want their beasts hideously tortured, they should do away with them. Though cruelty and trespass were still crimes, there had been no arrests in either case, and the news was full of masked terrorists stating their determination to wipe out all animal life on Earth and on any planet where humans lived or planned to live.

Only a few people were left at the temple pod stop, mostly cadre members who were taking a few extra minutes to don robes and veils for their trip into the urb. I located an eastbound pod and pulled my own veil from my pocket as I boarded among a scatter of others. I keyed in my tower stop absentmindedly and sat down near the door.

As the pod moved away, a voice came from behind me, "So you're a dog lover." A man's voice, hesitant but angry.

I caught my breath, held it, let it out slowly as I drew my veil over my head. "Not particularly," I took a moment to arrange my veil. "I've got an old friend who likes cats. Known her since we were kids."

Silence answered me. I looked at my wrist-link, holding it high enough that the lens mirrored the space behind me. His face was bare. Sulky-looking, with a wispy black beard and shifty eyes. Beard meant down-dweller. He was too far back to reach me without getting up, and I was closer to the door. I read the pod number from above the door and slid my hand into my pocket, gripping the vial of STOP that I had finally consented to carry. His move.

"I heard her tell you to hug the dogs!" The tone was jeeringly accusatory.

I'd anticipated as much and had my response ready. "She means my brothers. When we were little, we had a wagon, and the boys would pull us around in it down on the park floor. She used to call them our dog team, out of some old book she'd read."

He glanced over his shoulder at the other passengers, near the rear of the car. "You women ought to be ashamed," he snarled.

"Of what?" I asked in real surprise, keeping my voice level with an effort.

"That church!" he said. "That female, animal-worshipping church. It's ungodly!"

"It's not female," I murmured. "Lots of men belong, and we don't worship animals. We just recognize them as creatures created by God. Why? Do you think they were created by something else?" Moving as little as possible, I pressed the "next stop" button beside my seat.

"They were made for our food, and we were meant to do away with them as soon as we got many enough. You'll get what's coming to you, you know that."

I felt myself simmering. "Don't you think we all will?" I tilted my wrist. He was rocking back and forth, making unsettled noises, breathing angrily. The pod slid to a stop, and I rose unhurriedly and got out, catching a glimpse of the knife in his lap as the door closed. I'd depodded at a transfer station, empty at that time of night.

What had he been going to do? Skin me? My mouth was dry, though the hand clasped around the vial of STOP dripped with sweat. Anyone hit with STOP was down in five seconds, which was why it was the defensive weapon of choice for those who could afford it. The person who bought a vial of the stuff received antibodies against it that were unique to that preparation and that person. The compartment at the bottom of the bottle held the antidote. If the antidote wasn't provided within a quarter hour, the person hit with STOP was dead in thirty minutes.

STOP was legal because assault was about the only crime left that people could commit. They couldn't steal. Implanted identichips were used for all purchases. The chips would transmit an alarm if the owner was unconscious or drugged or in fear. Flits worked only for their owners. Apartments opened only to their owners. Entry to stores was blocked to those without the right credit rating. All items were identified by codes implanted during manufacture, and items were debited to the buyer's identichips in the exit lock of the store. Even store employees had to exit through the locks. With concs more available than air, why would anyone rape? Aside from the handful of intransigent misfits who lived habitually as I had done briefly on my way to Baja, everything was controlled except for madness, fury, and stupidity. For those, we had STOP.

I wiped my palm down my pant leg and transferred the vial to the other hand. The man was looking directly at me, scanning the lobby behind me. He saw I was alone and half rose from his seat only to fall back into it as the pod moved off. Looking behind me, I saw that the tower was derelict. No wonder I was alone. I took a deep breath and checked the time. He was one of only half a dozen people in Pod ARX99-3987 at precisely 22:14:30 on the current date, and the rest were all women. I linked ark headquarters and told them. All the ark and sanctuary workers noted and recorded every threat. Dame Cecelia wasn't the only one who could get hold of Past-this-point records, and we preservationists kept dossiers on every IGI-HFO we could identify.

I took the next pod, so rattled that I missed a change and had to go backward to get home. I had a headache starting as well as a case of the shakes. Unfortunately, the evening's confrontations were not over. Two stiff-necked men in uniforms were waiting in the library, being treated to coffee-14 by Paul.

"These gentlemen from Species Control want to ask you some questions," he said, ostentatiously putting an arm around my shoulders. "One of your trainers got picked up the other night."

I turned to the two men, eyebrows raised. "Not *my* trainer, Officer. He works for the Alred family canine preservation trust. But I do know about the incident." I shook my head sadly. "Poor Adam. The stress must have triggered a convulsion."

"Stress, ma'am?" the older of the two officers.

"Well, yes. Jarl Alred called him and asked him to come down and pick him up at some conc club or other, but he didn't wait at level to be picked up, so Adam had to park the flit and go to sub three to get him. When Adam and Alred came out, the flit had been vandalized, well . . . turned over, and a group of idlers, accompanied by some ruined concs, threatened a fight. Jarl was moodspray oblivious; Adam didn't want any trouble, so he pulled Jarl back inside. Someone had already called for help, luckily, for when Adam stepped outside again, he went into full-scale convulsions and woke up in the hospital. Poor man, he looks absolutely dreadful!"

The two officers looked at one another, one with the corner of his mouth twisted, both of them knowing full well who the Alreds were. Gritting my teeth at the pain in my head, I seated myself comfortably, hands folded in my lap, ostentatiously willing to talk about it all night if they wanted to. The older one shrugged and gave it a try.

"Thing is, some of the . . . idlers claim an animal attacked them."

"Really? A rat?" I said, puzzled. "I didn't know there were any left."

"There are some rats, ma'am, but it was something larger than that."

"Well, what in the world would that be. A feral cat? Something off-world? Something smuggled in by one of the alien diplomats?"

"There's no chance your trainer had a dog with him?"

"No chance at all!" I said, sitting up even straighter in outrage. "The trainers value their jobs far too much to risk the preservation license or their animals by doing that. The foundation animals never leave their protected site, and you should know as well as I do that they are identichipped just as we are. If there had been a dog there, you would be able to get a record of it." I frowned. "Besides, you know how cramped a two-seater flit is. Where would Adam have put a dog?"

The two shrugged again. "Maybe the kids got confused?" said one.

I shrugged. "It's possible, I suppose. Or, maybe someone was using too much moodspray, but whatever the local juvenile gangs get up to has nothing at all to do with the foundation. And by the way, when are you people going to start enforcing the ban on ruining concs? Adam says there were ruined concs in the group! Badly maimed! Doesn't treatment of concs come under Species Control?"

Both officers mumbled something quasi-apologetic and made hasty farewells, leaving me to shake my head and mutter about spoiled young men loudly enough that Paul heard me.

"Where were you this evening?" Paul asked, jaw clenched.

"I stopped to say good-bye to Margaret Olcot." Plus evading followers, attending Midsummer services, narrowly avoiding being assaulted or murdered, and finishing up by being misleadingly unresponsive with Species Control officers. All in all, quite time to leave the planet for something quieter.

"And when did you become spokesman for conc rights?" he demanded.

I turned on him, the whole day's frustration coming out in a burst. "Paul, you should be ashamed to ask me that! I know concs are the next thing to nonsentient, but cruelty is cruelty. You hurt one, it feels it. You maim one, it feels that, as I have very good reason to know! Causing pain for pain's sake is, in my opinion, the greatest sin a sentient being can commit, and now, if you don't mind, I'm going on to bed. It's been a difficult day, and there's at least one more like it before we leave."

He had the grace to flush slightly as I left him, but it was because I'd touched his pride, not his conscience, and he was already plotting how to put me in my place. Perhaps he would simply do without me in the future. That thought compensated slightly for the rest of the absolutely gluppish day.

⠿ Myra lived outside the Urb in the Hargess development, a dozen luxury residential towers grouped around the Hessing estate which stood among farms. Her home was on the top story of a seaside tower with no algae harvesters or treatment plants in view. The family was old money, old power, old politics, reinforced by profits from centuries worth of investments in off-world materials and fuels. Myra was not part of the Hessing line of succession, as Witt would have been, but she had the same Hessing kinfolk in all the right places. We sat at a small table set for luncheon, with the two mechs in the room shut down and the Quondan butler elsewhere.

Myra said, "Dame Cecilia heard you might be going to Moss. She asked me to ask a favor of you."

I set down my cup and took a sandwich, my eyebrows going up in surprise when I tasted it. It was delicious.

Myra murmured, "It's chicken liver paté, imported from Pharsee."

"Real chickens?" I asked, wonderingly.

Myra smiled. "Real, smelly, unsanitary, feather-molting chickens. I was speaking of Dame Cecelia . . ."

"I wish you wouldn't, Myra."

"Then forget Dame Cecelia. I'm asking a favor of you. I'm troubled by something, and I'm wondering if you could try to find out about it, on Moss."

"On Moss?"

"At the Derac outpost. A few of them have been left behind to keep an eye on the contractors. Have you ever seen one?"

I shook my head. "I've seen pictures. Vaguely humanoid, long tails, scaled, predators' teeth and talons. They're egg layers, carnivorous, diurnal."

"One never sees the females," Myra said, with an expression of distaste. "One understands the females are unintelligent, incapable of speech, and instinctively bound to nest behaviors." Again she made the odd expression, looking away from me as she continued. "When the female leaves the nest, the father is summoned. He picks one or two males from the brood to rear to adulthood, then eats the rest of the brood . . ."

I put down my cup, fighting a spasm of nausea. "His own . . ." I swallowed. "If the female babies are killed, where do they get females to breed?"

"I have no idea. Derac planets are off-limits to us, so what we know about them is made up of bits and pieces learned during diplomatic or trading meetings or recorded conversations. Sir Dawlish heard such a recording, between two Derac, during which one of them questioned the other as to whether it might be possible to buy human females."

"Buy them? For what?" I asked, amazed.

"They didn't say. The whole matter would have attracted no notice if the same Derac hadn't later asked a human official of the Board of Trade if it was possible to buy human females."

"That would be slavery."

"Not necessarily. Some races have indenture laws that are far short of slavery."

"Well, we don't and the Derac know what our laws are!"

"So do the Orskimi, but they have slaves, and that makes them the subject of endless discussion at every IC meeting. No one knows what to do about it since the Orskimi—and the Derac, as well—could do far more damage out of the Alliance than in it."

I chewed thoughtfully. "Is it possible the Derac might be trying to understand our views?"

"Father says no. He says they don't care about our views. He says the young ones are unbearable, and the old ones are incomprehensible, and they have one peculiar trait: Except when among themselves, they never mention females of their own race, though they refer to the sexes of other races, Tharstians, for instance."

"I didn't know the Tharstians have sexes."

"According to Father, they have five, all of whom get themselves ready for reproductive activities by lengthy joint bubble bouncing, which looks totally unsexual to us but is extremely erotic for them. Father maundered away about all this at the dinner table, and Dame Cecilia, possibly for the first and only time since they were liaised, was actually listening to him." Myra sipped her tea. "The business about buying human females upset her a good deal. So, when I heard you were going to Moss, I thought maybe you could find out about it."

I seethed. "Dame Cecelia as much as killed Witt, you know."

Myra sighed. "You may not believe it, Jewel, but Dame Cecilia now blames herself for what happened to Witt, which is rather nice for those of us in the family who have been accustomed to bearing all the family guilt. She's come to the conclusion that if she hadn't made so many difficulties about your liaison to Witt—including forcing Witt to go on that expedition in an effort to split you up—she'd have had grandchildren by now."

I said in a strangled voice, "Yes, Witt and I would certainly have had a child by now."

"She now believes she misread you completely. When you didn't have a baby, and you didn't liaise with anyone, she began to blame herself. I'm telling you this just in case you have any lingering animosity."

I went to the window, hiding my face. "Lingering is too flaccid and ephemeral a word for what I have, Myra. I *was* pregnant, though I didn't know it until some time after Witt left. When your mother had me harassed and threatened by her friends at BuOr, I had to get away. I was young and scared and my effort to evade her was . . . stressful. At any rate, some weeks later, I lost the baby."

"Lost . . ." Myra's voice was harsh with shock. "I never knew that."

"Ironic that Dame Cecelia probably caused the loss of that grandchild she wanted so badly. It was probably for the best. With Witt gone, they wouldn't have let me keep it. Hell, I couldn't even have paid the fine for reproducing without a coparent!"

"You could have found someone. I would have . . ."

"It doesn't matter. It was over very soon." I turned to confront Myra's sad face. "Afterward, I knew that if I'd had a child, Dame Cecelia would have taken it from me. She'd already cost Witt his life, I wouldn't have wanted her to have our child. My resentment is not merely lingering. It's entirely alive and well."

Myra cried, "Jewel, are you going to mourn your life away?"

This annoyed me. "Do I sound like I'm mourning? I'm not grieving, I'm angry! I'm angry at your mother. I'm furious at Witt himself. I get wrathful when I'm reminded, so I try very hard not to think about it."

"But you haven't had any other liaison . . ."

"That's true, but it's not out of any feeling of . . . fidelity. When someone male makes a move in my direction, all I feel is vacant. It may be chemical or aberrational or perhaps obsessional, but there's nothing I can do about it. Let it lie!"

Myra flushed. "All right. I understand. Will you do the favor anyhow, for me?"

I regarded her thoughtfully. "I'll do what I can if you will return a favor, which is what I linked you about in the first place."

"You have only to ask, you know that."

None of the Dame's actions had been Myra's fault, so I forced the anger out of my face and voice. "The ESC on Moss has discovered a group of old Hargess ships up on the plateau area. It occurs to me the ships may have ended up there the same way the Derac did, through some kind of spatial anomaly. It also occurs to me that the people in those ships seem to have disappeared, maybe in the same way Witt and his group did. Tell Dame Cecelia about those ships. Suggest that she use her influence to get them investigated by ESC because they may contain a clue to Witt's disappearance."

Myra looked as astonished as I had expected. "What do you want to know about them?"

"What will the Hessings want to know? Everything there is, Myra.

Where they were going, by what route, who was on them . . . everything. Send me the information through the ESC on Moss . . ."

"Mother doesn't deserve your help, but . . ."

I held up a threatening hand. "I thought we had it clear! I'm not doing it for her. I'm doing it strictly between us. I try to find out what you want to know, you get ESC to stay on that planet and investigate those ships."

⋮ On my way back through my Urb, I was only half-conscious of my surroundings. Outside the express pod, towers sprinted by, cross-street traffic Dopplered above and below while the pod made its unvarying rhythm, purrs interrupted by clatter. Talking about Witt always raised his ghost, though he was a fragmentary wraith at best, shreds and shards that never added up to a whole person. I couldn't dislodge a particular pattern of light and shadow falling across his cheekbone and eye, or the wide double curve of his mouth, like an ancient bow. His hair was deeply black and thick, an inheritance from an Asian grandmother, cowife of a far-traveled Hessing entrepreneur. I remembered his hands on me. He was a clumsy toucher, willing but not . . . empathetic. His hands never quite soothed, never quite rubbed out the ache, never quite scratched the itch. I remembered his smell, always waking with it still in my nostrils, not unpleasant, not at all remarkable.

That was it. The curl of an eyebrow and lip, an inept touch, a certain smell. If that was all I had left, where had the rest of it gone? Had there been any more than that? From time to time I had told myself we hadn't known one another long enough to build a complete memory of one another. Either that or that last day with him had totally corrupted recollection. Perhaps during those eleven days of our liaison I'd been dreaming my way into his life, not really looking at him at all. That was possible. I did that a lot, had done that since a child. It was far easier to make a pleasurable world and its inhabitants inside my head than to deal with what was real.

What was increasingly real was this amorphous cloud of apprehension I couldn't get rid of, this vague mental fog out of which some tiny voice whispered, "Danger here. Menace by something, someone. Peril coming." It had nothing to do with the ordinary, day-to-day concern about IGI-HFO. It felt like those times when one wakens in the morning inhabited by shapeless and totally reasonless fear, leftovers from dream terror that one cannot possibly recall. That terror dissipates, however, and this did not. On the podways I saw only the everyday, the normal, the usual. A veiled woman hurrying to catch the pod, followed by her package-carrying, ivory-haired conc. Crowds moving through the pod lobbies. Veiled people trailing one or more package-carrying concs like comet tails. Groups of bored young people chattering in corners, a trio of concs near the entry, singing for pod change. It suddenly occurred to me that concs who were, so to speak, still "unadopted" would need to eat! Did they live on pod-lobby food?

People moved in streams, tangling and untangling, up a level, down a level, into the pods, out of the pods, traffic as traffic had been for years. The singing concs swayed to their music, their treble voices insistently sweet, like holiday candies. One of them glanced across me, then back, its eyes fastening upon mine, eyes as opaque as darkness itself, limitless in depth, ageless in intent, regarding me from a distance that reduced me to ant size, a mere thinglet, a nonimportance.

As I dropped my eyes, I shivered, unable to help it. When I looked up again, the concs were wandering away, still singing softly, following their accompanist. The look it had given me had been one of total incomprehension, exactly what one might expect from a totally unrelated race of creatures, no more threatening or strange than the look one might get from a pet bird. Still, I had never seen that expression on a conc's face before. Of course, I hadn't spent any time looking at conc faces. Those who didn't like them tried not to look at them, and that included me.

At the sanctuary, where I stopped to see Adam, there was a certain restlessness evident. During the night, the guard told me, several strangers had tried unsuccessfully to force an entry from the flit lobby. They had threatened to return in force. "All the smaller dogs are gone," murmured the guard. "The lab is cleared out. The supplies have been divided up and shipped. They took your idea and smuggled everything out through the cargo tunnels. All the trainers are gone but Adam, Frank, and Clare."

"Three trainers, six dogs, is nine berths on a starship," Adam said, when I went to his suite. "Very expensive proposition. It's not sensible, but then, nothing makes sense anymore!"

"Of course nothing makes sense," I snapped. "Living creatures aren't supposed to live without breathing space."

He snorted. "Iggy-huffo says we'll all love one another once all the dogs are gone."

"Don't think about it, Adam, just do it. You three, the dogs, and all your supplies are leaving here by chartered cargo flit about midnight. You go straight to the ESC port. Paul and I will be joining the ship there at dawn tomorrow. How are the dogs?"

"Behemoth, Titan, and Wolf are a little nervous but otherwise perfectly splendid. Dapple, Vigilant, and Scramble likewise." He nodded in satisfaction. "All three are pregnant. Scramble will pup first."

"Scramble's the best one of all," I commented, fondly.

"She's certainly smarter than any two of the others put together." He sounded vaguely miffed at this. Adam preferred Behemoth to the others. At the time, I didn't know why.

One more thing had to be done before I left, letting Gainor Brandt know about my conversation with Myra, for he had impressed on me that ESC needed to know anything and everything, no matter how trivial, about the races they had to work with.

I linked him. He sounded tired and depressed. He was on his way to a meeting, but he could stop later in the evening to have a drink with me on my mercantile floor. I agreed and went home to join Paul for dinner. Since Paul was still full of talk about Moss, I was able to work the Derac into the conversation by asking, offhandedly, "Why did the Derac sell the moon?"

"The Derac always sell off a part of new discoveries, to pay back their Gathering of Elders, the G'tach, which subsidizes exploration."

"So, why don't they handle the compliance process themselves? Why contract it to ESC?"

He assumed his lecturing posture, head back, eyes half-shut, unshakably superior. "While you were still down in Baja, say . . . eleven years ago, the Alliance got around to formalizing the Deracan lexicon, and I was assigned as one of the assistants to the team who worked on it. I may have spoken of it to you."

"I recall your saying it was a miserable job."

His nostrils narrowed, signifying displeasure. "Everything with the Derac is a stinking battle, stinking in a quite literal sense! They 'cooperated' in providing the lexicon only because accurate translation is needed for them to trade with other races. They tried to keep us focused only on the vocabulary of quantities and merchandise. What and how many for how much. It was like deciphering a wall by being given every seventh brick. Humans can't speak Deracan because we don't have the throat sack they do. It's difficult for us even to distinguish individual words.

"Lingui-putes, however, have no such limitations. All they need is word meanings, so the four of us went to a Derac retirement planet with a dozen lingui-putes to spend some time with a few unwilling Derac. In practice what happened was the Derac pointed at his lunch, wrote a certain symbol, and made a particular noise, which our machines recorded as a sound pattern. We labeled that symbol and its equivalent sound pattern *Gak*—or something equally arbitrary—and when we talked about that sign or sound we said, the 'Gak sound' or the 'Gak symbol.'

"We guessed that it probably referred to food, but we didn't name the symbol *food*, because we might be wrong. It might mean *something I killed*, or *ugly animal* or even, *that's you if I catch you alone somewhere*. So, when we fed it to the lingui-pute, we directed the 'pute to look for Gak or its parts in other samples of the language, hoping the context would carry us into areas that would help specify the meaning."

I rubbed my forehead, just above my eyes. Paul's discourse often seemed to set a headache off. "What does this have to do with why the Derac don't do their own surveys?"

"I'm getting there," he said reprovingly. "My work on the lexicon is pertinent. We began to accumulate a lot of fighting words. Attack, take over, grab, steal. They had twenty expressions for thievery, over a hundred for robbery and assault. Essentially, they're pirates and adventurers who travel in Daj-Derachek—(that's our word for their word, you understand?) It means *shipclan*, a group that includes the males descended from one patriarch who occupy and run one ship, together with their whelps, or apprentices.

"When they discover something worth selling, three large shares go to the elders, the G'tach; to the members of the shipclan; and to the ship itself, for maintenance. Two smaller shares are given also: one to the parent ship, the one they were born to, and one to a fund for the new ship they will buy for their whelps.

"Every Derac carries a togro, a genealogy that goes all the way back to one of the seventeen racial patriarchs, and the name of that patriarch is the first part of each Derac's name, even if there are a hundred generations in between. As there were only seventeen patriarchs: there are only seventeen G'tach . . ."

From the center of my raging headache, I interrupted him. "The point you are reluctantly approaching, in answer to the question I asked an extremely long time ago, is that since whelps grow up in shipclan and are limited to shipclan, no Derac ever specializes in anything."

"That's right," he said, flushing slightly. "No surveyors, no biologists or zoologists."

I rubbed my forehead, interested despite the dagger stabbing my brain. "No physicians? No . . . designers or accountants? No cooks?"

"Derac cuisine consists of burning the fur, scales, or feathers off whatever they've killed, then eating it raw. Clothing is the untanned hide of whatever they've recently eaten, the smellier the better. Their word for famine is the same as their word for odorless, because when there's famine, they eat their clothing and don't smell anymore. They don't need accountants because every one of them can calculate in his head faster than you can feed data into a computer, including complex navigational computations and anything to do with money. You want to know how much your savings would be with variable interest compounded for a millennium, ask a Derac."

He shook his head, making a face. "Nobody I know has ever seen a sick Derac, so physicians aren't needed. They may well eat anyone who's sick or wounded. They farm out all specialized work. Your average Derac shipclansman—that is, the younger members of the race— are willing to spend about five minutes on any nonship problem. If they can't solve it in five, they farm it out. Derac start to fidget if they have to stay two days in one place. They have no infrastructure to support science, engineering, procurement, or training. They have no history of it, and it would take generations to create one, just as it took us. They became starfarers by the back door, by buying ships. They don't build anything for themselves."

I stood up. "I presume no music, no art."

"Along toward dusk, they did something they called singing. It was a kind of bellowing, actually. The elders spent a good deal of time sprawling about on warm rocks having what we would consider philosophical discussions, from what little we overheard. Why are we here?

What are we for? What should we be doing? We weren't invited to listen in, as the Derac are consistently aggressive, even in ordinary daily life. We concentrated on the job and left as soon as it was done, though *done* isn't the right word. We're still recording Derac speech everywhere we can, refining our own understanding of their talk and what they really mean when they talk."

I had been about to leave, but this stopped me. "We, being who?"

"The Interstellar Coalition Linguistics Board. Earth builds a lot of Derac ships, so the devices can be built in. Don't mention that to anyone, Jewel! It's against the IC conventions, and it's being done quietly, not only with the Derac, but with any race where understanding is questionable. The board feels it's better to breach the conventions to improve communication than have a misunderstanding start a war."

"As they all too frequently have!" I commented before excusing myself and leaving Paul to finish his supper while I went to my room and used a pain spray. If I was now at the point of getting a headache every time I was in Paul's company for more than a few moments, the coming trip to Moss would not be a festival. I lay down to let the pain spray work, which it did, before donning the requisite robe and veil to keep my appointment with Gainor.

I met him by the lift, and took him into the nearest bistro, where we could sit uninterrupted for a time over a glass of a greenish brew suitably called Alga-alka. Though some people confessed a fondness for it, I couldn't drink it. Most people ordered it only as an excuse for occupying a seat. We each took one ritual sip before I filled him in on my bargain with Myra Hessing.

"So, you'll get all the pressure you need to keep ESC on the planet for a while," I concluded, reluctantly taking another sip to wet my throat.

"Were you counting on her asking this favor?" he asked, turning his glass to watch chains of sluggish green bubbles ooze upward.

"Actually, I intended to ask her to do it as a favor. Her asking me for a favor came out of the blue. Anyhow, the thing I wanted you to know was this strange Derac thing, about buying human women. I got Paul to talking over supper, and from what he says about them, it's obvious there's no way I'd be able to find out anything about the Derac, even if there are some of them on Moss. He did offer one item of interest, however. Do we do any listening on Derac retirement planets?"

"What listening?"

"Oh, come on, Gainor. Paul mentioned the IC Linguistics Board recording conversations. Myra mentioned her father being privy to such recordings. I know it's against the conventions and has to be deniable, but still . . ."

He scowled. "No. We haven't listened on their retirement planets. There aren't any humans on retirement planets. The lexicon project may have been the only time."

"There have to be some other races who go there? The Derac aren't capable of building anything themselves."

He stared at me, eyes narrowed. "Why do you ask?"

"It's what Paul said. It seems the ships have a social structure so rigid that very few words are needed, but Paul says the Derac actually change at some point in their lives, and that's when they retire to a planet and adopt a new culture. Rather as humankind did, fifty thousand years ago when we all of a sudden acquired opinions and vocabulary. When the Derac reach a certain point in their lives, they do the same. They lie about in the sun and discuss their philosophy of life, so that would be the place to put your listeners. You're in good with the Tharst, aren't you? They build things for other races, and those orbs they float around in have veiling capabilities, don't they?"

He gave me a look, slightly surprised, slightly amused. "Jewel, I'm noticing a devious part of you that I had not seen before. Tell me, is Paul taking his concs?"

I gritted my teeth. "Naturally! My hope is he won't have time to pay any attention to them. They're so idiotic!"

Gainor grimaced, leaning back in his chair and folding his hands across his expansive belly. He dropped his voice to say, "You know, don't you, that concs are the real tabula rasa, the blank slate upon which anyone may write what he pleases. Or she pleases."

"I've only known Paul's, really. Oh, I've seen them in the pod lobbies and carrying packages, but . . ."

"Paul created their idiocy, Jewel, believe me. An acquaintance of mine has one that plays chess, rather well. And I know of one that dances beautifully. In each case, that's what the 'owner' wanted. Or needed." He sighed, stared at the ceiling for a moment. "Did you know the birthrate on Earth has dropped by some 80 percent since the concs were . . . introduced?"

I stared at him openmouthed. "Eighty percent? Are you sure?" I blurted it rather too loudly.

He put his finger to his lips and chuckled without amusement. "Oh, yes, Jewel, quite sure. Sure enough to make me wonder if they were put here for that purpose."

"By whom?"

His face went momentarily blank; one nostril twitched, as though at an unpleasant smell. "We're not certain."

"But you have an idea?" I pressed him.

He shrugged, the fingers of one hand making a rat-a-tat of discomposure. "We hear things. The Interstellar Coalition is a hotbed of . . . talk. I won't say rumor, because we're not at all sure it isn't fact. Whoever made the concs used Zhaar technology to create them. Most of the elder races have used it from time to time, but the race that uses it the most—that we know of—are the Orskimi."

"Why would the Orskimi try to reduce our birthrate here on Earth?"

"Maybe they're short of living space. They like the same environment we do. They might begin the game by dropping concs into Earth's populace, at first only a few, so they're not seen as a threat, then more and more. If this were any other planet, when the birthrate dropped, the population would dwindle enough to make eventual conquest easy."

"If this were . . . ?"

". . . any other planet, which it isn't. This is Earth. Every space not taken up by a local will be taken up by a returnee, so the population won't dwindle. A conc case takes up only about fifteen cubic feet, so the number of concs awake and moving around is only a fraction of the total present on Earth."

"Doesn't the government keep an eye on how many there are?"

He fixed his eyes on the ceiling, musing. "Conc cases are manufactured and sold by Worldkeeper, as a monopoly, so we know how many cases there are, but not how many concs. We should know, but we don't, and any effort to get a count is met with a certain degree of . . . obstructionism."

"From whom?" I demanded.

"Well, if I had wanted to introduce concs on Earth, I'd have hired a human agent to meet with certain Earthian legislators who are known to be for sale to the highest bidder. Posing as a friend of Earth, I'd have sold concs as a device to help Earth make more space for returnees by reducing the birthrate. I'd have explained that the system is foolproof because concs aren't human, they take up little human space and no human air, which is true, by the way. They respire, but only to produce speech, they don't use oxygen. They're like plants, they manage on our exhaled carbon dioxide. I'd mentioned that cellular makeup kills bacteria and viruses harmful to humans, so they don't spread disease or become ill, needless to say.

"And, if I did my job well, I imagine the people who were paid off would help me bring as many of them to Earth as they chose to."

"The Earth Congress has forbidden export of concs to other worlds," I said. "If tourists take them, they have to bring them back!"

"True," he mused. "I'm guessing the next move will be an amendment attached to some obscure bill that defines concs as property. Later there will be an equally obscure amendment to the export law allowing people who are moving off planet to take their property with them. Once there are a few concs on Faroff, others will show up, just as they did here on Earth."

"But all this . . . this strategy would take . . . a lifetime or more to cut our numbers, Gainor."

"That's the primary reason I believe the Orskimi are involved. They're the only race we know of whose strategies extend over millennia. Ask your brother, the linguist. What other people have an ordinary word in daily use like *Skitim-orskiantas-shampifa*, meaning *ultimate fruition of a plan laid by our early ancestors.* They're long-lived as individuals, true, but that doesn't explain how they can continue with these absolutely linear plans century after century, working toward ends that were decided millennia ago. How do they keep it going? On Earth, every time there's a new government there are new policies, but not among the Orskimi!"

"Who are suspected of using Zhaar technology."

"Because they have two slave races that are extensively modified in ways that scream Zhaar."

"But the Zhaar are dead, gone, lost. Nobody's seen them for aeons . . ."

He looked through me. "Not aeons, Jewel. More on the order of fifty to a hundred thousand years. So we're told."

His absent look made me uncomfortable. "I've heard that some elder races in the IC wiped them out."

He nodded. "So it's supposed, yes."

I sat back, sipping, trying to find my way in our conversation. "Gainor, are you hinting that the Zhaar are not gone? Dead?"

He stared over my shoulder. "I'm saying, simply, that when we were 'discovered' by stargoing peoples, we were told about Zhaar, but no one told us where they lived or what they looked like. We were told they were expelled from the galaxy. This one says a million years, that one says a hundred thousand or less. That's what the Tharstians say, so I go with that number. Each people is referring to its own years, of course, not ours.

"If we go to the IC Archives, we find a lot of Zhaar stories and things said about them by others, but no writings by the Zhaar themselves, no artifacts, because, so we're told, they were shape changers who could become anything they wanted to be. They didn't need tools, they became tools; they didn't create art, they became it. And even though they're supposed to be long gone, when a population suddenly disappears, as on Holme's World, everyone at IC starts nodding and whispering about the Zhaar having done it again.

"When the elder races, like the Phain or the Yizzang, are asked about the Zhaar, they say the question is irrelevant, the Zhaar are gone, but how could anyone know? If they were identity thieves, originators of a biotechnology that could modify any living thing, one of them might be sitting across the table from me at IC, looking me in the face, speaking to me out of a Yizzang or Phainic mouth."

I took a deep breath. "And we go along with the idea that the Zhaar are gone because . . . ?"

"We prefer to believe in a lot of things we aren't certain of. The goodwill and truthfulness of people we are negotiating with. The Articles of Confederation. Tomooze . . ."

I laughed. "Tomooze?"

"The Quondan believe it's a measurable quality. I say maybe it exists, maybe not, in the same way I say the Zhaar or some other race may or may not be sowing concs on our world as a takeover measure."

"Do we have any strategies to oppose their actions, Gainor?" I asked him. "Assuming it's all true, are we doing anything about it?"

He showed me his lopsided smile and shook his head slowly, side to side, his new hair waving gently around his ears. "Why, my dear, if we did, I certainly wouldn't talk about it."

That was what he said. What his face said was that whatever was being done, he didn't think it was enough. I started to protest, but he gave me no time to react. "Tell me good-bye, dear. I won't be seeing you for a while."

I was momentarily sidetracked, for it was true he would not be seeing me for a very long time. I kissed his cheek.

"Don't be late for the ship," he whispered.

"I won't, Gainor," I assured him. "Take care."

Reveiled, I went back to my floor, still possessed by that dreamlike discomfort I had been feeling for some time. As I left the local to walk back to the apartment, the feeling came into focus. Concs. Concs, too silly or infantile to cause fear; concs, adaptable, generally accepted, even enjoyed; concs, which were, if Gainor was right about them, as inimical as plague.

And four of them were going with me to Moss.

IGGY-HUFFO

⋮ While we were on the first leg of our trip to Moss, Gainor Brandt received a visitor in his office at Government Center, a slinking wretch whose appointment had been made through someone important in the legislature. He crouched across from Gainor, weasel snout twitching, skinny weasel claws grasping at air, hairy mouth uttering stupidities.

"The government requires an inspection of all animal-breeding facilities to assure they have been closed, as required by law. We do not understand why there should be the kind of foot-dragging that we at Federal Species Control have encountered." The weasel sat back, stroking his furry upper lip and peering through his implanted lenses like a stoat grooming itself after one blood meal while keeping both eyes open for another.

Gainor smiled sweetly. "Where's the foot-dragging? As I've said,

Citizen Gabbern, you're in the wrong place. I have no authority over the preservation sites, which are privately owned and managed. Here, in your presence not ten minutes ago, I linked the Alred canine preservation center and was told you are quite welcome to see it at your convenience. In pursuance of the new edict, it is quite empty."

"Empty?" the stoat actually squeaked, half-rising from his chair.

Gainor cocked his head, riffled the papers in front of him, cautioned himself as to manner and tone, managing to say in a calm, even voice, "The animals and trainers and support staff are gone. The center has reverted to the owner of it, in its entirety. In time it may be refurnished for some other private use, but I have no idea for what."

The stoat, Gabbern, who was indeed publicly associated with Federal Species Control, but more secretly and pertinently with IGI-HFO, glowered. "Inspection will at least tell us if this story is true!"

Gainor growled ominously, "It will indeed, so why don't you go and inspect it instead of sitting here insulting me? I can link them now and tell them you're on the way!"

"Will they have the locations of the animals which have been, as you say, *disposed of*?" the creature snarled, thrusting himself back in his chair, defensive and offensive at once.

"I doubt it. Can you give me the location of any relative of yours who has been recycled? The animals are gone. Done. Departed. Mr. Gabbern, why are you still here? Why aren't you on your way to the Alreds' place?"

"Because I am advised you have influence with these people!" snapped the stoat.

"You were advised incorrectly. The only people I can influence are those who work for me. The people at the sanctuary do not work for me. You seem unwilling either to take my word for it or to verify it for yourself, and I am at a loss how to help you."

"You could help me by forcing these damned animal lovers to stop keeping necessary space away from people and crops," the stoat snarled.

"What crops would you grow in the Alred mansion now the animals aren't there?" inquired the general. "Or do you wish to house people in the Alred mansion?"

"Too damned much room going to waste!"

"You wish to revoke the exempted estates laws? Is that a sensible ambition for someone in your position? Would you care to have that desire made public?"

Gabbern started to say yes, then no, then decided on saying nothing. Too many of those with exempted estates were contributors to the campaigns of powerful men. In some cases, those contributions outweighed the contributions from planets profiting from the Law of Return. The stoat muttered. "The numbers of humans requesting entrance to the home world continues to mount. We have to find space for them!"

"Do we?" the general asked. "Who says so?"

"Humanity says so," squeaked the stoat.

"Humanity has said so since time immemorial, but I would argue with the statement," mused the general. "Instead of saying, 'We have to make room,' I would say, 'We have to limit our numbers.' And I would say so because it is manifestly impossible for one planet to support the total number of people arising naturally from a fecund race occupying a hundred worlds on which they have killed off all their natural enemies." He paused, briefly, considering whether what he had said was honestly true, deciding to leave the Orskimi-Derac threat unmentioned. "Earth cannot support the great numbers of people who are sent here by the Law of Return. So long as we make it possible for the outer worlds to shift their burden onto us, they will continue to do so."

"We can support more of them once these animals are gone!"

"You have disposed of all the four-legged or winged creature left on Earth, but you won't be able to house and feed a dozen returnees with the space."

"You don't know that!"

"I do know that. It's my business to know that. I have testified to that fact before the Earth Congress, suggesting they should change the law." Which he knew they wouldn't. Even though legislators received enormous bribes from outlying worlds, it was less expensive for them than taking care of their excess populations.

Gainor continued. "Only when this constant immigration stops will people have room and water and enough air to breathe without using rebreathers." He went purposefully toward the door, flinging it wide. "I bid you good-bye, Citizen Gabbern. Go inspect the sanctuary for yourself. I am sure you will find it quite, quite empty."

Which he himself had seen it to be, early that morning. He almost wept, as he told me later, thinking about it. Empty. Labs empty. Trainers' apartments empty. Dog runs empty. Even Jarl Alred's pet poodle had been taken far, far away.

: At Alred's, the stoat was escorted around the 259th floor by a capable young assistant who showed him the kennels, the research center, the library, and the circle of residential suites around the atrium, now open to the sky, its vast sunscreen folded into a bundle at its center.

"These were the apartments of the trainers," the assistant said, indicating the doors.

"I'll see inside," Gabbern insisted.

"Of course. The doors are unlocked. They're all pretty much alike, but go through all of them if you like." The assistant seated himself on a garden bench and focused his attention on the reflecting pool, with its growth of lily pads. Listening intently, the assistant heard the Species Control officer bang his way from apartment to apartment. All of them were empty, stripped, and clean except one, which showed signs of recent occupancy. Gabbern spent a longer time in there before coming out to ask why the apartment seemed lived in.

"I think an acquaintance of Mr. Alred needed a place to sleep for a few nights," the assistant said. "The whole place belongs to the Alreds. They may use it as they like, so long as no animals are housed here." He led the way to the laboratories, which Gabbern damned with a cursory look, and "I can't see why they needed laboratories at all!"

"Nutrition, I think. Learning what food is essential and which is nonessential . . ."

"You need a DNA sequencer for that?"

"Sequencers are used for species preservation, but the only thing I ever heard about that had to do with removing deleterious genes. You'd have to ask someone associated with the program for details."

"Where would I find such a person?"

"You'd have to ask Mrs. Alred."

"And where is she?"

"Off planet for a time. Visiting family."

The stoat sulked. "We could house twenty people around this space."

He received a lofty look and a well-rehearsed answer. "If it weren't an exempted estate, you could, yes. However, the committee that over-sees your work is indebted to the Alreds. I don't think they'd want to see that support go to their opponents . . ."

The stoat, still manifesting annoyance, was shown to the nearest pod lobby. That was, however, not quite the end of that. Though he should have reported promptly to the office of Species Control, he went instead to an office in the upper floor of a large ex–urban storage warehouse near the bay.

"Gabbern to see Evolun Moore," he announced to one of the many guards.

"Business?"

"He knows. Just tell him I'm here," the stoat squeaked.

The guard went off down a long hall, past several other guards and watchers, returning after some time to gesture at a chair, where Gab-bern was told to wait.

Fuming, he waited. In due course, one of the guards came to fetch him and escort him down the long hallway through several anterooms decked with IGI-HFO banners, and into the windowless office of the great man himself, where Gabbern made his report, as briefly as was possible.

"It's really empty?" Moore asked doubtfully.

"Of persons and animals, yes, Great Leader." The stoat leaned for-ward, arms on Moore's desk, dropping his voice, "It is possible, how-ever, that it was temporarily vacated, just for this inspection. They got word we were coming, they shipped everything out temporarily."

"Who told them we were coming?"

"It could have been assumed, from what's been happening."

"And you think Brandt knew nothing about it?"

"He . . . may have known nothing, yes. He was irritated by my ques-tions, but he wasn't . . . fearful, as he might have been if he was worried about the animals."

"You planted the device?"

"Great Leader, planting the device was why we scheduled the visit!"

"Is it likely to be found?"

"No. It's in a ventilation duct leading to one of the trainer's apart-ments, which are at the center of the floor, as we planned. One of the apartments had been used recently, and I could stand on the bed without leaving any sign I'd done so. There'd be no reason to look for it there."

"Can it be traced?"

"No. It's from an XT source. It came pressure wrapped, I took the wrapper away with me, it's already been burned. And once it goes off, of course, there'll be nothing left to trace."

"You have the detonator the supplier gave you? The transmitter thingy?"

Gabbern removed the case from his pocket, opened it to show the device inside. "Here it is. Be careful with it. The Alred Tower is over a mile away, so you're probably safe here from flying glass, but I'd stay away from the windows when you use it, just in case. When will you . . . ?"

Moore said in a pontifical voice, "It will be used to announce our new campaign against the exempt estates. It will make our point very clear, and the troops will applaud the action. I will personally choose the time, just after an election, to insulate our legislative support from the consequences."

Gabbern nodded, but Moore did not notice. He was lost in the intricacies of his plots. He could neither ruin the opportunity with too much haste nor delay unnecessarily. This time no animals would be tortured. The public had not responded well to that tactic. This time, he would wait until a propitious moment, a time when something dramatic was needed, then he would blow the Alred Tower to hell.

"We were made in the image of God," he reminded his inner circle of friends and supporters when he informed them about the device. "We and only we. No other race in the universe is made in that image. It is our destiny to inhabit the universe, singly, wholly. We cannot move against the Tharst, the Quondan, the Derac, the Orskimi until we have cleansed our own planet. Then we who were made in God's image will move out into the star-lanes, colonizing as we go, until the entire universe is filled with that image. Such is our destiny!"

It was great stuff, and its familiarity made it no less moving. Every person assembled in the room felt he or she had been personally selected by God to achieve great things. It made veins swell and hearts thunder to hear it, resulting in an immediate cascade of volunteers willing to place other such devices here and there through the urbs and the exempt estates. Moore signed them up for later use, placing his hands upon their heads in approbation. Hatred had always been an easy sell, and the crowding among down-dwellers and even ordinary citizens made them willing to hate those blamed for their lot.

The uniform History of Earth used in school curricula devoted a short chapter on racial bigotry on Earth and to the fact it had been ended by contact with other worlds. In the face of alligator-like Derac, orb-floating Tharstians, tentacled Ocpurats, six-legged six-armed Orskimi, faceless Quondans, and the predatory Grebel and Xan, *all* humans were obviously In God's Image. All races with nonhumanoid forms had become the enemy, taking the place of the ethnic, religious, or linguistic scapegoats of ancient times.

The textbooks actually noted that Earthers, who could have benefited from a time spent rejoicing in their common humanity, had merely transferred their bigotry outward, as the Quondan had done during that epoch known to interstellar historians as "The Quondan Absurdities."

⋮ While Gabbern reported to his adored leader, the young man who had shown him around the sanctuary conducted a thorough search of all areas the stoat had walked through during his visit. Since the stoat had stayed longest in the slightly messy room, as the profilers had suggested he would do, that room was gone over first. An extremely sophisticated and powerful explosive device was removed from the ventilating duct. Further search found various tiny listening devices, but no other dangerous devices, so reported the searcher to Gainor Brandt.

"Good," said Brandt. "Where is the thing?"

"With our people, in a containment unit, in case Moore gets itchy-fingered."

"Can they trace its provenance?"

"It's definitely off-planet. They said they'd let us know."

"Gabbern was followed, of course?"

"Before he went back to Species Control, he went directly to IGI-HFO headquarters."

"Presumably Moore has the transmitter needed to set this thing off?"

"Gabbern had it when he went in, he didn't have it when he came out, so it's very likely."

"I'd love to put the device in IGI headquarters." Gainor sighed. "I suppose the collateral damage rules that out."

The assistant considered the matter. "Moore's office is swept three times a day. It's buttoned up like a level patroller's overcoat on a windy night. However, it's on the top floor of one of those multiuse buildings down by the freight transit center. There's a dead records storage place directly below it, and we could encase the device to make the explosion directional." He smiled. "It could blow 'up,' literally."

"Whose records?"

"Bureau of Order."

"What a nice idea," said Gainor Brandt.

THE DERAC

: Garr'ugh Center was a planetary system set aside by the Garr lineage of the Derac for use both as breeding grounds for the young and retirement centers for the aged, retired members of the Garr shipclans, those who had reached the life change and were thus capable of spending time in thought. Though youngsters considered the elders to be mere shells, no longer fit for anything useful, the changed ones thought of themselves as savants and sages, the brains behind exploration and conquest, even more valuable to their race as thinkers than they had ever been as fighters.

Though the elders spent much time in thought and converse, the habits of earlier years were not entirely eradicated. The traditional midmorning warm-sprawl still took place, though the retired ones relaxed upon the Sprawling Ground central to the "Retired Ships," as they were derisively called by the younger Derac, not entirely without reason. They were, in fact, ships that had been retired when their crews retired. Each retained its original heated sandboxes for sleeping, its convenient fire pits for burning the fur or feathers off edibles before consuming them, and its bridge deck, where the immemorial shipclan rituals were conducted at intervals. The engines still provided warmth, and only the cargo holds were empty, for the ships had been connected to central supply.

On the second and largest planet was the home of G'tach Garr, which had provisioned the exploration that had accidentally happened upon Garr'ugh 290. Though the amount advanced to the shipclan had been returned to the G'tach with interest—a satisfaction that was not invariably achieved—the G'tach continued to follow the fortunes of system 290 with great interest, for systems near wormholes, even erratic ones that only opened up every now and then, were useful during war, an occupation usually being engaged in by at least one or two of the seventeen tribes of Derac.

One of the members of G'tach Garr was Gahcha, who held this office by reason of his position as life captain of his Regional Retired Fleet, and Life Captain Gahcha was planning the greatest war in Derac history! Gahcha spoke of this future war at council meetings and, which amazed him, he did so eloquently. At his recent life change he had acquired a mental acuity, a revelatory sharpness that was as startling as it was unexpected. Games whose rules he had never understood he now played with both vigor and success! Conversations he might once have found impenetrable, he now comprehended. Deracat, the destiny of the race, a subject he had once found dull and obscure, he now gloried in.

Gahcha's clarity of mind and purpose had first been put to use when he had challenged the previous life captain to a test of strength and wits, during which the previous captain had been deposed by losing his captaincy along with his life. Now Life Captain Gahcha led his Regional G'tach, but soon he would head the G'tach Garr. After that, he would ascend to the Admiralty of the G'tach Derac in order to lead all seventeen clans into a Great Scaly Caough of a war!

Regional life captains determined the crews—for so they were still called—of Regional Home Ships, which housed several thousand retirees. Of that number, Gahcha's own particular Home Ship sheltered a carefully chosen few hundred, and of those, an even more carefully chosen few dozen were his daily companions. On a particular morning, Gahcha announced to these cronies that the large Derac contingent on Moss, where his son was currently serving a term as observer, was steadfast but uncomfortable.

"So what does your son say?" demanded one of his colleagues, curling his tail politely to give the life captain more room.

"He says the linguist from Earth will soon arrive," Gahcha replied. "He says living there is extremely unpleasant because moss grows on their skins all the time, and it's impossible to stay dry. He says they don't believe the Mossen are people, they don't believe they wrote any message, they think the Earthers wrote it themselves because they're mossenated in their minds."

"And what are the implications?" the colleague persevered.

The life captain squirmed farther onto the warm, soft sand to get some heat back into his belly. Something was wrong with the sandbox in his sleeping cell. Instead of being steadily warm and cozy, it had been cold as space all night and he'd had to sleep in a warm suit. He hated sleeping in a warm suit, always had, even when he was spacefaring, because it made him itch. Great God Ghassifec knew what the maintenance slerfs were up to, but it certainly wasn't doing maintenance! He would complain to the Orskimi. They had designed the slerfs, and had guaranteed their performance. They would have to refit them or whatever it was that Orskimi did to their bionic adaptations!

Setting his annoyance aside, he replied ponderously, "The implications of Moss really affecting people's minds could mean we will have trouble selling the planet, if we ever wanted to, which we don't. The implications of the Mossen really having a language would be that IPP wouldn't let us sell the planet, though we would receive the usual bonus for discovering a previously unknown intelligent race. The implications of having moss grow all over us would be that we wouldn't want it for ourselves, not to live on, though we will certainly use it for our purposes before we leave it!"

"By purposes, you mean, to start the Great War," said the colleague.

"Very soon, yes," said the life captain. "Before we go on to conquer the galaxy."

The others on the sprawling place nodded, making a gargling rumble that might be transliterated, inaccurately, as "H'hachap, H'hachap," which meant something like "Destiny comes." One Ghetset, the most vociferous colleague, and also the one in whom the life change had made the least improvement in intelligence, demanded, "Why will we start the war on Moss, Life Captain, sir? If we don't want it for ourselves?"

"We will need it as a staging area for our exploration of that sector. We intend to find the wormhole, which will take many, many ships."

"Then why did we give the Earthers a contract to start with?" demanded Ghetset. "Why didn't we just keep quiet about it."

"It is better to have Interstellar Confederation see us conforming to regulations than to have it suspecting us of wrong doing!" snarled Gahcha. "By calling in the Exploration and Survey team, we can seem to be in compliance with IC regulations while our plans go forward. If they found us on a planet that had not been surveyed for compliance, we might have to fight more than just the Earthers. Eventually we will conquer them all, of course, but not just yet."

Another colleague forestalled further questions from Ghetset by asking, "Oh, great Life Captain, tell us again how H'hachap will come about."

Gahcha lowered his neck frill and squirmed slightly deeper into the warm alluvium.

"To advance: Our knowledge of H'hachap began long circuits ago on Planet Gehengha. A Derac just coming up on the life change actually listened to the humans talk, a thing we do not usually bother to do. If anyone thinks otherwise, five minutes spent in the exercise convinces him of the wisdom of unhearing. However, in this case our kinsman learned of this law the humans have about returning." Forestalling questions, he held up a warning claw. "It means any human anywhere among their planets can go back to the original birth planet of the race if he wants to. This Derac..."

"What was his name?" asked a fellow lounger.

"Who? Oh. He called himself R'ragh."

"Thing fixer?"

"Ah...new-maker, reformer. He was later called R'ragh the Reformer, but that was after he became a follower of Ghassifec. To advance: R'ragh came to believe that this law was the source of the humans' power, the power we have sometimes envied, sometimes disdained. We have envied their inventiveness, their concentration. We have disdained the brief, very brief youth they have, only a fifth of their lives or less, compared to half or two-thirds of ours. Even while in the juvenile state, some humans think and study all the time, something no young Derac would conceive of doing. Nonetheless, they have inventions on top of inventions..."

Ghetset said, "They figured out the Plavite Compressor that we found on Garr'ugh 193. We found it, but they figured it out. Next thing you know, they were manufacturing the things by the millions on their factory planets, and what did we get out of it?"

"A royalty," said Gahcha. "Quite a substantial one." He used a Derac word meaning "enough and some left over."

"A royalty!" Ghetset flicked his tongue at an imaginary bug, showing what he thought of royalties. "We could have had the whole thing."

"We could have ... *if* we manufactured things. *If* we'd figured it out," said Gahcha, turning on his side to sun his left legpits. Several slerf efts crawled into the newly exposed area and began searching under the scales for itch-mites. Though no one present had reason to know it, they looked very much like klonzees. "The fact is, of course, that we don't manufacture things, and we didn't figure the thing out, and as a result, we buy our ships from humans or Ocpurats or Fifflizen. To advance: All of this was noticed by R'ragh the Reformer, who decided the very things we have disdained about the humans are the things that give them their advantage."

Ghetset raised his head, inflating his throat pouch, his wattles turning red. "He wanted us to build ships? Who's going to stay in one place long enough to build ships? We don't even build towns! The only thing we build are sprawling boxes for the little ones. Even our retirement homes are worn-out ships built by somebody else. We don't know how to build ships. We've always bought them from other people. The Fifflizen first, then the Ocpurats, the Orskimi, now the humans ..."

Gahcha bobbed his head repeatedly, meanwhile reviewing mentally just why it was he had selected Ghetset for this group. Ah, yes. To have someone to whom he could tell things he wished other people to learn of, whether information or disinformation. "Exactly. And why? That's the question R'ragh asked. Why? Why don't we start thinking earlier? Eh? Why do we need a youth that goes on so long? Umm?

"To advance: R'ragh sought answers from an Eetchie he had allowed family status ..."

"An Eetchie," cried Ghetset. "We do not grant Eetchies status as family. What kind of Eetchie was it?"

"This Eetchie was of the Orskimi, one who had been most helpful to R'ragh. It is not unknown to grant Eetchies family status, though it is done rarely and only to one who has done a great favor to Deracat."

Ghetset pursued the matter with a quotation from scripture. "In the beginning was the great swamp of unbeing, and from this swamp, in the time before knowing, the Derac were created by Ghassifec, in the shape of Ghassifec we were made. All others who swim and move and speak are Eetchies, unworthy creatures, not of the lineage of Ghassifec."

"So you quote accurately!" Gahcha glared at his associate. "But until the day when all Eetchie shall be cast into Ghassifec's fires of forever, they may still be helpful, and this Orskim was helpful. It was he who helped R'ragh find the truth about our long youthfulness. The Orskim told him the Derac stay young as long as we can because we enjoy breeding! We don't want to stop breeding! In the far past, we bred endlessly, and ogputi of our young were eaten by the Fez and the Grebel and the Zan, giving us even more reason to breed. Then the Fez were gone, killed mostly by the humans, though some by the Quondan and the Tharst. The Grebel and the Zan were no more, many eggs were laid in our nests, our young lived in great numbers, and we didn't have ships enough for all of them to grow up in.

"To advance: This, said the Orskim, is why we began what he called our current lifestyle, which began not at the roots of time with Great Scaly Caough and the Far-seeing Sixteen, but only an ugget generations ago . . ."

"So recently?" exploded Ghetset.

The life captain glared at him.

"To advance: The Eetchie Orski told R'ragh that our way of life was not ageless tradition, magma jelled into stone, but a recency, a change from an older system, one that could be changed back! If our females were more like human females, said the Orskim, if they had brains and talk and abilities, they could go with us on the ships. When we found new planets, instead of farming out the exploration to Earthers or Ocpurats, we could settle on the planet and do it ourselves. Also, with our females beside us, we could breed whenever we wanted to, and instead of the old ones taking care of the efts, the females could do it."

"H'hachap, H'hachap."

Gahcha nodded repeatedly. "The human females are receptive all the time. Even when they're already bred."

"That's disgusting," said a colleague from the edge of the group.

Gahcha acknowledged with a head bob. "Some Derac think so, yes. Some others of us understand what R'ragh the Reformer was telling us. He asked us to think about the time of Great Scaly Caough, the time when we had many young, and the predatory Zan preyed upon our ships, killing many of them ..."

"The Zan preyed on everybody," said a colleague. "Even the humans."

"True. But R'Ragh asked us to think about the time when all the Zan were killed, down to the last offshoot, when we suddenly had too many young, when they mutinied on ship after ship, and we ended up having to kill off most of them. R'ragh said that's when we moved the breeding function out of ships, onto retirement planets, and that's when we removed the females from the ships."

"What could we ever have done with females on ships?" asked someone at the edge of the group. "How did we put up with them? They can't even talk."

"I suppose we kept them in a special hold, or something," Gahcha replied. "R'ragh said when we moved the females off the ships, instead of breeding all the time we were *thinking* about breeding all the time, and that didn't leave any time for thinking about anything else. Which is why we don't invent things. It is only when we are past breeding that we think about things."

"To advance: What was it that R'ragh said we should do?" asked Ghetset.

"R'ragh says we should colonize the planets we find. The ship should make landfall and stay there, males, females, and young. Planets are big, the females can lay all the eggs they like. When we can breed whenever we like, we won't be thinking about it all the time, which makes us nervous and incapable of concentration! Even young ones will have time to think. And, if we change our females so they're more like human females, maybe we will have even better brains to use in thinking about other things, even when we're young! R'ragh taught that this is what we must do, so we can breed greater intelligence into our people."

"Why would we want to fix our females?"

"Because ..." The captain struggled to remember why that was.

"Because our females don't have any minds at all. If we're going to share a planet with them, they need some sense, you know, language, brains. R'ragh learned that female humans are smart, like the males, but in a different way, and having both kinds of wisdom directed at a problem increases the likelihood of its being solved. R'ragh told us we need to change our females so they think."

"We think!" objected one of the listeners.

"We all think like *us*, and we have to go to other races if we need our thinking checked, as R'ragh did to the Orski. What R'ragh wanted us to do is to buy some human females and pay the Orskimi to take their brains apart and use their DNA to splice to ours to make females who talk and think."

"That's forbidden technology," said someone, somberly. "They use Zhaar cells to do that splicing. The Zhaar were shape changers, and it takes shape changer cells to do what you're talking about."

"True," Gahcha responded. "But some exceptions can be made."

"Why buy human women? Why not just . . . take them?"

"Because then the humans would accuse of what they call abduction or slavery, and it's against their laws. You can't just take someone and cut them apart, not according to human law . . ."

"What do we care for human law!"

Through gritted teeth, Gahcha said, "We have to seem to care because human law is registered with the Interstellar Planetary Protection Institute! IPPI even made a fuss about the shipclan taking one of those Mossen creatures. Our brethren had to claim they found it already dead. Which it was, by the time they were finished with it."

"Your son Tachstucha told you about Garr'ugh 290, did he?" asked a lounger. "That's where he's assigned?"

"Yes, but he was here for mating. He spent three days over on the breeding ground and left this morning to rejoin his group on Moss."

"I've heard all this many times," said Ghetset, his voice so closely approaching the yowl mode that all the lizards in the circle began to raise their fins. "I personally don't see why we're waiting until we get these females. If we're going to conquer the humans, let's get at it! If we're going to take over the galaxy, let's get started"

"Well," muttered the life captain, licking his teeth insultingly, "if you go off starting things without a proper foundation, they will fail. As soon as we have the human women, we will give them to the

Orskimi, the Orskimi will tell us how long the project will take, and THEN we will begin the war. It's all planned and agreed to." The captain raised his dorsal fin, livid with bile, and whipped his tail so that it cast sand toward Ghetset, who barely blinked in time to avoid being blinded.

"Once we have our women changed, we'll need new worlds to live on, and the best planets available for us are the ones the humans have," trumpeted Gahcha. "The Ocpurats live in water, the Tharstians prefer light gravity, the others like things heavier or more methane in the atmosphere. No, the best planets for us are human planets, or Orskim ones."

"We sold most of them to the humans," objected a lesser lizard, one at the far, shady side of the plot. "And to the Orskimi."

"Everyone knows that," the captain asserted. "So, we'll have to take them back."

"Why don't we just rent them?" asked Ghetset, irrepressibly.

"Humans don't have space to rent because it was never revealed to them they should eat their young! They multiply like mold, until the area is contaminated, then they move and do it over again. Sharing a planet with humans would be impossible. We have to eliminate them entirely and take their planets. Then we'll breed up our strength and do the same to the Orskimi."

The captain stretched his snout high in the air and gaped, a signal that the topic was closed and he wished to meditate. Around him there was a murmur of . . . what? Agreement? Gahcha opened one eye to see bodies contentedly relaxed, faces innocently gaped toward the sun. He reflected what a pleasure it was to know that his colleagues, by and large, seemed to think his plan was a good idea. By the time he told the story a few more times, they'd think they'd thought it up themselves. Oh, he hoped he lived long enough to see the galaxy free of humans! Free of Orskimi, too, of course, though he imagined that might take longer.

⁞ We learned all this, of course, since I could not be writing of it otherwise, only because others were intent upon listening to the Derac. We were later to be grateful that these folk were friendly, if not with all Earthers, at least with Gainor Brandt.

⋮ At this point, it may be appropriate to introduce some of the people I would later meet on Moss, as there is nothing at all intriguing to say about our voyage to that planet. Grav-rep voyages are indistinguishable from one another: One takes one's soma and one sleeps; one then wakes, attends to sanitary matters, eats something tasteless, returns to one's bunk, takes additional soma, and sleeps again. Though I did not learn of them until later, far more interesting events were occurring on the planet toward which we were headed.

⋮ On Moss, if one left the PPI compound and walked eastward across the cushioned country in a steady but unhurried pace, one would come within a couple of days to the foot of a plateau, one of the two that soar upward from the more or less level plains of the mosslands. Even prior to landing, ESC had established that the monolith making up this outcropping extended all the way through the planet, emerging on the other side as another plateau of roughly equal size and altitude. Both escarpments rose sheer from the floor of the forest, greenly mossed and lichened at their bases, emerging darkly from that coating about half a kilometer above and ascending thence in bare, black, crystalline facets of basalt to the notched rim of the ramparts, often invisible behind the windblown spray that masked the massif poles of the world.

In its earliest embodiment, the gargantuan column had been the core of a volcano on an enormous rocky planet with a very hot core, a much lighter mantle and crust, and little or no water. This protoplanet had circled Garr'ugh 290's sun just inside the orbits of the gas and ice giants until it was struck by a fast moving and extremely massive body of rock and ice from outside the system. The resultant fragments that were not thrown out of the system or inward to the sun were spread widely in a thick belt of rubble that eventually coalesced into three planets and one moon.

The results were Stone, made up almost entirely of heavier, core material, too small and too close to the sun to retain an atmosphere; Jungle, a mixture of core, mantle, and so much water that it developed both oceans and a thick, dripping atmosphere; and Moss, largest of the three, which aggregated both rock and ice into one heavy little moon and, more or less spherically around the roughly cylindrical chunk of the former volcano, into a planet from which the volcanic ends protruded like enormous flat ears.

As part of the huge protoplanet, the cylinder had not been disproportionate. Skewered through this smaller world, however, it was incredible: a continuous chunk of rock, the ends forming circular plateaus with diameters one-twelfth the circumference of the planet, so tugged this way and that with each circuit of the heavy little moon that friction from the ceaseless stresses heated its central mass. Deeply buried water picked up this heat and moved it through cracks in the monolith to the surfaces of the two mesas, where it emerged as boiling springs, explosive geysers, and myriad simmering pools.

Despite these steaming flows, the heights were both cooler and wetter than the lowlands. Copious rainfall accumulated in sizable lakes, overflowed into streams, and ran outward to the rimrock. Some rivers on the lee arc of the highlands spurted clear of the precipitous walls to fall thousands of feet, as from great milky spigots in the sky, while on the weather side, violent winds vaporized the plunging waters into wavering veils wafting gently onto the mosslands below.

The plateau varied from miles-deep central glaciers to temperate edges, from pockets of deep and fertile soil to badlands of cracked ridges and scraggy peaks, many furred by dwarfed trees whose roots stubbornly penetrated every fissure. Many plants on the heights were found only there, including ubiquitous oval shields, like giant liverworts, that overgrew the derelict ships so completely they would never have been noticed except for the weak but persistent "downed ship" signals eventually picked up by an ESC orbiter. Aside from making one brief stop to record the presence of the hulks and to drop a few automatic data-gatherers, however, ESC had let the place alone.

The data-gatherers, called "fish," recorded the presence of shiny, crablike creatures both atop the mesas and in the mist lands at their feet, but no attempt was made to collect specimens or determine what kind of creatures they actually were. The contracts held by ESC and

PPI mentioned the highlands only as a postscript: areas to be mapped if and when the planet was found to be habitable and, even then, only after the lowlands had been fully surveyed.

No one at PPI or ESC thought the highlands would be worth anything except for mining, and not even that until the planet Stone, which was of much the same geological structure, had been reduced to gravel. Then, too, it was possible something inimical had happened to the people in the ships. The "fish" showed no survivors, no cleared lands, no roads, buildings, walls, or canals, no herds of animals grown for meat, milk, or hides, and, aside from the vulcanism, no evidence of the higher temperatures that usually betrayed the presence of human settlements. Even after the ships were found, no one supposed a human colony, and since the ships had certainly been human, no one supposed a colony of any other sort either.

⋮ Gavi Norchis, Chosen Ritual Mistress of the First Slumber, set her harp upon the stone floor of the bridal chamber and bowed to the Lord and Lady of this night: Lynbal, Chief Larign's son and Quynis, Chief Quilac's daughter.

"The song awaits your pleasure," she sang. "Deep into the rainbow lights of being, as you shall choose."

"Red," said the Lord, a trifle impatiently. "The red of appetite and conquest." He handed her a blood-colored capsule.

Gavi took it and bowed low. "And the Lady?" she inquired.

"Blue," whispered the girl. "The blue of peace and tranquillity, the softness of cloud." She, too, held out a capsule, this one blue as the sky.

Gavi found this disappointing. Both of them had taken their words directly from the Book of Colors. Doing so often indicated a lack of imagination but, in this case, more likely betrayed a deficiency of involvement. Looking at the Lady of the Night, Gavi was convinced of the latter. Poor little starveling girl. No more flesh on her than on a spider. Well, if tonight went well, she would fatten, her hair would shine, her eyes glow. Gavi often achieved that much with less attractive brides.

"As you choose," said Gavi, beckoning to her chair holder, Squint, who slipped forward with the stool, unfolding it beside the harp, placing the backrest and armrests as she had directed him, setting the candlesticks at either side, the scent table between them, then darting back to obtain the red and the blue candle chimneys from the Chest of Lights. His own low stool was already set beside his drums.

Gavi went on: "And the harmonizing principle?"

Most couples to be wedded said something like "Love," or "Forever," or "Union." These two merely looked at one another, a curious look, half-longing, half-forlorn. "What say you, Slumber Mistress?" the chief's son said at last. "What do you recommend?"

"You will leave it in my hands," she said firmly, not as a question.

"Surely," murmured the Lady. The Lord assented with a brusque nod.

"Share the waters of the night," she said, offering the goblet, ready prepared upon the table.

They sipped it, alternately, three sips each. Quite enough for the purpose. There was enough easepod in it to set them free from any embarrassment in bathing with one another.

"Bathe now," and she gestured at the curtains hiding the bed, softly made, and the warm bath, already drawn. "Remember that you must immerse yourselves entirely, including your heads."

Gavi had already inspected bed and curtains, finding them appropriate for her service, and she had covertly added her own secret substance to the bath. Privately, she called the substance "nothing," for it erased extraneous odors from whatever source, letting the thing bathed in it emerge with only its own intrinsic aroma. No matter how perfumed, a body bathed in "nothing" would smell only of itself, and the imprinting which would take place tonight would take place unimpeded by any former imprint of any other person's odor. After tonight, these two would desire only one another.

The two young people went silently through the curtains, and while the silence gathered, Gavi went to the scent chest to select from among the hundred or so materials there. Her chairholder-apprentice had already started the first burner-board by filling the channel that connected all the oblong scent pots with a length of slowfuse.

"Attend me," she said, as he crouched beside her. "Veilroot in the first and second cup, to dim self-consciousness and wipe out either intention or apprehension. Tonight we are allotting two full cups to veilroot, for the Lady of the Night is only a girl, given by others, without love or even attraction to guide her. Veilroot is what?"

"A smoke scent," he answered promptly.

"Correct. So we put it directly in the cup. It is slow to act but persistent in effect. The effect will last throughout twelve cups and perhaps more. We put hungerstem, also a smoke scent, in cup three, filling only the first quarter of the cup."

She watched as he placed the powdered herb in the cup and packed it neatly against the leading edge, where the fuse would burn first.

"That's it, a clean edge, made with the knife. Hungerstem is quick to act at first, but will diminish in effect if continued, so we want only enough to stir their senses. Cup four will be fireseed, which is?"

"An oil, to be heated."

"Correct. Fill cup four with hot-burn number three, which you will mix with one-third holdfast root, put an oil cap on it filled with fireseed oil, and here, between cups three and four, add a short length of quickfuse. Hunger and fire should follow one another at once, without pause."

"Do I take the other fuse out?" he whispered.

"If you attempt to splice the fuse, you may create a discontinuity. Simply lay the quickfuse on top and pack it firmly down with the stylus. It will ignite from the slowfuse below it and run rapidly to the next cup; the other fuse beneath it will burn more slowly, but it doesn't matter. The fuses are as nearly odorless as craft can make them, and neatness in a scent board is not a measure of its efficacy."

She watched him closely, gratified to see that he followed instructions correctly, without elaboration. When he began to fill the cups, she went on, "In almost every case with young people, fireseed requires tempering, which is why we have added holdfast root. Cup five also will be one-third holdfast with fireseed oil above."

"Will they take so long?" he asked, astonished. Squint had done the night dance a number of times, and it had never taken him that long!

"Taking not long enough would be the problem, leaving her unfulfilled, and she must be fulfilled . . ."

He flushed, not having considered this.

". . . So, then we place another length of quickfuse under cup six, half-filled with tempestweed, which is?"

"A smoke scent."

"Correct. And the quickfuse runs to powdered gum of ecstasy—this is the dried sap of the little jar tree, Squint, not the big jar tree, ever!—followed by sleepflower oil for five full cups, seven through eleven, which means?"

"The gum is a smoke scent, then we need hot burn under the oil pans."

"Very good. The final cup is one half-filled with wakevine, making the twelve. Now, important! Here are the capsules they gave me, blue and red. Empty them into a work dish. Add neutral spirits to make a small atomizer full, mark it into thirds, and place it on a stand beside the curtain, the nozzle extended into their private place. When the burn reaches the tempestweed cup, rise from your drums and squeeze the first third of the mist into the room."

"And what are the capsules, Mistress?"

"They are the essence of each of them, the unconscious longings, the single most important ingredient." This was false, or at best misleading, but she had no intention of revealing all her secrets to an apprentice, certainly not a new apprentice. "It is not burned or heated as an oil, but blown as a mist. Be sure you test the bulb for leaks before setting up! While I start with this board, make two more boards, the same as this, to be followed by a short board of sleeproot only. I will take them through their joy three times this night. Do you understand?"

"I understand, Mistress, but why three?"

She sighed. He was a good boy, but he lacked either intuition or the power of observation. "Because she is a virgin girl, because an heir is needed before the people go to war, and because the chief's soothsayers mark this night as the most propitious within the next three cycles. For these important reasons, we were chosen over the Lord's objection,"

"Why did the Lord object?"

Lord Lynbal's demeanor should have told him this. Gavi frowned slightly, "Think of his manner, boy! He believes he can set any woman on fire. He believes it because he is Lord and chief's son, and because no woman has told him otherwise!"

Squint flushed again, "Will the Lord and Lady remember this, Mistress?"

"They will remember it always, though differently."

The Lord would remember with disbelief and wonder, the Lady with thankfulness and joy. Though the chief's son had to beget an heir before he could make a chief's battle journey to the Other Mountain, he might have rejected her work if he had realized how efficacious it would be. It did not matter now, however, what he thought or what he might have rejected. Gavi's presence meant the end had been foreordained.

She carried the scent board to the table, lighted the candles, and set the smoking punk stick ready at hand. Observing that the smoke did not go truly toward the filmy draperies of the bedchamber, she took time to reset the fans. There was still splashing from the inner space. The time was not quite yet.

Beyond the curtain, the new Lady of Loam allowed the Lord to pour the warm, scentless water over her head and hair, to lave her shoulders with it while she accustomed herself to the look of him outside his shell. He looked very bare, as all people did when divested of their out-cave hard armor or their in-cave soft armor. Bareness was frightening. Bareness preceded birth and death. Bareness inside the cave left one vulnerable to treachery. Bareness on the outside left one at the mercy of the cold and the wilderness. Showing bare skin, except for the face and hands, was a sign of unworthiness on the inside. Only Bottom Feeders went bare. And wedded couples.

His fingers, touching her shoulder, were not unpleasant. That protrusion below, rather like a large finger, was no doubt the organ she had been told of. Surprisingly, the fact of its being there, so very overtly, did not worry her. As her mother had told her, everything was in the hands of the Mistress of the Slumber Time, whose task it was to make all things simple and easy. She need not think how or why or when or what to do. The mistress would take of all that.

The Lord ducked his head once more, then rose from the water, first drying himself, then holding out a great, soft towel. "Come," he said, disguising his annoyance at all this nonsense with some difficulty. "We must lie down before she begins." He had promised his father he would mate her well, a sacred promise, on the altar of the ancestors, like a child promising to be good! As though he needed anyone to help him do what the night required to be done! A chief's son could not join the army and march southward until he had begot an heir, so he would beget, though this one looked incapable of carrying a child. No meat on her. All bones. And all that nonsense about the capsules. He had slept three nights with that capsule in his bed as she had no doubt done with hers. By the heights and the depths, there was too much of this ridiculous stuff gaining credence among the Hargess. Too much back and forthing between these mistresses and the mosslands, consorting with moss-demons he would wager.

Their bed was warm. The room for first nights was carved into a wall of the Abyss where hot springs rose through the stone to the surface far above them, there to bubble and steam in countless pools and geysers before trickling down through the spongy stone to be heated once more.

The Lady found this a happy thought. When she was truly wed and pregnant with a son, she would be allowed to ascend to the surface and see the bubbling springs and all the deep-soil lands of Loam that were held by her new tribe. Until then she would be like a fledgling, confined to her nest, as she had been at home, as she had feared being forever . . . She lay down as she had been bid, dutifully drawing the covers to her throat, putting her arms at her side, trying to relax. He did not touch her, which helped.

Outside the curtains, the music began. Through the translucent folds she saw the red lights of his candles, the blue lights of her own. The music wove. She smelled something strange and intriguing, focusing her attention upon it. What was it? Something . . . very quiet and relaxing. As the music went on, her body went limp, feeling his beside her, as loose and relaxed.

By the time the urgency started, she was too warm and easy to let it concern her. Her body grew tense; a tingling spread across her belly, her breasts felt tender, aching, the feeling went on, growing and growing, building up inside her without any possibility of releasing it. She reached for him, coupling with him as naturally as though they were young trees growing together, one bark enclosing the two heart-woods. The smell of him entered through her nose but spread to fill her entire body, which pulsed and thrust of itself, no guidance needed, as the feeling went on and on and on until suddenly, the world exploded. She floated in an ecstasy that was without palpable end but passed sweetly into sleep, which passed into wakening and then into hunger and tension and tempest once more into sleep, and then all over again, and then sleep, only sleep.

Through all their waking moments, they heard the music of the harp and the drum and the two voices, the mistress's voice and that of her assistant, the words, the music, the scents accompanying their coupling as though the musicians could see them, as though they knew exactly what was happening.

During their final sleep, the mistress departed with all her accoutrements save the short-board of sleeproot, which would burn itself out before morning. It had been decorated with carved vines, twined together, and the names of the couple. Most brides kept it as a remembrance.

When the Lady Quynis woke in the morning, she took Lord Lynbal's face between her hands and kissed him awake. He seized her in his arms, straining against her, taking great, deep breaths of her, joining their bodies yet again with no Mistress of Slumbers present. Until last night, Lynbal had thought her plain. He had been wrong. He had thought her slightly distasteful. He had been wrong. He had accepted her as wife only out of duty to the tribe and to his place at the head of it. All of it wrong. She was the only woman in the world. He would never, never desire any other. He told himself he had decided all this, during the night.

The truth was, Quynis was plain. Her slight body, though it could look elegant when dressed, was bony and without allure when unclad. Her marriage had sealed the pact between two tribes, at Chief Larign's behest, though he had been dismayed when he first saw the girl. He had gone immediately to advise his son that chiefs could have more than one wife, several, in fact. Indeed, he had begun making a list of candidates, if only to placate Lynbal.

None of this would be needed, for Lynbal would lust after Quynis and she after him during their whole lives, never, never desiring anyone else. None of the participants to the bargain had made that decision, however. Only the Mistress of the First Slumber had done so, and though it was not something she decided in every case, this time she had done so, irrevocably.

⠇ Lord Lynbal left the bridal chamber late in the morning to keep to his usual routine with his body-men. Each midmorning they donned their armor and went out into the Abyss on patrol of their tribal lands and the neighboring crevasses. As his father, Chief Larign of Loam, was fond of saying, this routine was both traditional and sacred, no matter what else was going on. One patrolled one's territory, and one did it all the time, even when ill, tired, preoccupied, or newly wed.

As Lynbal passed the great hall, his father hailed him, and Lynbal swerved into the lofty cavern, lighted from above by light shafts that had been enlarged through natural clefts. Seated at a table close to the warmwall, Chief Larign breakfasted with Chief Quilac of Granite, who had escorted Quynis to Loam and stayed, with his men, for yesterday's wedding

After greeting his father, Lynbal turned to Chief Quilac. "I thank you for your daughter, sir. She is a priceless gift."

The two elders exchanged a covert glance of surprise, which Lynbal was too besotted to notice.

"Have you breakfasted, son?" his father asked, somewhat anxiously. The boy looked as though he might be feverish!

Lynbal smiled, a slightly lecherous smile. "Indeed, sir. I have breakfasted on ambrosia. Now, if you will excuse me, I am slightly late for morning patrol." He bowed and strode away, leaving the two staring after him.

"What was her name again?" asked Chief Quilac. "The ritual mistress."

"Norchis. Gavi Norchis. I'd heard she is quite remarkable, and in this case, it seems her reputation was warranted."

"How long will the effect last?"

"I didn't ask her. We spoke of an heir, you and I, and I told her an heir was necessary. She did say she could also arrange it so they would find it impossible to dislike or disrespect one another, which I thought a good thing."

"A very good thing," said Quilac. He was fond of his daughter. Quynis had a delightful laugh; she was almost always good-humored; and she could barbecue crab like no one else. Nonetheless, her starved sparrow look had persisted despite all his care or all her mother's ministrations, and Quilac had feared she might be rejected by her groom.

Chief Larign continued, "Norchis said as they live together, they will come to be of one mind about things."

"Thus supporting our alliance."

"Exactly. And since the Medical Machine found nothing physically wrong with either my son or your daughter, we can expect an heir shortly, one who will grow to be a natural leader of our combined clans."

They stared at one another, and at their cups, half in amazement at what they had achieved. Warfare among the dozen Abyssal clans had gone on since the finding of the Key, centuries before. Every twenty years or so, the tribes of the Night Mountain allied long enough to fight the tribes of the Day Mountain for possession of the Key, and between these great battles, the Night Mountain tribes fought among themselves, jockeying for leadership. Presumably the Day Mountain tribes did likewise. The Alliance of Loam and Granite clans was the first attempt at peace upon the plateau, and Quilac thought it miraculous they had actually reached this point.

He murmured, "We all have our scent rituals, we all have our scent mistresses and masters. They do much good, relieve much pain, assist in much healing, but I have never known one able to do this much. Could this Gavi Norchis do something that would bring other chiefs of the north to our alliance?"

"I don't know," said Chief Larign, with a carefully innocent look. "I never asked her." As indeed he had not. He had, however, told her what he wanted before she had worked her scent magic on Chief Quilac at the last Truce Gathering of the Clans. And here Chief Quilac sat, all unwitting, as a direct result of her craft. Since Gavi could do things no other ritual master or mistress could even attempt, her next duty would be to work on Chief Badnor Belthos of Burrow, to make him a peace lover and bring about the wedding of Larign's daughter, Lailia, and the Burrow heir, Balnor. The mistress would do it in the same fashion she had done this, and toward the same end.

"We should find out." Chief Quilac pursued his own question. "If we could bring Belthos in . . . Why, if we could bring ALL of them in, we might have a chance at conquering the Night AND driving away these invaders sitting on our shores."

"Do you really think that possible," Larign exclaimed, with every outward evidence of surprise. "I must ask her at the earliest opportunity."

"Don't ask, tell!" demanded Chief Quilac.

Larign shook his head, smiling ruefully. "She is an artist, my friend. They don't work well when forced. We must be patient, let her see how well this first step has worked out, how it helps us all. She much dislikes any idea of making people do things against their will."

"As I understand it, that's not what she does. She lets their own will make them want to do things!" He winked.

"Ah-ha. Oh, yes, ha-ha. Very good. We'll have to see what we can do." He returned to the herbal mixture in his teacup, a new tea the herbalists had put together. He had not yet decided whether he liked it. There was a spiciness that pleased him, but the underlying fungal tones threw it off . . .

Quilac asked, "What have you heard about the outlanders? Recently, I mean? Are there still as many of them?"

Larign set his cup down with a sigh. "Just as many, yes. Perhaps more. Strangely, however, almost all the ones who come are elderly, and they don't last long. It's as though they come here to die."

"They're taking risks with it, then."

"I have no doubt of it," Larign agreed. "Much else might bring them, but nothing else would keep them here."

"Don't they know what happens to people who do what they're doing?"

"They may not. They've only been here a few years, and they have a halfway sort of discipline that keeps them from the worst sort of addictions. They haven't witnessed anyone totally given over to it, haven't actually seen the death it brings. And, as I say, many of them are old, and it isn't a bad way to go, if you're old. Very little pain."

Quilac shuddered, making a gesture of aversion. "If one doesn't mind the horror of what comes after, that's true." He collected himself, allowed a moment's silence before changing the distasteful subject. "Do you think the decision made at the last Truce Gathering of the Tribes was a good one? Do you think they'll really leave on their own if we leave them alone?"

Chief Larign sat back in his chair, pursing his lips. "From what we have seen, their presence here is temporary. They've brought in no settlers. The old ones who came are gradually dying, without issue. I think it's wise to let nature take its course and remain hidden on our heights. When our army marches to the south, as it will do as soon as Lynbal begets an heir, we will have to detour around their encampment, but that's a small price to pay."

"Remaining hidden is sensible so long as those Derac are still here. Archives has much to say about the Derac, most of it bad."

Chief Larign nodded his agreement. "We don't want war with the Derac. Eventually, they, too, will be gone. Then we can begin colonizing down below."

"And if in the long run they don't go? If they find out what . . ."

Larign interrupted hastily, not wanting to hear it said. "They won't find out. If they did, we'd have to drive them out. And you're quite right. It will go better if we are all united in doing it."

⠇ Gavi Norchis never thought of herself as having been born into a family. She had been reared by a shifting scatter of human flotsam containing several free-floating females of various ages and a number of itinerant males who drifted in and out with the winds. The woman called Tela had definitely been Gavi's biological mother, though which male had been father, Tela swore she had no idea. Tela denned in a deep but narrow cave far down the Abyss, nearest the tribe of Loam but not part of it, a bit farther from the tribe of Granite, but not part of that, either. Such people seldom lived to be old, being as they were the many-generation descendants of engine room people and galley help, barely literate even then, totally illiterate now, people known as Bottom Feeders among the Abyssians. Gavi's folk were bottom-most among them, dwelling in depths where the Abyss narrowed to nothing among a great litter of boulders and sharp shattered stone wetted by curtains of steam and spouts of hot water from the springs. The one thing that could be said for being a Bottom Feeder was that one found no difficulty in staying warm.

Bottom Feeders lived by picking through trash and trapping crack rats for their skins. They drank the sap of the greater jar trees that grew in rock crevices, so called because the trunks swelled into the shape of giant ewers, anchored in place by long, twisted roots sunk deep into rock crevices. Greater jar trees gave off a thin, sweet sap that was both filling and dangerous. Though it gave a feeling of well-being and the energy to live, it slowly killed brain cells. People who drank only jar sap grew so stupefied that they did not eat or drink or move away from their beds to excrete, finally starving to death in their own filth. The fact that such fate was rare was due more to the difficulty of sapping the trees than it was to the good sense of the users.

When Gavi was four or five, something had gone wrong in the cave, something more wrong than usual. Gavi became aware of it only when the shouting escalated and she felt the all too familiar blow of a belt across her back, the signal to start running downward into ways too narrow for older people to follow. That time she had gone down farther than ever before, for her flight had attracted the attention of a band of young tribesmen, brainless young males led by a wiry, evil boy-child whom the others called Belthos.

It had taken almost all her strength to stay ahead of them, and finally, driven to the end of that childish strength, she had committed the foolishness of crawling into a crack with one turn so narrow that while the boy could not enter it, neither could she turn around. She had no choice but to go on, slithering and creeping, finally arriving at an opening into a smooth bubble in the stone, a spherical cell evenly heated by hot springs, a rounded den with no cutting edges and with three openings: the one she had come in by; another that split into two tunnels, one to the abyss she had just left, the other to a neighboring gorge in Burrow Tribe lands; and a third one, straight through the wall of the plateau onto rocky shelf above the mosslands, high enough to be hidden but low enough on the cliff that one could see what was happening down there.

This shelf was laid out in hexagons, the remains of the great basalt crystals that had broken off to make the ledge, one of them broken slightly higher than the others to provide a convenient seat. The ledge lay directly behind a cascade that had deeply notched the escarpment rim, a cataract so shredded by winds that long before reaching the shelf it had become a veil of fog, a soft screen through which one might observe the lower mosslands while remaining quite invisible . . . and wet. Moreover, from this lookout ledge a narrow and hidden trail extended behind pillars and through cracks down the face of the escarpment to an exit at its foot amid a tumble of boulders. Even the way out of the boulders was tricky, though Gavi knew immediately it had been used before. Intrusive rock corners had been knocked off purposely, with repeated blows, and a store of firewood was piled in a crack, protected from above.

At first, Gavi had used the warm bubble lair only as a retreat, a place to escape punishment or evade harassment. Soon, however, as she repeatedly explored the route down onto the mosslands, she discovered that living was much easier down there than it was on the height. It was warmer. Water was easy to come by. Food was more abundant. Some moss trees oozed delicious and satisfying sap that dried into ready-made candies. Some extended long, arched branches where tart-flavored fruiting bodies hung like rows of bells. There were many crabs, and some of the small, tan-furred creatures that lived among the moss were quite tasty when cooked. Even the fire was no problem. One had only to dig up chunks of old mossroot and stack them in any cave to dry. Moreover, in the moss forest she had no one to feed but herself. In this land there were no sullen drifters snatching her slender gleanings from her fingers before she had a chance to swallow them.

Each time she went back up to the lair, she carried a few flat chunks of broken stone, gradually filling the bottom of the spherical chamber to give it a level floor large enough to sleep on. This she covered with soft mosses brought up from below. She trapped crack rats and skinned them to make a cover for her bed and a coat for herself. She sneaked out in the deep night and stole clothing from caves high up in the Burrow lands, enough that she had a change of clothing when one set needed washing. All these things she had either seen done by others or figured out for herself.

Even during her earliest moss gleanings she encountered the Mossen. She watched (something she was good at) and mimicked (something else she was good at) and after a time she joined in their dances. She had no companions and no other amusement than what went on with them and their world. No human child had ever gone among the Mossen. No human child had ever learned the language of the Mossen, which could be learned only when one was a child. And, having learned that language, though she was not equipped to speak it, she applied the information it conveyed to problems she had, thus becoming able to do things others could not do, for she understood the reality around her as others could not.

The people of her plateau called themselves the Night people of Night Mountain, or sometimes, Abyssians. They lived in the darkness of the crevasses, warmed by the hot springs in the stone, illuminated by light shafts and by candles made from wax-vine. They wore crab armor when they made their rare forays across the moss world to battle Day Mountain people, who lived in stone houses atop their plateau, houses planted with vegetation which hid them completely. Day and Night were the two halves of one people, moieties of the survivors and seekers.

They all wore armor even when they went out onto the top of the escarpment near their homes. They could not feel the world through the rigid shells they shaped to their own need; they could not see it or smell it clearly through their masks, but since the people of the Abyss presumed that dreadful things could happen to humans among the mosses and were determined to prevent its happening to them, not being able to feel a dangerous world did not seem a disadvantage.

It had taken the child Gavi no time at all to realize that armor could be used as a disguise. When she grew strong enough, she found a young crab that had just shed its shell, and she killed it before the new one could harden. She cut and bound shapes of the shell around her arms and legs, her chest and back as she had seen the armor makers do, shaping it to herself. The crab head made her helmet and mask, and when the armor was dry, she polished it with stones, decorated it with fantastic designs, connected the parts of it with quilted fabric at neck, shoulder, and waist, at elbow, hip, and knee, and in this disguise she walked openly upon the paths of the Abyss. From behind the anonymity of her visor she traded skins and fruits at the market, acting as an adult among adults, though she was not yet fourteen.

She was quick to detect danger and even quicker to avoid it. Her lair was her refuge from males who pursued her, as a few of them did, attracted by her voice or her smell. Belthos was a constant harrier, an unworthy contender for her favor if that was what he was about. Time after time she lost him, and the others, in the mazes of the Abyss, and they never discovered her lair.

By the age of fifteen, she had accumulated enough coin to apprentice herself to the Guild of Scent-mixers, the most ancient of the guilds among the tribes. Apprentices of the guild—which had chapters on both Day Mountain and Night Mountain—could be anyone: Day people or Night people, old or young, male or female. During her three-year apprenticeship at the local Shrine of Survival, a place where all outward distinctions of gender, tribe, or age were set aside, she had learned and followed the rules without question. She learned the scent-mixer jargon, invented by the guild to disguise their almost total ignorance of the craft they were engaged in, just as the Mental-Medicine jargon covered an ignorance even deeper. During tests, she recited the guild's own gibberish back to the examiners, thus gaining their approbation. No one questioned her right to be certified as a scent-mixer, first class.

Once the certificate was in her hand, she set about forgetting everything they had taught her as she perfected the practice of her art. Her reputation grew. Others would willingly have learned from her, but she told them she had gone to the same school as they, omitting to mention the Mossen, intercourse with whom was forbidden in any case. Since her understanding came from the language of the Mossen and other persons did not know that language, teaching others what she knew was impossible. She would take apprentices, yes, in order to have helpers, and she would teach them what she did, but she could never teach them what she understood.

"Give me a child," she said to one eager importuner. "Give me a child three or four years old, and I will raise that child to know my craft."

So far, no one had felt driven to do so. Children were not numerous among the people of either mesa, and they were treasured as the rarities they had become. Time on time, Gavi blessed the inadequacies of her own childhood while remaining thankful that her family had all died of jar juice. Had she not been born among the Bottom Feeders, she might never have had the great fortune to grow up as she did; had they not died, she might have been encumbered by them. As it was, she was as she was, and there was no one to whom she owed loyalty, or love, or trust, no one to whom she was indebted at all.

I know all about her, and she about me, even those things we tried to hide from ourselves. Though neither she nor I knew it then, we were to become the dearest of friends.

⁞ Shortly after our arrival in system Garr'ugh 290, the captain announced we would set down on the moon, Treasure, to pick up some botanical samples for PPI. Paul was greatly annoyed by this, and his annoyance was, as usual, shared with others. For relief, I went to visit the dogs. They had traveled as we had, asleep when we slept, awake when we were awake. They and the trainers had a large suite—large for transport, that is—and the dogs were pacing the larger stateroom like caged animals, which, of course, I reminded myself they were.

"Awf!" said Behemoth, the moment I came in.

I shook my head, no. "This is just a brief stop, Behemoth. We'll be on the ground less than an hour."

"Owr ome," he said, facing me, eyes glittering.

"That's the plan, yes."

"Wan see."

"I know. But you can't see it without being seen by the crew, or by Paul, and that would ruin everything. Only the captain and a couple of his officers know that we're dropping off some cages. We figure six months, a year from now, this will be home for you, but it's not ready yet."

"Ow no rrrea'y."

"How? It's not ready because you'd starve to death. The animals we're dropping off need another year to spread and reproduce."

Scramble turned to Behemoth and rubbed against his neck. I felt the message she was transmitting somehow, by gesture, by scent. She was saying, "Be patient. It's all right. She's doing her best."

I left them as I found them, Behemoth impatient, Scramble counseling patience, the others willing to abide by whatever the alpha dogs agreed upon. On my way back to my own stateroom, the captain announced that atmosphere and gravity were suitable for type-C persons, and passengers could debark briefly, at their own risk. We had arranged this, so I could get Paul out of sight. I went to collect him, but, naturally, he didn't want to get off the ship at all.

"Think of it!" I said as charmingly as possible. "A small, heavy moon with a breathable atmosphere and almost earth gravity, a moon with rivers, lakes, and forests, a moon called Treasure, and we're getting to see it at no extra charge. Not a dozen humans have been on this gem of a moon, and here you are, one of them."

He brightened at this. "It might be worth an item for ICN, he murmured. "Bit of travelogue."

Nonetheless, once outside, he muttered, "Ridiculous," as he pulled his collar up over his ears. His irritation during and for some time after space travel came from his conviction that the medium through which we moved was highly inimical to human life and only constant concentration would hold him together long enough to arrive anywhere. "Couldn't they have run out here at any time to pick up their samples? Haven't they had years to pick up samples?"

"Presumably there was something in particular that was needed this time." I took his arm in mine and tugged him into a reluctant promenade, chivvying him ahead of me down the slope. "Come on, let's get a look at those bearded trees or whatever they are."

"Who owns this?" Paul demanded.

I shrugged, disclaiming knowledge. Who really owned it was nobody's business. The moon, gem that it was, had been snapped up the moment it appeared on the market, and rumors had been spread variously: that it would be a center of religious work, or a racial enclave, or a cultural, artistic, musical, sexual, dietary, financial, or fraternal group, or perhaps even a housing world for the elder elite of some overcrowded planet. Since it had been sold through several brokers and bought through several agents, no one knew who actually owned it, and the matter aroused as little interest in the PPI office on Earth as it did on either Moss or Stone. People there had more urgent problems to consider.

Interstellar Coalition protocols provided that moons or planets could be *sold* at buyer's risk without certification from PPI and ESC, but that no moon or world could be *occupied* until certification was received. The owners of Treasure had not asked for certification, and so far as anyone knew, the moon remained undisturbed except for ESC ships dropping in now and then to take botanical samples. This was generally true of most ark planets, but this was the first time I had set foot on one of them.

We soon were out of sight of the ship ramp and of Adam, Clare, and Frank, together with the two officers, who were driving a carrier down the ramp and away into the taller growth across the clearing.

I drew Paul's attention to the other direction. "This growth covers everything! I can see why no one found the Hargess ships on Moss until just recently. Did I tell you, I found out something about it from Myra?"

"Myra Hessing? What are you having to do with her?" He sounded not merely dismissive, which I might have expected, but miffed. Hearing the ring of temper, I concentrated on being casual.

"Oh, I ran into her at temple. She was quite nice, in a let bygones be bygones kind of way. You had mentioned the Hargess ships, and I, making conversation, asked her if she knew what ships they could be. She sent a communiqué to our last transship point."

"Saying?" he asked reluctantly, attempting to sound uninterested.

"Saying they could be part of a fleet of ships that was lost well over two centuries ago. Their last transmissions said they were taking a side trip, seeking Splendor."

"Splendor?" He shook his head. "What?"

I walked farther downhill, saying over my shoulder, "I first heard the words from Matty. She got them from a Zhaar translation of a Martian cave writing."

"Nonsense. No one ever translated Martian."

"It's in the IC Elder Races Archive," I said, firmly. "There were Zhaar seals all over the writings, and Matty paid an IC linguist to translate it into common speech."

"Matty? Don't be ridiculous."

He was making me angry. "She did, Paul. Joram, Tad, and I know all about it, but you never went to see Matty, and you seldom talked with Joram."

"You probably mean Saik Sp'laintor" he said, grudgingly. "The Saik Sp'laintor story was included in some unattributed writings that I translated as part of my advanced placement assignment. It involves a search for the spiritual home, rather like Eden in human mythology. I suppose the root words could be Zhaar, though I'd have guessed one of the ancestral languages of the Phain, among the forgotten tongues that IC has collected from abandoned planets."

"But to translate them, if the races who spoke them are gone . . . ?"

"Lexicons and grammars exist in the archives of other races who are still around. Writings of the Zhaar could have been translated into Sarpta, for example..."

I interrupted. "Actually, it was into Panqoin, from that to Tsifis, then Gendeber, then Phainic."

He ignored me. "What was the context of those words?"

"In a song that Matty sang:

"... *We here kept faith alive, but all the rest,*
the wisest and the bravest we have borne,
left faith behind to go out, seeking splendor..."

He stood with his mouth slightly open, staring at me while I recited the words, then snorted, "Ridiculous! There's nothing like that in the work I translated."

"Do you have the translation with you?" I asked, pretending interest.

"I suppose it's stored in one of the lingui-putes. I never throw anything away."

"Do you remember anything about it?"

"It was about a... mystic world, a place separated from the real world by a kind of veil. I read it as a metaphor, a typical evocation of the world of the dead, of passing from life into a spiritual world, with a lot of philosophical discussion about protecting that world from harm, from taint, from being polluted by... whatever." He snorted again. "It ran to several hundred thousand words in translation, but I've given you the pith of it."

"Saik Sp'laintor sounds like paradise. If you find your translation, I'd like to read it." We were far enough away, so I knelt to sniff at a particularly interesting blossom. "Oh, by the way, Myra says the people on the wrecked ships on Moss were employees of Fleurs de la Forêt."

"The perfumery planet?"

"These particular ones were leaving Forêt to set up a sister planet somewhere else, because Forêt had run out of room for the flower fields. That was always Forêt's selling point. Real scents from real flowers, not made in laboratories. Do you remember the scent my mother used to wear?"

"Matty? It was something herbal, airy..."

"It was called Prairie, and it was from Forêt." I noticed he was standing still, staring thoughtfully into space. "What?"

"You used the word, *paradise*, from an ancient earthian word meaning garden. Eden was a garden, of course. I'm trying to remember if Sp'laintor was supposed to be a garden . . ."

I said, "I have no idea. At any rate, the ships on the Moss plateau may well be the ships in question, because four of them were never accounted for. If someone would peel off the moss and get the registration numbers, it would help." I moved over toward some particularly extravagant growths, drawing his attention to them. "Have you ever seen so many shades of green or so many shapes? Leaves like cones, like cylinders, like needles, like threads, like short strings of beads! Look at that arched branch hung with tiny shiny bells! There's another, beyond, with bigger pendants! Here's a red bush, round as a ball, with golden tassels on it!"

I drew him along the edge of the elfin wood, chatting and exploring until the Klaxon sounded, at which point I cried, "There, samples all fetched. Not even time for you to get impatient." Smiling happily, I led him back toward the ship, only to be stopped in my tracks, gasping. An odor had hit me in the face like a slap with a rotten fish.

He turned toward me, looking at me curiously. "What's the matter?"

He didn't smell it, though it was coming from across the clearing, from behind the ship, blown by the wind, a rank and woody reek that struck with almost physical force. The stench ended as suddenly as it had begun, cleanly, as though it were limited at an edge. Another odor followed, this one soft, floral . . . no, not floral, not spicy either. I lifted my head, sniffing, trying to determine what it was. Sweet, but alien. Sickly sweet. Unfamiliar. And . . . threatening? Yes, threatening. Like a smile through teeth.

Ahead of me, at the ramp, Adam stood facing the miniature woods, face empty, nostrils wide. As we approached, he turned toward us, eyes glazed. "Get aboard," he whispered. "Quickly."

We scrambled into the ship, which only moments later lifted off, leaving the smells behind. I stood in the lock, eyes closed, visualizing what I knew was happening there.

Deep in the growth of the stunted forest, some of the cages the trainers had placed there had already opened. Small furry things in those cages had smelled danger and were crouched into the smallest possible compass, nostrils squeezed, breathing slowed. Gradually they relaxed as their noses tested ordinary air. Furry feet moved to the open door and through it. Long soft ears lifted high, bodies stood up on hind legs, eyes peered. Senses detected nothing but edible growth. For weeks they had been eating this same green, smelling this same smell.

Cautiously, the rabbits moved out and away, sniffing for water, hearing the drip of it somewhere nearby. The ship had landed near water, the site would not have been chosen otherwise. One of the rabbits, a pregnant doe, tried the soil with busy forefeet, hard claws chopping the moss and throwing it out behind her as she dug deeply into a deep bank of layered mosses. Fragments sprayed between her legs from the soft, friable substance beneath her. It held the shape she had dug, the round, clean beginning of a burrow. It was not sandy loam, but it was good for digging. Those who chose the site of landing had been careful about that as well, for pockets of deep soil were unevenly scattered upon this moon.

Rabbit instinct said, dig upward, into a hill, so the tunnel would not flood during storm. Instinct said, dig at the roots of something large and protective, roots that will support the overlying dirt and allow the excavation of sizable burrows. Instinct said, dig now, before the babies come, for a proper burrow will take time and only pregnant does dig burrows to house their bare, blind babies. The bucks made scrapes for themselves to lie in, relaxing in the sun or evening cool, but they did not excavate—which didn't keep them from crowding into the burrows when the weather was wet or cold or they wanted company.

Behind the doe, a woodchuck scurried from another cage and also tried the soil, finding both it and the greenery around it satisfactory. Woodchucks were egalitarians, both sexes dug and stood guard, as was evidenced by the animals who followed the first one, each standing erect and searching both sky and forest for danger, seeing none. No snake, no hawk, no fox. The next cage released hares who bolted from the cages the moment they opened: darting, doubling, switching, finding sheltered places and freezing into immobility, becoming invisible. The hares were also does, but they did not dig. Their life was on the surface, where they bore fully furred, open-eyed young. In this place they saw no threat, no threat, as yet . . .

Mice slipped from the next cage, out and away under the nearest something, behind the nearest something, crouching, black eyes swiveling, whiskers twitching, turning to smell the way back to the box, then a little farther away, and back, mouse-trailing out, returning, farther out, back, farther out yet, learning the way from safety into the unknown, excreting little pellets all along the way.

As the rabbits did likewise, choosing a place they would use for that purpose. As the hares and the woodchucks did, careless about the distribution. All the excreta were full of the tiny, hard-shelled seeds they had been fed on the ship, indigestible seeds of tasty, noninvasive plants that would suck up into themselves trace minerals the local growths had not evolved to use but earth creatures needed to survive.

The last cages opened silently, the first allowing a flutter of bright wings to escape into the air. Some flyers, others ground walkers. Warblers and quail. Hungry birds that pulled down the first head of seed they came to and began swallowing the seeds. Though Moss had no plants with seeds, Jungle did, and Treasure had borrowed from both. The other cages were larger, tall enough to hold speckled deer. Three adult does with their young. Two full-grown bucks in individual cages. Other cages with young of both sexes. They stepped out watchfully, ears alert, eyes searching the surroundings.

In the ship as we moved away, I turned to face Adam.

"What was that?" I asked. "That smell, just before we left?"

"Two smells! Did Paul notice?"

"I don't think he caught it at all. I wonder how the first odor managed to dissipate so entirely before I smelled the second one. As though it had an edge to it."

He put his hands on my shoulders, his nose twitching, his face seeming elongated in his effort to smell what it had been. "My nose even in the daytime, as you should know very well, is damn near dog nose, and I smelled danger."

"There are lots of stenches that aren't threatening, Adam."

"It felt threatening. We may have put those poor little critters at risk!"

"They'll make it," I said, striving for the calming voice I always used around the trainers and the dogs. Both sets reacted strongly and quickly to stimuli that I couldn't sense or couldn't interpret. High levels of threat and stress coupled to intelligences that fully apprehended danger meant they needed all the calm they could get. "If it was something big you smelled, remember that our prey animals have evolved to sneak around the borders of big stuff. Their ancestors outlived the dinosaurs, coexisted with cave bears, went right on breeding when coyotes and wolves and dogs were all over the place. We've made hundreds of drops on Treasure. All the prior ones have survived well. The deer are having twins and maturing fast. All of them have unlimited food and no predators yet . . ."

"That we know of," he muttered.

I pretended not to have heard him. "The native plants plus the seeds we've left give them all the nourishment they need. The mineral blocks in the cages will keep them going until the plants grow. Six pregnant doe rabbits, average litter of six, ready to breed at three months. Two buck rabbits. The others similarly arrayed. From this drop alone, assuming little or no mortality, several thousand doe rabbits, more or less, in a year or so. That's earth time, of course. The one thing we don't know is what the change in the seasons and length of days will do to them. The breeding stock came from a dozen different ark habitats. Gravity will be different for some. Because they're burrowers, living by smell in the dark a lot of the time, length of days shouldn't matter much. And they get Mosslight, at night."

"How long before dogs can be introduced?"

"We're not certain. A dog Behemoth's size would eat several rabbits a day. A pregnant or nursing bitch would eat more. The prey population was dotted all over the moon, and it's already widespread. There are still more drops to be made, and we'll have to risk being seen in order to make a few big, big deliveries. Thus far we've managed not to be noticed. A casual sampling stop en route to or from Moss attracts no particular attention. Only Gainor Brandt and our associates know that Treasure is owned by the arkists, so don't mention it . . ."

"What's that?" Adam asked, staring out the port.

"Where?"

"Back on the moon, just there for a moment . . . A flash of light like a beacon. Did you see it?"

I peered at the receding globe, seeing nothing except itself, a green orb with pools of blue here and there, wisps of cloud overlaying all. "Probably light reflected off a rock face. There's a lot of rock under all that green, and sometimes a face splits off. If the slope is steep enough, it will slide down and leave a bare surface for a short time, smooth and slick, like a mirror."

"You know all about the place?"

"I know everything ESC knows."

"From General Brandt?"

"He's a good friend, Adam. To all of us."

DOGS ON MOSS

⋮ An ESC shuttle brought us to Moss. From above, as we descended, I admired the textures and colors of the surrounding forest. The randomly patterned surface gave a subtle impression of movement, as an ocean does. The only landmarks that stood out were the shielded island where ESC held sway, and a large, dark-colored blot to the west, a charred clearing littered with ugly ships. One of the crewmen, noticing my frown, said, "That's the Derac encampment."

"The land looks cleared."

"Right."

"I didn't think IC members could do that, not until the planet is certified."

"The Derac read the regs differently. If their ships burn a clearing, that's an accident, and it doesn't count. And if each time the ship sets down, it burns it a little bigger, that's still just an accident."

"How many of them are on the planet?"

"Anywhere from half a dozen to what looks like several hundred, now. They've been building up, lately."

After we landed, I stood in the lock, trying to verify the movement I thought I had seen. Though no wind was blowing, a branch moved fractionally toward the ship, bringing its drapery with it. A mossy mass turned from a green that was almost black to a more brilliant hue as fronds turned to face us. The straight line made by three globular growths became a triangle as the center one edged forward. It was as though the surroundings had heard the shriek of the descending ship and were now in the process of confronting it, us, as avidly as I confronted this new world. Foolishness, of course. Building drama on insufficient foundation. Gainor, who claimed to have found this tendency in many of my reports, had warned me against it.

"Lonely children learn to do it," he had said with the tone of one who knew whereof he spoke. "They build enchanted worlds for themselves to replace unpleasant or impenetrable actuality. Unfortunately, living in fantasy doesn't equip them to deal with dangerous reality."

"You sound like my aunt Hatty," I had said, remembering that she had said something of the kind about not paying attention to the nudging of one's subconscious. Still, Gainor's warnings stayed with me as I went down the ramp, so focused on the forest that the appearance of the welcoming party struck me momentarily mute.

I hadn't seen them arrive, but there they were, doom written on their faces and phantom vultures nesting in their eyes. The foremost parted his lips and words breathed out like the whisper of a ghost.

"Bar Lukha. Lieutenant to the CEPO on this contract. At your service."

His eyes were set so deeply in circles of darkened skin that it was like looking down chimneys to find the light in them, sullen embers ebbing into darkness, brightening briefly at each breath. His cheekbones jutted over blue-shaded hollows, and his neck tendons stood bare as cables, seeming almost separated from the flesh beneath. Behind him were two more cadavers, each as remote, each smiling as grotesquely: three nodding skulls making a mockery of welcome.

It took all my self-control to respond in a flat, ordinary voice. "Delighted to meet you, gentlemen."

Lukha whispered again. "These are the people who will provide you with any assistance you need, Installation Manager Maywool, Commissary Manager Lackayst."

As I turned toward them, they shuffled a handbreadth toward me, exhausting themselves in the effort. I greeted them with the same hollow heartiness, turning to include Lieutenant Lukha, only to see him shambling slowly toward the moss forest, evidently having completed his duty as he saw it.

The gray-haired man, Lackayst, waved a leaf-thin hand toward an untidy pile of panels and fittings that lay upon the meadow. "We should ... ah ... have those put together by evening. Maybe the ship could stay ... ah ... in case we don't ... quite ..."

His voice wheezed into silence as he ran out of energy and stood paralyzed, lips still curved, face calm, a horrid simulacrum of a living man.

I turned wordlessly and strode back up the ramp. My belly and thighs said run, but I held myself to a walk and managed a gentle push to close the lock behind me. The captain stood nearby, looking at me curiously.

"Something wrong?"

"Captain, is there an ESC ship in system. I mean, something larger than the courier we came in?"

"The *Dorian* is in system, yes. It has another load of supplies to deliver here before going on to Stone."

"Can you put me in touch with it?"

He did so, and I spoke to the captain of that ship, who referred me to the construction chief.

"So what've they got done?" he demanded.

"Nothing. The panels are in piles. There's something very wrong down here. I need ... mechs, I suppose, under the command of someone who can figure this out."

Angry words came from the com. When they had run their course, I said, "Gainor Brandt told us ESC would do whatever was necessary to expedite our work. The ship we came on is a four-man courier, so you're the only ones in system I can ask. If you want to question Brandt's orders, you'll have to do it with him, so we'll go back up to our transport and message Brandt that we're holding them in station while you sort it out."

More angry words, less emphatic, to which I replied in monosyllables. Finally, agreement.

"What?" asked Paul from behind me.

"A minor foul-up," I said casually. "I'll take care of it, but you may as well relax until it's done. Our quarters in the PPI installation aren't quite ready at present."

Paul turned an ugly red and began to steam. Before he could work himself into a lengthy tantrum, I went to tell Adam, Clare, and Frank to stay where they were. When I went back outside, Lackayst and Maywool were still where I had left them. My return jolted the former into speech.

"... as I was saying ... I'm sure we'll get it ... sorted out ..."

"Don't bother." I smiled brightly. "The supply ship is sending someone down to take care of it."

The two stared at me without comprehension. It seemed to take forever for them to decipher where we were at the moment. Either it penetrated at last or they simply gave up, for they turned in a series of tiny, tottering steps and went off toward the installation, slow shuffle by slow shuffle, each movement the result of laborious maneuver. I could read the effort it took: "Now, move left foot forward. Put weight on left foot. Pull other foot up even with left foot, no, no, don't put it down, move it forward ..." Their hands hung loose on their wrists, as though barely connected, each hand trembling, quivering, reaching out and grasping at nothing, then falling limp before beginning the same motions again.

What was going on? Where were the local PPI people? Over a hundred people worked here, but not one was to be seen, though I stayed where I was for some time, looking, sniffing, listening, sorting out the directions. The expanse of low-growth "meadow" lay around the ship on all sides and extended its rippled, watery patterns westward to the shore of the large lake, where it met the surface of the real water without a visible seam. Water and meadow were twin surfaces, joined imperceptibly at their edges.

The farther shore was invisible, though I could follow the long curve of the nearer bank southward for some distance before it was hidden by mist. Straight out from shore, not far, the force fields doming the ESC island shimmered with light. The Derac were north of that, on the near side, hidden by the forest and by the curve of the lake. PPI's sober installation was strewn beneath the skirts of the forest to the south. All PPI installations I had seen had possessed walls or fences to mark their boundaries, but nothing separated these buildings from the growth around them. Above them masses of angular trees grasped at the sky, a gaunt scaffolding everywhere garlanded with moss, which also covered the buildings and the paths among them. Decorative clumps of the stuff had either been planted or had prettily positioned themselves here and there.

The smells were remarkable. The ship had crushed the foliage beneath us, and the area was redolent with an odor I could only describe as edgy or agitated, which contributed to the unsettled impression I was getting. On Earth, we arkists were used to vague menace and continual anxiety, but we knew our enemies and what they might do. This was different. This was an immediate, positive trepidation without discernible cause, an invisible someone shouting "boo!" Nothing looked threatening, that is if one ignored the vaguely monstrous shapes the shadowed mosses massed among the trees. No menacing sounds reached me, no monsters approached, my hair did not stand on end, but I was afraid in a way that seemed—ridiculously enough—entirely familiar.

I told myself in no uncertain words that I was dramatizing the situation, but the edginess continued. Finally, I shut my eyes and concentrated, trying to find the path through whatever emotional thicket I was caught in. Was it childhood fears? Monsters in the closet, under the bed? Abandonment horrors? Nothing resonated. Whatever it was, it had nothing to do with my past. It was of itself, of this place, a sense . . . It came to me suddenly. What I felt was awareness, not mine, something else's. The smell was part of it. It, whatever it was, knew we were here. It knew we had just come. It was fiercely, remorselessly interested! I stood paralyzed, eyes still shut, asking myself why I was thinking "it" instead of "they."

The scream of the *Dorian*'s descending shuttle put an end to this divagation. I went back into the ship and didn't come out again until the shuttle had disgorged a party of mechs commanded by a striped-sleeved, noncontact-suited officer. ESC regs required noncon suits on any planet that wasn't certified, no matter that it made conversation difficult.

"You're the one who called?" demanded the sergeant in a too-loud, surly voice. "Good thing for you we had to shift cargo. Otherwise, we'd have brought the last load and been gone by now."

"We need housing," I said, moving in close "Those seem to be the parts of it. I don't know what's there . . ."

"I do," he grated impatiently, still almost shouting. "We brought it here. It's exactly as it was when we unloaded it three days ago. What the hell are they . . . ?"

I stepped close enough to brush his suit-ear with my lips, lowering my voice. "Something wrong here, Sergeant. We need to find out what. Can't find out without someplace to sit down and study the situation. Can you put the thing together?"

He dropped his voice to match mine. "Putting the damned thing together is what we were supposed to do, and I told that fellow Lukha so, but he couldn't wait to be rid of us." He turned on his heel, striding away while shouting instructions over his shoulder.

The procedure was new to me. I watched somewhat bemusedly as the heavy mechs paced off distances and angles with monumental exactitude before placing three service cores and assembling the floor panels around them. When the last panel clicked into place, the entire floor leveled itself in a series of little rises and drops, bumpety bump, whompety, boom, done. Interior and exterior wall panels, some with windows and doors already hung, were slid into preset channels on this surface. Finally, the process was repeated with a shallowly arched roof, after which the entire structure shook itself like a dog, settling all the joints. I almost applauded. It had taken them far less than an hour to assemble a long, low building with three doors on its east-facing side and one door at the far, southern end. The mechs then opened the remaining flexi-crates of furnishings and carried the contents into the building.

As they were separating the empty crates into units for stowage, a man came out of the largest of the PPI buildings, stared in wonder at what was going on, then trudged up the slope toward me.

"What the hell?" he asked in a hoarse baritone.

"ESC has assembled our living quarters," said I, crisply. "I'm Jewel Delis. My brother is the linguistics expert PPI asked for. And you are?"

"Drom," he said. "Duras Drom. Chief Emergence Compliance Officer for this operation. Why in hell didn't they wake me?"

"You didn't expect us?"

"Not until . . . galactic date twenty-four thirteen, at the earliest. Was there no one here to meet you?"

"Someone named Lukha," I said. "Your deputy? Someone named Lackayst, someone named Maywool. All of whom, if I may say so, Chief, looked decidedly unwell and incapable of function."

Drom shifted from foot to foot, lips drawn back from his teeth, nose wrinkled, a futile snarl of exasperation? Guilt? Anger? I couldn't decode it.

"I've been working long hours," he said at last. "I told Lukha to wake me."

"You must have been exceptionally tired," said I. "It was 24:13 yesterday."

His eyes opened wide. "I slept through two days?"

"If you have the same disease as the ones I just met, I could understand that," I replied, searching his face. "What's going on, Chief? And where is everybody?"

Drom cast a surprised glance at me, as though I had said something bizarre. "Sorry?"

"I don't see any activity. Where are your crew?"

"Ah." He nodded, his eyes wandering evasively over the installation and the trees beyond. "Well, we spend a lot of time out in the moss. Taking samples. Identifying species. As for what's going on, well, ah . . . we have a project under way, trapping some small Big Crabs. I mean, that's what we call the type, the Big Crabs, but we want some small, ah, immature ones to analyze."

"What are they? Really crabs? Like on old Earth?"

For the first time, he seemed truly responsive. "They look remarkably like extinct earth shore creatures, as a matter of fact. Since we recently learned about the ships up on the escarpment, we've wondered if perhaps these down here aren't descendants of some that arrived in the cargo holds of those ships. If so, they've grown at an astonishing rate."

"How large are they?" I asked.

"The biggest ones we've only seen in the mist lands. From what the fish—I mean the floating data-gatherers—show us, they're a couple of meters long. The legs are much stockier than an earth crab's. I mean, proportionately, they'd have to be, to carry the additional weight, not that they're heavily built. The armor is chitin, fairly light, very strong, and there's not a lot of gut . . ." His attention veered to the construction party, now leaving the site. "I understand you've brought some animals?"

"Dogs. And the linguist's concs." If they counted as animals.

Drom flushed. "Right. PPI stewards' department will see to keeping your quarters clean, except for conc quarters: That's tabu territory for PPI personnel. Meals are available in the commissary or you can obtain foodstuff there and fix it yourself. By regulation, commissary's off-limits to anybody but humans, that includes dogs and concs." He glared briefly at nothing.

"I know," I said. "That's understood." I did understand it, but it struck me that this was the first time Paul had actually lived on a PPI installation. He might not be aware of the rules.

"Well then, I'll let you get moved in. We can complete the arrival routine when you're settled." He turned and stalked off toward the installation, his face darkened by some emotion I could not read. All in all, an enigma.

The sergeant came up the hill. "You've got a house, it's furnished, the service cores are working. The mechs are running a line from the water purifiers to the lake; you should have water within the hour. There aren't any pens for the animals yet, but we'll bring some fencing over from the island."

"The dogs'll do fine in the house," said I, distractedly. "Though a fenced area would be nice for exercise. We'll put up some kind of barrier to keep them out of Paul's hair."

"Not necessary," said the sergeant. "Mr. Delis's bedroom and study are at this near end, then a lockable door, then the great room and food service core, then another lockable door, then the other bedrooms. That's in accordance with the info we got from the general manager's office."

I smiled at this, wondering when in heaven's name Gainor had had time to specify the floor plan. "Grand. Sounds perfect."

Voices spoke behind me, and I turned to see the three trainers, each with a dog and a bitch on leash. The sergeant took one look, and muttered, "Great Mahalus!"

We had a protocol for meetings between the dogs and people who knew nothing about them. On such occasions they would play the part of pets, and I would play the part of master, though I could no more master these creatures than I could fly. They knew, as I did, that it was only play. I called to black Behemoth. Adam unclipped his leash, and the dog strolled over. When he reached me I put my hand on his neck without stooping. The top of Behemoth's head was well above my shoulder.

"He's a big one, isn't he?" I said in a doting voice, as Adam and Scramble approached. "Much larger than the original Great Dane or mastiff types, but with none of the bone or joint problems that used to be associated with large dogs. Life span is longer, too. Big dogs used to be old at twelve, but Behemoth will live to be thirty or forty at least, maybe a lot older than that! This brown bitch is his mate, Scramble."

Scramble turned her eyes toward me when I said her name, her jowls curved into a dog smile, mocking me. I turned to Adam. "This gentleman heads the ESC team that has put our quarters together. Sergeant, this is Adam Whitlow. The other trainers are his brother, Frank, and Clare Barkley. The white dog is Wolf, and the gray one is Titan. The spotted bitch is Dapple, and the red one is Vigilant. We call her Veegee. They're a bit smaller than the dogs . . ."

Adam nodded; Behemoth sniffed the sergeant's outstretched and gloved hand with magnificent disdain, then he and Adam rejoined the other dogs and trainers where they stood near the ship, all of them turning slowly, nostrils wide, smelling the world, reading its messages, interpreting its meanings.

"The females aren't all that much smaller," said the sergeant in some awe. "What are they doing?"

"They're just smelling the air," I murmured.

"The trainers, too?"

Indeed, the trainers, nostrils widely flared, were testing the air for smells.

I said, "We humans aren't totally without a sense of smell, you know. It helps if we can guess what the animals are sensing. Sergeant, please accept my sincere thanks for being so accommodating. I'm sure Gainor Brandt will be pleased to hear how helpful you've been. Now, though we don't have water yet, I think we'll get into our own quarters." I wanted to avoid any further interaction between dogs and persons. The less curiosity, the fewer tales told on shipboard or in ESC barracks, the better.

He sketched a half salute and took himself off. I located Paul, who was so busy repacking his equipment he had forgotten he was supposed to be angry. I pointed out the building into which Drom had retreated, said a few words about some of the personnel being ill and not up to their usual standard, and suggested he go take care of the formalities. Full of himself and his project, Paul stalked off toward the headquarters, not even noticing the dogs. So far as I could tell, he hadn't noticed them at any point in the journey, though they had all been awake and in evidence at transit points.

I caught up to Frank and Clare. "You all seem to be finding a lot to sniff at."

Frank nodded. "You should get some dognose, Jewel. You really should. You're a little old for it, but some of the cellular transplants would take..."

I murmured to him, "I have what will take, Frank, have had since I was sixteen. I volunteered for the original transplant study, but let's for God's sake not talk about dognose where anyone can hear us, okay?" I jerked my head to indicate both the ESC men behind us and Paul, who was entering the headquarters. "We'll have to learn to be quiet about things we talked about freely at the sanctuary. PPI is BuOr, and BuOr is enemy territory. Some of them might even be iggy-huffo. There probably aren't a dozen people on the planet we could call sympathizers."

I headed for the door farthest left, saying, "This should be trainers' wing. Four bedrooms here, plus whatever sanitary service core they've put in. Middle door will be living room with a food service core, and the other end should be Paul's quarters."

"Same building?" murmured Clare, her brow furrowed.

"For the time being," I said, ruefully. "That's part of what I meant by enemy territory. There's a door we can lock in between. We'll have to share quarters until Paul considers us inconvenient enough that he moves out, or asks us to. Don't worry about it now. Just do what we do and ignore him."

"Four concs are a little much to ignore."

I couldn't have agreed more, but that wasn't the issue. "Paul uses concs as advertisements for himself. He dresses them up and shows them off. Here, they can't leave their quarters, so, if he really gets involved in the linguistics bit, he'll forget all about them and leave them in their cases until the feeding alarm goes off. We can put up with a few hours a week."

Our door entered at the base of a wide, T-shaped hallway, with a bedroom-cum-study on either side. The sanitary core, between two more bedrooms, was on the far side of the cross corridor, which had an outside door at the left end and the lockable inside door at the right end. Deep storage closets lined the near side of the cross corridor, and each bedroom was well equipped with integral storage plus comfortable furnishings in a jumble of styles and colors that had obviously been dumped into the rooms more or less at random. I had long suspected that all ESC employees were as totally color-blind as dogs had once been.

The cross corridor was extremely wide; the dogs' beds were already along the wall. I noted the outside door had a lever type latch, one easy for the dogs to manage. Gainor really had thought of everything. While the dogs explored the rooms, Clare directed a shift in furnishings to make more harmonious groupings. The Whitlow brothers, Adam and Frank, took the rooms the other side of the cross corridor, while Clare took the one to the right of the entry hall, leaving the one to the left of the entry for me. It was the one I would have chosen, as it had a large window that looked out to the south, into the forest.

We had barely finished shifting furniture when a carryall brought our personal baggage, which didn't take long to sort out and store. As soon as I had my own belongings stowed and the empty cases stacked outside for pickup, I went through the building to Paul's quarters and helped with the disposition of his furnishings and belongings. Other conditions being equal, he stayed in reasonably good temper if he was fed regularly and his quarters were kept in order. I had time to put things where he would expect to find them, though I left the cases of references and equipment strictly alone.

Over at the headquarters building, I found Drom and Paul hovering over a table laden with stacks of recordings, logs, journals, and enough data cubes to build a play city. I had built many as a child, using Matty's DCs.

"There's plenty of room here," Drom was saying in a strained voice. "You can have an office here, at the headquarters."

Paul had donned his professional charm, a garb he usually wore with strangers, at least until he began to dislike them for some reason. "Figuring out a language is the kind of job where you do nothing but puzzle for days, then suddenly wake up at three in the morning with a clue in your head. It helps if everything is at hand. I have my own AI machines over there ready to digest most of this stuff as soon as I decide how to enter it."

"Any help we can be?" asked Drom, attempting unsuccessfully to hide his relief.

I picked up on Drom's reaction, though Paul did not. Inasmuch as

PPI had asked for Paul, it seemed very odd that they'd be relieved to have him separated from them. Strange. Eccentric. Or, from what I had seen so far, unnatural.

"I'll let you know," Paul replied.

He had no intention of doing so. Most places we had visited he had managed to find someone besides me to be his flunky, and it was seldom the person anyone else might have recommended. Though I am efficient, I am insufficiently adoring, so Paul usually picks someone to adore him. Since he'd brought the concs along this time, however, maybe they'd provide a satisfactory level of worship.

Paul and I carried the material back to his quarters, where the door now bore a neat little sign, LINGUISTICS. Inside, he dumped his armload of materials and looked around without comment. He took for granted that the place was orderly, seeming to believe it happened naturally, like a fall of rain. Two men from the ship on which we'd arrived brought the conc's sleep tanks and installed them in the dormitory room at the north end of the building, along with a store of conc rations. Concs could eat anything humans ate, but they didn't need to, and conc-kibble was cheaper. Mechs from the larger ship returned with a load of fencing and made a yard at the south end of the building. When the fence was complete, the dogs came out the door, raced around it in three strides each, jumped over it, chased one another through the shade of the moss trees, marked this territory by defecating at the edges of it, then jumped back in again to greet me where I stood in the doorway watching the ESC men, who were pointedly watching the dogs.

"Fence won't do it, ma'am," said the ESC sergeant, shaking his head. "We'll have to get some barrier fields from the island. They're not things we carry supplies of on board . . ."

It was a hurdle I had foreseen. "Dogs are built to run," I said in my most charming voice. "It keeps them healthy. These dogs are hunters, but there's nothing on the planet for them to hunt. They can't get lost, they won't hurt anything, so can't we just let them run?" My suggestion was, of course, in total defiance of all applicable ESC directives, but we were on PPI ground, and given the rivalry between the two, the ESC man might be quite willing to let PPI handle trouble.

He had a huddled conversation with another ESC man, then murmured into his com, shrugged, and returned to me. "The boss says okay, for now. We'll check with headquarters, and if something else is needed, we'll install it next time."

Once inside, I wiped the narrow line of sweat from my hairline. If we'd had to keep the dogs fenced in, it would have defeated the purpose of bringing them to Moss. Gainor and I had been prepared for me to kick the problem upstairs with the ESC people and let Gainor handle his opposite number at PPI, but with the PPI contingent seemingly oblivious to anything around them, we were home free. It was quite true that the dogs wouldn't hurt anything, though I reminded myself to talk to the trainers about dog pee. It killed many kinds of plants, and Moss was covered in plants.

The mechs reached the lake, installed the water intake, then returned to stow the packaging units before departing. The shriek and thunder of the shuttle's rising was succeeded by an absolute silence. I stood at the door of our quarters marveling at it. There was quite literally no sound. No wind. No wave. No bird calling from a tree. No mechanical thing. No voice. Heaving a breath that was half relief and half wonder, I turned around to watch the lineup of hindquarters in the hallway, six tails twitching, six sets of jaws eagerly wolfing food, six sets of jowls and noses being licked, six sets of paws groomed with efficient teeth before six large animals curled into huge doughnuts of various colors and fell asleep. I had a strong feeling that only the need for food kept them with us. If there had been prey on the planet, they would have gone the moment they were loosed. Except for Scramble, of course. She turned twice on her bed, then rose and came to me, reaching up to tongue my neck as she did, often.

"A good place for a while, love," I said. "Can you all be patient, just a little longer?"

"Ai whill," she whispered. "Ai no huwwy loos you."

"You'll never lose me, Scramble. Not if you need me."

"Lil wons com. Ai awais nee you."

At one time her words would have surprised me, but Adam had been right when he said she was smarter than the rest of them. She knew she was pregnant. She knew what that implied. She would need help, and she depended on me to provide it. I was, so to speak, grandma to the pack.

Scramble returned to her bed, and I went to mine. Thus far, Paul had taken no notice of the dogs, Drom had taken no umbrage at them.

Thus far, all had gone well, and I simply lay there, savoring the quiet, which remained unbroken until the commissary signal blared.

Adam, Clare, Frank, and I went outside to find Paul awaiting us, escorted by two prancing, giggling concs. I waved the trainers on, waiting until they were out of earshot before saying, "Concs aren't allowed anywhere in the compound except their own quarters, Paul. Neither concs nor dogs are allowed in the commissary. Also, conc quarters are off-limits to PPI stewards, so you'll have to clean up after them yourself."

He turned red. "They have no right . . ."

"It's in the regulations, Paul. I don't recall that you've ever stayed inside a PPI installation before. Concs are not allowed on PPI installations, period. Since you're a private contractor, so long as they're in your quarters, technically, they're not on the installation. They'll have to spend their time in the cases or with you."

"Who told you? About concs being off-limits?"

"It was in the briefing material." I had checked, and it was. Paul still looked doubtful, angry, or both, so I went on. "Drom reinforced the information when he saw the dogs and the conc cases."

He stalked furiously back into his quarters, Poppy crying, "Whassa madda, Pow-ie. Can' we go have din-din?"

I followed him to his door. "The conc protein rations are stored in their dormitory, Paul. Commissary meals are pretty much time-dependent. Try not to be too late."

"I'm not coming," he said sulkily, his face still red.

I gritted my teeth. "Well, there are also prepared meals in stasis storage in the kitchen. And if you're not going out, you can sort out your materials and put them where you want them before someone from PPI puts them in the wrong places." I left in a hurry, before he could reply. Whenever he was determined to be angry, I always tried to give him as many different things as possible to be furious at. A broad field of complaint diluted his concentration of fire.

The commissary staff was entirely mech except for two middle-aged female supervisors, neither of them at all vacant-eyed. I'd expected the food to be at best slightly better than Earth food, but it was astonishingly good! Fresh vegetables and fruits, newly baked bread, real butter! There was a fluffy dessert made of real chocolate with real cream, flavored with something wonderful! The meal alone was worth the trip, though the trainers and I made no progress in getting to know the PPI contingent. The twenty or so staffers in the room studiously ignored us, and Drom wasn't there. I noticed that only a few of the people at the tables showed the same symptoms as the three men who had greeted me, all to a much lesser degree. Whatever it was, some had it and some didn't. Or some had had it and were getting over it.

By the time the four of us returned from our meal, it was well after dusk. Paul had returned the concs to their cases and was busy with his equipment at the meadow's edge. My contingent gathered on the east side of the building, Adam and I with glasses of wine from the storage unit, Clare and Frank drinking beer, real beer from the commissary, not earth-stuff. The dogs lay behind us, chewing tough strands of flavored tooth cleaner, the next best thing to bones.

The lopsided moon bulged up from behind the tree line, its greenish light softening the forest. The dogs' noses twitched constantly, as did the trainers', though less obviously. I'd had more practice at keeping my nostrils quiet than they had. Paul was so busy setting his devices to record whatever was going to happen that he had no time to see or smell anything.

I didn't see the Mossen until Scramble nudged me. Following the direction of her gaze, I located a pallid blur against the darker forest. One blur became several, then turned into cone-shaped pearls of light, softly blue, only a few at first, then more, and more and more, necklaces of light-bubbles, gently glowing as they flowed from among the trees, strands of green-blue, blue-gray, gray-silver, silver-green, an ashen glimmer in Treasurelight. Someone in the compound turned on lights that had been hung in the surrounding trees, and what had been shadowy became bright, the creatures blazing with color as they massed in the center of their dancing space, the sequin lenses on their bodies flashing fractured light in all directions as they whirled and turned and milled about before unspooling themselves from the central grouping to move along the edges, lines of them traveling clockwise around the perimeter of the meadow. As each one passed, I murmured into my recorder its predominant color: ... orange-yellow, red, aqua toward the green, aqua toward the blue, deep purple, light fuchsia ...

The line returned to the center, then parts of it emerged again, keeping the same order ... aqua toward the blue, deep purple, light fuschia, pale green, citron, light pink, grayed purple . . . Sometimes the circle included all the Mossen in a single line. Other times, the lines were short, composed of ten or twenty Mossen, circling the edge while the others whirled in the middle. For a time, I went on listing all the colors I could see . . . grayed purple, six separate shades of yellow in sequence light to bright, then orange-yellow, red, lavender, harsh lime green . . .

When I had listed more than seventy colors, I gave up on it, no longer sure I was distinguishing individual shades, tints, or hues. The dance went on and on. For a time I closed my eyes, letting the odors from the surrounding forest summon up their own visions: a garden of fragrant blooms, a gardener's manure barrow, lavender, a shipboard pest killer, sage and marjoram, sweat, fresh dung. There were as many stenches as floral and fruit odors, lots of woodsy and herbal smells, some that were resinous or cheesy. No help there. I opened my eyes and peered at the dancers once more.

It grew cooler. A little wind came up. The moss edges of the meadow fluttered, the fluttering grew stronger, the wind went deeper, moving rapidly toward the center of the meadow to heave up the entire carpet of moss, curling its edges into flight. A single gust whirled the whole assemblage, moss carpet and dancing Mossen, high above our heads, where it simply disintegrated, silently, into pale fragments. Around us something pattered like a fall of rain.

The Mossen were gone. Flown away? Moved into the branches of the trees, while hidden from view? Blown by the wind to some other location?

I yawned gapingly, aware of weariness. The trainers and the dogs straggled behind me into the house. Within minutes all the human ones of us were in bed, three very soundly asleep. Not so the dogs. Through my open door and the window that opened into their pen, I heard them wandering in and out, over the fence and back, lying down, sniffing the air, getting up to get a better sniff, lying down again. Something was out there. Something they were not frightened of, not exactly, but something they very much wanted to know about.

Deep in the night I wakened to another presence in my bed. Scramble. She was lying with her back against my belly, and my arm was across her wide chest. She had done this on the ship a few times, seeking my company. I didn't know whether it was because she liked my bed better than her own, or simply wanted nondog company. I stroked down her side, murmuring something fond, and she sighed, her hide rippling. Then I fell really asleep and did not stir until morning.

THE FOUND
THING

⦂ Once when Gavi Norchis had been about twelve or thirteen, she had become disoriented on a return trip from the lands below to the plateau. She had walked a considerable distance in the wrong direction before catching herself and retracing her steps. When sunset came, however, she was still far from her own trail up the escarpment, though a group of caverns she had previously explored lay nearby. With night coming on there were certain dangers she preferred not to meet in the open, so she cut enough moss to make a bed and carried it well back into the coziest cavern, where she found a little side niche with a tiny steam vent and a narrow entrance she could block with a stone.

She gathered dry wood for a fire, an easy task since a tall scaffold tree had recently fallen nearby. She plugged the cracks with moss to keep the drafts at a reasonable level and lay down wearily, only to find something digging into her back.

A few moments exploration with her hands found the thing, a manufactured thing, stuck in the crack beneath her bed and protruding just enough to dig into her. She got it out, with some effort, feeling it to be a small cylinder with a button on one side. When pushed, the button clicked, a light came on in the cylinder, and on the rock wall before her appeared a young woman smiling and waving. She had yellow hair and very green eyes, and she stood in a window which looked out at ... towers and towers and more towers. The Loam Clan had many scenes of old Earth, but none like this. The Loam Clan people did not dress as this woman did, or as the man did who now joined her to turn and wave at the person recording the event. And what were they doing? Some kind of ritual?

Perhaps a harvest ritual, for now they stood beside a great pile of pastry, feeding bites to one another. Yes. Either a harvest ritual or a new year's ritual, when people wished sweetness upon one another. The pictures ended with the two of them in one another's arms, looking out across a city in the dusk.

That was all. Since the pictures did not look like the world her people had left, Gavi thought they had been made somewhere else. Everyone in the tribes came from Jardinconnu, the fragrance planet, and they had no places like these pictured ones. If this thing was human, then other humans had left it here. But no other humans except the tribes had been on this world until the Derac and humans came, a few years ago, and even they had not come *here*, to this particular place. One ship had landed on the plateau near the old ships, to release devices that swam in the air, no doubt reporting what they saw to another device, far away. Which meant . . . what?

It was too dark to make out the device in detail, though her fingers told her it was etched on the outside with words or a design of some kind. She put the thing in her bag and lay down, falling asleep almost at once. In the night, however, she awoke to a strange, humming tone that seemed to emanate from the stones around her. She peered at the openings into her den, into this crack and that one, tracing the sound to a crack halfway up the wall, one she had stuffed with moss. She pulled the stuffing away to see a light. People were passing to and fro. She could see their legs and the tops of their feet. The odd thing was the legs weren't moving. The people were gliding, and she could hear their voices.

"Along here somewhere . . ." A troubled voice, almost whining.

". . . been so stupid . . . told you a thousand times . . ." An angry voice.

"Forget it . . . probably not important anymore . . ." The first voice, almost as though it were weeping.

The light drifted to one side and went out suddenly. She returned to her bed as she might have done after a dream, falling into sleep and staying that way, untroubled for the rest of the night. In the morning, she woke with a most undreamlike memory of the incident, which only strengthened as she rose and went to the crack where the stuffing moss lay on the floor. Dark in there. She put her arm into the crack and her fingers touched the back of the fissure: stone. The crack did not open into space. It didn't open into anything. There was no way people could have walked past inside the rock.

So she had dreamed it. Either that or a place was there at night which was not there at other times. Either that or she was losing her mind.

She kept the device in her secrets bag: a finger-long tube, lettered on the outside with the words *Forever and a day*. Alone at night she sometimes looked at the images. The two people were in love. She knew of love, had read of it at least. She had seen none of it during her early years and little enough of it among the tribes, and that mostly in the lower classes, where it wasn't complicated by politics. She knew one provisioner and his wife who were happy as bugs on a branch in each other's company. It would be wonderful to be in love like that. Or, so she supposed. She could arrange it, of course. Arrange it for herself and someone, if she liked. It needn't be anyone who liked her, they would like her well enough after the ceremony.

Or perhaps she should grant the gift of love to those who found it hard to find? That sweet young woman who wove the beautiful tapestries, Gemma. The one with the squint, the voice like a frog, the horrible teeth, and the nose that went a little sideways. Her body was slender and strong, her hair was lovely, and her manner. She had a sweet sense of humor. Why shouldn't she have the gift of love as well as any other?

What person should she pick for Gemma? Someone she really liked. None of the official Loamers. Unfortunately, she could not think of a man she really did like. The only person she greatly liked among the Loamers was Chief Larign's daughter, Lailia, the one they called Brightfoot. Gavi's fascination began with the name, which flowed like water: lah-EEL-ee-yah. And then, there was the look of her, slender and graceful, yes, like most woman who carry water on their heads, but with something else, like pride or natural elegance or . . . like music, as though she were dancing to music that only she heard.

Naturally, since anyone would love Lailia, given half a chance, her father chose to mate her to a man she would be unable to love at all. Balnor of Burrow, son of Chief Belthos, as egocentric as his father had ever been, and even more arrogant and cruel. It had been Belthos, then about ten or twelve, who had pursued the infant Gavi into the depths of the Abyss some twenty-six or-seven years ago. He had loved chasing things, killing things, it didn't matter much what. Now he loved ruling over people, pushing them to see how far he could do it without their pushing back. Perhaps it was time she had her revenge on Belthos...

SOMETHING HAPPENING ELSEWHERE: DERAC

: Situated not far from the retired ships of the G'tach was the Derac breeding facility to which Tachstucha, son of Gahcha, had been summoned for the choosing ceremony. The young hatched from his last mating had been brought to the Ground of Ghassifec for selection. Tachstucha went there, stopping first at the retirement ships to visit his father, then going this place and that to pass out ceremony money from his fasgi pouch, paying local residents for their good thoughts during the selection process.

He was wearing an ancestral brood apron, one with five pockets. It was unusual for a father to choose more than two young. Three was an expression of pride, four of arrogance, but five was a signal of Ghassifec's regard. No Derac would choose five without a specific say-so from God. Ten years ago Tachstucha had chosen five at his last breeding time, and he could afford to do it again if he skipped a few mating seasons in the future. Some Derac wouldn't do that. They found the breeding enjoyable, so they did it, picked one or none of the offspring, and let it go at that. Tachstucha preferred to spread out his breeding and take all who were worth raising.

He hissed politely at the keeper of the shrine and went into the warm, brood-smelling interior, finding the nest as much by smell as by sight. There were eleven squirmlings, a goodly number, some already turning green, several with nose horns breaking the skin among the nostrils.

He opened the shuttered window above the nest and took the first male youngster in his hands. Quite active, green, eyes showing a fine opalescent sheen, tail limber and strong. Provisionally, he dropped the little fellow into one of the apron pockets, where it rolled itself into a ball and was quiet. Two more followed, each of a generous size. The eight remaining were smaller. He sifted through them, looking for any that might show signs of excellence, but there were none. Two were males, but very small. The others were quite pale, which meant they were probably female.

He left the shrine, telling the worker at the door to dispose of the rest. Some fathers ate them, but Tachstucha did not. When he was halfway to the gate, he reached for his fasgi bag, suddenly recalling that he had left it inside. He turned back the way he had come, entered the room, and came silently up behind the worker who had one of the young in one hand and a sharp instrument in another. The two males lay dead in the nest, but as Tachstucha watched, fascinated, the worker punctured the skull of the small Derac he was holding, then placed it, still quite alive, in a carrying box before picking up another.

"What are you doing?" Tachstucha asked.

The worker turned, paled, dropped the instrument, and thrust the young behind him.

Tachstucha felt his neck swelling, the membranes around his face filling redly with blood. "I asked, what are you doing?"

The worker mumbled something, stuttered, finally said, "They will kill me."

"Who will kill you."

"The breeders. The breeders will kill me."

"You're taking my little ones to the breeders? Which breeders?"

"The K'khassa Breeding Farms. The female breeders."

"Don't they have enough young? They need more?"

"They like . . . many. They like doing it. They . . . we've always taken the females if the fathers don't eat them."

"And what was that instrument you were using. What were you doing with that?"

"Fixing them, Explorer. Fixing them. So they wouldn't care. So they don't . . . think. We fix all the females so they can't think. We make them mindless. Don't say. Please. They'll kill me."

"I won't say. I won't say anything." As he wouldn't, for he was too confused to say anything. He had always known the rejected young were destroyed, which was sensible, though not something he cared to do himself. Natural predation had taken care of Derac young in the long ago, but there were no longer any predators, so the Derac took care of it themselves. Regrettable but over and done with, as the humans said. Forgettable. But this, this business of keeping the female ones. Not only that. What had the worker said? That he was piercing their skulls so they couldn't think? Or care? Females never thought or cared! They were genetically incapable of thinking or caring! They were mindless. He had mated often enough to know that!

Tachstucha went directly from the breeding ground to the G'tach of his father, found his father sprawled among company on the warm ground, whispered to him that he had information of a private nature to impart, and retired with him to his own sand bed in the retirement ship. There Tachstucha told what he had seen.

"Make them mindless? You're sure that's what the worker said? Make them mindless?"

"I repeat exactly, Honored Father."

"What sort of instrument?"

"A sharply pointed one. Like a claw. And he stuck it into the little one's head, through the skull."

"And he said they were sent to the K'khassa Breeding Farms?"

"He did. Because, he said, they, the farmers, like doing it."

"Breeding, he meant."

"So I thought."

"Ah. So, since it is the K'khassa Breeding Farms that supply females for the breeding of our shipclan, may we presume that some of those we breed may be our own sisters? Our own mothers?"

Tachstucha paled. "Ghassifec forfend!" The Derac had strong tabus against incest.

"Indeed. We have always been told that the females were bred from special lineages, that we were provided with ones unrelated to the rest of our population."

Tachstucha nodded miserably. That was indeed what everyone believed, what he himself believed. He well remembered his first episode at the breeding farm. An enclosure had been prepared for him, one with three females in it. He had engaged in the dominance activities of his race, subduing all three, then he had killed one and eaten some of it before breeding with the other two. He had not thought of them as Derac, but merely as vessels for his procreative function. Exciting vessels, truly, but that was merely a matter of smell and action and the sounds they made. If they had been able to speak, to think, to cry out words instead of mere whimpers of pain . . . Would he have killed that one?

It was hard to think about that. Each time the thought came, it slid away from him, leaving discomfort behind. He told his father so.

"Then do not think about it, my son." Gahcha had no intention of telling his son about the Orskimi and their plans, particularly inasmuch as it seemed the Orskimi had misled the G'tach G'gh'hagh, the Derac High Council. He would not even speak of this deceit on his own sprawling ground, for there were some among the retirees in that circle who had not left youthful unmindfulness behind them

"My son," he said to Tachstucha, "you must obey me in one thing. You must not speak of this to anyone. I will take it up with those in power, but it must be done with absolute discretion."

Seeing that Tachstucha regarded him with only partial comprehension, he tried again. "Do not mention this to anyone."

"Only my shipclan," replied his son. "Yes, Father."

"Not your shipclan," said Gahcha, angrily. "Not anyone!"

"But, Father, shipclans share everything."

"They do not share this! This is something you must forget you ever saw."

Tachstucha thought about forgetting. The more he thought about forgetting the more vividly the memory presented itself in all its details. The squirmling had made a sound of pain. The squirmling was his very own, and they had hurt it. Of course, if he had eaten it, it would probably have felt pain, too, but that had the sanction of tradition. "Father, I do not think I can forget it, but I will try not to tell anyone." He drew himself up with resolution. "I will try not to forget not to tell anyone."

Gahcha regarded him closely. Even for a youth, Tachstucha was not very bright. "Come closer, my son," said Gahcha. "Lean down to hear what I am saying . . ."

When the young Derac leaned down, Gahcha bit him through the spine, just at the skull, and held him tenderly for the few moments it took him to die. The ship was empty of other Derac, and its fusion furnaces were still functioning. Though it took Gahcha some time, he managed to lug the lifeless body to the door of the furnace, and it was then he saw the movement in the pocket of the brood apron. Before loading the corpse into the furnace, he removed the apron, chiding himself for the sentimentality of the gesture. Retired communities, however, could rear young ones just as well as shipclans could. He would foster them himself.

He took the squirmlings from the apron, admiring their strength, their flexibility, the intense green of their skins, the adorable buttons of the nose horns that sprouted below the protruding topaz eyes. Ah, well. By Great Scaly Caough, they would be a good souvenir of his dear, dead Tachstucha.

THE PUPPIES

: Scramble pupped in my room during her third night on Moss, while black Behemoth lay outside the door, fur and ears up, daring anyone to intrude upon the process. The trainers had brought collapsible whelping boxes with them, and within a couple of hours, seven little ones were born, three dogs and four bitches. All of them were dark, some were marked with brown. When Scramble had them thoroughly cleaned up, licked into shape, and nestled against her belly with one thigh protectively covering them, I opened the door for Behemoth. He greeted Scramble, nose to nose, then took a sniff of the puppies, pushing them this way and that with his huge muzzle. Scramble didn't object, and when he had satisfied himself that all was well, he went out to his bed, dragged it in through the door, and lay upon it inside the door, on guard.

"If it weren't for me," said I, "you'd be hunting now, wouldn't you."

"Yuh," said Behemoth. "Werna hyou, llon gone."

It was true. If he'd been wild, he would have been long gone, hunting food for his mate and the pups. If it hadn't been for me, or Gainor, or Shiela, or a hundred others. Of course, if it hadn't been for those of us who'd fought like devils to protect them, all dogs would have been long gone, on Earth at least. Those of us in the battle felt . . . no, we *knew* we had a debt to pay, one that extended at least forty thousand to fifty thousand years into the past. Dogs were part of the "Litany of Animals" we sang at temple.

> *"Bulky shouldered bison, built like a bastion;*
> *wily alligator, floating like a log;*
> *wolf in the wildlands, jackal in the jungle,*
> *dutiful and diligent, man's friend, dog."*

"We owe you," I said, "I know we still owe you."

"Yuh," said Behemoth, staring through me. "Oh, yuh."

I said, "Dapple will have Titan's babies next, then Vigilant will have Wolf's. Have you thought any more about switching mates?"

He gave me a stare, his fur all the way up, a low growl rumbling through his body, like a heavy piece of equipment idling, ready to roar. "Nah rran oomahns."

It was an insult, not unexpected, but the reality was more than a little scary. I said hastily, "Quite right, Behemoth. I knew it wasn't the right thing. The babies will mix the genetic pool enough when they grow up, among themselves."

His fur smoothed, and he began to lick his forepaws, turning them so he could get his teeth between the pads to pull out bits of moss, which he spat out, nose wrinkled.

"Don't like the smell, huh?" I commiserated.

"Rran," he growled, his word for rank, or stinky, or foul, though Behemoth thought some things smelly that I quite liked and vice versa. *Rran* usually meant *shit*, or something similar.

"Where'd you pick it up?"

He turned his head to the north, ears up.

"On the meadow? Where the Mossen danced."

"Yuh."

"What is it?"

He said something like Rrnn, or wrnn.

Shit. "Mossen shit? Show me where, tomorrow. I'll take a sample for analysis."

"Nrrr. Wrrn. Mhsn wrrn."

N, which Behemoth could produce, took the place of D or T, which he could not. "The smell is a Mossen word?"

"Yuh. Wrrn."

Yes, word. Now what did that mean? *Shit* was a word for shit? Which could be. Prelinguistic. The thing was the name of the thing. Show me a rock, I mean rock. This rock means all rocks. A kind of sign language? That's the way written language started with humans. Point to the sky. See sky! The point becomes word for sky. Draw the hand with a pointing finger up, it means sky. Over centuries it reduces to a slanting line with a loop at the bottom. A sack of wheat is signified by a clay model of a sack of wheat. To keep it secure, wrap it inside a clay envelope with a picture of the sack on it. Finally, realize the model is redundant, the sign on the clay is enough. Very interesting, but I was too tired to think about it.

"See you in the morning," I said, turning off the light.

"Yuh," said Behemoth.

⋮ I woke very early and went with five dogs for a walk in the woods. Adam, Frank, and Clare were still asleep. Behemoth was sitting guard over the puppies in my bedroom, and Scramble, for the moment released from motherhood, ran rapidly, nose to ground, moving away from our general line of travel then back to it, scouting.

During this first contact with the world, I tried to pay attention to everything. The extravagant variety of foliage and structure made it difficult. It reminded me of my trip to Quondangala, where their males adored their clothing as our males do their sports. It was important to the Quondan that no two be wearing the same arrangement of clothing at a gathering, as doing so this betokened a lack of originality, of artistry. The botanic inhabitants of Moss seemed to have the same tradition. If I stopped and looked around, I could seldom find two growths alike within view, but when I moved on, others of the same varieties would show up. Each thing was its own thing, among other, different things. Did each have a specific purpose? Was the arrangement organic? I hadn't a clue.

The mosses were of generally soft colors, greens, blues, grays, pale yellows, even paler pinks, but among them were occasional patches of brilliant blue, fiery red, poison green, and sharp ocher. The blues scalloped the sides of tree trunks, emitting a rich, fruity scent, their surfaces gemmed with drops of sapphire nectar. The poison green hung in fringes from branches, and I sneezed at the sharp vinegar odor. Pillows of the red mounded on the ground, smelling of . . . what? Baffled and unthinking, I reached down to touch a tiny patch of it, jerking my hand back when it tingled as though burned, a sensation followed immediately by a wave of euphoria, racing up my arm to my shoulder, into my neck, into my head. I stood there, cradling my hand, smelling that smell, lost in a totally ecstatic moment.

Minutes later, the feeling evaporated. I reached out my hand to touch it again and was thrust back. Scramble. Her head and neck making a barrier, pushing me away.

I took a deep breath, turned resolutely, and stepped away. "Not a good idea, huh?"

She gave me a look that made me flush. "Right," I said. "Not a good idea."

" 'Mell ain'erus."

"It is dangerous, no doubt. Glad you were here, Scramble."

The other dogs had spread away. I heard one or more of them moving, off to my left, so Scramble and I went in that direction. As I came close to the sound, I whistled. The reply should have been a short yap, once, to let me know they had heard. No reply. So the sound wasn't made by the dogs. The hair on Scramble's neck was up, her ears were forward. " 'Mell. 'Aim," she said.

Between me and the sound source, an ocher curtain draped over one of the skeletal trees. The curtain was actually woven, that is, strands of moss grew both vertically and horizontally, as though the fabric had been loomed. Or were a loom. Through a rent in this fabric I saw color first, a large bank of the redmoss, then movement: people, lying on the moss. Two. A man and a woman. They were naked and almost skeletal. Starved, but heaving slightly in gruesome charade, a morbid mockery of sexual desire. I had seen something similar in maimed concs, that same . . . grotesquerie. The figures before me shuddered, the sound went on, and I realized that neither sound nor motion originated with them but with the creeping mosses around them.

I waited. The two did not stir. I went forward, slowly, Scramble at my side, both of us stopping about an arm's length away. They weren't breathing. The woman lay sprawled across the man, her hair hiding his face. From beneath them the moss heaved itself, and it was this undulation that had given the illusion of movement to the figures upon it. Now it crept with a slight crackle, up their sides and then across, to cover them.

I took a deep breath, made sure the moss was not near the toes of my shoes, then reached forward and pulled the woman's head away so I could look at the man's face beneath. Bar Lukha. The one who'd met me at the ship. I dropped the woman's head and moved away slowly, searching the area. "Where are their clothes, Scramble?"

She quartered the area, barking sharply, "Eer." The clothing had been dropped in a heap, ID tags on top.

Leaving the clothing, I took the tags. "Call the others, please."

Scramble lifted her head and howled. Within moments the other four were assembled. "Danger," I said, pointing at the redmoss. They couldn't distinguish among shades of red, but they could certainly smell the stuff well enough to identify it and the fact that the people on it were dead. "Don't touch, don't let anyone touch. What will you call it?"

"Rrr-igh," said Scramble, two tones, one low and growling, the other a yelp ending on a high, choking sound, like a puppy, hurt or scared. It was not unlike the word they used for me, when they needed something. The low, growling note followed by a two-tone howl, rrr-aroo, rrr-aroo. Wherever I might be, if I heard that call, I knew they needed me.

"Rrr-igh," parroted I. "Listen, be careful."

They looked into my eyes, then at Scramble, as though for her agreement, before sniffing the moss patch and walking around it to sniff the other side before going back to their explorations. I, mean-time, took my tool kit from my belt and found a knife with which to collect a sample of redmoss, cutting it as far from the swallowed bod-ies as possible, putting the severed tuft into a leakproof bag. Even detached from the main body it kept making that tiny crepitation. As I sealed the bag, I noted something odd where I had cut the moss, a pro-truding something. With pliers from my kit, I pulled it out, a small bone. A finger bone. human-looking. I dropped the bone into another bag. Before I went on any more walks I would talk to Gainor Brandt's man out on the ESC island. Ornel Lethe.

Bar Lukha's fate, and that of the woman, made me feel numb, but their deaths had certainly been voluntary: the clothes removed, the identity tags on top. It made no sense to treat it as an emergency;

there was time enough to warn people after I returned to the installation. Assuming, I cautioned myself, they didn't already know.

I was more alert from that time on, more attentive. I behaved as I would at home, keeping my hands to myself, watching where I put my feet. Many of the same growths I had seen on Treasure were found here: the same arched branches hung with little teardrops, the same round red bushes with golden tassels. Well, I told myself, PPI has been on planet for several years, and ESC ships have gone back and forth, stopping on Treasure. They no doubt carried spores to and fro. It was a logical explanation that should have satisfied me but didn't.

Every now and then the wind shifted, and when it came from the north, from the installation or some point beyond it, it brought a peculiar odor that made me think of snakes. Each time, Scramble growled in her throat to signify danger, not imminent, but present. The third time it happened, I made a note of it in the little pocket recorder I always carried. Something to be investigated.

When the dogs and I had explored for another half an hour, I questioned, "Home? Guide please." Scramble turned to guide me back while the other four went on with their investigations.

The trainers were still abed. I went first to the kitchen, to start coffee, real coffee, which PPI seemingly had in generous supply, even though no one on Earth did. While I waited for it to brew, I returned to my room to show Behemoth the moss and bone, opening the bags so he could smell them. I warned him as I had warned the others, "Rrr-igh," I said. Scramble lifted her head from among the puppies and confirmed my warning by repeating it. Released from puppy watch, Behemoth went out the door at a run, following the scent trail the others had left.

Scramble said, "Unng-ee," and I fetched food for her, topping her bowl with a spoonful of calcium supplement. She made a face at it, but she ate it, interrupting herself to ask; "Mahs ar-kine?"

"I don't know what kind of moss, Scramble. Like nothing on Earth."

Frank came into the corridor, sleepy-eyed. "We having breakfast here or at the commissary?"

"Whatever you like," I offered. "There's packaged stuff in the radiated storage. I've put a pot of coffee on, a far better brew than we've ever had on Earth."

"PPI actually owns a coffee plantation on Orgrup III," he muttered, returning to his room to get dressed. "It's probably from there."

Through the open door into the living area, I saw Paul prowling toward the coffeepot. Damn. He could have heard me talking to Scramble. I had to get into the habit of keeping that connecting door shut and locked! In a moment, he prowled back to his own quarters with the pot, almost full, in hand. Enough for six, and he was taking it all. Typical. I returned to the kitchen—this time shutting the door behind me—found another pot, and brewed more coffee. When it was ready, I carried the pot, mugs, and sweetener down to my room, shutting and locking the door behind me. When I set the coffee on my desk, the aroma fetched all three of the trainers.

"We can have coffee here in the mornings," said Adam. "Then go to the commissary, get to know the PPI team."

"We can have coffee here or in the living quarters, but that door has to be shut," said I, putting my specimen sacks on the desk. "Look what I found."

"Human bone?" asked Clare. "There's been nothing said about fatalities on the planet!"

"Firstly," I murmured, "abandoned Hessing ships have been found up on the plateau. We have no idea what happened to their people. Secondly, this installation is obviously understaffed, despite the fact that preretirement people have been coming in for short stints with PPI for two years or more. Thirdly, this redmoss is a euphoric. A . . . remarkable and lethal euphoric."

"You didn't . . . ?" Adam said.

"Nobody warned me, Adam. I touched the stuff. It works on contact, and it wipes you completely off the charts for however long it takes to wear off. The immediate inclination is to do it again."

"Which you . . ."

"Which I didn't do, thanks mostly to Scramble. Look around us. There's supposed to be a large contingent here. Where are they? I see people who look half-dead, and I find finger bones in the redmoss." I drew a deep breath, "And I saw two people who had just died on it."

They let me tell it, not interrupting. "Their clothing's lying out there in a pile with the ID tags on top. Bar Lukha was one of them, a woman named Surri Ponak was the other. They hadn't been dead long when I first saw them, and I watched the red stuff crawl out from under them and crawl back to swallow them."

"How far out was it?" asked Clare.

"I was maybe half a mile or so into the bush, the forest, the what-ever. Behemoth had stayed with the pups while Scramble had a break."

"Anything besides the redmoss and the bone?"

"Just . . . beauty, and eeriness, and a lot of stuff that's fabulous, chimerical, bizarre . . . Pick any adjective, you'll find something it fits. If you go out, wear cover, no breves. If you're going to be touching stuff, wear gloves. Try not to let your skin touch anything until we find out about it."

"Could the euphoric effect be a defense mechanism?" asked Adam.

"It would certainly be a good one, defense or offense," I agreed. "Start to pick the stuff, or eat it, get it on your skin, then just stand there forever while it eats you. Anyhow, until we find something out about it, best keep hands off."

"How do we find out anything about it?" asked Clare.

"I have an appointment to meet with an ESC man out on the island. He has access to all the data ESC has collected."

"Nothing subjective, then," remarked Adam. "No impressions."

"Impressions!" I laughed. "I've got a few thousand, but none of them strike me as helpful. There's a peculiar smell out there that I catch every now and then when the wind shifts from the north. It makes me nervous; I don't know why. Some of the PPI people, Drom included, look underfed, with black circles around the eyes . . ."

"As though vampires had been at them," said Clare.

"A few days in the redmoss might do that to you. Bleed away your strength . . ."

"Saprophytic," murmured Adam. "Evolved to paralyze the prey and drink its vitality."

"Ah," I murmured. "I'll warn Paul about that." Just in case, though it was very unlikely he'd go wandering off by himself.

Paul didn't join us for breakfast. He was deep into the materials received the previous day when I knocked on his door, and he barely looked up when I warned him about the redmoss. The concs were still in their cases, and aside from making sure he had heard my warning, I was happy to leave well enough alone.

⋮ Along the sides of the little boat, water rippled clear as air; small almost transparent creatures swam beneath it, some scurried over the shallow bottom on walking fins. "Do you fish these waters?" I asked the PPI boatman, who had arrived at our quarters within moments of my return from breakfast.

"No sport and no food," he said. "They don't fight a line, and nothing that lives in the waters here tastes good."

"What about things that grow in the forest?"

"The blue drops are sweet, like fruit, and there are some things like mushrooms."

He wasn't a talker by any means, though his face did not show the starved look I had seen on Lukha. "So what grows here eats you instead," said I, deciding to risk it and see what response I got.

He turned toward me, surprised. "What?"

"The redmoss. It's eating people. Lukha. Maywool. Lackayst. Some of the others, no doubt. What do your medical people say?"

He looked away from me. I could see his hands shaking on the tiller of the little boat. "Pier up ahead," he said, keeping his face resolutely forward. "When I take you back today, I'll leave this little floater with you, so you can get back and forth on your own . . ."

So he would talk only about the boat. "Is it easy to drive?"

"Same controls as a flit, ma'am."

"Only there's no up and down."

"No ma'am. If you go up and down with this, you can pretty well figure you're in trouble. I'll set you down at the end of the pier, and I'll be waiting when you're ready to go back."

He bumped the floater into the pier, which automatically clamped the vessel to itself, allowing me to step up from the solidly anchored surface. The crewman busied himself, face still turned away, preventing eye contact.

I had been given a code for the call station nearest the lock. I used it; the lock clicked open; I covered my face with a mask, felt the air being pumped out, the sterilant beams encase my body, the new air pumped in. The lock door opened into a shabby lobby inhabited only by a dour, bony person who really did look like a priest of some particularly austere religion. Pole-thin, brooding-dark, heavy-boned, narrow-lipped, his coffin-shaped face ended in a forbidding jut of jaw.

"You're Delis?" he asked. "I'm Lethe. Follow me. Wyatt and Durrow are waiting in my lab."

We went quickly, I trotting to keep up with Lethe's much longer legs. The ESC ship sat at the center of the island with a dozen small enclosures around it, the separate work areas connected by lanes of resilient matting and heavy conduits carrying air and power. I saw no one except a few uniformed figures passing at a distance. The door to the lab enclosure opened at Ornel's voice, let us through, then closed behind us with the crunch of a lock mechanism driving home.

"Sybil Wyatt, Abe Durrow," said Lethe. "Jewel Delis."

"We received word you wanted to see us," said Durrow. "What about?"

His tone was both challenging and annoyed. I said, "Before we say anything more, will you please check your console for a message from Gainor Brandt. Code RY679ZZ."

The three exchanged glances.

"Please," I repeated. "He directed me to ask you to do that, first thing, before we had any opportunity to arrive at a misunderstanding, an impasse, or a mutual dislike."

Durrow turned red; Wyatt grinned. Expressionless, Lethe went to a communication bank on the far side of the room. While he was engaged with it, I examined the other two as they were examining me. Sybil Wyatt was a leggy brunette, her hair drawn back severely, no color in her face but the dark brows and suspicious gray eyes, dressed in blue overalls covered by a long white coat. Abe Durrow was short, stocky, and ruddy-cheeked though graying, with a cherub's sensual mouth and discontented expression. He was watching me the way the dogs watched their food dishes. Territorial. Who did they suspect me of being? What did they suspect me of wanting?

Ornel Lethe returned. "Perhaps you would be kind enough to tell me what was turned loose upon Treasure."

"Rabbits," I replied. "And hares, and burrowing rodents, deer, mice, and quail. Earlier drops have been made of larger prey animals, including some large swamp-living rodents for certain areas."

"It seems she really is from Brandt," he said to his friends. "Not someone sent to dig us out and burn us for supper."

"Who burns whom for supper?" I asked, amazed.

"The Derac," murmured Wyatt, pursing her lips. "But only the fur-bearing parts of us."

My eyebrows went up. "You're not really afraid of the Derac?"

Lethe pointed to a group of chairs around a table, and three of them sat down while Durrow fetched coffee. "Yes, I am afraid of the Derac. I am afraid of even one Derac, if it's where I can't see it and don't know what it's doing. I have seen places where Derac have recently been, and you would not want that to happen to any feeling creature. When we came there were half a dozen Derac stationed here. They had a small ship, little more than a shuttle, at the north end of this lake. Not long after we got here, new ones started arriving. They've got a dozen ships down there by now, and may have as many as a thousand crocs. We're badly outnumbered, so yes, I'm afraid of them."

Abe Durrow said, "At first, two of them dropped in every now and then to see what progress we were making. They behaved as Derac always behave, with an assurance totally unmodified by thought. Derac do what Derac do, they don't question it, and they don't worry about it. They asked questions, we answered, and they made reports to their G'tach in very simply coded Deracan, which we always intercepted and translated. Among other things, the Derac here are very vocal about their desire to capture and eat some of us, just to see what we taste like. In response to that wish, the G'tach orders them not to do so *at this time* as there will be plenty of opportunity later."

I felt a prickling along my arms. When I looked down, I saw goose-flesh. Ornel's words had been completely flat and unemotional, but they conveyed threat quite well. "Do they smell?" I asked.

"The Derac? Why do you ask?"

"When the wind shifted from the north, I kept getting this smell. It made me think of snakes."

"They smell, yes. I don't know how you could pick it up at this distance, though."

I didn't tell him how. I just shrugged, as Abe Durrow returned to the subject at hand. "We have considered that this expressed desire to eat us may really be an attempt to find out whether we're reading their messages. If we get irate, or fearful, they'll know we are."

"Could it be a joke?" I offered, from a dry mouth.

"Derac don't joke," said Lethe. "They have no motive to attack us that we know of, except for hunger, of course, but attacks usually follow Derac buildups like this."

"And you suspected me of being their agent? Do I look like a Derac?"

"No. We thought you might be somebody reporting to PPI," said Durrow. "We have certain administrative difficulties with PPI."

I shook my head, amused by this. "I have no reason to love PPI, believe me. We're only housed with them because the linguistic work my brother is doing can't be done from inside a force field. I'm sure you know all this."

"What we hear and what we know are often different things," said Lethe. "What is it we can do for you?"

"Several things, actually, some to our mutual interest, some personal. I hope you have information on the differences between Moss flora and Treasure flora, and fauna—if any. The animals we've been dropping off on Treasure will reach a sustainable population level very soon. If there are mosses there like certain ones here, it may put the dogs at risk."

The three stared at me, watchfully.

"Why do you say that?" asked Lethe.

I was caught by surprise. I'd been certain they already knew about it. Temporizing, I asked: "How big is the staff at the PPI compound."

Wyatt strummed her fingers on the arm of her chair, "Fifty-two in the first group, and seventy-five arrivals since."

"How many are here now?"

"No one's gone . . ."

"Have you checked how many are here now?"

"No reason to," said Durrow, with a sneer. "They're PPI."

"Do you have any *way* to check how many there are now?" I persisted, frowning.

"Send each one a message," jeered Durrow. "Something requiring an answer."

"Ask to speak to all of them at a meeting," suggested Wyatt, grinning.

I grimaced and stood up, at which point Lethe waved me down, saying, "Everyone over there is supposed to be wearing a link. If necessary, we could run a check of active links."

"Can you do that *now*?" I insisted, not sitting down.

My suggestion bought me a skeptical look, but Durrow and Lethe rose reluctantly and crossed the room to the console, conferring under their breaths. The screens before them flickered. Durrow exclaimed abruptly.

Wyatt said, "You think they're going to find something, don't you?"

"I know they're going to find some of the PPI personnel are missing."

"None of them have gone on a ship . . ."

"I know."

Lethe returned to us, white-faced. "How did you know?"

"The first three people I met here looked like something was eating them alive. Our group ate at the commissary last night and again this morning among a mere handful of PPI agents and staffers. I walked around the compound and saw very few others. The man who brought me over to the island looked okay, but he won't talk about what's eating his colleagues. How many active links did you find?"

"Forty-seven."

"Out of a hundred twenty-five," murmured Wyatt.

I nodded, rummaging among the contents of the deep pocket of my jacket. "There's a kind of redmoss out there. I've brought you a sample. I believe it's lethal, not all at once, but gradually. It's also a euphoric. I touched it by accident, and it was very difficult to keep myself from doing it again. That single exposure was enough to give me a craving for it. I don't want to do anything about the craving, which is still going on, because it'll be useful to find out how long it takes to dissipate, if it dissipates. I believe every time a person uses it, a little of the person gets killed off, until there's not enough left to go on living. The effect must be cumulative over time. I should imagine the stuff would kill a rabbit or a small deer almost at once, assuming it does to other creatures what it does to humans. That's why I said the prey animals may not be able to survive on this world."

"Where are the missing people?" Wyatt asked the air.

"Possibly lying on a bank of the redmoss, or in it, maybe nothing left but bones and a pile of clothing," I offered, dumping the pack rat contents of my pocket on the table. Pocket recorder. Matty's recording and her last work. Comb. Nail kit. Vial of STOP. Odds and ends, including the envelope I was looking for. I handed it to Wyatt. "There's a human finger bone. You can test it along with the moss sample, run it against personnel genetic records, find out who it belonged to. And that's just one growth. What about all the rest? That's what we need to know for the animals on Treasure, and for me, personally, I'd like any information you have on this world."

Durrow peered at the sample of redmoss before replying, with a glance at Lethe as though asking permission. "PPI has sampled the area around the installation extensively, and they've sent all the samples to us. We have complete genomes for most of the stuff that grows around here, but I don't recognize this redmoss at all. Sybil has traced the family . . . wouldn't be family tree, would it? The family moss: what's related to what and how long ago. There are several separate genetic lines. Nothing we've tested is harmful, we've handled it all.

"The trees are not related to the mosses. We hypothesize that the trees were at one time the majority species, and the mosses took over later. Needless to say, PPI never sent us a sample of this red stuff . . ."

"Which could mean it was there and they just missed sampling it," said I, holding up a finger. "Or it wasn't there until recently." Another finger. "Or, it was there all along, but they didn't want you to know! At least three possibilities."

Durrow nodded. "My guess would be that last one."

Sybil said, "To add to the list of what we have so far: We have a census of the fauna, not much of it, frankly, and there's a question whether any land animals originated here. We thought so at first, since Moss wasn't known to have been visited by anyone but the Derac before we got here, but that was before those Hessing ships turned up on the plateau. They were merchant ships, not explorers, which means they weren't X-teed to get rid of any organisms. Most merchant ships are contaminated with critters, depending on where they've landed recently or what they're carrying in the holds. There are no land fauna here that couldn't have come from those ships if we accept very rapid evolution. Little crabs that got packed in with seaweeds are now bigger crabs. Little mice became several things like bigger mice, and differently shaped mice, and aquatic mice. A few tiny lizards gave us some small and large scaly tree climbers. A few pet birds, or wild birds being carried as cargo, gave us half a dozen types of avians, most of them brightly colored. We have dew-eaters, moss-creepers, leaf-suckers. Except for the crabs that still need to spawn in water, all the other water animals are truly Mossian, native to the planet."

I was amazed. "All this in a few hundred years?"

Sybil said, "We don't know the mechanism. Something here promotes mutation, we have no idea what."

I considered this. "But you're trying to find out."

"Of course. We began by looking at the environment, including air, water, food, a combination of all those, plus perhaps radiation of some kind. Vacuum-driven evolution is known to be quick, to be sure, and these creatures definitely entered a fauna vacuum—no land animal competition at all. Still, we usually talk in terms of a few thousand years to get speciation like this. Two hundred years is ridiculous. We're still looking for a reason. We haven't given up."

I said, "That brings me to the personal things I'd like to know. Have you made a search for survivors from those Hessing ships? I mean, of course, descendants of survivors."

They looked at one another, shaking their heads. No.

Lethe said, "You know the primary objective of any resident program is to find, identify, and categorize native intelligent life, then all other life. The creatures we call the Mossen showed up early, here and there, a half dozen, twenty in a row, elusive as shadows, and they were as they are now, discrete mobile forms that moved in orderly ways. Whether that signifies intelligence toward the mouse level, or intelligence toward the man level, or toward any intelligence at all hasn't been determined. Not long ago, they started dancing on the meadow over there. Subsequent to that, PPI claims it received a message. You can't prove it by us."

"You haven't seen the message?"

"We have not. ESC doesn't take risks, and as a result we've lost no personnel. Our job is to wait, to weigh, to infer, to describe. Ordinarily, by this time we'd at least have had some opinion as to the intelligence of what we're studying, but on this world we've reached no conclusion at all. We have lots of records; we've tried the usual protocols; we've watched one group closely to see what it does, then compared that with what other groups do, trying to distinguish between instinctive and learned behaviors. On Moss, who knows? We see them dancing, but they all dance. What do they do when they aren't dancing? Haven't a notion because we've never seen one not dancing.

"We assumed they have some other life in the forest, when they're unobserved. So, we programmed fish to record sounds from the forest, hoping they would pick up something from the Mossen we couldn't see. We got a wide variety of what we'd call nonindigenous noises. Hammering. Bells ringing. Occasional complex sounds that were almost words. Derac noises—at times when the Derac were nowhere near. Women's voices. Children's voices . . ."

I said thoughtfully, "Children's voices?"

"That's what I said," snapped Burrow.

I smiled. "All the other noises could have been mimicked in the time since you and PPI got here, but you've never had any children here, have you?"

Lethe opened his mouth and forgot to close it.

Wyatt said, "No, we haven't."

I let the smile become a grin. "So the creatures couldn't have heard children's voices unless those Hessing ships had survivors."

They stared at one another. Finally, Wyatt said, "And if so?"

"So, if the sounds are made by Mossen in the forest, or by anything else, they may be nothing but pure mimicry."

"Why?" asked Lethe, almost angrily. "Why mimic human speech?"

I shrugged. "I don't know, though I suppose it could be evolution- ary and totally unconscious. Like some mutated butterfly being hatched with spots on its wings that look like bird eyes; birds don't try to eat it, it has offspring with the same spots who also don't get eaten. The mimicry of sounds might be something like that. Mimic the sound of the thing that might eat you . . ."

Lethe said slowly, "More likely the thing that might eat the thing that eats you. Or even, the thing you'd like to eat. On Earth, people used to go hunting for water birds, and they'd make the sound of the bird they were hunting to attract the prey."

I nodded. "Sounds logical."

"What's a butterfly?" asked Wyatt.

I said, "An insect that used to live on Earth, with beautifully col- ored wings . . .

"Ah. I'm sorry. I'm not an Earth native, and while I support the preservation effort philosophically, I know very little about Earth fauna."

"There's damned little to know, these days." I stood up, suddenly decisive. "I can't keep that poor PPI man waiting on the pier any longer. Will you report this to ESC, or shall I?"

Lethe said, "We'll draft a complete message from you and us, copy to you, adding our study results, such as they are."

"Now that I have a boat to use, I'll drop over in the next few days. Link me if anything happens."

Sybil Wyatt came with me to the lock, scuffing her feet on the path, looking down at her shoes, murmuring, half to herself, "You must think we're completely oblivious, not wondering about the presence of children's voices or knowing about people disappearing from PPI..."

"Why should you? It's no part of your directives to keep track of PPI, is it?"

"Not since Jungle. There, they were based in our space, and we were supposed to protect them. Which we couldn't do once they went out in the tangle. Since then, ESC has refused all responsibility for PPI contingents."

I stopped short. "You were there?"

"On Jungle? Yes. All three of us were. It was Lethe's first command. Why?"

"One of those who vanished was Witt Hessing. He and I were liaised. He was ... very important to me ..."

I don't know why I felt it necessary to add that last. Surely the fact we were liaised was enough to legitimize my concern. We stared at one another, my anger confronting her pity, inconsequential as a rock hitting a pillow. Something moved in her pocket, and she patted it until a tiny face peeked out.

"Gixit," she said, as explanation. "We were the only two things left ..."

"On Holme's World," I said. "I know. But that was years ago. Small animals don't usually ..."

"This one seems to have a long life span," she said, as the little beasty leapt out of the pocket onto her shoulder, large eyes watching me with intent curiosity, all four hands busy holding on, wide ears pricked.

"You mentioned the attack on Holme's World. That's what it was like on Jungle. There was nothing wrong there on Holme's World.

One minute we were all celebrating the final stage of terraforming, the next minute everything on the world was dead but me and Gixit. There was nothing wrong on Jungle. One minute everything was fine, the next minute eleven men were gone.

"Gixit came with me back to Earth. When I was a lot older, working for ESC, I got hold of the genetic material saved before terraforming and created several more of his kind, male and female, hoping I could find somewhere to turn them loose. Moss is the best bet I've seen so far, but that's not important . . ."

"You have the others here?"

"Oh, yes. Most ESC staffers have some kind of pet or hobby. Living inside a force field isn't terribly fulfilling. Anyhow, that's beside the point, which is that we don't know why Holme's World was hit, and we don't know what happened on Jungle."

I said firmly, "We may not know why, but there are Hessing ships on the plateau, so we know people have disappeared from up there, too. All of which says this system needs to be investigated. I don't care what the IC protocols say about surveys, intrusive or otherwise. We've got to get PPI off dead center."

"Lethe said we'd report to General Manager Brandt."

"Wrap it and put a bow on it for him. Tell Gainor Brandt if we're to save the PPI contingent, it will have to be quick, and the orders will have to come from outside. Please don't just wait and weigh about this one, Sybil. Try to get some action."

⋮ During the Mossen dances over the next several days, I went on listing the colors and the order of the dance; daytimes I took the dogs on long walks in the forest; and Paul fed his computers with everything he could think of, concentrating on the sounds the fish had picked up in the forest. Early on the fifth morning, when I happened upon him in the kitchen, he was beginning to snarl.

"I was talking to one of the PPI kitchen people the other day," lied I. "He's a hobbyist, extinct fauna. He happened to mention protective mimicry among prey creatures. It got me wondering, if those sounds are made by the Mossen, could they be protective mimicry?"

Paul stopped what he was doing and became very still. "In what way, protective?"

"Well, mankind can be dangerous. Perhaps by assuming our sounds, the Mossen are less exposed to predation by something else."

"PPI hasn't found any predators."

"I know. But they haven't really looked at much of the planet, either."

"Besides, mankind has only been on the planet a short while. Wouldn't these creatures have needed much more time to evolve . . ."

"It could be like birds. The organs required for singing probably took a long time to evolve, but once they could do it, new songs might take no time at all. There used to be birds on Earth that could spontaneously mimic whatever they heard, voices or bells or sirens."

"In which case," Paul said in a deadly tone, "my work on the sounds these creatures make would be totally wasted."

I cursed myself silently. "Oh, I doubt that, Paul. I just thought it was an interesting idea. Probably nothing in it at all."

As there probably wasn't. Any more than my report to Gainor Brandt had anything real in it. Surely ESC wouldn't simply let the entire PPI contingent kill itself off! Unless Botrin Prime had kicked up a fuss and demanded Gainor keep hands off. Which wasn't impossible. Assuming that might be the case, and even though it broke protocol rather seriously, I decided to talk to Drom himself!

I found him before his console in the headquarters building. Lukha's chair—at least I supposed it had been Lukha's chair—was empty. Drom himself looked more troubled but slightly less ill than when I had seen him last. I pulled a chair over and sat down beside him. When he pretended to ignore me, I pulled his chair back and faced him, saying, "You have forty-seven live PPI people left on the planet. Did you know that?"

His shocked dismay told me he had not. "Out in the mosses . . ." he whispered.

"No, you don't have almost eighty people wandering around out in the mosses. Many if not all of them are dead. What's going on here, Duras? Why did all the oldsters come here? Was it to die?"

He turned away from me to bend over his console, almost resting his forehead on the work surface, taking a breath like a sob. "Most of them."

"Why?"

He knotted his hands together, clenching his teeth, almost shuddering from the effort to control himself Then he took a deep breath, let it out in a long sigh, and said, "You probably won't understand. People don't, not unless they're . . . PPI. It's a tradition with us, we've always done it. My own father. His father . . ." His knotted hands beat his knees, punishingly.

"Talk to me," I urged. "You've got to talk to someone."

He took another shuddering breath. "I know. I told myself that, sometime ago . . ."

"What has PPI always done?"

"When we get too old to do the work, when we look at retirement, being planetbound . . . it's fine for some people, some even look forward to it, but a lot of us can't face it. We want to go on doing what we've done all our lives. See new places. Learn new places. We don't want to live shut up in four hundred square feet of an anthill on Earth, we don't want to die like that."

"So. You say 'always'?"

He took a deep breath, stood up, walked away from me to stare out the nearest window. "There've always been planets or moons where it was easy to die . . ."

"Dangerous planets."

"I didn't say easy to get killed on. I said easy to die on. Go to Borderland 13, sleep out in the open, you don't wake up in the morning. Flying night creatures come to suck your blood, but they do it without your feeling it, and they inject a chemical that gives you lovely, euphoric dreams while they're doing it. It's painless. Easy. Nice, if death can be nice. The largest moon of Chime 30 is a lovely place, beautiful views, light gravity, easy on old bones, old hearts, and a kind of happiness in the air. You wander, feeling happy, not even tired. About fifty, sixty days after you arrive, you've forgotten everything except the inclination to wander. You don't eat, or drink, you just walk and chuckle and walk and chuckle until eventually you fall down dead. There's a spore floating in the air that settles in the brain. That's all it takes.

"PPI men, they know these places. The word gets around, just like it did about this one. I've lost fifteen people from my original crew out there. Some of the retirees have filled in behind them, the ones who're still in good enough shape that they'd rather work than die. The three you met—Maywool had an ET disease, one we can't cure yet. Lackayst was within two weeks of retirement. Lukha . . . he just got in too deep, that's all . . ."

"Lukha died with a woman. I saw it."

He turned toward me, shaking his head. "It isn't sex. I did it enough to know it isn't sex. That's not what it's like at all. If you lie on the moss with someone else, you seem to dissolve into one another. You have a whole new world in your mind, another person, memories, ideas . . ."

"You did the redmoss?" I asked.

"I was an addict," he said stiffly. "But I broke the addiction when we decided to send for . . . for someone. I got all the crew together. We identified the users, including me. We used the med machines to fight the addiction. I figured when the linguist we asked for arrived, it'd get reported, and besides, it was interfering with my job. I like my job. I'm not ready to die yet."

"No more addicts among the people here?"

"A few recovering from it, like me. We did a general warning. If I see any sign of it in people, or they see any sign of it in me, a med-modifier gets installed until the next ship, then out. The warning couldn't apply to Lukha and the others like him because they were already too far gone. It didn't apply to the temporary duty people, old-sters who didn't want to go back to Earth. I wasn't about to sentence them to that. The moss was the only good road left for them."

"Didn't want to go back to Earth? Did they come from there?"

"No. But they came from planets that get rid of anyone over eighty-five. Most of the men and women who came here were close to that. They couldn't face fifteen or twenty years of pensioned-off hell!"

"So, what does PPI think about this?"

"PPI! That squeezer, Prime! He pretends it doesn't happen, pretends he doesn't know, but every pension he saves, he gets a bonus from his board of directors."

"If the people have pensions, then why would they be sent to Earth? They could support themselves anywhere!"

"Hah! The planets with living costs low enough for a PPI pension to be adequate don't admit retirees. Old people cost a lot more than young ones, that's all. Some of the ones who disappeared here brought their husbands or wives with them . . ."

"And they're all dead."

"You said they were dead, but it's not necessarily true. If they took off their links so nobody would bother them and went off into the moss, they could live out there. Blue moss jellies are delicious; the lab says they'll sustain life indefinitely. There's fruit on some of the trees. The climate's gentle. You can dig a soft shelter into a moss bank. If you stay away from the redmoss and a handful of other dangers, the place is safe."

I stood up, sickened but not surprised at what I'd heard. During the year after Witt had gone, before Paul had invited me to join him on that Quondangala job, I'd supported myself by working at one deadly dull job or other, and my only pleasure had been the time I spent at the Baja animal sanctuary. If I had lost that singular joy, I might have wanted to die. If we tower dwellers have nothing that delights us or amuses us, it's like living in a jail cell or a coffin. Confining. Anonymous. Lonely. And life among the down-dwellers, in all that noise and dark, that is a foretaste of hell. Drom was right about that.

"You might consider borrowing a power cannon from ESC and getting rid of the redmoss near the compound."

"I have considered it. It's against PPI policy. We honestly don't know how the redmoss fits into the ecology here. We tried building fences around them, but the mosses crawled out from under them."

I left his office to stand outside, totally undecided. The link on my wrist vibrated. Lethe was linking me. I didn't want to talk to him where I could be overheard, so I returned to my room before answering it.

"We've got word from Brandt," he said. "Can you come over?"

"I'll be there soon." I jotted a note to the trainers who were out with the dogs and stuck it on one of the corridor closet doors—our improvised bulletin board—checked on the puppies, who were asleep, then went down to the shore where the little boat was moored. It was as simple to operate as I had been told: One could set the course and leave it alone. As it purred its way toward the island, I scanned the surroundings. If I half squinted and ignored the scale, this could be an Earth scene, forests retreating up slopes, far mountains, the lake was an ocean with sandy shores and a romantic sandy spit extending into the waters where eight large dogs emerged from the moss forest and drank from the lake.

I opened my eyes wide and sat up. They saw the movement and

vanished into the moss. I clenched my teeth and felt my hands shaking. Not anger exactly. Anxiety.

At ESC they gave me Brandt's message, one forwarded from wormhole to wormhole on the way out, with a few consequent faded spots, nothing they couldn't make out.

"Dame Cecelia Hessing has learned about the Hessing ships, and she thinks the disappearance of their crews and passengers has something to do with Witt's disappearance. She demands we investigate.

"If that weren't enough, the revelation about the PPI contingent is causing a meltdown here. Botrin Prime wants to forget it, bury it, pretend it isn't happening, because it's evidently a kind of . . . accommodation that's traditional in PPI. First I'd heard of it, but he knows all about it. Any enlightenment you can come up with would be welcome. Dame Cecelia won't let him cover it up, says it may be connected to all the disappearances. Interesting for you, her harassing him for a change. Shoe on other foot kind of thing.

"Expect my arrival. The *intricacies* of the situation require personal attention by someone authorized to deal with the Derac. Have information about their increased numbers. Botrin Prime will probably send someone also, don't know who at this point. I had all I could do to talk Dame Cecilia out of coming herself.

"Be careful. Brandt out."

"What *intricacies?*" asked Lethe.

"All of them," said I. "The dogs, the Derac, Dame Cecelia—she's Witt Hessing's mother, and Witt disappeared on Jungle. Then there's ESC's relationship to PPI, and PPI's unstated policy of encouraging suicide."

Lethe erupted, "What did you say?"

I told him, quoting Duras Drom as accurately as I could. "Gainor used the word *accommodation*. That's more or less what it's viewed as. If I'd been head of PPI, I'd have taken possession of a garden planet somewhere along the line and set it up for retirement, so my people would have something to look forward to. This is a manticore egg . . ."

"Which is?" asked Sybil.

"Something that will hatch a very scrambled beast," I rejoined. "That's what happens when science gets mixed up with politics, you get monsters that eat good sense. Especially if what Drom says is true about Botrin Prime getting bonuses for saving pension money."

"Any progress on the language business?" asked Durrow.

I shook my head. "Paul's finding nothing. His machines correlate nothing. I mentioned the mimicry idea to him, just to get him off high dead center."

"We wish him luck," said Lethe.

"I've had another idea," I murmured. "What if their language isn't oral."

Abe Durrow sat down beside me. "You mean sign language? The Zhaar are said to have had a sign language, a batch of them, as a matter of fact. Each of their shape societies had its own, in addition to the general one."

"I don't know about the Zhaar," I confessed. "I was thinking more in terms of color, actually. I've been looking at the individual Mossen. There are at least seventy shades, tints, and hues. When there are more than one of the same color in a dance, I notice that the belt around them seems to be identical. I've taken images, blown them up, and compared."

"Belt?"

"That stiff section around their middle. It has . . . what would you say, raised areas? Like something embossed: letters or words. So far as I can see, each belt is different, like a fingerprint, except for the identically colored ones. If they are really identical, then we have things that grow to a pattern, maybe as many different patterns as there are colors."

"Not one race of creatures?"

"I wouldn't say that. Humans are one race, but we have different fingerprints, different DNA. We grow to a pattern, but only clones would be identical."

"So the communication might be by . . . ?"

"By order of the colors. If we have seventy distinguishable colors that could be something like a syllable, the order in which they arrange themselves might convey the language, mightn't it?"

"That would imply a positional language. Maybe," said Sybil. She muttered quick notes into her memo pad.

I went on, "So the Mossen might mimic us to attract our attention, and then arrange themselves to convey a message."

"They mimic us?" asked Lethe. He sat back in his chair, eyes unfocused. "If that's true, if they're using our sounds to get us interested:

Firstly, why don't they do it when and where they dance; and secondly, who did they talk to before we came?"

Long silence.

"Well, where did they dance before we came?" asked Sybil. "We haven't looked into their activities before we arrived, but there were survey fish on the planet for almost a year before we came, and we have those records."

"It's only a suggestion," I offered. "If I suggest anything to Paul, he spends more time debating the proposition than he does working with it, so the best I can do with him is drop a hint he can later claim as his own idea."

"Tell us something about the dogs," said Lethe.

The answer to that question had been carefully composed, rehearsed, and was even largely true. "Geneticists selected for size, longevity, and strength. They're better able to communicate and possibly more intelligent than natural dogs were. They were bred this way with the idea of giving them even more survival skills, for when we turn them loose."

Sybil murmured, "You said 'selected.' Was that done with Zhaar technology?"

I responded stiffly. "Use of Zhaar technology is against IC law."

"The Orskimi use it," said Abe.

I said, "All I know is that Gainor mentions recurring top-level IC discussions about the technology and about other races using it. If the Orskimi have the stuff, it's logical to assume others might get it, too. I can't swear nobody on Earth has ever touched it any more than you can."

"How about PPI?" Abe asked.

"I can't swear to that, either. I can only swear that I have no personal knowledge of anyone using it."

"Ah," said Abe, sharing a glance with his colleagues.

I said, "Gainor has told me what's said about the Zhaar, about their being shape changers, able to change themselves into anyone or anything they wanted to, able to infiltrate any group, mimic any person, any race. They're rumored to have stolen secrets, killed for pleasure. They could have anything they wanted simply by becoming the owner of whatever it was, committing piracy by becoming the crew, committing genocide by becoming the settlers of a planet. But then, it was said to be the Zhaar who wiped out Holme's World, so if anyone from that world is a Zhaar, it would be you, Sybil."

"Fat chance," she snarled. "If I could change my shape, I'd have done it long since."

"The other thing that's said about the Zhaar is that they're dead and gone. Gainor says whoever or whatever made the final decision to commit genocide on the Zhaar, assuming that it actually happened, probably saved millions of lives."

"And who's alleged to have done it?" asked Sybil.

"Gainor says some of the elder races may have done it."

"See, that's what I can't figure out," Sybil complained. "The Zhaar are gone. But the rumor is the biotechnology still exists. How can they have the one without the other? I mean, the shape changer matrix was in the Zhaar bodies, not stored in a laboratory somewhere. Whoever has it, they had to have taken some of the people . . . alive. And if they reproduced by budding, as is said, if you've got one live one, you could soon have thousands."

"I don't know," said I. "Maybe I don't want to know because having Zhaar technology implies we might still have Zhaar as well."

"So you'd be against using the technology?" asked Lethe.

"Philosophically, I'm against it," I said. "But I'm told, the use of Zhaar net tissue would enable amputees to produce new limbs and people with broken spines to be healed and disfigured people to be pleasant-looking again without the long time lapse and repeated surgical interventions we used to do to get lesser results, and without cloning ourselves in order to harvest parts, with the attendant ethical complexities. So, practically, I might feel differently."

"Ah," Lethe said again, this time more warmly.

"But," I said, "I try to keep in mind that though philosophical absolutes prevent practical solutions, practical solutions can involve insuperable ethical dilemmas. For some people."

Sybil gave me a quizzical look. "In other words, you're on the fence."

I laughed, ruefully. "I'm the kind of person who opts for practical solutions in particular cases, then feels guilty about it later."

Lethe said, "There was that attempt to give animal senses to people, back . . . oh, when, fifteen years or so."

"I'm one of those they tried to plant dognose in," I said quietly. "I volunteered for the experiment when I was sixteen. There was no danger involved; the cells would grow or they wouldn't, but they weren't invasive, and I have no idea whether any Zhaar technology was involved. The cells did grow, but not a lot. I have a hyperacute sense of smell, but it still isn't anywhere near that of a dog, much less a dog like Behemoth or Scramble."

"How acute is hyperacute?" asked Abe.

"Blindfolded, I could identify you three from across a room, and who's been here recently. From fifty feet away, I can smell what kind of mood my brother's in or smell something very strange and dreadful in the PPI staffers who are using the redmoss. What I can't do, and the dogs can, is say whether you are afraid of me or not, whether you are a danger to me or not."

"To their world, we're deaf and dumb," said Lethe.

"Just about, yes. The sense hasn't been notably useful to me, not on Earth, at least."

They promised to let me know as soon as they had an arrival time for Brandt. I got in my little boat, backed it up, and turned to go back to shore, seeing once again the spit of land where I had seen eight dogs. "Damn," I said, feelingly. "Damn, damn, damn."

⋮ "I went out to ESC," I said to Adam, later that afternoon. "On the way, I looked down the shoreline, and what did I see? Eight dogs, lapping water from the lake, like a pack of myth-wolves. It was I in the boat, counting dogs, but it could have been anyone, counting dogs."

Adam flushed. "I knew you'd be angry, but he said they expected us to go along. I really couldn't say no."

"Say no to whom?" I demanded, outraged.

"Behemoth. Well, him and Titan both."

As that penetrated, slowly, I felt my mouth hanging agape and snapped it shut. "I thought we were the ones who decided what was best, Adam. Are the dogs running things now?"

Instead of remorse, I saw amusement. "Of course they are! What makes you think they haven't been running things for a long while?"

Now I really was stunned. "Explain," I said, afraid I'd get started on a rant if I said anything more.

"Behemoth and Titan and Wolf have been in charge of their own lives since they were about . . . two years old. We don't give them orders because they won't follow orders. We ask them if they will comply with suggestions, and we tell them the reasons."

"Such as?"

"Such as, will they pretend to obey orders to impress some visiting arkist who's likely to be a big donor. Will they be friendly with Shiela, whom they dislike, because she can turn us out on the street if she wants to. Will they please be nice to Gainor Brandt, pretty much for the same reason."

"They dislike Shiela?"

"They say she smells of too many layers."

"Are they being nice to me because maybe I can help them?" I asked, my throat dry.

He shook his head. "No. They've never even questioned anything about you. They never questioned anything about Jon Point, either, while he was alive. If they help you or obey you, it's because they see you as a pack somebody. Not the alpha dog, Behemoth's definitely that, but a somebody, nonetheless."

I felt the fume building up and fought it down. This was no time to get stirred up. "Can they count, Adam?"

"So far as I can tell, they're discalculic, almost completely. They can distinguish between one and several, few and many, however. The pack has a certain weight or aura or completeness, and they expect that attribute to be there when the pack hunts. When something upsets the aura, they howl, sometimes for a long time. Frank and Clare and I are sort of pack adjuncts, so we're part of the whatever, but we are definitely on the bottom rung. Not that they abuse us. They don't need to because they know we're no competition."

With an effort, I pulled myself back to the original topic. "Remember the fix you got in the night you went to pick up Jarl Alred? There was a hostile crowd, you got all fired up, and you shifted to dog shape in order to break up the crowd. You were seen. The species police were all over the place and all over me. You were too far away today to be recognized as individuals, but you weren't so far away that someone couldn't count from one to eight! Six big dogs is all there are right now. Once Scramble's puppies are grown, it'll be harder to determine how many in a group. And once Veegee's and Dapple's puppies are born and grown, there'll be even less likelihood. Until then, you must not let more than six animals be seen at one time, less however many are back at the house with puppies!"

He flushed. "And how do I explain that to Behemoth."

"You don't," I replied. "I think I can explain it to Scramble. I'm not angry about your shifting, but I am angry about your letting yourself be seen. Your shifting could be very helpful. I'd like you to smell the redmoss and the area around the meadow, but you mustn't be seen doing it, not even at a distance."

"Well, I did smell the redmoss." He lifted one nostril. "The smell is distinctive, very attractive, but I don't think anyone with less than dognose would realize what it identifies."

"You mean, people might smell it, but not know it?"

"Yes. Humans react to things they smell all the time, even when they don't know what they're smelling, or even *that* they're smelling. They do weird things and don't know why."

I thought for a moment. "Is it an attractant to the dogs?"

"No, and for us when we're in dog shape, hardly at all." He flushed. "We'll be good, Jewel. If Behemoth insists again, I'll refer him to you. Now, when is Gainor Brandt getting here?"

"Ten to fifteen days. Our trip out took about twenty-five days, of which we experienced less than three. Gainor has access to faster transport. It won't be long."

"The dogs think, that is, we were all thinking, talking . . . It would be interesting to go east of here, to the foot of that plateau. The guy in the PPI garage says if it's related to the project, we can take one of the floaters. You could use that, the rest of us can run . . ."

"How do I relate it to the project, Adam?"

"Our project? Or Paul's?"

"Paul's project is the one PPI knows about."

"Maybe the Mossen dance other places. Maybe they make other noises other places."

"The noises don't seem to be related to the message. It might be color . . ."

"Well, maybe they have different colors elsewhere."

"Ah," I said. "Where would we have heard that?"

"One of the guys who goes into the moss a lot. One who isn't here right now." He was inventing, but since I needed only an excuse, it didn't matter.

"And what is *our* project, Adam?"

"The dogs have never had time or space to do long-distance runs. Both they and we need to know how good they are at cross-country. Just a test, Jewel."

This was all true, and it would give us a chance to see more of Moss, so I went to inform Paul, finding him busily entering information into his lingui-putes. When I came in, he hastily covered what he was working on, something to do with Mossen belts. "Paul, would recordings of belt patterns and colors in other groups of Mossen be helpful to you. I mean, groups other than the ones that dance here?"

He glared at me, irritated at the interruption. "Are there other groups?"

"One of the PPI men says there are. East of here, toward the plateau. The trainers and I thought we'd make a little trek that way tomorrow, just to take a look at the cliffs and the falls. If it would be any help to you, I'd take a recorder along."

He considered it, a tiny tic jumping at the side of one nostril. "Maybe I'll go with you."

"Oh." I didn't need to simulate surprise, though I did need to counterfeit pleasure at the prospect. "That'd be wonderful! We're taking a floater and sleeping on the ground. Bring your antibug stuff, some of the local ones bite, but there won't be many until we get into the real rain forest at the foot of the plateau. It rains a lot more over and near the plateau, so you'll need waterproof gear, too. I'm glad you'll join us. It'll be fun."

He thought about it, the tiny tic leaping and leaping, the way it always did when he was planning to manage me. The twitching subsided. He had decided against it. He didn't need me for anything just then, and the trip would be uncomfortable. He didn't like being uncomfortable.

"No," he said, finally. "No, I shouldn't interrupt what I'm doing. Yes, it would help if you record the colors and belt patterns elsewhere, to see if they vary from those here. If there's something interesting, I can make a trip there later with one of your fellows to guide me."

"All right," I murmured, trying to sound disappointed. "Whatever you like."

Normally, when I accompanied Paul on his contract trips, I served as his hostess in entertaining the locals, his surrogate in being entertained by the locals, in either case keeping them off his back while also taking care of the details of daily life. Here, there was no entertaining. Here, the details of daily living were reduced to a minimum and provided by PPI.

I told Drom I was going to the plateau, asking his advice.

"Early on we made a few trips out that way, nothing too lengthy. The waterfalls are remarkable, well worth seeing. There are gemstones in the streams, near the falls, but be careful. Wear protective clothing. There could be some other redmoss kind of thing out there."

I thanked him. On my link, Lethe said more or less the same thing, as well as insisting I take spare power cells for everything. Adam and I got everything ready, so we could leave early the following morning.

In my room, that night, when everything was quiet, I talked to Scramble. I just talked. I told her about Adam getting into trouble back on Earth. I said, if anyone saw him or Frank or Clare when they were changed, it might cause a lot of trouble for them as well as for me. It might threaten her and the puppies, and the other dogs. I said humans were in the habit of counting things because we had good eyes but inferior noses. I asked if she could keep Behemoth and Titan from getting the trainers into trouble. She listened.

When I had finished and was about to turn out the light, she said, "Wy?"

"Why? Why would it cause trouble? Or why do Adam and Frank change into dogs?"

"Wy engh humahn?"

"Why do they change back? Into humans?"

She fixed me with her unblinking eyes, waiting.

"They change into dogs because Gainor got some stuff through the Tharstians in order to make dog surrogates, so when you were puppies, you could learn from example how to live as natural dogs do live, in packs, with leaders, by hunting. We had no wild dogs for you to learn from, and that was the best we could do. Also, we thought we could learn more about dogs from people who were being dogs."

"No."

"They're not dogs?"

"No."

"I know, not real dogs, but they thought they might learn something more."

She went on staring. I said, "You want to tell me something more, something you may not have words for? You want me to guess, so you can tell me when I'm right?" She stared, licked her jowls, went on staring. I sighed. "All right. You want to tell me . . . they haven't learned."

"Es."

"They haven't learned. Because . . ." Because why? "Because they can't forget they are human?"

"Es."

"And they're not going to find anything out. It's just . . ."

"Pay."

I thought about that one. "Play?"

She nosed the puppies and lay down, flat, the conversation over. I turned out the light, but it was some time before I went to sleep. The sense of it was, if they had learned anything about being dogs, they would not change back into humans. So long as they were willing to change back, it was only play, they hadn't really learned anything. I tried it in reverse. If I were a dog who could change into a human, but I preferred being a dog, would that mean I knew nothing about being human? Or, too damned much?

⠸ Shortly before leaving the next morning, I uncased the concs and fed them. They were as unhappy as concs could be, wanting to play, to go outside, to eat something different. I was firm with them, putting them back into their cases, though it galled me to do so. They were the way they were because that was how Paul wanted them, infantile and cute, and totally subordinate. It seemed unfair to lock them up because they were as Paul had made them. Of course, if he really struck a stopping point, he might uncase them for a while. Otherwise, they were likely to stay in those cases the entire time they were on planet, except when being fed every six to eight days.

All the dogs went along, the puppies in a covered basket on the floater, which was supplied with dog and human rations and a modest supply of water, easily renewable. Water ran everywhere on Moss, and it was everywhere potable, according to the ESC people.

The trainers and I rode in the floater until we were deeply into the forest, well out of sight of anyone from the compound. There the trainers stripped off their clothing and walked beside the floater as they changed. Adrenaline could make the process happen quickly, rage or great excitement could make it happen in minutes, but when things were calm, jaws and tongues slowly lengthened, eyes shifted subtly to the sides, ears rose toward the top of the skull, forearms and shoulders shifted. Genetically they did not change. They became quite doglike, except for their high-domed heads, far too rounded for canines though not terribly unlike the old, large-headed dogs: St. Bernards, golden retrievers, mastiffs. At a distance, they would pass for dogs, particularly if they stayed in dog form long enough to lengthen their coats. At first their fur was merely an all-over fuzz. Adam was the same shining steel gray as his hair, with a darker gray stripe down the spine. Given long enough, he usually grew a mane. Clare was evenly brown with red glints in her fur, and she would acquire feathers on her legs and tail; Frank was a mottled gray and black, plain black at a distance, with a close, short-haired coat. Getting the coat to grow wasn't voluntary. It simply grew, like claws, like teeth, like tails. If they stayed dogs for several weeks—which was the longest it had ever been tested—they would have full coats, long tails, longer legs, fangs, and hard claws for digging. Whatever technology Gainor had obtained, it was limited to soft tissue and young bones. At some point, Adam, Clare, and Frank would be too old. Their bones wouldn't make the shift. I'd heard them discussing how careful they'd have to be later in life, to prevent their being dogs when that final moment came. Funny. The conclusion I drew now from that remembered conversation was quite different from the one I had drawn at the time.

It took several hours before they felt ready to run, but once they did, I lost all sight of them. The floater hummed beneath me, a vibration more felt than heard. The wind waved moss banners from every tree. I heard an occasional chirp or flutter but was otherwise alone: No other person was within sight or sound of my voice. I halted the floater and gloried in the quiet, focusing on the surroundings.

My world had always been narrowly circumscribed. On Mars, one saw caverns. On Earth, one saw the walls of the towers. In both cases, our perceptual world had finite boundaries. On Moss, I stood at the center of a transparent and expanding balloon that was itself unconfined. Each barrier my eyes touched became the threshold to something farther on, each perimeter pressing outward as the tenuous fabric of perception reached and then encompassed another layer of the endless series of mosses, trees, hills, and distances, ending eventually in the shifting mist at the limit of my sight, itself unconfined in any direction. I felt ridiculously, ecstatically happy.

The iggy-huffo people talked a lot about their religion of killing animals to manifest man's God-given dominion, but they'd never known what dominion was. They thought it meant shutting everything out but themselves. The glory of Moss meant letting everything in, all this space with the plants and animals interwoven into it, only myself fully aware of the fabric of it. No, no. Unthink that. I had no idea who or what else might be as aware as I or even more aware than I. In any case, I was willing to cede the primacy of knowing, if I could only keep the feeling of ecstatic freedom that had wrapped around me like protective wings. Never in my life until that moment had I felt both unobserved and totally encompassed.

There were only a few moments of this exhilaration, all too brief a time. Scramble returned to the floater to check on the pups, leaping aboard and nosing me affectionately, letting me know I was still her puppy, I guess. The pseudodogs tired more quickly than real dogs, so they were next to return. Adam leapt back into the floater, soon followed by Clare and Frank. They didn't change shape, just lay there, panting. When they had rested enough, they leapt off and ran once more.

The floater was equipped with directional finders fed by the orbital surveyors. I kept the line of movement generally eastward, seeing the escarpment rising gradually before us as though all that immensity of stone were growing taller the closer we came. Once in a while, trees or taller growths made us veer to one side or another, but there were no long detours. We made excellent time, stopping for lunch and water when the dogs came to run behind the sled, panting heavily.

By evening, we had approached closely enough that the scattered mists from the waterfalls occasionally wafted over us. I parked the floater and laid my bedding on a nearby moss bank. The dogs, nine of them, curled up around me, though Scramble would not settle until she and Behemoth had moved the puppies into the midst of the huddle. The winds fell with nightfall, and it became warmer without the mists. I lay with Adam's back curled against mine, Veegee on one side of my legs and Wolf on the other. All the dogs, real and unreal, slept at once, but I remained awake for a time, staring up at the treetops where fringes and curtains of moss moved of their own accord, slowly though perceptibly changing their patterns. An opening was first a star, then a circle, then a more complicated star with fringes. I considered setting up a time-lapse recorder to preserve the effect, but I was too warmly, comfortably joyous to move.

BLISS

⋮ Quynis, bride of Lynbal, Lady of Loam, almost immediately after being married had formed the habit of sleeping late and eating huge breakfasts. It was said among the kitchen people of Loam that she had gained one quarter of her weight over again in the first flush of honeymoon. Certainly, she was a far better-looking woman than the starveling waif who had first arrived. Now she was pink, becomingly rounded, with shiny hair and glistening eyes, the object of her young husband's complete devotion.

"Marriage suits you," her father told her as she was helping him pack for his journey back to the Granite Caves of his tribe.

"Will you ask Quillan to come visit me?" she begged. "I have something important to talk to him about."

"Now, why should your twin be visiting you so soon? Ha? He just left, ten days or so ago. One would think you should be contented with your new husband for a time, not needing a brother for anything useful."

"Oh, Papa, but it is for something useful. He says he's ready to decide upon a bride, so he'll be needing to come back very near here, won't he? To the gem mines? To get stones for an offering bracelet?"

He looked into her eyes, finding only an innocent joy welling there. Now why hadn't the rapscallion mentioned it to him if he'd found a girl? "If you say so, daughter. He tells me very little, and most of that unimportant."

"Well, he did tell me. So, ask him to stop and visit me on his way to the mines. Tell him to do it *on the way*, not after he's been there. Now that you and Chief Larign are allies, he may come through Loam lands, mayn't he?"

He chuckled to himself. The minx wanted gemstones for something. Something for that cock-o'-the-heap of a husband of hers. Well, why not. Quillan had attended the wedding, but he had returned home the day following. He was the heir, and it was considered good sense not to have both the chief and the heir gone from tribal lands for any length of time—except during the decennial wars, when everyone left except the women, children, and old people. Such folk would stay safe enough so long as all the predatory types were part of an army, and the army was elsewhere. At other times, leaving tribal lands untended gave too much temptation to greedy neighbors. If Quillan was ready to decide upon a bride, however, custom demanded that he make a trip to the gravel mines in the rivers at the foot of the plateau and there search out stones to make an offering gift. Offering gifts denoted sincerity, a willingness to make a considerable effort, and though only chiefs' sons had the tradition of acquiring gemstones, even lesser men spent a good deal of time and thought on such matters.

Lynbal had given Quynis a necklace of greenstones set in gold, a goodly gift, yes, but it was said he had had someone else find the stones for him. Quilac had worried a good bit about that. Suitors who were sincere would let no hand but their own touch the stones until the gem cutter got them. Lyndal might have been casual, even contemptuous before; he certainly wasn't now. Now Quilac's mind was so set at rest that he could bid his daughter farewell with an untroubled mind. Surrounded by his men, he set off for home.

That afternoon, one of the more influential men of Loam sent a messenger to Gavi Norchis, asking her to come treat his wife for what he, himself, thought was an imaginary ailment. Gavi came to Loam, diagnosed the ailment, which was far from imaginary, and told the man to take his wife to the Medical Machine as quickly as might be. The Medical Machines from the old ships still worked, though they were reserved for serious illness or accident.

As she was leaving by way of a winding and deserted hallway that would let her out near the trail to her favorite dwelling place, someone pssted at her from a doorway, and she turned to see the radiant face of the bride, Quynis, who laid a quick hand upon Gavi's arm and drew her into the small room.

"I need to speak with you privately," she said, beaming from ear to ear. "Scent Mistress, I waited, hoping to see you. Can you tell me what fee you would charge to assure one would look upon my brother with loving eyes?" The words came out all at once, in a spurt, followed by a little laugh. "I didn't mean to blurt at you like that. It's just . . . I'm so happy. I want my brother Quillan to be happy, too."

Gavi seated herself on the only piece of furniture in the room, a small, low table, and gave the girl a good looking over. Oh, yes, she was much improved. Pregnant, without a doubt. "Happy, are you?"

"Oh, Scent Mistress. So happy."

"Is your brother Quillan much like you?" she asked.

"Oh, no." Quynis shook her head violently. "No, Quillan is handsome and strong and tall. He's pleasant, too, to everyone. But the woman he is in love with is very lovely, and it may be she might be . . . She could . . . Perhaps he wouldn't be . . ."

"Perhaps he wouldn't be her idea of a perfect husband?" asked Gavi.

"Yes. He might not be. Granite is not such a rich place as Loam. To be Lady of Granite might not be . . . as attractive as being Lady of some other place."

"Who is the woman?" Gavi asked, cutting through all the circumlocutions.

"Lailia. My new sister. My brother saw her. I've never seen anyone go into it like that, so quickly. He was just . . ."

"Ah," said Gave. "He was taken by her, yes?"

"At once. One glance. I saw it happen."

"Well. Let me think on that."

"Can you tell me your charge?"

Gavi smiled, hiding the little flames in her eyes by casting them downwards, modestly. "For true love, perhaps there would be no charge. But I would need to see him first."

The girl crowed, "He's coming here, to visit me. Can I send word to you . . . ?"

"That won't be necessary." Gavi smiled. "People in the market let me know all the gossip, who is going where, and why, and when they will return. He's a good boy, your brother?"

"Oh, he's not a boy at all, Scent Mistress. Truly. Though we were born at the same time, he grew into a man far quicker than I grew into a woman. Until I came here, that is. I was stuck, somehow. I could feel it, the being stuck, unable to go on growing inside myself. Now I feel myself becoming more womanish every day, but Quillan has been a man a great while, and he is a good man, yes. The people love him."

Rare and wonderful indeed to have a chief's son who was loved by his people. Gavi smiled encouragingly. "Indeed. I will see you both, then, when he comes."

She stood, patted the girl kindly on her shoulder, and took herself off while reflecting upon the vagaries of fate. She was determined upon squaring her account with Belthos of Burrow. She believed Chief Larign had his eyes on Belthos's son for Lailia. She approved of alliances, but she did not approve of Balnor marrying Lailia. She did not approve of Balnor marrying anyone, except, perhaps, one of the moss demons.

How could she do this and this without doing that and that, ah? A lovely puzzle. One that might keep her awake many nights running, figuring it out.

WALKING SUNSHINE

⋮ Walking Sunshine had sprouted as an ordinary willog, that is a whilesome talker, one who spent its youth making little messages: more fire smell (warmer) less fire smell (cooler) more receding smell of frond (longer) more approaching smell of treetops (higher). As it matured, it had grown its share of long messages: "Attention all moss, types briefstink, gooplop, rottenwood, and jellydrip. At the next warm send sporelings southward for a general remossening around Lake Stinks-of-Toothy-Things."

Walking Sunshine had enjoyed being only a talker, though, inevitably, the time had come when it felt it wanted something more. That, actually, was its first inkling that it was, in fact, a willog, as willogs were notorious for wanting something more. To signify the change in status, it took the name Walking Sunshine ("Walky" to itself), and while it was still light in weight and agile in limb, volunteered as a thread-moss gatherer. Thread-moss grew everywhere in the forest, though mostly on lower limbs of trees, where it hung in festoons and veils, filtering both sunlight and moonlight, forming a backdrop for the messages that came through the mosslands. Thread moss gatherers climbed into the trees, broke the moss from its anchorage, and transplanted it to the treetops, stretching it from tree to tree to make a sunshade for the sporelings planted in the soil beneath. Walking Sunshine did this work for some years, until it grew too heavy and the trees complained.

By that time Walky was in late saplinghood, time to seek out some Mossy-Longtime-Rooted, where it would learn the logic of word formation, vocabulary, synthesis, order, and clarity. After a sometime search, he found such a Mossy one, already attended by a group of young willogs, among whom Walking Sunshine rooted itself happily, amusing itself and them by composing poetry, purely for their own amusement, of course. No late sapling would thrust its own compositions before the perceivers of a Grown-one, but making poetry was practice in the art of language, and practice was laudable.

Several sizable beds of eatmoss grew in the area, where elderly willogs came to lie a pleasant time in renewal and reformation. On one eventful day, however, a walking-bad-smell had come to lie there, a new walking-bad-smell, not one of those from Tall Rock. The bad-smell stayed on the eatmoss a while, then went away, but soon it was back again and again, and as the moss gradually ate it away, Walky's curiosity had moved it to run its rootlets up into the bad-smell for exploration. Wonder of wonders, with roots deeply embedded, it had heard! It had seen!

A revelation! A miracle! Walky had studied the eyes and ears until the walking-bad-smell had dwindled, then it had waited impatiently for other walking-bad-smells to lie on the moss. The fresher ones were easier to study, and Walky had grown eyes at once, not very good ones that first time, but workable enough to see color, and shape, and distance. Oh, marvelous distance! Challenging color! Intriguing shape! But that was only the beginning. Ears were next, and with the ears, sound.

All willogs had pretended to stay far away from bad-smells since the Tall Rock bad-smells had threatened willogs with fire. They could only pretend, not actually do, because the World needed them for things, and they had responsibilities. Once Walky had ears and eyes, however, it gave up any pretense of avoiding bad-smells, uprooted itself, and went in search for more seeings and hearings, finding them in abundance at the bad-smell place beside Lake Stinks-of-Toothy-Things. There Walky *heard* things: Bells. Buzzers. Howling when ships came down. Hammering. Yelling. Singing . . . oh, singing. And whistling, too.

Keeping well hidden, Walky rooted itself to listen and to see, days on days. It saw bad-smells using their eyes toward pieces of stuff with marks on them, it heard them making sounds at the stuff, then others came and made the same sounds at the same marks. So it was Walky learned how words were written by the sounds they made and knew immediately that the World must be told of its discovery! At once, Walky shifted to reproduction mode and began growing messages, self-reproducing messages that came up already messaged from spores! Walky's messages, no matter how many generations later, said what the original message had said: "The bad-smells cannot detect our words. If we wish to understand the bad-smells, we must grow new organs. Genetics for new organs included in this message."

Even while engaged in this flurry of information, Walky was learning more and more human words and how they were put together. As it learned them, Walky grew the words and sent them out, into the world.

Also, he continued to frequent the eatmoss beds—redmoss the bad-smells called it. Sometimes "crabs" got into the moss, and "beetles," and "mousy" things. All of those creatures had eyes and ears, oh, such wonderful gifts. Crab eyes. Mouse eyes. Beetle eyes. All to be added to bad-smell eyes. Some eyes could see color, others not. Some were for seeing moving things, others to see still things. And a new creature had come, as well. A thing called dog by the bad-smells. Perhaps dog eyes would be different yet.

Walky's messages spread widely. Many of its messages were examined by other willogs, who thereupon grew ears and eyes for themselves. Now, even some of the mosses had eyes, mouse eyes or crab eyes or beetle eyes. What wonders the bad-smells had brought!

Perhaps, Walky decided after much thought, it was not polite to think of them as bad-smells. They spoke of themselves as humans. Perhaps it would be more tactful to call them that.

THE MEETING

: In the middle of the night I woke, my face wet with tears and an impossibly familiar voice coming from behind a screen of trees. Wolf had rolled away from my legs, giving me room to stand. Pulling my loosened clothes around me, I moved toward the sound.

Behind me, Adam said, "Wha?"

"I don't know," I murmured, almost moaning. "Oh, I don't know..."

He uncoiled himself and padded beside me, moving gradually in front of me to sniff the way toward a luxuriant drapery of mosses that glinted with sparkling point of light. When I separated the strands with my fingers, I saw a pale vertical surface alive with movement. Alive with... my own face! And Witt's. There we were at our wedding celebration. I was feeding him wedding cake. He was laughing at a joke someone had made. These were pictures from the album Taddeus had given us; the album I had pressed into Witt's hand the day he left...

I lunged through the hanging screen, seeing only his face, crying, "Witt. Oh, Witt."

Someone nearby exclaimed in surprise. I whirled to confront a terrible... a monstrous... stalked eyes that glittered... a dreadful... spikes like daggers... A scream gathered in my throat.

"Hush," said the terror, taking off its horrible head to reveal a woman's face. "Be not screaming, please."

I swallowed the scream and collapsed on a fallen trunk, staring wet-faced as the woman in the shell came closer, holding out a hideous hand, which she pulled off to show the human hand beneath.

"That is you in picture, not? You look more old. I watched you setting up camp. I thought I would look again being sure. But then, you were hearing voices. I misremember picture being so loud . . ."

The woman spoke clearly but slowly, as though considering each oddly accented word before she uttered it, as people did who had been reared in the far colonies where dialects of common speech were spoken. Her olive-skinned face was crowned with dark hair braided in a high coronet. She had dark eyes, a wide mouth, and a beaky though shapely nose with the nostrils widely flared in excitement. The rest of her was bound and corseted in tough shell, some kind of exoskeleton with a row of extra legs hanging at either side.

Adam thrust his head and shoulders across the trunk, beneath my arm, a low growl in his throat, the fur on his neck up. I stroked him absently, murmuring, "It's all right, all right."

"What's that?!" demanded the stranger.

"Just a dog," said I. "My dog."

The woman shook her head in wonder. "I have not seen dog. We are told of dog, of course. One of six faithful Earthian friends, not? Cat, dog, horse, cow, sheep, goat. So legends say."

"Where did you get that album?" I demanded, pointing at the device in the woman's hand. "Those are pictures of our celebration, Witt's and mine. That thing in your hand is our photo album." My voice rose. "Where did you get it?"

"Shhh," said the other, maneuvering the clumsy shell so that she could sit beside me. "I will also sit. This is wonderful enough sitting and acquainting, not? Coincidence, not? I found thing here"—an emphatic down gesture of both hands—"in one of these caverns, along this wall"—fingers pressed together, both hands making pecking motions along the wall. ". . . It is mine some time now . . ." Hands pressed to the carapace over her chest. ". . . Yours, I know" —a sweeping gesture toward me—"but I found it, so thought it mine." Her hands relaxed in her lap. "I thought maybe it was celebration of new year, not unlike ours. But you say it is something else? What is pastry for?"

"Our wedding cake. An old custom. We still call it that, even though they aren't really weddings anymore."

"Ah. We have wedding pastry, but ours are ring-shaped buns with sweet filling." Gavi searched my face, put out a gentle finger to touch the corners of my mouth, the lids of my eyes, as though to reassure herself I was real. "So you wedded this man . . . ?"

"My husband, Witt, was never on this planet," I said. "He disappeared! Where is he?" It came out almost angrily, as a demand.

"How long ago?" the woman asked. "How long he went away?"

"Oh, long, long ago. Twelve years ago he disappeared on Jungle."

"Where is Jungle?" asked the other, hands raised, palms up denoting doubt.

"The next planet in, toward the sun."

"There are two planets between us and sun. Ruby and Emerald." Her hands spun in orbits, her fingers darted, spelling.

"Then Jungle must be what you call Emerald," I said. "It's a green world. My husband was there, with an exploration team. And he disappeared along with ten other men, and they've never been seen since, and he had that photo album with him. How did it get here?"

"Have not one thought concerning it," said the other, still peering closely into my face. "My name is Gavi Norchis, thank you."

"I am Jewel Delis, with the Planetary Protection installation here."

"Ah, our world needs protection? I did not know. I am of Abyssians"—wide gesture, up, ending with index finger pointing high—"people of Night Mountain."

" 'Shish," said Adam. "Ais shish."

I nodded. "Right, Adam. The Hessing spaceships, up on the plateau. Those were your people?"

Gavi stared at the dog. "He talks?"

"They speak words they can manage to enunciate. Their genetic makeup was manipulated to create speech centers in the brain without changing the anatomy much. Once they have the speech center, they can invent words for both intra- and interspecies communication. Like their word for redmoss." I growl-yelped, "Rrr-igh."

"A warning-pain combination," said Gavi Norchis.

I nodded. "If they follow their usual pattern, *rrr-igh* may become their general term for anything dangerous on the planet, or maybe for any dangerous thing that lies in one place. They will add other elements to specify which dangerous thing it is, depending on how many varieties of danger there are."

"Is wonderful," she cried. "Was not aware dogs talk." Her hands went to her head, then away, fingers fluttering, miming no thoughts.

"Do all your people talk with their hands?"

Gavi looked at her hands as though unaware of their existence. "Ah. Silent talk, for when we must not be overheard. It becomes habit. Especially when using . . . old language."

"Are you descended from the people in those ships?"

She folded her hands, making much of the act as she gave me a sly look from the corner of her eyes. "Yes. We were on way to Hidden Garden, Planet Jardinconnu, our new world. On way, we went aside looking for Splendor, and anomaly caught us. We had not one idea how getting back, and ships were damaged, so could only stay here. Two shiploads stayed on Night Mountain, two shiploads trekked over to Day Mountain. Our people claim half of world, other half belongs to Day Mountain."

"Whai?" asked Adam.

The woman regarded him with interest and some confusion. "He is asking of me . . . ?"

I said, "Why. Why does half belong to you and half to them?"

"Because, Planet Forêt is sending out one Hargess cousin and one Hessing cousin for heading new colony. Much rivalry. Hargess chief wanting boss-ship of this world; so is Hessing chief. Both men fighting great duel, both now longtime dead, so we could as you might say . . ."

"Reunite?"

"Be one people, not? No good. Small customs piled for long time become mountain of tradition, now too late backening and restarting. Menfolk place much value on . . . warlikeness?"

"Belligerence?" suggested I.

"Strut, you know. Like roosters." She smiled secretly to herself. "Very important for male pride."

"Nobody knew you were here," I cried. "There's no sign of you except the ships."

"We hide," said Gavi. "Ah. Here are more of dogs."

Clare, Veegee, and Titan had come through the moss forest to sit down near Adam, thoughtfully regarding the shell-clad woman.

I asked, "You hide? Why?"

"Because we do not want being harvested," she said, getting slowly to her feet. "You are here only short time, not long enough knowing much about mosslands. Come! Nearby is pleasant cavern. We can built sit-talk-fire, keep warm, avoid harvesters." She locked the question at us, head cocked.

Adam nodded, so did the other dogs, who returned the way they had come. Within moments they returned with their kindred, each of the dogs carrying a puppy by the head.

"Little ones!" cried Gavi. "Tiny ones!"

"I'll get the floater," said I, rising.

Gavi Norchis came with me. "We had floaters. But they were stopping much time ago. No machines now, except Medical Machines, from ships. Those we keep working."

"How do you live?" asked I, dazed. It had occurred to me that I might be dreaming, for the encounter had the dimension and aspect of dream. None of it seemed real. I stooped to gather our blankets.

"As people lived before machines," Gavi answered, taking the other end of a blanket to help fold it. "So our wisewomen say. We gardening where is good soil, plentiful rain, high up, over places where is heat. Warm soil making up for cold air. We living inside warm rock, where hot springs keeping us comfortable. We spin clothing from thread mosses, made, so wisewomen say, for that purpose. We come down from top for shearing thread trees, when thread has grown long but before it grows thick, except we take some thick thread, also, for making armor lining."

"Who harvests you?" asked I, piling the blankets in the back of the floater.

"Who is knowing but God, and perhaps not He. Great mystery. Harvesters coming in bright light, so much light we cannot see, and when they are going, some of us are going as well, but only here, in low places. If watchful, if in armor, we see light coming and crouch down, arms and legs tight, look like crab, and light goes over us, not touching us." Gavi placed her load of blankets in the floater, climbed in beside me and pointed: "That way."

I parked outside the cavern. Its narrow opening led into a wider, sand-floored area with a half circle of fire-blackened stones marking a hearth against a cracked and darkened wall. A small supply of moss chunks and dried wood lay against the wall. Gavi carried it to the fireplace, suggesting to the dogs that they might gather what wood they could find nearby in the forest. Several of them promptly did so, dragging in some sizable branches, which Gavi broke up and added to the pile before covering the entry with a blanket hung over a use-polished sapling trunk mounted above it. She lighted the fire with a striker, flint and steel, a device obviously handmade.

Other evidences of long habitation stood about. A water jar in a niche. A pile of stones that had probably been removed from the otherwise comfortable sand floor. We gathered around the warming flame as Gavi pointed out the features of the cavern.

"Small waterfall outside when it rains. Take water jar out, fill it, bring it back in. Deeper inside cave is good warmwall. Always we look for warmwall, warmfloor, warm place. We can sleep there. Fire is only for pretty and light, for seeing by. Near warmwall is small hot-water place, big enough for bath, not good to drink. You do not want sleeping outside in moss. Still are moss demons out there. Some of our animals turning to demons, that is how we know."

"Moss-demons?" I asked. "What is that?"

"You have people doing redmoss?" asked Gavi. "I know you must do, yes, for you know of it. So you know they lie on moss, moss eats them, all but bones. Then, later, moss uses bones for shaping new thing that is rising up in likeness of that person, having that person's voice, everything. Nighttime it comes hunting for more persons. It says sweetly to your ears and your nose, it is lying down on you, and in morning, nothing, no more person, not even bones. Just one more demon, or maybe bigger demon, full of two people. You must trap them, burn them. Our people were burning one that had six people in it."

"How did you know?" asked I.

"It was talking to us. All six voices, six names, six sets of people it was crying to us, 'Do not burn, please do not burn.' We were burning it anyway, but that was long long ago."

I poked the fire with a stick, considering. This could be campfire talk, scary stories, not greatly different from those Joram used to tell. "I was talking to the people back at camp about this business of predators attracting prey. Predators don't evolve attractants unless there's something attractable in the environment. So, before people came, what did redmoss eat?" I half expected Gavi would take time to invent something, but the response came immediately.

"Willogs." Gavi poked the fire in her turn. "You have likely not seen willogs. We chased them south of where you are."

"Plant or animal?"

"World says maybe half and half. Sometimes willog ups roots for walking around, grows long branches, thin like whips, for catching things it will eat. Catches them, wraps them, holds them until they die, then drops them on ground and runs lots of little rootlets inside them. Other times willog roots itself and grows a long time in one place, talks to itself, talks to word maker, talks to other things, makes poems, declaims in sounds, becomes point of interest."

"Willogs make sounds?" I said, feeling a chill. "In the forest?"

"When first we were coming to planet, we were living down here, where is warmer. Some of us were going into redmoss. Some, willogs ate. So, we were moving up, high, into the caves, but we were keeping watch on willogs. Somehow they were learning sounds from our people. We were not staying in the moss long enough for them to learn much. When we chase them away, they can only make a few words, sounds like bells, like children playing . . ."

So there was more than one intelligence on Muss. "We haven't seen any . . ." I faltered

"Oh, no. Sneaky things, willogs." She paused, thoughtfully. "I was saying something . . ."

"About the redmoss eating willogs, and then the willogs became moss demons?"

"Sometimes. If redmoss had crabs in it, new thing is being part willog, part crab. If redmoss had birds in it, new thing is part bird. Cannot fly. Bird bones very fragile, do not last when redmoss eats bird, so few bones for building on. Sometimes willog demons living like . . . do you have flat pastries, made on . . . a metal plate made hot on fire?"

"Pancakes, yes. On a griddle."

"Griddle, yes. Sometimes willogs are young, have few bones, redmoss eats them, makes demons squirming on ground like pancake. If combination works, sometimes willog becoming new thing that is living for long time."

I looked around to see how my fellow travelers would react to her words, only to find they had more or less fallen asleep around the fire. Only Behemoth lay at attention, eyes fixed on the two of us. I asked, "And if the redmoss had a person in it when it ate the willog?"

Gavi shrugged. "Never happened. Long, long ago, we chase willogs away from Night Mountain. We told them staying away or we burning them all. So, no willogs here falling into moss with persons in it."

"When was that?"

"Oh, hundreds years ago, I am guessing. Before Day Mountain people went away. Too much trouble, willogs. First one thing, then another thing. Good poets, though."

"A hundred years or more," I marveled.

Gavi nodded. "We had chronometers on ships. Some still working. Now we measure years by sun. A year on Moss is having days less than year on Earth, but Moss day is longer. Time of year about same. Jardinconnu had long years but no wintertime, books say. Good for growing flowers."

"You said the willogs caught things to eat? What things?"

"Our animals. Goats. Cats. Some of us before we were knowing about them."

"What did they eat before you got here?"

Gavi furrowed her brow, stroked her jaw with one finger, puzzled. "I am not knowing. Never asked."

"You've never seen any fauna, any animals, birds, fish?"

"Are being small birds, yes. Fishes, yes. Crabs. Mouses. We are thinking they were being on our ships when we came."

I took a deep breath. "Well! Do you introduce me to your people?"

Gavi shook her head, very seriously. "I think it is being wiser not."

"Why is that?"

She accompanied herself with hand gestures once more. "My people are fighting evermore, this tribe against that tribe." Hands darted at one another, inflicting blows. "Every ten, twenty years, Night Mountain tribes put away fighting each other, join together to have big battle against united tribes of Day Mountain. They fight for key . . ."

"What key?"

"Key to Splendor." Hands raised in adoration, invocation.

"What? To Splendor? There really is a Splendor?"

Gavi's eyes shifted away, then back, looking earnestly into mine. "So chiefs say. Other people say it is only symbol, but important to chiefs! For making strut, you know? Wartime is coming very soon. Already preparations are making. So, I am introducing you, one chief may keep you, sell you to your people for weapons for using against other chief. Or, chief could try using you some other way, probably nasty. They do not want you here. We have peace with Moss. We stay where we are, planet leaves us alone. So, my people are staying hidden hoping you will go away . . ."

That terribly sincere look, directly into my face told me at once that she was lying. Or perhaps, merely withholding part of the truth. I kept my eyes fixed on hers, smiling only slightly, skeptically, letting her see it. She flushed, glancing around at the others. Even Behemoth had his head down, his eyes closed. She murmured, "There is another place here. Separate. The night I am finding your album, I was being wakened by voices. Looking through crack in stone, I am seeing people, legs only, but people legs, not walking. I am hearing man's voice saying 'It was along here, right here.' I am hearing another voice saying, 'How could you be so stupid. I have told you a thousand times.'

"The legs were not walking. They floated . . ."

"Where was this?" I asked, almost in a whisper.

"In the rock. Inside the rock. When morning was coming, there was only rock, but I was not having dream! I was seeing it! I was! And I was thinking, this is Splendor, this place. To get there, one must be having key, so . . ."

"A spatial anomaly," I breathed. "We all know there's one here, close by. The Derac fell through it. Your ships fell through it. And your chiefs fight over it?"

"When your people are arriving, down by the big lake, my people, both Mountains, are deciding there is nothing here making your people stay very long. Many dangers, nothing valuable. My people think we let you alone, you will go soon, but if your people are knowing about us, you will not go, and our planet will be visited so all the worlds know what only our chiefs know. Chiefs do not want visitings. That is why I will not tell them of you."

I marshaled my thoughts, wanting to be as truthful with her as possible.

"I'm not sure I want to tell our people about you, either. Not all of them, at any rate. Some of what you've told me is valuable; I'll have to pass it on some way, but I can do it without mentioning you. I'm what is called an arkist, a preservationist. I brought the dogs as a preservation effort, an experiment to see if they can survive and reproduce on their own. This isn't the place we intend them to live, but this world is very similar to the place we planned for them, and we needed to see how they adapt to this kind of environment.

"I don't want to endanger that project, and I don't want to interfere with my brother's contract. He's trying to learn the language of the Mossen, and he hasn't had a chance to gct anywhere yet."

"What are Mossen?"

"The things, the flame-shaped things, the ones who dance in a circle, different colors."

Gavi laughed. "You mean words!"

"He's trying to learn the language of the Mossen, yes."

"Not language of words. Words are language."

"Ai sai," said Behemoth. "Wrrns."

Gavi looked at him. "You smelled them?"

Behemoth replied. "Ess."

"The dog did not tell you?" asked Gavi.

"He did tell me," I snarled, enlightenment hitting me in the face like a splash of frigid water. I was furious at myself. "Behemoth told me, and I wasn't listening! Not properly. It isn't color, is it? Each one of them has a different smell!"

"True," said Gavi, with dancing eyes. "You know! How wonderful. No one up there knows. I learned their talk when I was tiny, only little child. Come out, I am showing you." She lifted the blanket and moved out into the night, calling back, "Bring your light thing."

I brought my torch. Gavi was across the clearing, amid a thick growth. When I approached, Gavi took the torch, and said, "There. See!"

The plant had a rosette of huge, basal fronds, longer than I was tall, from the center of which grew even longer, arching stems, with a row of tiny bell shapes hanging under each one.

"I see it," I growled. "There was something like that on the moon."

"This is talker," said Gavi, pointing at the plant. "Those hanging down are words, not ripe yet. They grow in order, each one set of smells, each one word. They swell up, they make gas inside like balloon, they get little tentacles at bottom, for holding them down, little tentacles on sides to hold other words on each side, each one fitting only between fore-word and after-word, they get ripe, all at once, break free and they go dancing, dancing, all across world, telling World what is message, getting riper and riper, being smellier you know? When all ripe, they float up, go pop, seeds fall, new talkers grow. These ones, they are message from World."

"In smells!"

"In smells, yes. Until we are getting here, mosses did not see, did not hear, but they could smell. This is message to World saying maybe, 'Eat human beings,' or maybe 'No more moss-demons,' or something else."

"And you can . . . sniff these words?"

"When they ripen. I have very good nose. All our people have very good noses. That was our profession, long ago, being noses. When I was very, very small, I come down from up there to here. Baby is no threat to anything. Baby only plays. So, I learned all smells. A smell like morning means *morning*. A smell like death means *death*. *Death* also means *stop* or *finish*. *Morning* means *start, begin*. Each person has smell, but there is also a smell for all of us. That smell says *human*. Smell of blood means *hurt*, or *kill*. World can make words saying *kill all humans*, or *some humans*, or *single ones of us*."

"Or to let us live."

"True, but maybe not . . . dependable. This is why our people live up in abysses. They do not know moss language, as I do, but they know it is safer up there. We stay up there, nothing bothers us. When army comes down, very soon now, everyone is wearing armor and going forced march, very fast, so by time message growing against them in one place, they are gone already. When they are coming back, they are coming different way, where no messages are. So we are doing it, each time."

"What do you know about the moon?" I asked.

"The green moon? It is growing and shrinking like stories of Earthmoon. Only this one turns around, so it isn't always same side we see. Sometimes we see light flashes on it, like harvesters . . ."

"You said, you came down here as a child. Alone? Ah. Then you had parents like mine, gone or dead or something?"

"Something," said Gavi, solemnly. "Yours?"

"Dead. When I was young."

"Ah. So you are lonely child. Then you find him, your husband . . ."

"Witt. Yes. Then I was not lonely." At that moment, I was sure that this was true. Or should have been sure.

"But he has been gone many years. Can you not find someone else?"

I stared at her, seeing nothing there but compassion and true interest, to which I answered truthfully. "No. No one else is even . . . interesting to me, in that way . . . I have tried a few times to become interested, but, it doesn't work. When Witt went, I think that part of me went, too."

"Ah," said Gavi Norchis. Then she was silent for a moment, looking thoughtful. "He was first man for you?"

"Oh, oh yes."

There was a momentary silence. I broke the quiet. "What do you do now? What is your work?"

"I am scent mistress. It is laudable calling. We are regarding scent very highly, as science. So, I am scent mistress, and I use scent for moving people, for curing, for calming, for making them fall in love, making them hate, too, if I choose." She drew herself up, proudly. "I am best one, because I understand what I am doing, and others do not. Others make up words, this smell is label *ak*, that one is label *uk*. Then they make rules about *ak* and *uk*, *ak* is of category *warm*, *uk* is of category *cold*. *Ok* is of color *red*, *ik* is of color *blue*. Rules meaning nothing, just someone making up system. Like in olden times, people making up rules about stars, planets, called . . ."

"Astrology," I offered.

"That, yes. This star influences that, this planet something else. Even on Jardinconnu we were having them: 'For many credits, I will do plan of stars and planets for you to keep away from danger.' Foolish men are always buying such things. Ha-ha. Mankind does that, makes up systems, even when no sense in them."

I smiled, knowing she was right. "Our need to control our future by understanding the rules is greater than our need to know the truth."

"Is being true!" Gavi laughed. "When they follow system that means nothing about labels meaning nothing, they are feeling good even though achieving nothing except by accident. I use language belonging to World. I achieve much."

"You're speaking very frankly."

"We are two women, not? Meeting strangely? I give your wedding thing, I show you where it was. You give me your swearing you will not speak of me to anyone. Also, if one day you meet my people, you do not speak of me to them. I have been saying much to you! Too much. Our meeting here is secret thing."

"Will you teach me Moss's language?"

Gavi considered my request, head bowed, forehead furrowed. "You should learn it yourself for understanding best. Rise early, smell dawn, ten mornings. Ten mornings is one word, subtle variations. Common smell is all mornings. Variations are other words: rainy morning, cold morning, sunshiny morning. Smell where tree is dying, until it is dead. You will have several words. Fated to die. Started dying. Almost dead. Dead. Rotted. Follow words dancing in woods, be seeing what happens where they dance. Does this growth start and that stop? Is redmoss dwindling into nothing or growing into huge levee. You will see, and you will have message. From that, you can make meanings for words. This is what I did, as child. If you reach hard place, I will help."

"The words are dancing over and over again in the meadow near our camp. From the colors, I think it was the same ones in the same order every time."

"Ah," said Gavi. "Telling you something important."

"Whatever it is, we are not hearing it. Can you at least tell us what that message is?"

Gavi shook her head. "That message is where you are, and I do not have one idea. I would need to be smelling for myself, and I am not safe going alone so far."

"If we smell the message, back there, and then come here and tell you the smells . . . ?"

Gavi shook her head. "How can you tell me? Some are easy. Rotten meat. Smell of apples. Smell of smoke, fifty different kinds . . . But others, how define?"

"We need a machine," said I. "Something to measure the smells, analyze them, reproduce them, in order. If we had that, could you tell us what it means?"

She nodded. "If you could be doing it quietly, without telling bad people."

Clare asked plaintively, "Where did you get the seeds and tools for your gardens?"

I looked up, confused. There Clare stood, fully clothed, having changed back into her own form and dressed herself without our noticing. Her face, however, was still changing. Gavi leapt to her feet, crying "Demons! Moss-demons!"

"No," said I, catching hold of her. "No, no. They . . . they have two forms, that's all. One doglike form, one human form. Clare has changed back as we have been talking."

"All of them?" Gavi shivered.

"No. Just three. Adam, Frank, and Clare. The others are true dogs, the puppies are true puppies. They are smarter than dogs used to be, and healthier, and they live longer, but otherwise they are dogs in every respect."

"Why?" Gavi cried. "This is evil thing!"

"No," said Clare. "This was to help dogs and learn about dogs, and we volunteered. I asked about the seeds."

Gavi answered, mechanically. "We had supplies, seeds, farm tools, small farm animals. We were moving to Jardinconnu, for living on new world, necessary food growing, necessary flower planting. Our people said on way they would make detour, seeking Splendor, for Hessing headman had old map given him by Tharstian. It was joke! No one was really believing it. It was kind of playing they did, my ancestors. So, our people were misbehaving, making little side trip, getting caught in space hole, and then this place and no way back. Ships had what we needed for planting, growing. Later, when Day Mountain went away, we shared supplies with them."

Clare nodded. "What animals do you have?"

"Chickens, for eggs. Goats, for milk and leather. Some goats got away, one time, and redmoss ate them quickly. Goat moss demons came home, crying for letting in. We burned them, crushed bones. Now we are very careful with livestock. When I learned moss language, words say to me no goats, goats eat talkers, eat other necessary things! We have also cats. No dogs."

Clare said, "You could come with us on the floater, smell the message in the evening, stay with us, then we would return you."

Gavi thought about it. "I am trusting you. I am not trusting others of you. Things happen. Maybe others would find me there and would not let me come back. No. I am telling you. You have things that make fires in sky? We had them, long ago."

"Flares? Signals?"

"Signal flares, yes. I am explaining something: On Forêt we were not speaking common speech each day. Learning it in schools but not speaking it. So, when our people are coming here, so many words we do not use anymore. We read aloud to each other from old books for not forgetting, but we do forget. What is plumbing? What is computer? What is hot pan ... griddle? Now I am speaking to you in Standard, but our talk being much changed. I am remembering book words, how they go together. Probably I sound strange ..."

"Only a little," said I. "You were asking about signal flares."

"Yes. Red, I am thinking. From where I live, I can see your sky. Today, just past, is day one, day of our meeting. You are counting, I am counting. On day seven, I am watching your sky when dark is coming. If you want meeting me, make three red flares in early dark. Be doing this several times in evening, if I do not see first time, I will see later time. If you do not, count again, seven days. Each seven, I will be looking at sky. If I see flares, I will be coming down in next day or day after. If you are alone or with these people or dogs, I will find you. If you bring other people, you will not find me."

"Dogs?"

She rose to her feet. "Protecting you, yes. Dogs are ... fine. Now you come to bath place and warmwall!"

Gavi took me deeper into the cave, showing me the bathing place and the warmwall as she spread her own blankets against it. She pressed the album projector into my hands before rolling herself against the wall, eyes shut, already seeming asleep. I returned to the outer chamber, where Adam had joined Clare in human shape. His muzzle was also very slightly extended. Changing the jaw and reshaping the tongue always took time; the calmer the situation, the more time it took. Being very frightened or completely enraged made the change happen so fast they didn't have time to undress first, as when Adam had changed on Earth that time, almost getting caught at it.

"What do you think?" I murmured.

"She smells perfectly honest," said Clare. "Friendly. Not hiding anything or falsifying anything. Usually, we can smell that."

"I was thinking more about what she had to say. Moss-demons. Willogs. Both might be dangerous to dogs. Moreover, she identified a plant as the message grower, and it looks exactly like one I saw on the moon, only larger. There was a smell there, Adam, remember? Just as we left, like an assault!"

Adam said slowly, "Moon, planet, both from same source ..."

I nodded. "During formation, meteoritic ejecta went from Moss to moon, from Jungle to moon, and vice versa. Possibly it still happens, now and then. Will we find willogs all three places? Moss-demons in all three places? Is that what happened to Witt? Is there redmoss on Jungle? And how did my little album get here? He had it in his hand when he left . . ."

"Space anomaly," said Clare. "We knew there was one. The Derac fell into it."

I stared at the device in my hands. "Keep in mind what she said about harvesters. 'They come in much light.' We saw a flash on the moon. The people on Jungle saw a flash when Witt and the others disappeared . . . So much information! How do I pass it on without mentioning her?"

Adam yawned, moving his shortened jaw from side to side to settle it into place. "You can tell Gainor. He'll keep his counsel, and he'll know what to do, won't he?"

I nodded. Gainor had been at this longer than I had. Perhaps he would. "If you don't mind, I'm going to use that nice hot-spring place to take a bath."

Adam waved me off. "We'll come make up our beds shortly."

Gavi was kneeling beside the stone trough, her hand in the water, when I approached.

"Oh, sorry," I said. "I was going to bathe in it. I thought you were asleep."

"Oh, yes, you must bathe." Gavi smiled. "I was falling in sleep, then I thought of putting some scent in it for you. Nice, not? Is excellent for relaxing."

"That's very kind."

It was relaxing. The scent, whatever it was, for I could barely detect it, seemed to penetrate to my very bones. I did something I had not done in a while: took Matty's album, the Seventh Symphony, from my pack and let it play softly as I soaked. I opened my eyes to see Gavi leaning against the wall, listening. I smiled, letting her know it was all right to share it with me as my very bones softened, and my thoughts softened, flowing together. I found myself following odd chains of associations that had no meaning for me. No matter. I felt wonderfully clean and totally limp. I dried myself with my shirt and put on a clean one before leaving the hot-spring area to lie down.

As I was doing so, Gavi approached. "The words they sang, to that music. The words about being forsaken, will you tell them to me again?"

I said yes, I'd tell them to her, and she went away. I slept soundly and long, only to come straight up off the blanket to the sound of a strangled howl. One of the lanterns was alight, on dim, and I saw Gavi rising and starting for the cave entrance. I leapt up and followed, hearing that strange, strangled howl, now accompanied by a wild outcry from the dogs.

As I went through the outermost cavern, I picked up a lantern and turned it high, pushing past the hanging blanket into the barely lighted world beyond. I saw the struggle immediately, Behemoth, caught in something that was strangling him, the other dogs attacking the something, without success. I saw Behemoth's legs leave the ground, he was hanging by his throat in sort of thicket . . .

And then Gavi went past me with the water jar from the cavern and flung the contents over the strange growth that was killing my lovely dog, and it shuddered all over and went limp. Behemoth fell in a heap, I yelled for Clare and Frank, both of them came running and we struggled to get Behemoth breathing again. At some point, I heard the thicket growl and shake itself, and when I finally looked up, it was gone.

"What?" I demanded of Gavi.

"Moss-demon," she said. "Mostly made from willog! This is why we are sleeping inside! This is why we are not going sticking noses in things outside at night!"

"What did you throw on it?"

"Stuff to make it tangle itself, forget what it was doing," she said, her manner indicating it would not do any good for me to ask for details.

Behemoth's neck was scratched, but he was otherwise unhurt. Scramble was licking his muzzle and whining softly to him. I contented myself with saying, "Gavi saved your life, Behemoth. Maybe someday we can return the favor."

He gave me a look that said, "I am aware of my obligations." We all went back to bed. Gavi Norchis woke me early to tell me where I could see the most spectacular falls and the most interesting growths.

"When we come here," I said, "We have to spend at least one night sleeping out. How do we protect ourselves . . . ?"

She handed me a tiny pottery bottle, stopped with a cork. "This I am making for you this morning. Rub on before sleeping. Is taking only tiny bit. Moss-demons are not liking it, and enough is here for several trips. Now, please be telling me the words in the music you were playing."

She had certainly earned that and a good deal more. She had a quick memory. I needed to repeat it only twice.

She left me, saying, "I am telling you, do not bother talkers! Moss is not liking people bothering talkers."

I took the words seriously enough that I searched out a talker, one with slightly unripe Mossen on it, and showed it to the dogs and train-ers so they could sniff it from the end of one long stalk to the other.

"The smells are already there, a little," said Adam. "Like fruit not ripe, it hints what it's going to be. Why didn't we figure this out before?"

I said, bowing toward Behemoth, "Behemoth did. He tried to tell me. I even smelled the succession of odors myself, when they were dancing, but I thought the smells came from the forest."

Behemoth's nostrils quivered, but he took no other notice. We spent the rest of the day sight-seeing. I found what I was almost certain were gems in the dry gravel bed beneath a sometime fall, not clear stones, of course, only large pebbles with the dull matte surface created by cen-turies of tumbling in gravel. I spent a pleasant morning, overturning rocks and looking at those beneath, pocketing a selection of the largest gems in green, blue, and red. Emerald, sapphire, and ruby were chemi-cally allied, differing only in their trace elements, and I had no doubt that's what these stones were. The plateau was of the same source as Planet Stone, after all, which was full of huge, pure gems, so the dis-covery didn't surprise me. What did surprise me was how different the plants were, here where the mists fell. They were huge in comparison to their counterparts in the drier lands, and they were alive with small animals, crabs, mice, other rodenty-looking things, birds of at least ten different kinds. I asked the dogs to collect samples—gently, please, without biting them in half—and even though I'd brought the sample boxes along mostly for show, by evening we'd filled them all and were putting the overflow specimens into the collection bags I'd carried in my pockets.

We saw no dancing Mossen, though we did record some remarkably musical bell sounds that went on for some time during the dusk.

"Willogs," I murmured to myself, totally convinced that Night Mountain had not chased the willogs as far south as they had assumed. The sounds weren't near enough to worry about. We slept warm in the cavern for the second night and left Gavi a note of thanks before departing the next morning. That night, halfway back to the base, we were considerably less casual about sleeping in the open than we had been on the way out. Two of us stood guard, turn and turn about.

WALKING SUNSHINE AGAIN

⋮ Once Walking Sunshine had ears, it knew it needed a voice, but need makes no pattern, as the World said. Only trial and error does that! It was difficult. The eyes and the ears had been only receptors of a kind. The World was familiar with receptors, and so were willogs. Easy things. A bit different, but not difficult. But a voice that would do bells and singing and declaiming and so many other things. It took forever!

The only easy parts were the air puffers. Every word had lots of air puffers to emit the smells, and anything a word could do, a willog could do. Voice boxes were very much harder. There had never been a pattern for voice boxes. There was no pattern for tongue! For lips! How did one make them to move quickly, flexibly, to curl and shape and lift, both sides, front and back! Walking Sunshine had grown a tongue fifteen times! And the lips, even more. Walky had done them over and over and was still not satisfied. The result was getting close. Close enough to summon many friendly willogs and share spores with them to show them how it was done. Now the pattern was there, all the spores had that pattern. The new sprouts were few, still, but they would be many soon. Soon, many willogs would be sprouted with eyes to see, ears to hear sounds, and voices to make sounding words. Much nicer to have the equipment in place rather than having to grow it all, bit by bit.

In recent days moss messages had come and gone, flowing from north to south. Humans, only a few, from Tall Rock were moving toward the wonder place, chopping signs on trees, piling stones to make markers. Walky had seen this happen several times before. The few humans would go to the wonder place and then back to Tall Rock. Then, more humans would follow the trail to the wonder place. Perhaps this would be a good time to introduce oneself and all the other speaking willogs. As was widely known, Tall Rock had one human who could hear World talk. Surely that human would walk with the others, and if Walking Sunshine were there, too, things could be explained! Not only Walky-self but the other speakers.

Walky lifted its talker branches experimentally. The latest crop of messages, concerning the advisability of having voices, was almost ripe. In fact, one branch was ripe! Walky shook it a little, loosening the first word, which, attached as it was by its tendrils, pulled the second one loose, then all the others in sequence. By the time the first message had danced off, several others were swelling into ripeness. Walking Sunshine shook its branches, loosening them all. When the last one had disappeared into the forest, it stepped out of its talker leaves and strode northward on nimble roots, toward the wonder place.

DURAS DROM

⋮ The evening that we were on our way back to the base, as I learned later, Drom called his people together and announced formally, for the record, what had happened to their vanished colleagues. No one seemed particularly surprised until he mentioned the number.

"Eighty people have gone," said Drom. "There are only forty-seven of us left here. Most of us have spent some time out in the moss; some of us have done the redmoss; those of us left here have been able to stop doing the redmoss even though a few of us had to be locked up for a while to break the habit. We're five men short of the original strength, and as I'd asked for ten more, we're actually understaffed by fifteen. I'm going to report the redmoss to ESC . . ."

There were indrawn breaths from a few, only a few.

He continued. "They know about it by now, because Jewel Delis found out about it, and their group reports to ESC. The only way we can keep ourselves employed is to report it and report it as an inimical force."

"Because there are no penalties for falling to inimical forces?" jeered a voice.

"That's exactly right," Drom replied, affably. "We incur no penalties for falling to an inimical force we did not know was present when we came here or did not know immediately was dangerous while we were here. We knew it was addictive as hell, but we didn't know it was fatal until Jewel Delis saw it eat Bar Lukha. If I report only to PPI, they'll continue sending retirees because BuOr management won't admit to knowing what's happened here. We all know why. Reporting to PPI and ESC both will keep our hands clean, and probably Earth Enterprises will do something about it."

"What's the linguist come up with?"

"Nothing, so far. It's been suggested that the noises we hear off in the forest are the Mossen mimicking us, so we'll come to their dance."

"Why?" demanded a commissary worker, from the back row. "If they get us together to talk to us, why don't they talk?"

"We can't answer that question! That's why we sent for a linguist. Perhaps the Mossen usually make their noises to attract something that serves a purely botanical purpose, in which case, there may be no language and the message we found, the one written on bark, could have come from . . . someone who's gone off in the mosses, gone off his head, and is dead now."

"You mean it was faked!" someone cried.

Drom frowned, shook his head, said unwillingly, "I'm accepting the possibility. I got you together tonight in order to reinforce what was ordered earlier. Stay away from the redmoss. To that, I'll add, get all your records in order. Bring everything up to date. Earth Enterprises will probably pay us a visit very shortly, and we should at least look like we know what we're doing."

His instructions evoked some grumbling from the commissary and maintenance workers, who said they didn't need reminding, they did their jobs and their work was always up-to-date. Which it was, Drom conceded when they mobbed him after the meeting, and why shouldn't it be? Their routines would be the same on Moss as on Stone as on Earth. Drom hadn't been talking about them, he said. They were only asked to the meeting so they'd know what was happening.

Mollified, they went back to their up-to-datedness, while other staffers began grumpy, in some cases frustrating or futile, nightlong searches for mislaid, postponed, and misfiled records and reports.

Drom was already as up-to-date as he could be. He went back to his quarters, took a long, warm soak in the steeping bath, made himself a pot of tea the med tech had recommended for stress, and got into bed with a fileboard full of other people's reports he had to read and initial. He'd planned to stay up and wait for Jewel Delis's return from the plateau, but there was no guarantee she'd get back this evening. One day there, one day to look around, one day back had been the plan, but they could just as easily have decided to spend two days there, especially if they found something interesting. He decided to leave the shutters open. If they did come back before he went to sleep, he'd see the lights.

The reports were the same old stuff, nothing new. No new species, no new ideas, nothing happening on the linguistics front. At noon, the linguist, Paul Delis, had shown up at the commissary with all four concs, and the man in charge had had to threaten him with arrest if he didn't put them back where they belonged. Delis had stormed off in a fury. Temperamental man. Like a kid who'd never grown up, never stopped having tantrums. He hadn't put the concs back in their cases, hadn't even taken them into the house. Late that afternoon, Drom had seen all four of them running through the mosses with Paul Delis egging them on. He should have arrested the guy, rounded up the concs, but it was late, he was tired, he had the meeting coming up. He decided to let them riot. Maybe, if he was lucky, the redmoss would eat them, or the concs, at least.

He read and initialed, surprising himself by feeling drowsy. The med tech had perhaps, just perhaps, known what he was doing. He dropped the fileboard on the floor and lay back, dimming the light. After a little time he slept, knowing he was sleeping, glad of it. His dream was full of wonderful smells, like good food and ripe fruit and being home on Dabber's World, the way it had been when he was a kid . . .

When the door opened, he was glad of that, too. Something smelled wonderful, very calming, pleasant. He opened his eyes just enough to see who it was . . .

"Lukha," he murmured. "Lukha. Glad you've come back . . ."

THE MOSS DEMON

: The dogs, the pseudodogs and I had an uneventful trip back to the encampment, arriving about when we had said we would, late evening, still not totally dark though close to it. I drove the floater while the trainers sorted through the specimen boxes and the dogs padded along behind.

"I'll go past the headquarters' building," I murmured. "If Drom's around, we'll let him know we're back."

"It's dark," said Adam. "Nobody there."

I drove along the building, noticing the amber glow from a large window, incurious about it, but brought to sudden panicky awareness by Behemoth, who erupted into a fury of growling and barking at the dimly glowing window. Something moved inside. I halted the floater, staring, unable to accept what I saw. Lukha. Bar Lukha. Bending above Drom on the bed, lowering himself over the sleeping man, Lukha, the dead man.

Enlightenment came, late but complete. "Moss-demon!" I screamed. "Behemoth smells it."

Adam had seen it, too. All four of them ran for the door, along with all the dogs but Veegee and Scramble, who remained standing over the puppies, Scramble's lips drawn back to show every tooth at full length, Veegee's head thrown back as she uttered a wavering, ululating howl. Adam ran through the office door and kept going toward the door to the bedroom, I behind him, bursting into the inner room, the dogs' nails rattling on the hard floor. Clare and Frank were behind us, shouting, all of us making as much noise as possible to rouse someone, anyone in the encampment.

"Pull it off him," I cried, at the top of my voice.

Behemoth was already doing so, mouthful by mouthful, for the thing came apart under his assault, little rootlets pulling out of Drom's flesh with a tearing sound. All the dogs were at it, biting and spitting, then clawing at their mouths to remove tendrils that tried to root there.

"Gloves," said Adam, drawing on his own to pull handfuls of the stuff from Drom's face, his mouth and eyes. "Put on gloves, or it'll root in your hands."

Drom's mouth came clear, and he gasped weakly.

I had attacked with my bare hands and was now trying to rub the stuff off, for it was rooting into my fingers. "Dogs," I cried. "Back off. Don't get it in your mouths."

Growling, the dogs backed off, clawing at their mouths. Since Adam and the others were busy with Drom, I pulled the tendrils out of my hands, put on my gloves, and pulled the tendrils out of the dogs' mouths and tongues. They came loose easily, unlike the ones on my own flesh, as though they found the dogs' flesh unsuitable. Perhaps the moss-demon had to seek human flesh because it had human flesh in it. Wasn't that what Gavi had said? It created selves like the things it ate?

Something moved at the corner of my vision, and I saw a chunk of moss inching its way toward me. I cried, "Wolf, get a disposal bag, quick. There's a pack on the floater." As he fled, I chopped off a chunk of the approaching moss, fished a specimen bag from my pocket, and sealed it up with great care before kicking the crawling stuff away.

Wolf returned in moments with a box of disposal bags in his mouth, half a dozen PPI men following him, alerted by the howling and shouting. Adam, Clare, and Frank were still busy pulling the last of the stuff off Drom while the gathered workers stuffed the writhing moss into disposal bags.

"God," said one. "There's bones in this stuff."

The med tech yelled from the door, "Who's hurt?"

I called him over and spoke rapidly, suggesting that he use magnification to be sure all the tendrils had been removed from Drom's body, that what they had pulled off was some kind of moss monster, that they had to dispose of all parts of it at once by burning.

"Including the bones?" he asked, staring at the chunks of material being bagged, wriggling moss with thighbones in it, rib bones, a skull.

"Yes," I said, shivering. "Including the bones." My mind went off on a tangent. There had been two people in the moss when Lukha was eaten. He and a woman. "How many sets of bones?" I cried.

"One skull," someone grunted. "One set of legs and arms."

Lukha. Why only Lukha?

One of the PPI men went off to get the flame cannons from the armory, items they had never had to use. When he returned with the equipment, Adam went with him to supervise the burning while I helped the med tech find all the tendrils on Drom's face and chest, arms and legs. It was like pulling hairs, except that these hairs wriggled and tried to reroot themselves. As we worked, Drom gasped and blinked and eventually was able to tell us with reasonable lucidity what his name was, what his job was, and where he was at the moment.

"Lukha," he said thickly. "I saw Bar Lukha . . ."

I had been thinking up a story to deal with this inevitability since I had begun pulling rootlets out of the dogs. "Yes," I told him, raising my voice so Clare, Frank, and Adam would hear me. "We all saw Bar Lukha. We might not have been so quick to realize what we were seeing if we hadn't run into one of your old fellows out there in the moss. He told us when the redmoss eats a person, later it takes the form of that person." I'd decided on this story to warn the people at the base without betraying Gavi's trust.

"Who was the person who told you?" Drom asked in a feeble voice. "Which one of our people?"

"Have no idea," I said, still loudly. "The dogs were all off running, and the others had hiked up to one of the falls. An old man came and talked with me for a few moments and warned me about the moss-demons, and when he heard the others coming, he ran off. He didn't mention his name."

"Moss-demons," said the tech. "What next? This is the craziest world . . . Wait. Hold still. There's a few of those damned tendrils still wriggling in your navel . . ."

I excused myself as the tech began an intimate survey of Drom's nether parts. I had to be sure all my people and the dogs knew the story I had just told. I had to take the sample of moss material and tendrils to the ESC so they could compare it with the earlier redmoss samples, and both things had to be done at once. It had been a long several days.

Outside, half a dozen men were burning the pile of moss chunks. Though the pile was not large, it showed a sullen insusceptibility. Every chunk had to be pulled apart into smaller and smaller bits with the fire kept on each bit until it turned unequivocally to ash, after which the men poured flammable substances on it and burned it again. The bones stood out against the dark ashes, pale blotches on the ground. One of the men marched into the space and tramped them into fragments, all but the skull, which resisted breaking.

Lathey, the man who had taken Lukha's place as Drom's deputy, asked, "Should we treat the ashes, you think? We've got acids we could use. Or barrels of wet-set we could mix the ashes with. You know, I keep thinking of spores . . . They can be really tenacious of life. Some won't even burn."

"That sounds like a good idea," I mumbled, half-paralyzed by the idea of fireproof spores. "Pour the wet-set right on top of the ashes, and stir them in. Be sure to get all the bone fragments in."

A sensible thing to have done in the first place! If the spores were fireproof, they would have spread for miles. Could the thing regrow into another Lukha?

Lathey went off, shouting orders. I found Adam, who had been outside when I spoke, and told him what I had said and why, asking him to reinforce it with each of the others, including the dogs.

"We'll do it together," he said. "I'll get them rounded up . . ."

"You do it now, Adam," I said. "I have to get out to ESC with this sample of moss demon."

"You kept some of it?" he whispered, eyes wide. "You kept some of the damned stuff?"

"I think it's safer to have some and know what it's doing than not have some and not know, Adam. I hope it didn't escape your attention that since a good number PPI men or women or wives of PPI men were lost in the moss, we may have that many more of these things wandering around out there. Plus, if, as Lathey suggested, the thing had fireproof spores, the possibility of thousands more."

⋮ Lethe woke reluctantly and took some time to be convinced I needed to see him at once. When I arrived at the island, he had Darrow and Wyatt with him, and we walked to the laboratory in virtual silence.

"Tell us," Lethe said, when we were seated inside.

I told them the current version, the old man and his warning, what we had seen on our return, what we had done.

"I brought you a sample," I said, laying the wrapper on the table. "I would suggest you treat it as hostile, certainly don't touch it with bare skin. I think we got all of it out of Drom, but I'm not positive. It kept trying to crawl back onto him or onto me even after we'd thrown it some distance away. We've burned all the rest, and I've suggested the men stir the ashes into wet-set. However, Drom's deputy, Lathey, mentioned fireproof spores, and if there were such things, they've been spread with the smoke. Please see if this stuff has spores. If it does, we need to know if they burn, and if they don't, we need to get the hell off this world."

"It actually looked like Lukha?" asked Sybil.

"It actually looked like Lukha, not just shape and size, but facial features and the way it moved. Do I know whether it actually looked like that or only made me feel I saw that? No, I don't know. So far as I could see while we were ripping the stuff off him, there was no part of what we tore away that was as smooth as skin or in long filaments that resembled hair. The old man said they came at night, so the effect may depend upon a lack of light and the use of shadow or suggestion combined with some kind of chemical hypnotic released into the air. I don't know. I know it's called a moss-demon, I know we all saw it as Lukha, and I brought you a sample, and that's the limit of my information."

"Gainor Brandt will be here tomorrow," said Lethe. "He's brought some new technical help."

He sounded resentful, but I wasn't. "Ornel, be glad he's bringing help. It's no reflection on you, and at this juncture, we need all the help we can get. I have some other news for you. The language of the Mossen is not color. It's odor. The Mossen that dance on the meadow are not separable things. They're all one message. They are created at the same time, in a certain order; they keep that order, because that order is a message conveyed in smells."

They looked at me as though I had lost my mind.

"Smells," said Wyatt, skeptically. "And you know this because . . ."

Since I could not tell him the truth about either Gavi or Behemoth, I had invented a story for this as well. "Because I saw a message being . . . born from its parent plant. They grow, as a group, all in a row. They're botanical. They create some kind of gas inside themselves, hydrogen, I'd suppose. They have little tendrils at the bottom and the sides to hold themselves down and together; they come off the plant all in one string; and they sort of float-skip themselves away, still in the same order."

"Of course you recorded this?" asked Lethe, dubiously.

"I did not," I said, gritting my teeth. "I was walking around, just sight-seeing, and I'd left all the paraphernalia on the floater. Once I knew what I was looking at, I stayed right where I was, so I wouldn't miss any of it. I'm sure we can find another one to record. I've seen the mother plant around here, I just didn't know what it was at the time."

"Around here?" asked Durrow. "Really?"

"A basal rosette, rather thick, with leaves as long as I am tall. No. That was in the mistlands. Things grow bigger there. Maybe not that large around here, Abe. Anyhow, out of the center of the rosettes come long, arching stems with the little bell shapes hung beneath them in a row. You may already have samples in your collection, but listen, this is important. We must not collect any more of them. The plants that grow the messages must not be bothered. We didn't disturb the Mossen because we thought they might be people, might have language. They aren't people, they don't have language, but something upstream of them does. We have to shift our scruples to whatever creature or being is actually speaking. Once the message is . . . born or detached, we'd probably be safe in capturing the whole string if we had to."

"If we had to?"

"I don't think we have to. All we have to do is set up an apparatus that can analyze and reproduce the odors produced by the Mossen, one at a time, as they pass. If PPI doesn't have any such paraphernalia, surely ESC does, or you could get it . . ."

Wyatt said, "Of course we have scent analyzers. It's part of regular survey gear, used in identifying botanicals, determining emissions, perfumes, if you will. We gather the same data on insects, birds, animals, as pheromones are often important for reproduction."

"But you've never used it here? Why not?"

Lethe shot the words at me one at a time, like bullets. "Because, dear lady, we have not done a survey here. Not until we have the permission of the local population."

I was too tired to get involved in whys. "In this case we'll have to do the survey to identify the local population. If you can get the equipment set up by the meadow where the dance goes on, we can analyze the smell of each one of the things as they pass. Does each smell produce some kind of symbol or chart that can be used for comparison?"

"A profile, yes," said Abe Darrow. "Made by its constituent molecules. Of course, they may be mixed with ambient odors from the local vegetation. They may be hard to isolate."

"They don't mix," I said. "I've noticed several times that odors on this planet are as limited in duration as tones played on a . . . a flute or a trumpet. You get a note, then the next one, and not a mixture of the two. So we get the charts or symbols or whatever, then we can give those charts to Paul."

"To Paul," Lethe said coldly. "Why?"

"Because he knows how to figure out languages," I said. "And a word is a word is a word, no matter how it's conveyed. Right?"

"I suppose," said Lethe. "We'll let Gainor decide."

"Let him decide," I conceded. "But in the meantime, get that equipment over to the meadow so it will be ready when he gets here."

⁝ Paul was in his bed, as were three concs, sleeping in an untidy sprawl of appendages. I stood in the doorway, staring at the pile. Things weren't going well on the language front, obviously. Now I had to get Paul thinking about a language of odors without telling him. Unless, perhaps, he should just be told. I couldn't go on forever stroking his ego. Eventually he had to learn about cooperation. Or was that thought fatuous?

I shut the door and left him as he was. The day had contained quite enough excitement. The next would no doubt offer its own challenges, and, one hoped, its own solutions. Halfway back to my own room, I hesitated. Three concs. I tried momentarily to convince myself that the other one, whichever one it was, was back in its case. Or under the bed. Or somewhere.

Shaking my head, I retraced my steps, tiptoeing into his room and peering into the closet, under the bed, behind the table where he'd been working. No conc. I went into the conc dormitory, so-called, where the four cases sat on low stands. All of them empty. The food bin full of food but empty of conc.

I searched the bathroom area, the living room, kitchen area, went through the door into the dog wing, woke the dogs and asked them to search.

"Whigh?" asked Behemoth.

"He wants to know which conc," Adam translated from the door to his room, where he stood half-asleep.

"Does it make a difference?"

He merely looked at me. I flushed, went back the way I had come, into Paul's bedroom once more. Of course the concs smelled different. The one on top with purple hair, that was Lavender. Beneath it was yellow hair, Marigold; and on the far side was Salvia, blue. The redhead, Poppy, was missing.

I went back again to give Behemoth the information. He and the other dogs, except for Scramble, went through the bedrooms, through the closets, then out the door and over the fence. They were gone for some little time, returning in a group, Behemoth's hair raised around his neck, his lips drawn back from his teeth.

"Rrr-igh," he yelped.

"Poppy was in the redmoss?"

"Ess. Wahs. 'awn."

"He means she's gone," said Adam. "He smelled her trail, into the redmoss, but now gone."

I went at once to the administration building, where the med tech and several of the staffers were still lingering while four men mixed wet-set into the ashes.

Lathey was among them, and I drew him aside. "Did you see my brother or any of the concs outside today?"

His lips thinned, he frowned.

I said, "It's all right. I know he does stupid things. Tell me."

"He brought them over to the commissary and got run off. The man in charge threatened to put him under restraints if he didn't get the concs back where they belonged. Later we saw him outside, in the moss, chasing all four of them, laughing like a maniac. Drom said let it be until you got back, then he'd decide what to do."

"One of the concs evidently was ... uh, eaten by the redmoss. It's missing, and the dogs tracked it to the redmoss."

"Bones?"

"Haven't looked, but as I understand it, concs don't really have bones. More like, cartilage. In which case ..."

His face hardened. "In which case we could have something looking like a conc come around real soon. And before that happens, I'm taking the concs that are left and putting them in stasis. Our damned linguist, pardon me, ma'am, I know he's your brother, but he'll just damned well have to do without them."

⋮ The concs could not be removed without waking Paul, who was not cooperative. I had foreseen as much. Paul was removed by Frank and Adam while the concs and their cases were taken from the building and put somewhere else; I didn't ask where, and no one told me. I did ask the men to take the conc food, as well, and I reminded them the concs needed to eat every seven to ten days even when in stasis.

"How dared they!" Paul shouted, when Frank and Adam went off on business of their own and Paul was allowed to return to his own rooms. "How dared they. Well, they can damned well solve their own linguistic problem. I'm sick of it. Sick of this place."

Thus far during his tantrum, I had followed my usual habit of patient soothing and sympathizing. The rage went on without tempering, however, and finally I reached the point I had always sedulously avoided: I became angrier than he was.

"They'll learn who they're dealing with," he shouted.

"They already know," I said, coldly. "And they're sick of you. They don't care if you leave. They wish you would, so they can get someone else who will solve the problem. The head of Earth Enterprises is due to arrive any day. They're going to ask for your contract to be revoked so they can issue a new one."

It was the first time I had seen Paul speechless. He actually turned pale. "They're what?"

"I think you heard me, Paul. They have grounds. You disobeyed the regulations, and in doing so you've endangered every person on this base."

"Don't be ridiculous," he sneered.

I told him what I suspected as though it were proven fact. No point in temporizing! "You told Poppy to lie down on the redmoss."

He flushed. His mouth twisted.

"You told it to. What was it, an experiment?"

". . . see what happened . . ." he mumbled. ". . . tired of it . . ."

"Well, you saw what happened. No more Poppy. Now let me spell things out for you. It's widely thought that the concs are created by Zhaar technology, that is, with the use of shape changer matrices. We also found out recently that when someone or something living is absorbed by the redmoss, the redmoss makes a simulacrum of that person, and it comes back looking for other people to eat. It happened here, tonight, in the headquarters building, while you slept through it. A simulacrum of Bar Lukha came back and tried to eat Drom! It was scary. At one point I had moss crawling after me trying to get onto my skin again.

"Now, can you imagine a simulacrum of Poppy with a shape changer matrix in it coming back for you? Or wandering around out there building an army of Poppys? Can you imagine how your career is going to go down the tube when this little escapade of yours is known throughout ESC and PPI and every commercial agency they've ever worked with?"

He sat down, abruptly.

"You have one chance to save your reputation. I found something out on this trip. I found out that each Mossen is a separate word in a message, with a particular place in a word order, and each word is conveyed by odor. ESC has equipment to detect the odors and analyze them. They're going to do it tomorrow night when the Mossen dance. Then they'll give the information to you. I may even have a clue as to the system. Just like spoken language, it may have evolved as mimicry. The word for death smells like something dead. The word for rain smells like rain. What they do for verbs, I haven't a notion, but presumably you're bright enough to figure it out."

"How . . . how did you find that out?" he said, his face very red, rage simmering just under the surface.

I told him the story I'd told everyone else, concluding, "They opened up one at a time, starting with the one farthest out, and as each one opened, there was a separate, distinct odor . . ."

"Before, you said it was color, patterns . . ."

"I didn't say it was color or pattern, I said the colors and patterns were unique and interesting. They also happen to be associated with particular odors. Pink ones do seem to smell alike, so do blue ones, and so on."

"Why odor, why *not* color?"

"Because until humans got here, this world was blind and deaf," I shouted, angry, mostly at myself for not having realized this immediately. "It couldn't have had language dependent upon seeing or hearing, because nothing native to this planet has eyes or ears!"

"You're saying they had noses?" he screamed.

"Chemical receptors, which is the next best thing. Most plants do."

"Go away," he said, petulantly. "Just go away."

"Fine. Take the chance or don't take it. By tomorrow night, it'll be too late to change your mind."

I left him. I also locked the door on my side of the living room as well as the outside doors, telling the dogs to wake me if they needed to go out. Since Gavi Norchis had described willogs, since I myself had seen a moss-demon, the planet Moss seemed much less friendly than before.

Certainly *I* was less friendly than before! I had never talked to Paul like that, never threatened him, never indicated that I thought him less than brilliant. Siblings were supposed to feel rivalry, which I had carefully avoided by giving him nothing to rival. I had always been compliant, indulgent, obliging. What on earth had happened to me?

A DECISION
IN *CHAGGA*

⋮ Life Captain Gacha was a member not only of the Gar G'tach but also of the G'tach G'gh'hagh, the supreme council of the Derac people. Not all tribal life captains were members of this group, which selected only Derac who were of abstemious habits and able to keep their jaws locked, thus minimizing the betrayal of secrets when one was far gone with what the humans called "moodsprays," a product of Earth Industries much in favor with certain aged Derac who had received little or no mental benefit from the late life change.

The meetings of the G'gh'hagh were rotated among the seventeen planets or systems used by Derac tribes as breeding and retirement sites. They were held at specified, infrequent intervals, though special meetings could be called if necessary. At Gahcha's summons, and as soon as was possible following the disposal of Tachstucha, this grand council met in the old wardroom of the retired ship named *Chagga*, or "Slammer." There Gahcha repeated what he had been told by Tachstucha concerning the Derac females. When he had concluded, he lay back on his warmed cot and waited for reaction, which was not slow in coming.

"Your son. He'll tell everyone," said one member.

"My son will tell no one," said Gahcha in a soft but very meaningful voice.

Silence fell over the group. There was some shifting about, some muttering. Finally, one member growled, "Someone had better take care of that breeding facility worker. He'll get spray crazy some night and spill it all."

"Already done," said Gahcha, who had made an unscheduled inspection of the breeding facility the morning following Tachstucha's disclosure. The worker hadn't even fought back, had, in fact, seemed almost grateful that his terror was soon to be over.

"This means we don't need human women," said the largest among them, a ponderous oldster with a low, growling voice. "Also, it means the Orskimi knew we didn't need human women."

"You're sure?" asked another, pale chartreuse with age. "About the Orskimi?"

"This is the kind of thing the Orskimi are sure to know in great detail," growled the large one. "Was not R'ragh the Reformer educated by the Orskimi? Did not our idea of H'hachap come from R'ragh? All along, have we not felt little Orskim pincers at the edges of events, nipping here, pinching there?"

"They have a plan," said a third member. "They always have a plan."

"Can we determine their plan?" asked Gahcha. "They have suggested, and we have agreed, to attack the human installation upon Moss. Then . . . of course, we will be at war with the humans . . ."

"And while we are at war with the humans," said the ponderous one, "the Orskimi will no doubt slip into all seventeen retirement systems and wipe out every one of our breeding centers because we have foolishly allowed our females to be concentrated in a few locations, where they may all be easily killed."

"All!" Gahcha was outraged. He had not thought of this, but it was certainly likely. What a blow! With all females gone . . . Great God Ghassifec forfend! "It would be the end of our race."

"Let us make our own plan," said the ponderous one. "For the moment we must conceal our knowing of what the Orskimi intend. We must seem to be proceeding as they expect us to do. Let our warriors upon Moss fall upon the outpost and inflict damage. Then let one of us—it will, I fear, have to be one of us, not a simple warrior—be captured by the Earthers or perhaps the Tharst. When we are captured, we will confess that the Orskimi paid us to do this thing because the Orskimi want to take over all the Earthers' planets . . ."

"Why only the Earthers?" asked another. "A small raid upon a Quondan planet, with another such confession. Another here, another there, and we could have half the races in the IC united against Orskim interests."

"I fear, as their putative instrument, we would be considered as culpable as they," said the ponderous one. "A small incursion, against an unarmed Planetary Protection team, that is not a big matter, particularly if we do not kill many of the important ones. An attack on a populated world would be of greater consequence, and would require the sacrifice of many Derac warriors at a time when all are needed to attack Orskimi. An attack is necessary, and while we are proceeding as planned on Moss, we can be deciding where and how it should take place." .

"What is left to be done on Moss?" asked the ancient.

"A few more of our warriors are to arrive with the heavy armament needed to knock out the shields at the ESC post. We have built our strength slowly, over time, not to alarm them, and we won't destroy the ESC post, just scare the softskins half to death so they'll get the message out."

"How many of them are you going to kill?" asked the ancient one, running his old tongue reminiscently along his teeth.

"A few," said Gahcha. "We'll kill quite a few ordinary men. There are no young ones, but there are a few females we can kill. Killing females and young upsets the softskins greatly, but they forget as quickly. Kill their important men, they remember it forever, so we don't want to do that."

A long silence followed, at the end of which, Gahcha slapped his tail twice upon the drum section of the cot, and announced, with great satisfaction, "Done."

THE ARRIVAL OF GAINOR BRANDT

⋮ Early in the morning, I told the trainers what Paul had done, urging them and the dogs to keep their eyes and noses alert for any conc-looking thing that might be wandering about. On my way to the commissary for breakfast, I saw the odor sensors being set up on the meadow by a noncon-suited ESC team, Sybil among them. She waved to me, coming over to say that Gainor Brandt would arrive mid to late afternoon, and he wanted to have a conference in the ESC bubble ASAP thereafter.

I had a quick breakfast, then went through the specimen boxes and bags I'd brought back from the plateau area, feeding and watering live critters before taking a maintenance floater full of them over to Sybil.

"Can you take these over to the island with you? They're specimens from the plateau area, many of them alive, and there may be some new things among them." She gave me a doubtful look, so I added, "Collecting them can't have been intrusive because most of them are exogenous to begin with."

She peered more closely, with evident interest, and agreed to take them to the isolation lock where all ESC specimens were stored. When I looked out half an hour later, the ESC people were gone except for one man testing the sensors, and another crouched over a multisense recorder, making tiny, repetitive adjustments.

The ship arrived as specified, midafternoon, setting down on the usual landing spot above the meadow. I was waiting for it, along with

Ornel Lethe, Duras Drom, and Paul, who had at the last minute decided he needed to present a good front to keep people from talking behind his back. I knew he intended to tell General Manager Brandt what *he* had discovered, and he had no plan to mention me as having had any part in the process. His intention was immediately frustrated by Brandt's opening statement:

"Mr. Delis, I need to talk with you, but I'm going over to the island at once. I need Jewel to come along, as I have some information for her from the sanctuary on Earth. I'll speak to you when I return."

Paul fumed while we departed, for Gainor took Duras Drom as well. Later I learned that he stalked angrily up and down the meadow for a time, then announced his intention of concentrating on how verbs might develop in an odor language, particularly inasmuch as that was one thing "other people" had no idea about. He was also heard to mutter that his sister had no right making off with Gainor Brandt that way. Gainor Brandt was his contact, not hers.

I had forewarned the trainers to be on the lookout for what Paul was likely to do if frustrated. Whenever people seemed to know things Paul did not know, he did his best to find them out so he could "manage" them. When we were much younger, he went through my belongings regularly in order to know all my secrets and keep me in my place. He was never in the least remorseful about doing it. He was convinced it was his right as the smarter, more able person to control others who were less intelligent and less able. I remember once Luth asked him why he did this.

"Father meant for me to take care of her."

"Your father? You were only three when he died, Paul."

"He still meant me to. He had her for me, so I'd have someone who would be smart enough to help me but not smart enough to do anything very important on her own."

"I thought he and Matty had Jewel because they wanted a child?"

Paul had snorted, "Oh, Matty wasn't important. My mother was important, but Matty was just someone to look after me. Like Bonner is."

Some years later, Luth had repeated this conversation to me. "I thought you needed to know."

I had replied. "That's another one of Paul's 'memories' that simply isn't true. Paul builds his dream castles in an interesting way. It starts with his wanting the castle. He knows such a castle can't exist without a foundation, so instead of admitting there is no foundation, he goes searching through memories and conversations for words or phrases that might be twisted or interpreted as a reference to his castle. When he finds them, he 'remembers' the foundation, and his castle is suddenly real."

"He really believes it?" asked Luth. "Believes his father said that?"

"Of course he believes it," I replied. "After a while, he believes anything he has said is true, simply because the words came out of his mouth. If you accuse him of lying, he's outraged."

Paul believed it no less on Moss than he had when we were children. In order to find out what I was keeping from him, he tried the adjoining door in the house (Adam heard him), only to find it locked. He went outside and found the east-facing door locked as well, and the south one, inside the dog pen, though Adam opened that one, when Paul rattled it.

"Something I can do for you, Paul?"

"Why is everything locked up?"

"I thought Jewel told you. We no longer leave anything unlocked. Moss demons are not something to be taken lightly. Anything else?"

Paul said no, nothing else, and walked away, looking slightly angry and slightly fearful. Adam told me later that he thought Paul had actually forgotten about moss demons until that moment. However, as he walked away, it probably occurred to him that if a moss demon like Poppy did come back, it would come looking for him. Concs habituated to the person who fed them, and Paul had had Poppy for several years.

Adam watched him standing outside his own door, which he had left open, shifting from one foot to the other. After dithering for some time, he came back to ask Adam to look around in his quarters, which Adam did with the utmost gravity. Adam felt about concs very much as I did, though his dislike was based on the way they smelled, which made him no less offended at Paul's having put Poppy into the red-moss. "A little panic, perhaps a good dose of terror might serve the bastard right," he told me when I returned.

On the island, meantime, Gainor had called his meeting in Lethe's lab, the first order of business being what Drom and I had to say concerning the previous night's incident. Since Drom and some unfamiliar ESC people were present, I stuck to the story I had told previously, and when the likelihood of an odor language came up, I once again said that I had seen it myself.

Gainor Brandt fixed Duras Drom with a pointed forefinger and said, "I think it's time we see this message the PPI force is supposed to have received."

Drom nodded. "It's been in the commissary."

"The commissary?" blurted Lethe. "Why?"

"It was written on bark in some kind of fruit sap. We put it under refrigeration to preserve it, but I brought it this morning. I knew you'd want to see it."

The rest of us waited while he went out to get it, then gathered around the table when he placed his burden on it and began to unwrap it. A chunk of bark, about two feet square, with one smooth side where it had been peeled away from a tree, and on the smooth side, the words, "Thankful, thankful, peoples here wanting know many more peoples." The letters were a little ragged, but quite clear.

We stared for an extremely long time. Something jostled in my head, and I asked, "Have these words been in evidence at PPI? In written form? Not in files or on forms, but on something obvious?"

"There's a notice board outside the commissary."

"Is it ever read aloud?"

"Occasionally, I suppose. 'More people,' appears every now and then, as in, 'The cleanup crew needs more people for duty next shift.' One man might read that off to another man."

"Thankful?" asked Gainor.

"The circuit riders from the Ethics Commission come by every now and then. Sometimes they do rituals. You never know who it's going to be, sometimes a Tharstian, sometimes a Fenbar or an Ocpurat. Human ones sometimes post a notice announcing a thanksgiving service."

I gave Gainor a curious look. I'd never heard of the Ethics Commission. He caught my glance and shook his head slightly, meaning let it go for now. "So these words, all of them, could have appeared . . ."

"Look," said Drom, "if you want me to be sure, I'll look it up and see. We keep copies of everything."

"Fine," Gainor said. "You do that, bring me the copies, and meanwhile I'll finish up my business with the people here."

That got rid of the extraneous people. When I was alone with Brandt and the trio I was accustomed to meeting with, I said, "I have some sensitive information, for your ears only, Gainor, unless you choose otherwise."

"I think we're trustworthy," said Lethe, in a dry voice.

"I think they are, too," said Gainor. "What's happened?"

"I haven't been telling the entire truth," I began, going on to supply the details about the journey from Forét, the spatial anomaly, the Night and Day Mountains, the tribal structure, the mysterious key, Gavi Norchis, the mention of Splendor, and the possibility that it was here, close, perhaps interpenetrating us as we spoke. Mouths opened as I told the story, and they remained open when I had finished. I felt laughter welling up and choked it back with an effort. It was a ridiculous tale. During the telling, I had been quite aware of how crazy it sounded. Nonetheless, the ESC people, who had been annoyingly smug during all our previous encounters, looked considerably shaken when I had finished.

"But you have no evidence of this," said Lethe. "No physical evidence.

I fished the little photo album out of my pocket. "Gavi Norchis found this at the foot of the mesa not long ago, and that evening she saw and heard the people in the rock—don't ask, I can't clarify that for you. This thing, however, happens to be a photo album of my wedding celebration with Witt. He had it with him when he left for Jungle. Presumably, he had it with him on Jungle. How did it get here?"

"By the Muzzle of Great Mahalus," murmured Brandt. "By the Twenty Toes of Tongal."

Lethe turned a curious glance his way.

"Tharstian gods," said I drily. "Gainor has taken to swearing by them recently, ever since a Tharstian High Priest told him Great Mahalus has no racial bias."

"The Great Mahalus," Gainor intoned, "is possibly the only supreme being in the universe who never created anything in its own image. Jewel, what have we got here?"

"I've been thinking about it for a couple of days," said I. "If we prefer to disbelieve, we have to come up with a simple, nonmiraculous way this album got to Moss. The first possibility that crossed my mind was your ESC people; some of them have been both here and on Jungle. Did one of them, perhaps, pick this thing up after Witt disappeared then drop it on this planet?"

"We were never out of noncon suits on that planet," said Lethe. "All the belongings of the men who disappeared were packed up and returned to Earth except for what they had on them when they vanished. On this planet, we've never left the compound to go any farther than the shore, as we did today."

I nodded. I had thought as much. "If we rule out meteoritic ejecta, since the album shows no signs of burning up in atmosphere, then I'm left with the album's being further evidence of the spatial anomaly the Derac ran into. Perhaps a branch of that anomaly connects the two planets and the moon."

"Why the moon?" asked Gainor.

"Because Witt disappeared on Jungle, his keepsake was found on Moss; because Gavi Norchis spoke of 'harvesters' here on Moss who come in a flash of light in which people disappear. Adam and I saw such a flash of light as we were leaving Treasure, and there was said to have been a flash of light on Jungle when the eleven men disappeared.

"Also, I found many of the same plants growing on Treasure as are growing on Moss, and while spores might have traveled the distance, it's a bit much to swallow. Since we already know as a fact that a spatial weirdness exists, the simplest hypothesis connects the three worlds by that means."

"And where does Splendor fit?"

"Assuming it isn't a purely religious or mythical place? If the tribes have gained access to this weirdness, it may be . . . what? Are there surfaces in an anomaly? Could it be dimensional or might it pull in a planetary surface as a nexus? Wormholes sometimes look quite splendid from inside. Might someone go through a door here, arrive on a surface called Splendor, then go from a door there to Jungle? Gavi spoke of a key. The two tribes or Mountains go to war over it every few decades, and they're due to start another one momentarily. Doesn't a key imply a door one can go through to somewhere?"

Gainor heaved a sigh. "As usual, Jewel, you've given me a good bit more to chew on than I . . . well, have appetite for! Assuming you're right in the main, even if not in the details, one thing we do not want to happen is to have any kind of spatial link to fall into Derac or Orskim hands, since we have recently learned the Orskimi have been pushing the Derac to declare war with Earthers in order to take over the human planets."

There were assorted expressions of outrage, surprise, and dismay, several of them from me.

"Derac don't live on planets," objected Abe, loudly.

Gainor said soothingly, "Except during retirement, quite true. The Orskimi, however, have also suggested Derac females should be hybridized with human women, to make them more intelligent, after which the Derac will live on planets."

"You found that out because of what I told you!" I said.

"You were one of the more important informants, Jewel. You're owed a vote of thanks." Turning to the others, he explained, "We've been recording Derac speech for a very long time, but we made little progress on understanding it because we put our recording devices in their ships, and the shipclans use only a few hundred words, total. It's like listening to the scatological cackling of carnivorous hens. They are not given to subtlety. Turns out, the best place to put our ears is on their retirement planets, as Jewel suggested."

"The Tharstians did it for us?" I asked.

"When I approached the subject with my Tharstian colleague, invoking the Great Mahalus as my witness, he told me they'd been doing so for at least a generation, and they were gratified to learn we were finally catching on to what the Derac and Orskimi were up to. At that point my Tharstian friend paused significantly, looking expectant . . ."

"How does a Tharstian look expectant?" Sybil asked. "They float around in those glassy orbs all the time. You can't even see them!"

"The orb is actually a biological membrane that closes around them to filter alien air. The orb is quite expressive. It flushes, turns pale, freezes when surprised, quivers when the occupant is interested in something. At any rate, when the Tharstian quivered, I put on my enigmatic face and nodded thoughtfully, as though I knew all about it. As a matter of ethics, Tharstians don't tell other races things the other races don't already know. They think of it as interfering. When it's a matter of stopping an interstellar war before it starts, however, they let the policy stretch a little around the edges.

"To advance, as the Derac say, my Tharstian friend decided I knew enough about it that he could speak without sullying his sense of honor. The Derac are counting on the Orskimi for two things: to hybridize human and Derac females and to be their allies in taking over all human planets. The Orskimi are planning, however, that when the Derac-human war starts, they'll move in and take over *both* territories. It's something they've been planning for ages."

"Who knows this besides you?" asked Lethe.

"The information has been sent to the chairman of the Racial Relations Board of Interstellar Confederation; I left copies to be sent to half a dozen other IC agencies if I don't get a response. And, it went to the ET Committee of the Earthian Congress, as well as to World-keeper Defense Mobilization."

"Admitting you sneak-eared the Derac?" asked I.

"Saying we'd been informed by a friendly power who shall remain nameless. Actually, the Tharstians gave me proof: a recording from a mortuary temple of the Orskim home planet. The Tharstians have informed us of Orski duplicity before. If anyone requires proof before acting, we can show it to them. I would, however, prefer your kind of story, Jewel, mostly true, with just enough fabrication to minimize damage."

"Then the Derac are a real danger," I said.

"The Derac are definitely a real danger. Yes. We've got that base of theirs ringed with observer fish. When things start to happen, we'll know about it. Right now I'm wondering how we should act toward those people up on the plateaus. We can't pretend we don't know about them forever."

"Let's do the natural thing," I suggested. "The only person we have to protect is Gavi Norchis, because she gave us some sensitive information, but if we go visit the derelict ships, we will no doubt discover her people as a consequence of that visit. Accidental discovery will leave her in the clear."

"I have a more immediate problem," said Abe Burrow. "If the Mossen aren't people, but merely the utterance of people, then are the word growers the actual Mossen people? Or is there another link in this chain? Does some other thing make the thing that makes the plants that make the Mossen? Several times, Jewel, you mentioned this Gavi person as saying, 'We have peace with Moss,' and 'the planet leaves us alone.' Did you see any redmoss around the plateau?"

"No. I didn't."

"Perhaps that's part of leaving them alone? I'd love to know, who the actual speaker is on this world."

I had considered Gavi's words to be merely a figure of speech, as I myself might have said, "Earth suffers from too many people," and though I'd wondered who the real speaker might be, I hadn't gone so far as Abe had just done.

"They may have . . . parts underground I didn't see," I offered. "They could have huge roots. What might we be looking for, a kind of vegetable brain?"

"If it's underground," said Sybil, "then it might be a network, several of them or maybe one enormous network that extends all over the planet. New plants sending down roots to join onto old ones?"

"Or equally," said Lethe, "the talker part could be responding to instruction from some other organism. In the absence of any data at all, we don't know."

"Until we know," Gainor Brandt told them with some emphasis, "we don't destroy or hurt anything. What we will do is send an ESC team onto the plateau to look at the ships. When we find some evidence for survival of the crews and passengers, we'll start looking for them, and we'll send a statement to IC saying Earth has a prior claim on the planet."

"Pretending we don't know that something on this planet has the only legitimate claim?" I asked. "That is, assuming the bark message wasn't written by some PPI oldster who wanted to stir things up."

"A prior claim by Earth can serve as a . . . transitional belief," Gainor said affably "We'll support that claim only until it's proven that an indigenous intelligence exists. The Derac will make enough out of the system either way. They made a big profit out of Treasure, and they'll still be doing very well out of their bonanza on Stone."

"When the Hessings get involved, they'll want to search for Witt," said I. My face felt odd, as though it might be frozen.

"If we can establish that the connection exists, they probably will,"

Gainor agreed, giving me a quizzical look. "You look rather reluctant, Jewel."

I shrugged, unwilling and unable to put my feelings about it into more specific words, but reluctance wasn't far off the mark.

THE LANGUAGE

: The odor sensors set up by the ESC, so the crew chief remarked to me, could detect and analyze over a million odors that had been identified by any one or more of the 512 races who had nose equivalents, on any of the 9052 IC member worlds. All these odors had names; in some cases, such as one odor called variously "burned dung," "sweet-weed," and "dead body," widely variant names assigned by different races. For nonlabeled odors, the chromatograph units on the smellers simply identified the chemical constituents and the molecular structure, compared it to those odors that were chemically closest, and assigned it a name as descriptive as possible. In this they were aided by lexicons of terms used to describe wines and perfumes as long ago as the twentieth century.

By evening, the equipment had been thoroughly tested. I had suggested that they space several detectors around the circle, at some distance from one another, to determine whether, in fact, each Mossen delivered multiple scents. Lethe and Burrow had decided to link the odor apparatus to the visual and aural recorders, so that analysts would have access to simultaneous sight and smell.

During all this process of setup and conference, Paul was notably absent. Once evening fell, however, he came out of the house dragging a chair, seated himself upon it, folded his arms, and paid attention to what was happening. Seeing him, Gainor Brandt strolled over, hunkered down beside him, and exchanged a few words in a pleasant voice, to which Paul replied volubly, with gestures.

Gainor returned to the group of noncon-suited ESC people near where Frank and I were leaning on the low limb of a convenient tree.

The dogs lay in a wide circle in front of us, noses ready. Gainor moved about, eventually stopping beside me to say, sotto voce, "Your brother claims he'd have made more headway if he hadn't been distracted by those dogs of yours. That annoyed me, so I told him you'd found out about the odor language because of the dogs, that we were considering using dogs in our own linguistic work."

"And how did he react to that?" I murmured.

"I don't think he liked it, but he shut up. Is he really good at this work?"

"He really is, Gainor. If we can give him anything decent to work with, he'll probably come up with a lexicon for you, and possibly a syntax. He's just . . ."

"A pain in the ass," grunted Gainor. "Where's Adam? And Clare?"

"Down at the far end, away from people," I said. "Seeing what they can . . . detect."

"Good for them," grunted Gainor, as he turned to rejoin his ESC people.

"Why doesn't he wear a noncon suit?" asked Frank.

"I don't know," I replied. "I do know he wants to change the ESC protocols on planets where both ESC and PPI are working, but the Earth Enterprises medical committee won't do it. They say the risk of transporting a slow virus back to Earth is so enormous that it's foolhardy to give up any protective measures unless the ESC plans to stay in quarantine whenever they're on Earth, the way the PPI do. If all life on the planet is botanic, rather than zoologic, they can cut that time way down."

Frank said, "With all those crabs and beetles and mouse types you brought, plus the survivors up on the mesas, it's clear this isn't a purely botanic planet anymore."

I replied, "The survivors have been here for a couple of hundred years. A virus slow enough to exceed twice the normal life span can't do much damage, which is probably what Gainor thinks, too, though he did point out the survivors have been up there, not down here."

"Look," whispered Frank. "Here they come."

And they did come, the usual pack of them, though now I saw them through informed eyes not as a disorderly milling of individuals, but as chains, all about the same length, some of them connecting with others during their assembly in mid meadow before spooling out, one after the other. Little lights came on in the equipment around the meadow. The dance began, and I noted almost subconsciously that the order was the same as it had been, at least in color. The same sequences went by, departed, joined others that went by and departed, again and again. I also noticed that the Mossen turned in the dance, rotating their bodies with successive sets of tendrils, a different edge or side of them facing outward until they had turned completely around, repeating and repeating. It wasn't an obvious turning. I had to watch for sets of tendrils letting go to be sure of the movement. Finally the Mossen began to swell. I actually saw it. I noted the slight puffiness of outline, the slight increase in buoyancy, saw the tendrils straighten to make more room between them, more room between themselves and the moss carpet beneath them. The wind lifted the carpet; the whole thing fluttered upward before exploding, softly, breaking into shards of rosy amber. One of them fell near enough that I could pick it up and sniff it. Something rank. I dropped it and wiped my fingers down the seams of my trousers. All around us, falling objects pattered to the ground like hail or a fall of nuts from a tree. I searched the ground, finally finding several hard, hexagonal seedpods that I gathered into my pockets.

The meadow had not been floodlighted during the dance. Only a few isolated lamps had illuminated the spectacle. The ESC technicians were busy with the equipment again. Gainor came to my side, whispering, "I've asked Lethe's people to come up with a synthesizer, a kind of odor organ that can be programmed to issue the dance scents in order. I thought you might take it to your pal up by the plateau and see what she thinks of them."

"Seven-day interval," I replied. "That's the earliest I can signal. That'd be . . . let's see, this is day five. If I want to meet her as soon as possible, I leave day after tomorrow, and you signal that night. We may have to wait one day at the other end, but there's a chance she'll meet us a little early."

"That should give my people time."

"Thanks, Gainor. And thanks for not making me break my promise to Gavi Norchis. I have a hunch she'll be of great use to us if we can let her do things her way."

Gainor nodded. "I'm going to tell Paul we'll have something for him tomorrow. Do you want to sit in on the results? You might have some insight. Lethe's already sure we're getting multiple scents from most single Mossen."

"What did he see?"

"Those things we thought might be eyes seem to be emitters arranged in six vertical zones around the body, each separated from the adjacent zones by rows of tendrils. The body is actually hexagonal, though the angles are softened when the body is inflated. As the body turns, it presents different sets of emitters, and sometimes the same smell is presented several times during one pass."

"I saw that, too, Gainor. Is a doubling like a double letter? An emphasis? A doubled meaning?"

"I have no idea. Do you want to sit in?"

I shook my head. "I'm intrigued, but not tonight. I'm . . . wearier than I should be. Too many things happening. I'd rather spend tonight with the dogs."

He lowered his voice. "They may have something to tell you, in any case."

Which was what I had been counting on.

⋮ Adam and Clare returned to their quarters the long way around, through the forest, and in through the southern door, which could not be observed from any other place in the compound. Both were still in dog shape, though they began the process of returning to their own form as soon as they were inside, with the doors closed. By unspoken agreement, they chose to do so in the hallway, where there were no windows, and I compulsively checked the doors several times to be sure they were locked. When they were changed enough to put their clothing back on, they went into their own rooms and lay quietly, letting their bodies change themselves. Only when their mouths and palates had returned to virtual normal did they come into my room, to sit against the wall and share the experience.

"It was . . . remarkable," said Adam. "For the most part, we have no idea what they were saying, but Clare and I agree there was a carrot and a stick in the message. We detected smells like a slap in the face, like the one on the moon, as well as enticing smells. Don't do this, do that, seems to be the message. Dead body smells could be interpreted as either a threat or a warning, I suppose. There were sweat smells, a hell of a lot of sweat smells.

"Effort," I said, after a moment. "Humans sweat when they work. Plants don't. They've picked up our smell for work . . ."

"Which would explain that ambient sequence. Sweat, then the ambient odor, then nothing, then sweat again."

"When you say 'nothing' . . . ?"

"We mean nothing," said Adam. "Among their odors, they have one that simply wipes every smell away. It's like being in a sterile glass bottle unable to smell even yourself. It gets rid of everything, even the ambient odors of the planet. Since I doubt it could really overcome the ambient odor, what it no doubt does is block our sensors for a brief moment. You'll get a sniff of an odor, then get hit with nothingness, then another sniff the same, and again nothingness."

"So that sequence you mentioned might mean . . . ?"

"It might mean, it's a lot of work to make a world," said Clare.

"Or," Adam said, "It could mean persons, human, are working too much in the world."

"Or," said Frank, "that we ought to get our stinky selves gone and leave the world alone."

"What do the dogs say?" I asked.

Clare replied, "Behemoth says it's talking to us, not angry. Scramble says it wants to talk to us and has been working hard to reach us, but we don't respond."

"Scramble said all that!"

"Scramble said the message was: moss try talk, no talk, try talk again very hard, no talk, why no talk."

"And how do they say talk?" asked Frank.

Clare said, "Scramble says their smell (evidently the Mossen have a smell of their own that's distinct from the ones they emit) and then our smell and then them and us and them and us."

"Talk," I marveled. "Though it could equally well be fight, or battle. Them and us or them versus us. No. Battle would involve death, so there'd be dead and blood smells. Gainor's bunch has a synthesizer they'll program to emit the message we got tonight. We'll leave for the plateau day after tomorrow, and he'll signal Gavi Norchis that night, by which time we ought to be near the plateau. Did anyone notice how many chains it took to make the whole message?"

"A chain being?"

"The number we saw on the branch. That'd be one chain. Some of them hooked up with others, I noticed."

"The ESC can probably tell you," said Adam. "The whole thing had a lot of redundancy."

Tomorrow I would ask Gainor Brandt, and I'd tell him what interpretations the dogs had come up with.

⋮ The morning after the Mossen had danced, Gainor came over to Paul's quarters carrying several large data boards displaying the smells emitted the night before together with notes (including some unattributed ones from the trainers and the dogs) that identified some smells or the category of the smell, or, if category could not be identified, giving it a label. Also included were lists of the smells in order, including repetitions and separations from individual Mossen as well as from Mossen chains that were duplicated.

"On the theory," Gainor said, "that each Mossen is a word or short phrase and each chain is the equivalent of a sentence."

I stood in the door, listening, as Gainor went over the material with Paul, concluding, "Both the ESC and the PPI people are exploring the nearby moss forests with scent detectors, recording different smells and what they are. For example, you'll find a series in there that seems to be varying stages in moss rot, starting with the fresh and concluding with compost. We'll do some digging and see if that interpretation is accurate. We'll find out if fresh redmoss has a smell. We've already established that the moss-demon did have a smell. Jewel was thoughtful enough to grab a sample while the grabbing was going on.

"One of the odors they used quite a bit was human sweat. We don't know, of course, what it means to them, but since they also used our own clean body smell, sweat smell probably doesn't mean human."

"Work," said Paul. "Effort. Exertion. Struggle."

"Quite possibly. Or, weight lifting, or building, or running, or . . ."

"I'll get to work on it," said Paul, dismissively. He had that look on his face. This was the first real material he'd had to work with since getting to Moss, and I could see he was eager to begin.

Gainor bowed himself out and we went down to my quarters, where we found Scramble sitting in the sun, surrounded by puppies.

Though they were too young to sense it as anything beyond warmth, she had brought them out into the sunshine.

He joined me on the ground. "Scramble's litter," he observed. "What about Dapple and Veegee?"

"Any day now. If they have five each, we'll have over twenty dogs here, Gainor. I've been concerned about pollution, so I took a walk early this morning, to see what happened where they've been defecating. Everywhere they've been, the moss has covered it. Where they pee, on the other hand, there is some damage to some organisms and no damage to others. So, I'll tell them to pee where it won't hurt anything."

"Lethe told me about the conc business," Gainor remarked. "About Paul putting one of his into the redmoss."

"I didn't know whether to feel outrage or pity," I said.

"Whatever's in the conc cellular makeup that kills bacteria and viruses might keep the redmoss from duplicating them," he mused.

"Possibly. The dogs haven't found anything that smells like Poppy except the redmoss where it lay down."

"I wonder what the Orskimi made them from, assuming they did make them," Gainor mused.

"God knows," I said, feelingly. "I was thinking how good it was they didn't spread disease, but that could be changed in the wink of an eye, couldn't it? As disease disseminators, they'd be perfect. I'm thinking back to the AIDS and Ebola epidemics of the twentieth century."

Gainor said, "If they start to show up in the colonies, I think we can accept that we're under attack. There's no doubt the Orskimi are using Zhaar technology."

"You mean to modify their slave race?"

"Races, plural. One of them is a kind of sucker fish that hangs on their bodies and eats dried skin or detritus. They call them klonzi. Also, as I learned recently, their legs are actually the leg segment of another race that's been beheaded and fitted onto each infant Orski."

"When the Zhaar did stuff like that, somebody wiped them out, Gainor."

"That's what is said, though equally, they might have gone away," he said in an expressionless voice. "If they were wiped out, you'd think someone, some race would have taken the credit for doing it."

⋮ Both Dapple and Veegee whelped during the night, seven puppies in Adam's room, eight in Frank's. Wolf and Titan did as Behemoth had done, staying on guard in the rooms most of the time, leaving only to eat and drink and go out into the forest to relieve themselves. Whenever the bitches departed on the same errands, the dogs lay next to the box where the puppies were sleeping. Dapple and Wolf's puppies were lighter-colored than she, but with darker markings. Veegee and Titan had produced a litter of brindle pups, several with red or gray masks around the eyes.

I increased the bitches' rations and added supplements. Gainor came to look at the pups late in the afternoon, asking if Adam and I would like to join the ESC team that would investigate the old ships.

We left early the following morning, making a single wide spiral to gain altitude and a shorter one to set the shuttle down. It was my first unhurried look at the planet from the air, and I was surprised to see how clearly the moss-covered PPI installation showed up against the homogeneous pattern of forests. The Derac base was considerably larger than when we'd landed, a charred scar at the north end of the lake. Elsewhere, except for the occasional wide stretches of meadow and the linked lakes or seas that more or less girdled the planet, the world was covered from plateau to plateau with the same growths, repeated in variations so minute that they produced an overall impression of absolute uniformity.

We landed near the covered ships. They weren't grown over with moss, as I'd supposed. The plant that covered them grew in flat, overlapping shields, almost like scales on a snake. A crew bearing torches and cutters began at once to uncover the areas where they were most likely to find ship identification. While they were occupied with that task, Gainor and I wandered around the area, recording the surroundings in some detail. While examining a particular view, I became aware I was looking at a garden. Beckoning to Gainor, I walked him through it.

"Look here, a cluster of root vegetables. I've never seen them grow, but I've seen pictures. There, corn, maize, at the foot of that tree, on the sunny side, and the vine growing up the stalk is a legume. That level space with the marbled texture is also a mixture of several vegetables, peppers, I think, and melons, and something I don't recognize at all . . . "

"It doesn't look like agriculture."

"It doesn't resemble our idea of field crops, no, but it does remind me of something I've read about, the forest culture of a people who once lived in Middle America. The type of farming was called micro-culture, each plant set in a pocket environment that would support it. A tall sun-loving plant being used to shade another and to support a vine, for example, or one plant fixing nitrogen for another type planted next to it. Different plants were grouped together if they would benefit one another. And, of course, it looks very natural, as it should, since each thing is growing in a tiny space well suited to it. I guess that explains why no one noticed it from space."

"I wouldn't have noticed it from three meters away, if you hadn't pointed it out," he said, patting me clumsily on the shoulder. Nocon suits were not designed for caresses. "But then, it's just another example of how helpful you can be. When are you going to accept my offer of a job with ESC?"

"Soon," I said, stopping with my mouth open. Now where had that come from? I'd been saying no for three years. I confronted Gainor's piercing look.

"What changed your mind?" he asked.

"I don't know," I confessed. "It's just . . . being here. Suddenly I know I'd enjoy it, and there seems no reason why not."

"I've been saying exactly that for some time, but you never believed it, or accepted it. I always thought you were still hoping against hope that someone would find Witt."

Not hoping exactly, I thought. More that Witt had been in my mind all the time, like a wall around me, a tall barrier I couldn't get over. "I guess I've given up."

"The moment you finally have a hint of his continued existence, and you've given up?" He regarded me with puzzled scrutiny that made me uncomfortable.

I turned to hide my face, noticing as I did so a huge crab creature crouched in low, furzy growth among some thorny shrubs. "Look, Gainor," I said. "It's huge!"

He turned and regarded it. "Huge indeed," he said. "But we have no time for zoological divagations at the moment."

I blinked at the crab, not calling Gainor's attention to the fact that several of the legs seemed rather lifeless, then followed Gainor as he tramped back to the abandoned ships. A worker beckoned from a cleaned section of hull and pointed to numbers that told us these were indeed the Hargess-Hessing ships from Forêt. Three other men were working on an airlock, which opened reluctantly, with a shriek of corroded metal. The inner lock was forced open in its turn, and we went through. No bones. No signs that anyone had been inside recently, though the stripped interior spoke eloquently of people having been in the ship when it landed and for some time afterward.

"I think we have our evidence," muttered Gainor. "A garden, recently planted. A vacant ship, stripped of all usable items. Under the circumstances, anyone would agree that exploration, even intrusive exploration, is now required."

"PPI or ESC?" I asked.

"PPI," he replied. "I've been looking for an excuse to get them away from the moss forest. The growth up here is quite different."

As it was. Some of the ewer-shaped trees gave off pungent smells and were interspersed with areas of waist-high, green-twigged growths bearing parallel rows of flat, shiny leaves that continuously though imperceptibly turned toward the sun. Beneath these, in the shade, violet-stalked creepers wove tough networks across stones and tree roots while liverworts—which is what one of the workers said the ship coverings most resembled—shingled the areas between. Where this dense coverage was interrupted by stone outcroppings, every hole and crack in the stone was fringed and crosshatched with patches and lines of low, wide-bladed grass that carried a spike of dark, prickle-headed seeds.

"Are you going to move the whole camp up?" I asked.

He nodded, somewhat regretfully. "The whole camp, yes, and almost immediately, before the Derac get the word to attack. There's no reason for them to have increased their numbers here unless they intend to do just that. With only forty-seven left in the PPI contingent, they'd be far safer up here. I've got fish watching the Derac; so far they have no heavy armament."

He mused for a moment, then said, "So, we'll start by keeping a shuttle on the ground at the installation, so we can leave at a moment's notice, and meantime we'll move all the records and most of the buildings plus a sizable team up here to look for survivors. As soon as you get a translation of the message from your friend, we'll take decisive action. Meantime, I'm sending word back to IC that Hargess Hessing has a prior claim on this planet. The people from Forêt may not have found the Splendor they were looking for, but they didn't come up empty-handed.''

I thought privately that they might have found Splendor, too, though perhaps they didn't know it yet.

THE DOOR TO SPLENDOR

⠿ One of the original settlers of Night Mountain had been a worker in glass who had made perfume bottles on Forêt. During the early exploration of the plateau he had found a large cavern with several lava chimneys that would serve admirably as glass furnaces. He named the cavern Lace Rock, after a huge stone formation along one side of it, and settled in with a few associates to make bottles, drinking glasses, and glass for windows or skylights, products that were traded and sold among the Day and Night Mountain tribes.

Some long-gone Loamer chieftain had used Lace Rock glass to fenestrate the irregularly shaped slits and holes of a large bubble contained in a lava fist that jabbed upward above the Fortress of Loam. This hidden room was floored level with sand and carpeted with thread-moss fiber rugs. Uniquely among the fortress chambers, it had a hearth and chimney, from which the seeping smoke rose invisibly among myriad other smokes and steams that fumed the plateau.

When a chieftain made his way through the lengthy natural passages and the several heavy doors that led from the fortress to this chamber, he was in the most private place in Loam, so it was there that the current chief took his son, Lynbal, to discuss the coming battle with Day Mountain.

"Our scouts have marked the way to the battleground. About a two-day march," said Chief Larign, referring to a hand-drawn map covered with many notes and emendations. "We'll need to go a bit wide, to avoid the fanged ones." He pointed to the lake, a long oval stretching from the northeast to the southwest, and then to the north end of it, where the Derac camp was shown by a number of concentric, ever larger circles. "Normally we'd go to the lake at that point, since it's closest, and we'd follow the shore around to the west, but with more of them camped there every day, we'll have to loop a bit to the north before we head south, directly to the battleground."

"Won't we attract their attention when the battle starts?"

"Not likely. A day's travel through the forest is far enough. Now, it's time you heard about the key."

Lynbal adopted a serious expression and sat very straight. This, he had always been told, was one of the important moments in his life, and he had given much consideration to the demeanor and attitude that would be appropriate, deciding on silence, respect, and appreciation of the honor.

"When our forefathers first landed here," his father said, "they did some exploring, of course. They were particularly eager to look at this lake, the only one within a day or so travel. Probably thinking of fish. They'd found no animals we could eat: no crabs then, no land animals at all, and they couldn't afford to slaughter the few farm animals they had with them for food.

"So, they set out for this lake, got to it, and went around it to the west, and in half a day or so came to this place . . ." He fell silent, staring out the nearest window at nothing, as though he had passed into reverie.

"This place . . ." prompted Lynbal, softly.

The chieftain came to himself with a start. "I suppose you'd call it an amphitheater, a mile or so across. It's a bowl, set into the land, absolutely smooth, absolutely round. The moss inside is blue, very short, velvety, like a rug. At the top, there's a circle of trees, hundreds of them, exactly alike. Every branch. Every twig. Every leaf. As though they were . . . I don't know, identical clones governed by the same forces. If a bug eats a leaf on one, another bug eats the equivalent leaf on each of the others so they stay the same. One of our people tried breaking off a twig, one time. The minute the twig was in his hand, every tree in the circle dropped the same twig, and on the way home, that man was eaten by willogs. Just a word of warning there."

Lynbal swallowed deeply, wondering if this cautionary tale was fact or myth, deciding that no answer he might get would ameliorate his discomfort.

"In the middle of the amphitheater, at the bottom," his father went on, "there's a stone pavement, say a hundred feet across, and at the center, a crystal of basalt about six men high with the key hanging near the top."

"You mean you hang it there?"

"I mean it hangs there, always."

"You leave it there?"

"It can't be removed."

"Then how can we say we have it?" Lynbal cried, forgetting about silence and respect. "I thought it was something you won, something you carried around."

The chieftain bestirred himself to annoyance. "Pay attention, boy! This discovery was before Day Mountain split off. When the explorers told the tale, both Hessing and Hargess went to see for themselves. There it was, bowl, pavement, pillar, key. Being Hessing and Hargess, the two mucky-mucks decided they had to have the key, so they cut wood, built a ladder, climbed up it, and laid hands on the key."

"And?"

"And a door slid out of the pillar edgewise, and then something stepped out of the door."

"What was it?"

"Nobody knows exactly. The men saw it, or them. They could remember seeing it, or them, but they couldn't remember what it looked like."

"And that's it?"

"Not quite, no. Whatever it was, it told Hargess and Hessing that one person could use the key every year. Only one for the whole year. Some one person, if he came with at least a dozen others, could use the key to ask if he . . . or she . . . could go through or if some other person could go through. And whatever answered the door would say either yes or no . . ."

He fell silent again, lips pursed, brow furrowed, sighing heavily. "While this was going on, the people with Hessing and Hargess were looking through the open door. Later they said they couldn't even blink their eyes for fear of missing some of it. They said it was paradise."

The chieftain looked expectantly at his son, who nodded but said nothing. After a moment, the chieftain went on:

"So that's the way it was for a while. The Hessing chief and the Hargess chief took turns, year by year, sometimes nobody could go through, sometimes the gatekeeper let all twelve people go through, and Hessing and Hargess went on hating each other, and the place was always in an uproar! After three or four turns each, the head Hargess demanded they draw straws to see which group should stay and which should move out and leave the other in peace. Hargess chief lost the draw and decided to move down into the mosses. Right away, he ran into moss-demon trouble, so they moved farther south, more moss-demons, and farther south yet until they ended up on Day Mountain. The two sides agreed to meet each year at the bowl and battle for the use of the key."

"Each *year?*"

"Well, we say year, it may be something other than a year. It's a span of time for the people behind the gate, is what it is. It has been as short as seven of our years, it's been as long as seventeen. We know when the time is coming, from the flashes."

"Flashes," Lynbal managed to say from a dry throat.

"Flashes. On the moon. In the moss forest here. When it starts flashing several times every night, that's time to get ready. We've still got a few of the old communicators, though we have to charge them by pedaling a generator, so we only use them when we think the time is coming, to say when the battle will be."

"But Day Mountain has to come all that way!"

"Well, they lost the draw, so they've got nothing to complain about. Anyhow, with the Hargessites, inconvenience doesn't mean anything. It's winning that's important. Even though the Hargesses and the Hessings are long dead, it's still important with them. It's traditional."

Lynbal sat with his head in his hands for some moments before looking up. "Let's see if I understand this. Every year, not our year but somebody else's year, Day Mountain and Night Mountain fight for a key. People get killed . . ."

"Not too many," said his father, casually.

"People get killed," Lynbal repeated. "When enough have been killed, then the winner has the right to use the key for a year to open a door. When he opens the door, the people on the other side of it may allow people in, or they may not."

"That's right."

"And why do we want to do this?"

"Because it's paradise. Splendor. Marvelous beyond all telling."

"You've seen it."

"Yes."

"What was it like?"

"I can't describe it. Just, wonderful."

"And you can't remember what the people look like, beyond the door."

"No."

"And who knows this, this story you're telling me?"

"The chieftains, of course. We lead the men in battle. Plus most of the men who've fought there. They've all seen what I've seen at least once or twice."

"Except for Lace Rock Tribe, which doesn't battle."

"Right, but they don't get to go through the door, either. Even though we don't let the men hear what we say to the beings inside, we let them watch when the door opens, so they can see through the doorway. It motivates them."

"Have you ever seen anyone go through?"

Chieftain Larign nodded, though sadly. "Yes. I've been the leader of the Night Mountaineers, and during my time I went there several times with a dozen men. Both times, the people beyond the gate let my men through, but not me, of course. I was just the opener. And then, a few times we've taken dead or dying people there. They'll always take the dead or dying. I took my father there when he was dying, and they took him."

"But if one of our women, say, died in childbirth. We wouldn't take her, would we?"

Chief Larign shifted uncomfortably. "It's quite a long way, so we don't bother for ordinary people. We usually take chieftains. And heroes. And anyone who's died during the actual battle, of course, Day or Night Mountain." His eyes shifted away from Lynbal to search for nothing along the arc of the room, murmuring, "Having the battle to train for and look forward to gives the men something to keep their minds and bodies occupied, so they're not always fighting each other.

Besides, they've seen through the doorway. They've seen their dear comrades go through. Any of us would risk a great deal to go through there."

Shaking his head, Lynbal stood up and went to the door. "I think I'll make the rounds of the guard posts, Father. I need to . . . think this over."

"Do that, son," said the chieftain. "I'll just sit here a while and look at the gardens. If I can figure out where they are. Ha."

The young man took himself away. The older man lay back in his comfortable chair and, in a very short time, began snoring.

At which point, outside the windows, a woman in crab armor rose from the ledge where she had been crouched and began the tedious and risky climb to the ground. Gavi Norchis had once more extended her intimate knowledge of the world in which she lived.

THE MESSAGE
FROM THE WORLD

⋮ Having observed a crouched and watchful crab, I knew the people of Loam had seen us on the height. It was likely Gavi would know we had been there. Adam and I made a fast trip to the falls while Clare and Frank stayed behind to look after the dogs and puppies. Gainor had wanted to come with me, but he had taken my word that Gavi had forbidden any contact except those of us who had first met her. We did little or no sight-seeing on the way, though we did stop to record the "birth" and the smells of a frond (sentence? phrase?) of words that happened to ripen as we were passing by. That night we stayed in the cavern Gavi had shown us on our first trip, which is where she found us the next morning. While Adam took a recorder and went in search of words being born, Gavi and I sat by her fire and talked.

"My people were being annoyed at you," she informed me. "You were pointing out our gardens so quickly, when they thought we were having them well hidden. So I was hearing in the halls of Loam."

"I knew we were spotted at least once," I said.

She nodded. "I was being in Loam to share a meal with Quynis and her brother Quillan of the Granite Tribe, along with Lailia of Loam."

"How many tribes are there, Gavi?"

"On Night Mountain? Seven. Loam, Granite, Burrow, Cavern, Pillar, Falls. And, Lace Rock, though that's being only a sort of tribe."

"Meaning?"

"It's artists and people having strange sex habits. They make clothing for us and glass, and paintings. They arrange spectacles and pageants. They don't fight, not usually, anyhow."

She confided this to me as she might have done to a friend of long standing, though I realized she was doing so only because I had no standing whatsoever. She was desperate to talk with someone, and she could not safely share with anyone in Loam her thoughts, her motives, her hopes, or her methods. I had come all this way to talk of the Mossen dance, which she knew as well as I. If she wanted to talk about something else for a while, so be it. Her willing cooperation was too important to risk through impatience.

"I interrupted you," I said. "You were telling me about your dinner party."

"I was arranging it," she said. "I was deciding Lailia should fall in love with Quillan now, before Lailia's father is telling her she must be marrying Balnor of Burrow. No one was noticing that drink and cakes I am giving to Quillan and Lailia are being different from ones I am offering to Quynis or the ones I was eating myself. They are looking the same, certainly, but I am taking great care that only Quillan and Lailia are eating or drinking the special ones."

I nodded and tried to look interested.

"When Lynbal was arriving, we are eating dinner, with wine I am bringing. Only having few sips of this and everyone is becoming warmer and more jovial. You say jovial?"

"Sometimes," I smiled. "A little drunk, you mean."

"Only a little. After supper, I am playing harp for them and using scent board. I have funny song about willogs and a moss-demon man whose wife was thinking herself well rid of him until he is coming back. While they are all laughing, the scent board is doing its work."

I rubbed the lines on my forehead a little fretfully. "Making Lailia fall in love with Quillan?"

"Finishing of that, assuredly. When they are bidding good night to their hosts, I am following them home. Quillan was going into Lailia's rooms and staying there until morning." She smiled, a very satisfied smile. "Very early, Quillan was departing from her, eyes being all dreamy, so I am having only one task remaining. I am going into dining hall, just about time Chief Larign is thinking of ordering tea. I am saying I will get his tea along with mine, and I am bringing him very special tea indeed.

" 'Ah, Mistress,' he is saying. 'What brings you to my halls this morning? I hope we have no folk ill among us.'

"I am telling him not at all, that I am having supper with his son and son's wife, so comfortable the evening being, I did not go home afterward but am begging a bed at a Loam warmwall. He is drinking tea, making smiles on his face, and I am knowing the tea is pleasant for him. So, I am speaking of Quillan and of Lailia and of marriage between them and before many minutes, he is thinking this is his idea, to make alliance between Loam and Granite tight as a crab's shell breastplate!"

Now, I was interested. "How did you do that?" I demanded.

"The scent of the tea is . . . what would you say . . . hypnotic agent? What I am saying goes into his head, and he is believing idea is starting there. So, into my teacup, I am saying: 'Then you make an ally of Belthos some other way, not? But only after everyone else is in alliance. That way, Belthos cannot bargain. Belthos has nothing to bargain with. If he had Lailia, he could threaten harm to her if you did not do as he wished.'

"And the chieftain thinks this is his idea, also. Then are coming Quillan and Lailia, hand in hand, feelings all over their faces, and Chief Larign is taking the news with much good nature.

"So, then into my cup I am murmuring, 'Since you have no heir as yet, Quillan, you won't be joining the battle for the key. Your father will no doubt want to leave you in charge of Granite tribal lands. Your marriage should occur at once, so Lailia may accompany you there . . .'

"And then the chieftain is saying, 'Better get you married off at once. Can't have the lovelorn drifting about during the key-battle time, can we?'

"The young couple are agreeing, not? 'But, I must make a quick trip below,' Quillan is saying. 'To the gem deposits at the foot of the falls. I will not have Lailia wed without an appropriate bride gift.'

"And I am saying, 'May I accompany you, chief's son? I am having urgent business of my own there, collecting healing herbs.' As I was having, though it was really for meeting you I am coming. Quillan is finding gems very early and is climbing halfway up Night Mountain by now, very eager."

I said, "So they'll be married."

"Yes," said Gavi, with a smirk. "And, if I am Mistress of the First Slumber, I will guarantee they stay as fond as they are now." She paused for a moment, then said, "I am telling you now of conversation I am overhearing between chieftain and his son . . ."

She told me to my amazement, making me glad that I had not pushed the matter of the message. There was still time enough for that. "When are the men going?" I asked.

"The chieftain says the army goes in a few days by the western route marked by the scouts, and he is not even knowing he tells me. I am intending to go after him. I will be seeing this door, this key, this battle. Besides, if there are being men wounded, they will be needing someone to heal them, or to let them go, painless."

"How long a journey is it?"

"Later I am finding out, two days' hard march, three if they go slower or have to go farther north to avoid the Toothies. The scouts have come back, already, after marking southwestern trails to go and western ones to return. Our warriors want to reach the battleground when the moon is full, giving them more light to fight by. Day Mountain is coming for a long time already. It is a great distance for them . . ."

I said, "Your people have seen us, up on the Mountain. They know we'll be coming. With a meeting between us inevitable, will they still go off to war?"

"After I am settling matter for Lailia and Quillan, I am asking about that. Chieftain says if you find us, you find us, with warriors or without warriors, no big difference, but if Night Mountain is not in time for battle, it is making great difference! If one side is not showing up, is forfeiting a turn. Besides, our watcher heard you strangers say the names *Hessing* and *Hargess*, and chief says you will do nothing evil to upset Hessings back on Earth, for only our being here gives Hessing-Hargess right to this world. Otherwise, this planet belongs to the toothy stenchfuls."

"True," I said, with admiration. "I hadn't thought that far."

Adam came through the woods at about that time, bringing the device he'd used to record several more talker fronds, turned to me immediately, and asked if Gavi had received the message.

"We've been waiting for you, Adam," I said, as he hurried to set up the scent organ and begin the sequence recorded on the meadow. Gavi sat silent, sniffing it all the way through, then twice again.

After the third time, she said, "How wonderful the machine is being. Oh, if I am having one of these, what wonders I might be working in this world."

"It sounds to me as though you've already worked wonders," I said. "You heal people . . ."

"Oh, yes, if they are not being too seriously ill, but the method is being so cumbersome by comparison. Gums for burning, powders for burning or spraying, oils for heating, each one being gathered and prepared with great labor then stuffed into scent boards with even more labor and care. Here, is only the pressing of a button and the machine is making the word."

Adam shifted from foot to foot, impatiently. "The important thing is, what's the message? What have they been saying to us!"

Gavi nodded, "Ah. Well. The World is asking that you be speaking to it. The World is asking that you be speaking to it before you are doing anything more to the plants and the creatures, for you are not fitting this world at all. This world is having no place for you on these mossy lands. If you are wanting World to be making a place for you, you must be speaking to the World, describing selves, no . . . not selves, describing wantings of selves. World is saying now, today, you people must be going up to the heights where are more like you and where no destroying happens. When others come, other kinds, they must stay on heights, also. Heights are . . . not . . . speakable with. Is that word?"

Adam and I shared a glance before I said, "You might say, 'conversable.' Is that all of it?"

She shook her head, looking slightly confused.

"World says 'We wonder about four-legged kind. Are they wanting going now or waiting until later?' "

"Going where?"

"I am faulty in understanding. These are new words. The word for go, I understand. Dog smell, receding, receding, something shutting it off, that is smell of going, and the odor of bruised moss as things go through it. I am not being certain what this means."

"We might be able to figure it out if we knew who is speaking," I said.

"World is speaking." Her gesture was wide, including all the growths around us, the sky, the stone ramparts looming above. "World is speaking."

"From . . . where?" Adam asked. "Where is the brain, the thinking part?"

"All is thinking part," she said. "No. All is part of thinking part." She looked puzzled. "Now, that is strangeness. Message says, 'We.' Smelling of mosslands, smelling of something not quite mosslands and smaller, smelling of something stronger, bigger. Message says, 'We wonder.' "

"How the hell do you get wonder out of a smell?" demanded Adam.

She pondered this. "Wonder is like question smell. Question smell is complex but familiar smell with part missing or strange new part included. Your mind asks, 'What is missing?' or, 'What is that doing there?' That is wondering."

I blinked. When had I encountered that before? Of course. Each time a mother dog nosed her puppies, to see if anything in that complex smell was missing, she was wondering . . .

Gavi stared at the sky, obviously puzzled. "I have not been smelling message to outsiders before. World was never thinking I was outsider. I have been smelling only little messages, from part to part. Like . . . like your eye telling your hand to reach out, catch something. Like your skin telling your finger to scratch an itch."

"But slower," said Adam.

"Yes," she agreed. "Ten or twenty days from sprout to finished words, another ten or twenty before ripe words do last dance. But then, we have short lives so move fast. World lives almost forever, so is moving slower."

"How do we speak to the World?" I asked. "How do we learn the language?"

"You are teaching me how this machine is working, and I am making message for you. You have something more for me to sniff?"

We said yes, and put in the message we had seen being born on the way to her as well as the ones that Adam had collected that morning. I was watching her face, and it went ashen.

"What?" I cried. "What is it?"

"World will not wait any longer," she gulped. "World says, badness, badness, you will go or you will be driven out. Now, World says. No more patience."

I might have scoffed at this except for the look on her face. She was terrified, not for herself, but for us. Adam and I shared a long, troubled look, and my mind clicked into panic mode. "A message, Gavi. Make us a message. Right now. Here's the machine, here are all the logs . . ."

"Too long, it will take too long . . ."

"No. It won't take too long. The message should be simple. 'We hear . . . that is, we smell you. We will obey you at once.' " It wouldn't be at once, of course, but it was obvious that whatever was speaking to us had an extremely flexible notion of what constituted promptness. "Here's the index. All the smells. With names. You hit the number of the smell you want on this keyboard, and it will emit. If that's the right one, enter it over here, on this other keyboard. I'll help you."

We worked until noon. The sun was directly overhead when we had the message ready. 'Humans understand you. Humans will obey at once.' She had done it a dozen times over, refining it each time.

"Let the machine send this smell over and over," she said. "Tomorrow, when you start back, keep sending it. When you get there, keep on with it."

"You don't answer the message back to the message carrier?" Adam asked.

She shook her head reprovingly. "Think! Ten, twenty days to make question. Then ten, twenty days to make answer. Words are gone by then. Sniffers are being everywhere in forest. Willogs sniff. Some mosses sniff. Some trees are good sniffers. Somewhere, here or on way, one will sniff the message . . ."

"But who gets the message?" I demanded. "Willogs don't run the world, do they?"

Gavi gave me a hurt look. "I am saying many times, World sends message, World hears message. You are asking where is World's nose? I am not knowing! Now is not time to be worrying about it. You have much work to do. Who is knowing what your wantings are? Every person is having different wantings. How am I saying your wantings. What are words for your wantings?"

"We probably want Splendor, too," grunted Adam. "We want heaven."

"Who has the key now?" I asked.

"Key is at battleground, but Night Mountain is having . . . owner-ness?"

"Ownership."

"Yes. Soon the men will be marching away, going to fight for it."

"All the men?" asked Adam. "If so, that makes this a very good time for us to come to Night Mountain doesn't it? Fewer people to worry about meeting?"

Gavi wrinkled her nose. "It is not mattering, good time or bad time or impossible time. You must come, now, soon. Otherwise, it will be bad for you. I am wishing I could answer for you, talk to something for you. Why is the Mountain being not conversable, I am wondering."

"Rock," I said. "The rest of the world is probably covered with a network of living material. It extends under the rivers and seas. Any-place there's a crack it can get through. But the rock that makes up the plateaus goes all the way through the world, and it's solid basalt."

"So," Gavi said, rather sadly. "This is why the World lets us be. Because we are out of way. I was thinking it was because we are living in respect of it."

Adam asked, "What's the smell for *go*."

"I smell your smell receding, that means you go. I smell sharp, nasty smell, meaning 'pay attention!' added on, and whole smell means, you will go. That message you had me sniff, it says you will go to Mountain. Now."

"How do you smell now?" he persisted.

"Evening smell, cut off. Little before evening smell, cut off, earlier time yet, cut off. Meaning, do not wait, not even a little. Do it now."

"And the word for the heights would be the smell of the heights," said Adam.

"Yes," she agreed. "It is having a different smell from here, colder, with more leaves in it. And jar trees. Jar trees are very strange-smelling, smell is very . . ."

"Pervasive?" I offered. "It spreads out?"

"Oh, yes. Big jar tree is being dangerous. People are drinking sap, after time, they are becoming limp, senseless. After much time, they are dying. Small jar tree is being more useful."

"So, if a good many of the PPI people move up onto the plateau . . ."

"Staying away from jar trees and gardens," said Gavi, firmly.

". . . staying away from gardens," I agreed.

"I am drawing you map to make sure," she said firmly, taking writing materials from the bag she carried and explaining as she drew: southernmost was tribe Loam, farther west was tribe Granite, farther east, tribe Burrow, others here, and here, there are gardens, and here, only here a good place for ships to set down on rock, disturbing nothing. The settlements took up only a small segment at the edge of the great plateau, though she mentioned that all the edge and part of the center had been explored by young men with nothing better to do.

"Will your people welcome us?" I asked.

"While most all the strutters gone, yes," she said. "Then, when they are returning, we must be using your machine on them. Make them peaceable."

"You can do that?" I asked. "Really?" And if she could, I exulted, could I take the method back to Earth and use it on the iggy-huffos?

"I can do it, if I am having help. If they will accept idea of sharing key."

"Will they win the battle?" Adam asked.

"Oh, yes. It is our turn."

Adam regarded her quizzically. "You mean, the battle is more of a ritual than a reality."

She shook her head. "Is being very real, but ending is foreknown. Night Mountain is owed three wins, this is second one, so we will win, but people are still dying. Without blood, without dying, there is no battle."

"It surprises me they keep it secret," Adam said. "If it's such a big thing, one would expect it to be discussed, all the details recounted . . ."

"Oh, they are discussing," said Gavi. "Over and over. This one was at the battle, he is saying this happened. Chief Such-such was almost dead, key was used, bright light came, chieftain was gone. That one was at the battle, he is saying 'No bright light, nothing happened, except body was gone.' This one saw the door open, that one didn't. This one saw something inside Splendor, that one says there is no seeing inside Splendor. What is being true, what is being false? Who can tell?"

"Well, some few things are probably true," I said. "There really is a key. It opens something. There is a where, there. Some people or bodies of people can go into that where. And there are beings or inhabitants in that place . . ."

"And the place isn't in normal space," said Adam. "Obviously."

Gavi looked thunderstruck. "If that is so, then I saw it! That was place I am seeing inside the rock. That place."

"Yes," I agreed with her. "It may have been."

We took our leave of her and started back to the installation, emitting our message continuously as we went.

⁝ Where Walking Sunshine went, words came fragrant through the forest, scented sermons, odorous orations, redolent rodomontades, syllable on scented syllable proclaiming the beauty of the World. The morning message might call attention to the scented blooms on the zibber trees. The afternoon message might remind one of the moist smell of mosses beneath a fall. Lately, the words had grown annoyed, irritated. Sharp smells protested the unresponsive creatures, men! In the forest north of the lake, following the trail the humans had made toward the battle place, Walking Sunshine sniffed the words with some concern, worried over their content, for (blasphemous as it would be to put it into smells) Walking Sunshine knew something the World did not.

Such a thing was unsmelled of! For any creature to presume it knew more than the World knew was heretical, disorderly, unwillogish, and being unwillogish took some doing, for willogs were a widely differentiated lot.

Nonetheless, Walky had come to the realization of a great oddity. Although humans could sense odors—badly, but they could do it—when words were sent to them, they did not smell the words. Conversely, though humans spoke words, the World neither heard nor heeded the words the humans spoke. Badly needed was a creature who could both talk and emit! An interspeaker! Though there might not be time for an interspeaker to do any good, for even then, new words came marching, not merely the constant trickle of them that was usual, but great chains of them, everywhere. Strong words emitting across mosses, reeking along ramparts, venting along valleys, stinking beside streams; they ripened, rose up, and exploded in showers of seeds from which new talkers sprang up in tens, dozens, and scores where only one had been before, all to grow the same messages that were jiggling here and bouncing there, multiplying as they went.

"Rottenness, rottenness to be rooted out, to be extirpated, removed from the circles of this world that the tranquillity, the long quietude of Moss be not disturbed.

"Is this not the footstool of heaven? Is this not the gateway to paradise? Is it fitting this monstrosity should continue, this moving creature that will not talk and will not listen, this thing called man? Is it fitting, this green toothy thing that burns the forests?"

Walky had never encountered a dilemma before. He had taken the word from men, who often argued about dilemmas, and the concept had been difficult for Walky to enfold. On the one hand, the World was the World. On the other hand, givers of such great gifts as eyes and ears should not be destroyed. Walky's willog soul denied this order of destruction. Its willog sap ran warmly at sensing these words. What thanks would that be for the gift of color? For the sound of bells. For the miracle of singing! Walky had grown three voices in three separate registers in order to try it for itself! Walky sounded lovely, simply lovely!

Walking Sunshine knew what response it would receive if this argument were put into words. Willogs could use their own words, of course. When they wrote poetry, they used their own words, but one could never use words that contradicted the wisdom of the World. Walky had told all the creatures to grow ears! Had that contradicted messages already received? Walky shivered all over as it thought back over its history. Surely, surely it had learned something, sometime that would be of help in this terrible predicament.

Though, on further thought, perhaps his words were not a contradiction of the World's words. Not really. Ears did not contradict noses. Ears were simply facts. Things the World should know about. Eyes were facts. So were voices. Something had to be done to let the World know what was true and factual, but what could it be?

In the Derac camp, the warriors were preparing for an assault.

"Clean armor," said one to another, who passed the word on, "Clean armor." The throaty gasps ricocheted around the wide and blackened clearing as groups of warriors set themselves to the task. Clean armor would be followed by other readiness commands, the series of commands that was always uttered in the days before battle. The heavy armament was due to arrive that day, along with the last clan-ship of warriors. In two days, three at the latest, they would attack the humans by marching down the west side of the lake and around it to the south, to fall upon the encampment from the south. No one would expect it, not from that direction. No one would see them until they had their teeth in the throats of the humans. Battle day was a day all the Derac were looking forward to. There was no meat on this planet at all, and they were heartily sick of eating rations.

The commander of the last shipload of Derac to arrive had said something about an aged one coming in the final ship. Usually aged ones did not leave their G'Tachs.

"Why is an aged one coming here?" asked one of the warriors, busy polishing his sword.

"To give us a talk," said the nearest Derac. That particular group had arrived in the last ship, and they had picked an unburned spot at the edge of the forest to work, because it was shadier. "Sometimes they do that, give us a talk if there's something special they want us to do."

"Like what?" asked the first, a somewhat younger warrior, with far less experience.

"Like if they want us to kill all the females first."

"There aren't any human females here."

"Oh, yes there are. They look like the males, that's all."

"If they look alike, how do we know which ones to kill first?"

"Jabucha says we just kill them all very fast, that way we're sure to have done the females as quick as anything. Nobody can tell which were first and which were next."

"Can we eat them? The females?"

"I suppose so. Nobody has said we can't."

Behind the warriors, at the edge of the forest, a particular copse took note of what was being said. The copse was indignant. These toothy ones had contributed nothing! They had burned the forest and reburned it every time someone tried to get closer to learn about them. They slept in their ships, with the doors locked. They wouldn't share the pattern of their eyes or ears. It had been very difficult to learn their language because they did not help by writing things. They did not share anything! A fungus upon them, the copse thought to itself, emitting the spores that would guarantee an itchy mold on the newcomers to match the one suffered by those who had arrived earlier.

Humans should be warned about this battle, this attack. They should be told, loudly, firmly, in words! So thinking, the copse faded, sapling by sapling, back into the forest, creeping away unseen, until it was far enough that Walking Sunshine could begin to roll, quickly, toward the battleground where it knew the humans would be. There, at the battleground, it would announce itself as interspeaker for the World.

⋮ We pushed the floater hard to get back to the PPI installation as soon as we could. We didn't make it by dark, so we rubbed Gavi's monster-off stuff on us, slept lightly, and rose very early to make the installation shortly after noon. I linked ESC and said I was on the way, please get yourselves together, and when my little boat arrived at the pier, Sybil was awaiting me inside the lock. We said very little on the way to the lab, where the others were gathered. The story didn't take long to tell.

"The World wants us to move," Gainor repeated the gist of what I'd said. "It wants us to do that immediately, it has lost patience with us. And you've told it we would."

"I've emitted Gavi's message all the way back here, and the scent organ is still poofing away on the meadow. We put it at the edge of the forest, hoping there are sniffers in there. I assume with only forty some odd PPI staffers left, moving won't take any great time."

"We can make a start today," he said. "Enough to indicate a good faith effort." He grinned to himself. "And won't the Derac be surprised when they find we're gone."

"You think they're planning to attack us?"

"Certain of it. Probably within the next few days. We've spotted their scouts at various places along the eastern edge of the lake, no doubt laying out the attack route. You think the World is planning to attack them?"

I shrugged. It was entirely possible. I couldn't imagine Moss would tolerate all that burn off and scarring, all that buildup of troops. I unrolled Gavi's map.

"Here's the place on the plateau Gavi picked for us to set down, destroying no gardens and infringing on no tribal lands. Naturally, we don't let on she gave it to us."

Gainor walked me back to the pier. "What are you going to tell Paul?"

"Same old story," I said. "Invent an old codger out in the moss who claims to be able to translate. Tell Paul what he said. I've got a word-for-word translation that Gavi dictated to me, plus a more idiomatic translation. Gavi says there are almost no Mossen words that cannot be conveyed by natural smells on this world except a few Derac, human, and machine smells they've borrowed from us recently."

"Almost?"

"She said 'almost,' " I affirmed. "She said there are a few language smells that she herself has never smelled, not from anything here on Moss. She says, however, that doesn't mean they're not a natural smell somewhere else."

"Did you ask her which ones?"

"As a matter of fact, I did, Gainor. She found a few on the odor organ and noted them down for me. One is a kind of cinnamon burned sugar smell. Another is a dark, sulfur rot smell. It's in my report."

"Very well," he said, patting my hand. "Tell your group to get packed, and I'll tell PPI they'll be lifted first, with their equipment. We'll do Paul and his equipment next and leave you and the dogs until last. That'll give you time to talk to them and work out a plan for moving them."

I went to Paul's quarters first. He was deeply involved, with several machines running, and it took a few moments to get his attention. When I gave him the story, he took the papers I gave him with only a trace of his usual sneering reluctance. After looking at them for a few moments, however, he said, "Right, right. Of course. Yes, this is on the right track." He stabbed at a word with a forefinger, shaking his head. "Not completely accurate here, I don't think, but the next bit is fine. Good. Good. Leave it with me." And he turned back to his work.

"They want to move you, Paul."

"Fine, fine. Whenever."

He was accomplishing something, which meant he would be making no trouble for anyone for a time, at least. Since Gainor would already have communicated with the PPI installation, I went to the trainers and dogs next. Adam had already told them what had happened; I had only to let them know what Gainor planned to do.

"He's leaving us for last," I said.

"Wan see," said Behemoth. "See war."

I looked uncertainly at Adam, who flushed a little and said, "Behemoth wants to go to the place where the war is going to be fought. I mentioned the business about . . . you know, the dogs."

It took me a moment to remember. Gavi had said the words wanted to know about the four-legged creatures going somewhere. "Why there?" I asked, stupidly, only to have Behemoth give me a look. It was his don't-be-stupid look that reminded me why there. That's where the door to Splendor was.

Adam said, "He wants them all to go, including the puppies."

"That could be dangerous," I said. "I don't know what weapons the Derac will use, but . . ."

"Na now," said Scramble, sounding anxious. "Affer war."

"When the fighting's over," Adam offered.

Scramble was looking at me intently. I was reminded a little of the way Scarlet had looked at me, long ago, when I had saved her puppies from Jon Point. "You all want this?" I asked.

Low, rumbling growl from the three male dogs. The females did not signal anything. They just sat there, looking at me.

I thought about it. I was as curious about the place as anyone, perhaps more than most, considering its possible connection to Witt's disappearance, and it would be very easy to find. We could get there without any trouble, so long as we didn't get mixed up in the battle. And the Derac, so Gainor had said, would be coming down the east side of the lake, well away from where we'd be.

"We'll need a big floater," I said. "We'll have to carry food for the dogs and ourselves, plus all the pups. We'll need to scout the area before anything happens, so we're sure we're safe and secure when people start fighting. If Gainor will let us, I'm willing to try."

Gainor proved to be out of touch, so I explained to Ornel Lethe what we wanted to do. He said he'd get the message to Gainor. Five minutes later, Sybil linked, asking if she could add herself to the party, and I said sure, I could use the help. Only after she'd gone did I remember that three pseudodogs would be along, something Sybil wasn't supposed to know about. Well, maybe it was time she did.

Almost immediately thereafter, an ESC ship arrived. Mechs poured out, and one set of them began taking the installation apart while another set packed up the contents of the buildings. There were eight buildings in the installation, and within an hour, four of them had been loaded on freight floaters and tugged away north by low-flying and virtually soundless mechs. In the midst of this, Gainor arrived to talk with me.

"We're not letting the Derac see us leaving," he said with a wolfish grin. "Nor see where we're going. The mechs will take the floaters to the plateau and go up via a deep canyon that's shielded by rock from any detectors. They'll go to the spot your friend picked out and set up everything just the way it was here. Now, what's this about the dogs wanting to see the battle?"

"Not the battle, Gainor. Splendor. They want to see the door to Splendor."

"Why?" he asked, amazed.

"I don't know," I confessed. "But Gavi did say something about words inviting four-legged ones to go through. I didn't tell Adam not to mention it, and even if I had, he might have done it anyhow. Behemoth is alpha dog, and that means he rules Adam, too."

Gainor's eyebrows went up. "That's interesting," he said, whistling soundlessly through his teeth. "How long has that been going on?"

"For some time, I gather. However, I understand their curiosity. They want to see, and so do I. We shouldn't miss the chance."

"Tell them I've said no, not just yet, because of the Derac. After this whole Derac nonsense is over, you can all go there, if you like, and take Ornel, Abe, and Sybil with you. She says you've already agreed she can go along."

I nodded, swallowing my misgivings.

"All right. Then you get your materials packed. We'll go ahead and move you, like everyone else, but when the battle is over, we'll let you have a floater to come back and see the battlefield."

I carried this word back to our quarters, emphasizing, as Gainor had not, the Derac heavy armaments that could make the whole area unsafe for anyone near it. Behemoth wandered off for a while. When he returned, he had evidently decided the plan was agreeable to him, for he sniffed my hand in passing. He usually made this gesture only when parting company.

By that evening, the rest of the installation had been moved. The following morning, our building went after the others. By noon, Paul and I were at home once more, though in a completely different location. By that evening, the ESC fortification had been reassembled not far away, though it was separated from us by deep chasms in the rock through which steams rose like tribes of troubled ghosts, almost hiding the force fields behind them.

"Are you sure the Derac don't know we're gone?" I asked Gainor, whom I encountered wandering around the installation, examining the weird jar trees and the immense liverworts.

"We're receiving from the fish around their base," he said in an uninterested voice. "They're going right ahead, preparing for battle. If they knew we were gone, surely they'd be doing something else."

I remembered what Paul had told me about the Derac and thought it entirely possible that Derac warriors would continue doing whatever they were doing until someone told them to stop, regardless of what might have changed in the meantime.

"The Night Mountain warriors have reached the bottom of the plateau and are on their way to the battle," Gainor said as he fingered a thick, juicy-looking leaf that smelled strongly of mint. "It occurred to me you might want to offer Gavi Norchis an opportunity to see what goes on there. You're both welcome to watch the monitors in ESC."

"I'd make the offer if I could," I agreed. "If I knew where to find her. She said something about following the Night Mountain warriors, and that's likely where she is. By the way, when do the dogs and trainers get up here?"

He turned to face me with his mouth open. "What do you mean? They came this afternoon!"

"No," I said. "They didn't. Adam said they were coming in the last shift."

"And someone told me they were already here," he snarled. "What's going on?"

He headed toward the ESC installation, and I went to the house, where I found Clare stretched out on her bed. When I came in, she sat up, saying, "They're gone."

"Where did they go?"

"Behemoth wanted to see the battleground. Adam borrowed a floater. He and Frank and all the dogs have gone."

"And you're just telling me about it now?"

"I didn't know until a few moments ago when I came in here and found Adam's note." She offered it to me, and I read it, cursing silently. I should have paid more attention when Adam had told me Behemoth was the alpha dog!

"Adam says they're going south around the bottom of the lake and then up the west side," I said. "I imagine we can find them."

"If you think that's wise," she said.

I sat down. "Sybil, the Derac have heavy armament, and they'll use it at the least provocation. If the dogs are in the way, they can all be killed, and if so, that's it for the dog project. Years of work for nothing. All that work stocking the moon, for nothing. If they keep the puppies safe, but the adult dogs are killed along with Frank and Adam, that's still it. The puppies aren't weaned. Even if we raised them, they wouldn't be able to hunt without learning it from someone, just as the big dogs learned it from you three, two of whom would be dead."

"I wasn't very good at it, either," said Clare. "All I had to do was chase along to illustrate pack behavior. Adam and Frank make much better dogs than I do."

"I'm going to link Gainor," I told her. "Wait here. Don't, for heaven's sake decide to go off on your own. I think Gainor is going to want to go with us."

I had some difficulty explaining to Gainor why Adam and Frank had behaved as they did.

"When they're in dog shape, they're dogs," I shouted, finally, after trying several times without shouting. "They think like dogs. They believe they are dogs, which is why the trainers were modified in the first place. We believed we needed a role model for the puppies! Adam and Frank taught Behemoth and the rest of the pack how to hunt! You can't expect Adam and Frank not to act like properly subordinate dogs when they are dogs. Subordinate dogs follow the leader, and Behemoth is the leader."

He cursed under his breath, calling upon several Tharstian gods.

"You'll have to go after them without me, because I have to stay here to oversee contact between our people and the current residents. I'll send Ornel and Abe and Sybil . . ."

"Not in noncon suits, Gainor. We don't have time to fiddle with stuff." Eating and excreting were equally difficult in noncon suits, not to speak of the limited time they gave people before the suit had to be flushed and resupplied. Gainor mumbled for a while before deciding I was right, and less than half an hour later the three ESC people were on a floater outside my door, where Clare and I joined them. During all this, I don't think Paul was aware of anything except what he was doing. I had heard recurrent gleeful shouts from his quarters, his usual habit when something he tried came out right, so I presumed he was making good progress on the language.

The floater we had was a giant step up from the little one we'd used previously. It had both high-speed and high-altitude capability, which enabled us to fly low over the plateau, angle downward through the canyon, and then speed at low level toward the former PPI site, arriving there in only an hour or so. By that time, it was getting dark, so we descended into the forest and used our landing lights to pick up the trail of the other floater. It didn't take us long to find rumpled mosses and broken twigs leading more or less southwest, around the edge of the lake and far enough from it that no one would have observed them from the shore.

Ornel and Abe took the first watch; Clare, Sybil, and I curled up on the cushioned floor and tried to sleep. There among the trees, our speed couldn't be any greater than those we were following. Every grove and tree meant a detour, and the trail itself wasn't straight but wandering, as though the dogs had gone first, sniffing out things that interested them, while the floater followed, bearing puppies and occasional nursing mothers.

Every time I thought of the puppies and the Derac anywhere in proximity, I got a sick lump in my throat. We had all worked so hard to give this race of animals a place of its own, and now that work was threatened in a way I had never foreseen. Behemoth and the other dogs were no doubt intelligent, we could all testify to that, but they were uninterested in or impatient with things like politics and human conflicts. They simply didn't recognize that dogs were at the mercy of human problems.

At about the middle of the night, Abe woke me and Clare, and we took over for him and Ornel. "We're headed up the long northwest shore of the lake," he said. "But it's still a wandering trail. I spoke to Ornel about just striking a line directly to the place they're headed for, but he thought it was better to follow them, in case something happened to them en route."

I agreed with Ornel, so I drove while Clare used the night-vision screen to find the trail. We came to a stretch of unforested country, all low mosses, and made good time crossing it, only to be slowed down again when we entered the forest on the far side. It was getting light when I stopped the floater so I could go off into the shrubbery for a few moments. When I returned, Abe and Sybil had broken out the rations and made coffee in the food service unit built into the floater.

When Sybil sat beside me with her plate, I noticed her pocket moving and touched it questioningly. A small head poked out, fuzzy, with large ears and huge eyes.

"Gixit," she said. "The rest of the family are up at the ESC."

The little creature gave me a look of surprise and dived back into her pocket, from which it peeked at me at intervals, accompanying itself with a long soliloquy that sounded to me like speech. "Do they talk?" I asked Sybil.

"They chatter," she said, dismissively. "It isn't language."

I regarded the little thing with a skeptical eye. It had certainly sounded like language to me. Perhaps it was the result of my having lived with Paul all those years. Anything sounded like language. We didn't take long with breakfast. By the time the sun was above the horizon, we were on our way again.

Our positional navigation system put us halfway up the side of the lake when we spotted something ahead that was not moss or tree. We stopped the floater and went forward on foot. The something turned out to be the other floater, half-covered with leaves and moss branches. I heard a welcoming woof and turned to one side to find Scramble in a mossy nest, well hidden behind a half-rotten tree. She was guarding all three litters of puppies.

"Scramble," I half shouted. "Why are you all risking the puppies like this? Don't you know they could be killed? There are Derac out there. I'm sure they'd love puppy for dinner, and maybe dog, as well."

She gave me a long, level look that told me I was overreacting. After all, here she was, with all the puppies, and nothing disastrous had happened.

The look wasn't enough to stop me. "And if Veegee and Dapple get killed? I suppose you have enough milk for all three litters!"

"You ahv," she said.

I trusted she didn't mean me, personally, but the resources of the base. Since she wasn't at all remorseful, yelling at her would do no good.

While the others brought the floater up, I sat down on the fallen tree, wiping my face with the backs of my dirty hands, surprised to find that I'd actually been weeping. It was relief, I suppose. I'd been half-convinced we'd find them all dead.

"What is Behemoth after?" I asked Scramble. "What does he want?"

"Hearsh oishes," she said.

"Voices? Whose?"

She shrugged. "Hearsh in win. Shay comm."

"When did he hear these voices in the wind?"

"Heer, mahsh."

"Here on Moss? Since we first got here?"

She nodded.

The dogs had good ears, but then, so did I, and I had heard nothing of the kind. Unless, of course, the sound range had been above human hearing, in that particularly shrill range that only dogs and bats can hear. Or unless . . .

"Hear, Scramble? Or maybe, smell?"

"Smell," she conceded. "Mai'ee."

This was an all-purpose "maybe" word meaning she didn't know, wasn't sure. My mind was full of ugly visions, visions of the other dogs being slain, hurt, incapacitated, and Scramble left here alone. She whined, and I looked up.

"Ai no yu comm," she said. "Always no yu comm."

"Yes," I whispered to her, putting my arms around her. She knew I would always come to love and protect her. I knew she would always come to love and protect me. We were friends, and she had depended on that.

Also, she'd been reading my mind, as usual.

I dropped my voice to a whisper. "You were the one who decided to stay here, with the puppies, because you knew I'd come? You knew they'd be in danger. You didn't want Behemoth to take them in the first place?"

She looked away from me with that impenetrable gaze she sometimes wore. She agreed with what I'd said, but she wasn't going to be disloyal to Behemoth by admitting it.

I put my head against hers and murmured nothing at her, letting her know I understood what she'd been up against, letting her know she hadn't betrayed our friendship, not in any way. She put her nose against my neck, just below the jaw. I think it was a way of saying, "You're safe with me here. I would take the throat out of anyone who harmed you . . ."

Clare and the others brought our floater up. She and I held a brief colloquy about what should be done next. I wanted the puppies up on the plateau, where there were people who could feed them and care for them if something happened to their parents, someone who would know exactly what to do, even if no adult dogs were . . . available, ever. I spoke through my teeth, trying not to make unseemly noises of grief. The very thought hurt.

Clare said, "It's got to be me, Jewel. There are only two of us here with any idea about it, and you need to go on, to see what's happening. If someone will go with me to drive the floater, I'll take the puppies back to ESC."

I put the matter to Abe and Sybil, and Abe agreed eagerly, giving me the strong impression that the sooner he returned to the protection of the force screens, the happier he would be.

I explained to Scramble, asking her if she wanted to go with them or go on farther, with us. When I assured her the puppies could be fed and cared for, she said she would go with us. She meant, go be with Behemoth, and we both knew it.

"Abe," I said, "keep low and stay away from the lake until you're well back on the other side. We don't want the Derac to see you."

"Don't they have traffic screens?" Clare asked. "We'll show up on them, no matter how low we are."

"They may have, but we've had ships landing fairly regularly, plus floaters going here and there. Remember how we traveled to and from the plateau yesterday, and keep yourselves at treetop level until you're shielded by rock. A long diagonal line from here to the top of the plateau will catch their attention where a low-flying floater won't."

"You want me to come back with the floater?" Abe asked, somewhat grudgingly. "There may not be room on that other one for all of you."

"I'm sure Gainor already has fish watching the battleground. Ask him to keep an eye on them, and when things settle down, after the battle, we'll expect someone to come pick us up."

The four of us who were left took up our packs and began following the trail on foot, Scramble in the lead, Sybil and I behind her, and Ornel bringing up the rear.

TOWARD THE
BATTLEGROUND

⫶ We made better time than I had expected, as Scramble was able to differentiate between a dog detour and a trail that went continuously forward. We climbed for the first part of the journey, a gentle rise that continued upward for some time before descending again almost to the level of the lake, which sparkled at us intermittently, off to our right. The sun swung above us and as our shadows began to lengthen toward the east, I felt a sense of oppression, a kind of smothering weight on the eyes and the ears, a stuffed-up feeling. I wasn't alone. Ornel cursed under his breath and stopped at the edge of a small clearing to dig through his pack for some kind of medicament to clear his eyes.

I said. "I feel it, too. It could be some kind of . . . scent curtain, perhaps. Can you smell anything?"

Though he said he couldn't smell anything, I certainly did, an elusive and wholly novel odor, not nasty or disgusting, but admonitory, all the same. I called to Scramble, and when she returned to us, I asked her what the smell was.

"Is laish lon umun," she said.

"This place belongs to someone," I translated for Ornel's and Sybil's benefit. "It's a keep out sign. No trespassing."

I wasn't sure they heard me, both of them staring at Scramble as though she'd grown another head. Finally, Sybil shook herself, saying; "We must be getting close to the battleground. I doubt the warriors will smell it if we don't."

"But wouldn't they be likely to?" I asked. "Gavi Norchis told me they were all 'noses' back on Forêt."

"She was also telling you not to talk about her," said a voice.

We turned. My two companions gasped as Gavi herself edged into view from behind a nearby tree, complete with crab armor except for the hideous head, which was under her arm.

"I am meeting you strangely, Jewel Delis," she said.

"I am meeting you happily," I responded, surprised at the jolt of pure joy that had struck me at her appearance. "We were just talking about the smell. Scramble says it means keep out."

"It is meaning that." She shrugged. "But it is being only a caution smell, not a punishment. It is warning World is using to keep creatures from danger. Battleground is dangerous, so, it warns creatures away."

"Are the warriors already there?" I asked.

"No. When they are camping for the night, I am continuing along trail. I am always liking to know what is around, what kinds of things are growing, where are hiding places, where are trees for climbing. When I am getting to battleground, I am deciding to go around it, to be seeing what is here on every side."

"What about Day Mountain? Have they arrived?"

Gavi shook her head. "Not yet. Who are these people?"

I apologized for not introducing her earlier and promptly did so. Ornel bowed over her hand, Sybil nodded as Gixit looked out of her pocket and trilled. This enchanted Gavi, and nothing would do but that we sit down in the clearing, build a fire, brew tea—to counteract the stuffiness, so Gavi said—and play with the little creature. I had to confess, we were all in a better mood afterward, including Scramble, who let Gixit lie on her shoulder and talk into one velvet ear, occasionally rumbling a response.

Gavi questioned what we were doing there, of course, so I told her about Behemoth's adventure. "Adam repeated what you said about the dogs being included in the message from the World, and I guess Behemoth was determined to see for himself."

"I have been sniffing same message several times since," Gavi said. "Always, they are emitting question about four legs. Do they wish to come through. They are not saying come through what, and it is confusing, not?"

"You didn't encounter the dogs on your way here?" Ornel asked.

"No. But I have not yet been going all around battleground," she said. "If dogs are wanting to watch, they would be going westward a little, where is being higher ground."

Gavi and I put the paraphernalia away while Ornel drowned the fire with what was left of the tea. We were just about to pick up our packs and proceed once more when Gixit squealed and ran for Sybil's pocket. Scramble put her head up, drew her lips back, and rumbled a warning as she stared through the trees toward the glimmer of the lake. In a moment I caught a wave of scent, pleasantly resinous. We all heard something moving, and then, music!

Instinctively, we backed farther from the trees, out into the clearing, as we tried to locate the source of the sound. There was movement in the woods, something invisible moving small trunks and branches, the music getting louder, and then, all at once, a copse of trees came lolloping into the clearing, leaflets burgeoning along every tendril, curved rootlet after curved rootlet turning and heaving like wheels, the whole in flourishing motion as it bugled and banged a marching tune that seemed to set the pace for the whole flower-embellished ensemble.

"What is it?" grated Ornel in a panicky voice.

"Willog," gasped Gavi. "Is being a willog, most strange!"

The willog no doubt heard us, for it stopped in its tracks with a silvery shiver of foliage and regarded us for a long moment with what felt like either expectation or exasperation. I, having felt that same kind of look from a good many animals requiring acknowledgment, said, "Good morning."

"Good, wonderful, most elegant morning," cried the willog in several melodic voices that bonged and thonked like a chime of bamboo bells. "A good morning to be meeting peoples. Is one of you the person who sniffs the world?"

We were for a moment confused by this, but Gavi shuddered briefly, cleared her throat, and said, "I sniff the world, usually."

"I am willog self-named Walking Sunshine," it said. "I am first willog with voice! Be congratulatory! I am creature of speaking words!"

"We congratulate you upon your achievement," I said, not knowing whether to laugh or run screaming. It sounded totally nonthreatening, but it was so very large, so twiggy, so full of offshoots and wiry-looking twiny bits that it was difficult to believe it was harmless and impossible to know where the voice was really coming from. Politeness be damned, I had to know: "Where are your . . . eyes and ears and mouth?"

An agile tendril zoomed toward me, stopping just short of my face, and from its swollen tip a large blue eye regarded me with interest. The eye had an eyelid with lashes that batted flirtatiously, seeming to wink at me, enjoying its own joke. That tendril was immediately joined by several others bearing either human-style ears or assorted types of eyes, some of them not at all mammalian-looking.

"Voice box, puffers, and tongue assembly do not fit on small parts," said the willog. "I have them inside main trunk, issuing through new mouth parts!"

Somewhat reassured by its manner, I said, as calmly as I could manage, "I am told that willogs are good poets."

"Some very good, yes," said the willog.

Its words were completely clear, with only a hint of echo, though with that intriguingly wooden sound, like an old musical instrument . . . a marimba! That was it.

It said, "I do make poems, but it would be prideful of me to claim they are good ones."

Gavi regarded it gravely, "Will you recite one for us?"

The willog extended two fronds, each with a set of seven words hanging from it.

"This is verse number one of my favorite own poem. It is a double seven."

"A double seven," Gavi repeated. "Which means?"

"Which means I have made it in moss words and in human words, one moss word to each line of the seven. In this way, we may say it, and see it, and hear it, and also smell it!" Its voice rose with enthusiasm. "How marvelous to have ears and eyes. How marvelous to have voices."

With an exuberant gesture, it shook the foremost frond until the word at the end came loose. It tugged the other six after it, and, instead of dancing off as I had seen happen before, the group began to circle and enlarge. There was an audible crepitation as they swelled in size, dwindling to a slight rustle.

"Poets grow them so," the willog whispered in a very stagy aside. "So they will recite for peoples, not go waltzing off to nowhere. First, hearing words!"

Taking a deep breath, the willog recited:

> *"Here*
> *we stand*
> *digging down*
> *within the mold*
> *of infinite leaves*
> *budded, aged, fallen*
> *sustaining each one of us."*

"That is sound speaking of first seven of poem," said the willog, turning toward me. "Now smell! The first word has one smell, the second word two smells, and so on up to seven smells in the last word, conveying the entire verse."

I looked helplessly at Gavi as the words began to circle. After one or two turns, she spoke, rather hesitantly:

"First word. The ambient scent of the world, meaning *here*. Second word: the scent of this willog, and of a healthy tree, with no separation, meaning *we stand*. Third word: Ah. What's this? Surprising! I am understanding it though. The three smells are herbage, then sweat, then damp earth. To get that sequence, one would have to be *digging down*.

"Fourth word: A surface moss and wood smell, a smell from inside the moss, a smell of roots, a smell of rotted mosses. The combination takes one *into the mold* itself.

"Fifth word. A set of mixed leaves . . . I am not identifying. Another set, another, another, a fifth one. Ah. Far too many to distinguish or count, therefore *of infinite leaves*.

"Sixth word. Ah. Yes. Now that I am knowing how the sweat smell is used, word six is not being difficult. Bud smell, old sweat—meaning past tense—leaf smell, old sweat, and dead leaf smell, old sweat, *Budded, aged, fallen*, six smells in all."

She looked at the willog with what seemed to me respectful admiration as she continued, "Seventh word, first smell: dawn smell. Second smell, same, and third smell, same, the third time with a moist soil and sweat scent added. Once is meaning once, of course, as twice means twice, but three times is meaning some or many. Just as *many evenings* is meaning the past, so is *many dawns* meaning the future. Soil and sweat smells are indicating a future with work in it. *Sustaining*. The fourth smell is of the drack tree . . ."

"The drack tree?" I croaked, totally lost.

"A resinous, thorny tree, very rare, which is always growing alone, a separate thing, an *each*. The fifth smell is of this willog, *one*; then a separation. The sixth smell is of many willogs, separation, then the seventh smell, a repeated one, again many willogs, the meaning of six and seven together, *of us*."

She nodded, saying to the willog in an interested though rather judgmental voice, "Is being very . . . demanding. The word *sustaining* is requiring considerable reach of understanding."

"Oh, yes," the willog agreed. "Growing a seven poem is very demanding. How to get the talker roots to grow the last word correctly so it does seven different things before popping, that is difficult." An ambient eye turned toward me. "A seven word must always use at least one smell more than once because the words have only six sets of emitters."

"If you can grow it to do all that, why don't you grow one with seven sides?" Ornel asked.

The willog shuddered all over, as though wracked by an icy wind. "Oh, do not say. Please, do not say. To say is . . . impropriety, unnatural, perverted. Even master poets who do eight and ten smell poems, do it with only six sets of emitters. Though," the willog looked somehow thoughtful—"Sometimes such poems are so distantly allusive as to be barely possible of apprehension. Always before, the work smell has been very difficult to make and to recognize."

"Moss's beings don't smell when they work?" I asked.

The willog shook the upper part of its largest trunk from side to side, disclosing as it did so several apertures high on the bole that might be its sound emitters. "We work slowly, effortfully but not strenuously, and our odors are extremely subtle. When men came, however, we learned the smell the humans give off when they struggle to do things, and that has given us many new *doing* words. Now we have also speak words, making many things easier to understand."

"What I don't understand," I said, "is how you have acquired so many human words. This acquisition is recent, is it not? How did you come up with this vocabulary?"

"Ah. In bad-smell . . . ah, that is, in human place by Lake Stinks-of-Toothy-Things, one could see places called notice boards, one could hear humans reading of them. So, Walky is gaining some words. *Attention* and *Personnel* and *Commissary* and *Language*. Evidently, master person is making rule against bad language. Walky rejoiced in this. Bad language is ruinous to speaking creatures. Like fungus growing on spirit. Then, Walky is seeing human place labeled *linguistics*. I, Walking Sunshine, read this as similar to word for language, and watched through window as the human using machine brings forward a thing called *Dictionary*. At night, when the human is asleep, one ear tendril goes through the window, one eye tendril goes through the window, one more tendril to push the buttons. Walky pushes button, machine says word, says what word means. I am reading at same time. Soon, I have memorized it, some of it, well, a portion of it. It would take many nights to remember it all."

"You must be very intelligent," I said.

The willog drew itself up. "I am intelligent, of course, as willogs must be. Willogs have many responsibilities. You have heard only the first seven of my poem. It is a double seven, but the second verse is not quite ripe. Nonetheless, I will recite to you second verse:

"They
who lie
below us
deeply buried
have no knowledge of
our speaking thanks in words
for food drawn from their bodies."

"Very true," said Gavi. "There is much buried on Moss, and much going on above it that is mysterious. It is a good poem."

The willog preened itself at her praise, leaves lifting and resettling into place with a silver shiver of pleasure. "No willog else has ever done a double-double seven in both smell and talk, with one sound of talk for each smell, the two meaning the same thing. No willog else has ever done a poem one could smell and say—in human words, of course, for they are the only sound words we have—and also hear and even see what it looks like when Walky's own words dance it or when it is printed in human words with a stick in the bare mud of the river shore or in berry juice on a sheet of bark as Walky did with the message Walky made and left for the human people to find . . ."

It wheezed to a stop, having run out of air. It had obviously not yet learned to breathe between words.

"I thank you, Walking Sunshine," I said. "Particularly for telling us you left the 'thankful, thankful' message written on bark. The one that said you people wanted to know more people."

"More peoples," it corrected me. "Humans made no answer, but Walky understands. Poor human people cannot send words the World can hear, and human people did not think to write a message Walky could read. Oh, poor humans who cannot speak. Unless we prevent, World is going to do something dreadful to you because you are smell-less! I have been telling World you have no noses. I am praying World will heed!"

I heard a movement behind me, then Behemoth's voice. "Noh, av 'mell."

Every part of the willog heaved upward and made a clockwise flailing motion except for one sturdy root, on which it spun. A palpable pirouette. "Ah. Dog! We are hearing very much about dog."

Behemoth stared his "nasty" stare at Scramble, who whined, deep in her throat, rather anxiously.

"Clare took the puppies back to the plateau," I said firmly. "They are safer there. Even if your being here gets you all killed, they will still be safe!"

Behemoth turned toward me, a rumble deep in his chest. Scramble put herself between me and him, and I smelled . . . some sort of interchange between the two, so subtle a flow of scents that I was not even sure I had detected it. Whether it was real or I had only imagined it,

Behemoth stopped glaring at her as the others came out of the woods, Veegee and Dapple, Wolf and Titan, the two pseudodog brothers behind them, packs on their backs.

"Many dogs," said the willog, surprised. "I am Walking Sunshine." He bowed to the assembled animals before I had a chance to say anything.

I moved forward and introduced the dogs, as each made a slight movement of acknowledgment along with, again, some very subtle odors. They were introducing themselves by smell! How did they do that? Scat and urine were the usual smell markings, but they were doing it some other way . . .

When it came to the trainers, I didn't know quite what to say, and Walking Sunshine spoke before I said anything.

"These are not dogs. Smell is not right for dogs."

I cast a sideways look at Sybil and Ornel. Well, it would do no good to try and keep the secret any longer. "No," I said. "They are not dogs, not really. They are really humans whose names are Adam and Frank."

Ornel's jaw dropped open. Sybil merely opened her eyes very wide and stared first at them, then at me, in angry disbelief.

"False dogs," the willog said. "But not made from redmoss. Something like redmoss. Something better, not so fibrous. Oh, how wonderful is such substance for making replicas!"

"Aren't you the clever one," Ornel said to me, in a hard, disapproving voice.

"There was a good reason," I said. "One you would approve of. We were breeding dogs for a world of their own, and we had no role models for them. We had no mature dogs to show them how to hunt and how to dig dens, how to act as a pack. If they hadn't had someone to show them, we'd never have been able to turn them loose on a world of their own."

Ornel did not change his expression, but his stare shifted to the willog, which was continuing its exposition.

"Replication is most interesting. Out of thankfulness for eyes and ears, willogs have let humans alone, for humans do not like being replicated. At least," it stopped momentarily and focused several eyes on Gavi, "not those humans who live high on the rock, where willogs do not go." It turned its eyes toward me. "Other more recent humans, however, have been old ones who enjoyed going into the moss and being remade, though their people do not want them to return afterward, to remake others . . ."

"The people have been remade?" blurted Ornel. "They are still alive?"

"Oh, yes, very alive. Still with same thoughts, same memories, but no more pains in bones, no more sadness. Walking Sunshine long ago has sent message to all redmoss, 'Do not remake humans to go back for others.' Silly for replicas to go back, to offer remake to others, and get burned dead for their trouble." At that point the blue eye stared at Gavi, letting her know it was her people who had committed this indecency, before it went on: "Humans would be far happier being remade as part of world instead of just sitting on top of world as they are now."

"All the old people from PPI are still alive?" I asked. "They are still . . . functioning?"

"Function?" said the willog, in a thoughtful tone. "What is function? They are not interested in doing things they did before, writing on papers, putting things away, making reports, all those things. They are wandering, tasting, smelling, talking to one another. Is this function?"

I didn't know how to reply. Ornel, however, said, "I would need to talk to one of them in order to know whether they still function or not."

The willog nodded, an all-over up-down motion. "We have had messages for some time describing this new dog creature. So far, no replication of dog had happened, but forest is alive with anticipation."

"No magh us," said Behemoth, with a snarl. "No mahs."

The willog actually recoiled at this. "Very well. You have only to say what you prefer. It isn't necessary to be abusive!"

Behemoth subsided with a rumble, and I spoke quickly into the uncomfortable silence. "We're forgetting why we're here. We came to watch the battle over the key to Splendor. If we want to be on time, I suggest we don't delay finding a place to watch from."

Behemoth's obvious truculence was more than a little disturbing, but I didn't want to query it at the moment, not with this completely unknown creature in our midst and large numbers of warriors coming toward us from several directions.

Gavi said, "I think I am already finding a place big enough for all of us. On west side of battleground, I am seeing a stone outcropping on the high ground, high enough to be seeing over the trees." She turned to the willog. "There is being room for you there, as well. Unless you want to try to get closer."

"With you will be good," it said, inclining several trunks in a bow. "Hearing conversation is good. Thank you for the invitation."

With Gavi in the lead, our now augmented group plunged back into the forest, with the male dogs following Gavi, Frank, and Adam close behind, then Scramble, Veegee, and Dapple. Ornel, Clare, and I were at the end of the line, followed by the willog, who, or which, had stopped making martial music and was contenting itself with a pleasantly harmonic humming in its several voices. I spent the journey trying to catalog impressions and draw conclusions that might be useful. The willog did not seem dangerous It responded with annoyance only when its intelligence was questioned. It had a strong sense of personal worth, which ought not to be disparaged. As for Behemoth, I was at a loss. Adam's subservience I could understand, it fit into the usual pattern for canine packs, but Behemoth's sudden exercise of authority had me baffled. He knew this wasn't the world we'd planned for them; he knew there was no prey here to keep them alive. Surely he wouldn't risk the ultimate freedom of a world of their own for some interim display of curiosity? Since that's exactly what he was doing, I could only assume something was going on that I knew nothing about.

We made a considerable loop away from the lakeshore, and by late afternoon, we had come to the back side of the outcrop Gavi had mentioned. There a long, bare slope stretched upward and eastward to a line of broken stone. The sun threw our shadows before us as we went up quietly, even the willog silent. The distance was greater than it had appeared from below, and we had gained a considerable height by the time we reached the top, a jagged cornice of fractured stone stretching widely to either side. The crevices we could see through appeared to lead out into the air. Nonetheless, the dogs threaded their way into the maze and very shortly found a sizable ledge where the shattered rimrock had fallen onto the scree below. When we all found our way through various cracks, we had an excellent view of the battleground below.

The moss-carpeted saucer was just as Gavi's informer had described it, though Gavi had not used words like *mysterious* or *eerie*, both of which applied. The moss was indeed blue because it was either fluorescing blue light or was bathed in blue light from some other source, a luminescence that most resembled a pool of shining, sapphire smoke. The paved center of the great dish lay like an island in this gleaming pond, no smoke obscuring its rocky surface, which reminded me of the roads on the Phain planet in being leveled by nature rather than art. The trees around the rim of the dish were also as described. Through my glasses I saw a perfectly uniform fringe: each twig repeating the pattern of each leaf; each branch reproducing each twig; each tree restating each branch.

In the center of the paved circle stood the hexagonal crystal of stone, tall and dark, with something extraneous mounted near the top of the southernmost face. I could see it only edge on, for we were almost due west of it. If I had had to label it from what I could see, I would have called it a medallion, perhaps, or a mask rather than a key. Though golden in color and appearing circular, I could not distinguish its details.

There was no sign of anyone approaching. Gavi murmured to me that the men from Night and Day Mountains might possibly arrive during the night. I conveyed her words to the group, and we all decided to get some sleep, including the dogs. The willog thrust some of its roots into crevices in the rock before arranging itself against the stone and becoming one with the landscape. When I had spread our sleeping mats, Scramble came to lie down beside me, with Gavi on the other side of her. As I dozed off, I heard Gixit's tiny, tremulous voice talking of . . . something, interrupted occasionally by Scramble's rumbling mutter.

AN UNEXPECTED ENCOUNTER

⠒ The full moon was low in the west, its light blocked by the stones behind us, when I was awakened by a stink. We had slept away most of the night, though it was still quite dark. I could hear Gavi breathing, but Scramble was no longer curled against my body. I sat up, eyes gradually adjusting to the combination of reflected moonlight and the blue radiance that bled upward from the giant moss saucer below. Gavi was still there, as were Ornel and Sybil. All the dogs were gone, how-ever, both real and pseudo, and something nearby was generating a feculent, powerful stench.

I rose, careful to make no sound, crouching low as I went to the ledge and looked down. There at the center of the pave, staring at the erect crystal and the surrounding trees were a company of . . . lizards? Alligators? No. Of course not. Derac! Erect, but with sizable tails they used as props when they stood, as balances when they moved at any speed. Knobby-skinned. Jaws protruding under a siz-able snouts. A forehead of clustered eyes, three horns sprouting below them. Fangs, yes, their glitter visible even from this distance. They were also heavily armed and armored. I couldn't tell whether the armor was natural or manufactured, but the weapons were large and complicated-looking.

I crept back, put my hand over Gavi's mouth, and shook her slightly. She came awake without a sound, her face crumpling at the odor. "Wha?" she started to ask, but I muffled her as I whispered into her ear. She rose, and the two of us woke Ornel and Sybil.

"We should get out of here," Ornel whispered, when he had had a look below.

I shook my head at him, putting my lips near his ear. "We don't know how many there are, or where they are. We're probably safer here than we would be trying to get away."

Gavi nodded in agreement. "We should be very quiet," she mur-mured.

"Where are the dogs," asked Sybil. "Where's Gixit?"

"Gixit was with Scramble," I said. "I imagine the smell woke the dogs, and they've all gone into the forest. It would be natural for them to do that. Probably Gixit is still with them."

We stretched out on the ledge, pillowing our chins on our arms to keep watch on what went on below. More Derac came down from the northern rim of the bowl, and more yet. After I had counted two hun-dred and there was no diminution of the flow, I gave up the count.

"Where were they headed?" Gavi whispered.

"Gainor thought they'd come to the installation east of the lake. He was wrong."

"A thousand of our people are coming here," Gavi persisted. "They need to be warned. I'm in armor. I can go . . ."

"No," I said. "Gavi, there's been a huge buildup of the Derac forces. They're probably scattered all through the forest along the lake, maybe on both sides. You don't know where your people are. Won't they have scouts out?"

She shrugged, her hands struggling with one another. "I don't know. Why would they . . ."

"I can go," said the small grove of trees that stood beside us on the ledge. It looked so natural there that I had quite forgotten what it was. The willog!

"These toothy ones will not even pay attention to me," it said, "and I have friends in the area."

"Please don't talk," I said. "Or sing. Or hum."

"You don't want me to have any fun," it said in an accusing voice.

"I don't want you to be chopped up for firewood," I said. "Those lizards are carrying axes, among other things."

"I was making joke," said the willog, in a slightly offended tone. "Of course I see they have axes. My eyesight is marvelous, fabulous, spectacular . . . ah, that is almost pun! My sight is better than yours. I have human eyes, also mouse eyes, crab eyes, some bird eyes. Oh, how wonderful to have eyes!"

At the threat of its becoming rapturous once more, I shushed it with a final: "Please, don't attract attention, or we may all end up dead."

One of its eyes zoomed toward my cheek, fluttered lashes against it in a butterfly kiss, then retreated as the willog trundled away through the stones. I dug my link out of my pack and attempted to reach Gainor. Though I keyed the link several times, I couldn't get through. Ornel was watching me, nodding as though he had foreseen the problem I was having. "The radiation from down there," he said. "It may foul up any attempts at communication."

"It has to be biological," I complained. "Not electromagnetic."

"You're assuming the two are exclusive," he said. "It could be biological and electromagnetic. We've encountered a good many such. There's a kind of fish on Thorgov III that . . ."

"Not now," said Sybil. "It doesn't matter what the effect is, we can't link outside, and linking outside is the only way we have to get some help."

"They'll leave," said Ornel. "If we just stay quiet and don't attract their attention."

"That's not the point," I said. "The people from Day and Night Mountains are approaching from the south and north. No matter which direction the Derac go off in, they're likely to encounter one or the other. That's why the willog went northward, to warn the Night Mountain people."

"Since the Derac came from the north, the southern way is probably clear," Gavi said. "I'll go that way."

She stood up and reached for her helmet, readying to go, when we all heard a scrabbling from the rocky slope we had ascended earlier. Gavi disappeared into a crack between two stones, the rest of us followed suit, along with our packs and sleeping mats. We had built no fire, so there was nothing to say we had been here, if whoever . . .

Whoever was the Derac. Some ten or a dozen of them, filtering in through the cracks in the rim wall, going to the edge to stare down and bellow at their fellows in the battleground. I wished I had one of Paul's lingui-putes. I would have loved to know what they were saying to one another. About half the group went back the way they had come, but six of them stayed where they were, poised at the rim, occasionally turning to left and right to look out over the forest north and south, as though they had been posted as sentinels.

My narrow crevice had no escape route. It made a nicely angled bend, one large enough to hide me completely, but there was no opening through the rock behind me, and I was too close to the Derac to get out without their seeing me. Peeking around the corner, at the stones opposite me, I saw Ornel slide out of concealment and fade back into a large crack toward the west. A little later, I saw a suspiciously crablike creature move in the same direction. That left Sybil and me. If Ornel got far enough away, he could link ESC on the plateau. If Gavi got away, she could warn the people coming from the south. All Sybil and I had to do was stay put, if I could keep my mind on that fact instead of the confused swirl it was in at the moment!

Scramble hadn't wakened me, hadn't warned me! None of the dogs had warned any of us! I had rather depended on them to do that. Being deserted by Ornel and Gavi left me feeling angry and insecure, but Scramble's leaving me was like being wounded! I would never have thought she could do that. Not if she had a choice. Well, she couldn't abandon me, so she'd had no choice. She'd been lured away somewhere, somehow. Probably by Behemoth. When we came, I'd thought we were in this together, that we were agreed on what our aims were, and all of us were hoping for the same ends. Perhaps that had only been my assumption. Behemoth had never said in so many words that he approved of our plans. And he had never said he would not make plans of his own . . .

I reminded myself that the puppies were safe. Clare would know what to do for them. Probably the dogs were safe as well, and they knew where the floater was if they needed to get to the plateau. Adam could fly it if he decided to stop being a dog. Unless, for some reason, Behemoth wouldn't let him stop being a dog.

The faint moonlight faded to the west. The blue glow from the moss below was also fading. Along the eastern horizon, a pale greenish line widened like a window being opened. Dawn wasn't far off. I thought it probable that when daylight came, the Derac would continue on their way south, then Sybil and I could escape.

It wasn't to happen. Voices came clearly through the quiet air, people, talking, singing, making a racket. At first I thought it was only from the north I heard them, but it was soon evident that the sound was coming from both directions. The sentinels at the ledge stood up, peering in both directions, then looked down as they made wide arm gestures. Evidently they received silent instructions in return, for they dropped among the stones, weapons at the ready. Now, for a moment at least, they could not see me, and I slipped out of the crack and back among the stones toward the slope. Sybil saw me go by and came after me, a bit wild-eyed, but quietly enough that they did not hear us. We got as far as the back edge of the rim rock, where the downward slope began, when all hell broke loose behind us. Weapons began firing, people were yelling, the Derac were roaring and coughing, and we stepped out onto the hill to confront half a dozen more Derac coming up the hill at a dead run, jaws agape and slavering.

I have no idea what made me put my hand in my pocket. I didn't consciously reach for anything. I had no picture in my mind. My hand just went there, closed around the vial of STOP that I have carried for years, thumbed up the cover, and as the Derac reached us, stretched out my right arm and spun to the left, throwing an arc of the stuff outward in their faces.

They were moving so fast that they ran over us, carrying us down with them. Some of the stuff got from them onto Sybil. They were choking, she was choking, the thrashing body on top of me was beating me this way and that as it struggled to breathe. I managed to turn half on my side and flip the vial over. Sybil's face was not far from me, under another Derac body. The antidote is a spray, luckily, and it reached her agonized face. She breathed in, then began gasping, little, tortured gasps. I sprayed her again, this time murmuring, "Play dead, Sybil. Lie quiet and play dead!"

I didn't realize the Derac we'd left up on the ledge were joining their kin, but they were on top of us in moments. I shut my eyes and played dead, the vial shoved under my body. The dead Derac on top of me was heaved up, then dropped. Through slitted eyelids I saw the one on top of Sybil also heaved up, then dropped. A burst of babble came from the uphill contingent as I was heaved over a leathery shoulder and carried off, able to see only briefly that Sybil remained where she was. Then my carrier went so quickly around a stone that my head swung against it with a mind-stopping thonk, and that was the last I knew for some time.

⋮ When I came to, more or less, I was lying in the middle of the saucer, to the south of the column and not far from it. The sky was light, but the sun had not yet risen. I didn't move. There were a dozen or so other bodies around me, most of them in crab armor. One of them might have been Gavi, but I couldn't see the faces. The Derac, such of them as I could see, lay at the rim of the saucer with tails stretched behind them and weapons pointed outward, a fringe almost as fractally regular as the trees above them. I moved my head very, very slowly, to see if there was a guard nearby. Not that it made any difference. The cordon of Derac at the rim was quite sufficient to keep me from going anywhere. Seeing no one on guard duty, I crept to the closest body and put my fingers to the neck of it, pushing them under the beetle helmet. No pulse. I tried again, and again, finally finding one faint pulse among them. So. Perhaps we were considered dead and had been laid aside for supper.

I turned over slowly, looking upward along the cliff to the ledge we had been occupying. It was a considerable distance, and I couldn't make out any details. I swiveled my eyes toward a faint sound and confronted the monocular lens of an ESC surveillance fish. ESC might be watching, but more likely the output from this fish was merely being recorded to be scanned at some later time. I made the ESC "help" signal that Gainor had taught me years ago, and the thing came down, near my face. "Emergency," I said. "Top priority. Get this entire scene to Gainor Brandt." It lifted, did a complete turn, recording everything around the rim, then zoomed off toward the north.

When it left, I was lying on my back, looking almost straight up at the top of the pillar, where the "key" was, by then close enough to be seen clearly. As I had thought, it was sizable and shaped more like a medallion than a key, a medallion bearing a symbol or picture that was startlingly familiar to me, though it took a moment to figure out where I had seen it before. Fuzzy thoughts came and went, my mind dealing them out like a hand of cards. This one? No? Then this one?

It finally came to me: I'd seen this same glyph among Matty's notes for Lipkin Symphony no. 7, third movement, "The Ancient Wall." A heavy, square outline with rounded corners. Inside that, a stylized image of a Martian and his dog, a dog that looked a lot like Behemoth. The resemblance was in the way the head and ears were held, the angle of the tail, the shape of the muzzle, the comparative size of the two figures. Though greatly foreshortened by the angle I was seeing it from, it was perfectly recognizable in both senses: as a copy of a Martian glyph and as Behemoth himself.

I was stewing away at some web of correlation, something to do with Zhaar technology having been used on the dogs and the trainers, and the Zhaar seals in the Martian cavern, and the translations that Matty had paid for . . . I couldn't make it all add up to anything. "Fanciful impressions allowed to take precedence in the absence of hard evidence." That was what Gainor would call it, but then, I'd had a bang on the head, and it hurt abominably. One or several Derac bellowed into the surrounding forest, receiving no answer. Why were they just lying there?

I fixed my eyes on their tails and tried to count one quarter of the circle. I started over about five times, but eventually counted 150, more or less. Which meant there were six hundred or so all the way around. Which meant . . . the Derac were outnumbered! They hadn't known about a thousand warriors from each Mountain. They'd come to take out a few people at the ESC installation and only forty-seven at PPI. They'd managed to kill a few scouts from one Mountain or the other, before the full armies arrived and what? Surrounded them? It certainly looked like it.

A faint whine. The fish was back. It zoomed down near me once more, and I heard a scratchy voice say, "Play dead, Jewel. We'll be there shortly." Gainor, probably. I let my eyes almost close and concentrated on the headache. Sometimes I could make pain go away just by thinking my way to its source, which in this case was at one side of the back of my head where it and the rock had briefly collided.

I was looking sideways at nothing through slitted lids when I noticed a change in the fringe of trees around the rim. They had been symmetrical before, but now each tree was lopsided, as if it had lowered its right side. Which it had done! Each tree was lowering several branches from among the foliage above, lengthy, ropy extensions, with no foliage, like whips. The tips of them came down, and down, alongside each Derac, then . . . where? All at once, the branches drew tight, snapped upward, and there were the Derac, every blessed one of them suspended by his neck.

The trees hadn't been just trees! They'd been willogs! Walking Sunshine had said it had "friends" in the area. Even so, the lizards weren't easy to kill. Their huge, muscular tails thrashed wildly, whipping at the tree trunks. Their clawed arms and legs raked the bark until it shredded. Other whip-thin branches snaked out and caught arms and legs, to hold them fast. Here and there, bodies went limp as a roar of human voices came from beyond the rim, and in a moment there were human figures among the trees, a full circle of them around the battleground, many of them busy stabbing at the pendant bodies of the Derac. One of them, in full crab armor, without hesitation started a run down into the saucer. Gavi, no doubt. And where were the others? Where were the dogs?

Dreamily, I noticed that the northern group of warriors carried flags of black bearing a green moon. The southern group carried yellow flags with green trees. Both groups wore small flags of the same colors on their helmets, and they intermixed and moved quite amicably together as they finished off the Derac and came down into the battleground, some of them paying more attention to the surroundings than to anything else. First-time warriors, I thought. Those who hadn't seen the battleground before.

The forerunner had been Gavi. She reached me, took off her helmet, and knelt beside me. "Are you being badly hurt?" she asked, almost in a whisper.

"I got a bash on the head," I answered. "I'm not dying, but my head hurts."

She felt of my head, reacting when I winced. She found a small jar in her pack and applied its contents to the bruise and under my nose. "Be lying here and letting it work," she said. "Our people are bringing our dead down now."

"You weren't in time to warn them?"

She avoided my gaze. "I was being not quite quick enough. The lizards were ambushing the tribe of Burrow when I arrived. Chief Badnor Belthos and several of his close kin were being killed." She looked upward, all innocence.

"You were . . . fortuitously delayed," I said.

"Only a little," she admitted. "Badnor was not being a good man."

"He's the one who harassed you when you were little?"

"That one, yes. At any rate, now he will be going into Splendor."

"They'll open the gate now?" I struggled to sit up. "Before the battle?"

"There will be no battle. Enough have already died. It is not necessary to battle and be killing each other if someone else is doing the killing already."

She left me sitting there and went among the bodies lying around me, checking to see who was dead and who alive. I noticed for the first time that they included both Day and Night Mountain warriors. Several were alive, and she treated them, with one thing or another. Though I'd already come to respect Gavi's skill, I was still amazed at how quickly the pain went away, taking the dizziness with it. Soon I was able to sit up and watch the warriors filing down into the saucer, bearing their dead on hastily contrived litters. After adding the twenty or so already beside the pillar, there were more than fifty of them.

The system seemed well understood by the participants on both sides. When all the bodies had been laid at the foot of the pillar, six Night Mountain warriors came down the slope carrying a tall ladder. Since it would have been completely mossened and rotted if left long in the moss, I assumed that either they had brought it with them or their scouts had built it anew when they had finished laying out the trail. The ladder was erected at the south face of the pillar by a committee of warriors who paid considerable attention to the distance from the pillar to the foot of the ladder, evidently a matter of significance.

Gavi came to sit beside me. "They are saying door will come out of the pillar, not always on same side," she whispered. "If the ladder is too close, the door might knock it down."

"Who goes up the ladder?" I asked.

"Chief Larign," she told me.

There was a brief delay while the warriors of both sides assembled in a great circle around the pillar. Chief Larign then scrambled up the ladder, positioning himself three steps from the top, one hand holding on while the other reached out toward the key. He leaned forward to press on it, three times.

The bottom of the pillar was suddenly perforated with vertical slots. Radiance and a smell poured out, washed over us, and filled the saucer. I saw it as a discernible fluid, flowing from the pillar, filling the saucer up as far as the rim before it stopped flowing. The moment the radiance stopped at the rim, the door came out of the side nearest me, a flat plane of brilliance, two-dimensional, flat, bright on one side, dark on the other. The inhabitants who emerged from the light side were solid. I saw them perfectly well. I saw the country beyond them, a place so beautiful it drew my eyes until they felt as though they were being plucked from my face. I saw the people there, I did, I saw them. I remember seeing them perfectly well, but I could not put into words what I saw. Into smells, yes. Into words, no.

Teams of warriors picked up the litters, carried them to the nearest doors, and pushed them in. They gathered up the bodies that lay at the foot of the pillar and pushed them through the doors also. When this was done, they merely stood there, staring. The people from inside the pillar stood as well, looking out toward the edge of the place. I followed their eyes and saw the dogs coming down into the saucer. Behemoth. Titan. Wolf. Dapple. Veegee. Scramble . . .

They walked directly to the door and went in. Except Scramble. She saw me. She broke loose from the others and ran to me, taking my arm in her mouth, tugging me erect. She followed the others, pulling me with her. Across her head I saw Adam and Frank being held by the warriors. Gavi was near the gate. Then the people from inside were reaching out to Scramble, she was going through, Gavi grabbed at me too late, for I was already being dragged through the door.

⠇ For only a moment I had looked up to see an armed ESC shuttle close above us. My eyes slid across Gavi's horrified face. Then the door swallowed us, and everything vanished. My mind was unfathomable as mist, vacant as air. I had no words. No nothing.

Sometime later, the nothingness separated into chunks of cloudy stuff that dissolved to make room for thought. I pushed myself away from the hard, painful corner I'd been crumpled against, a place where a stone floor met equally stony walls. Barred windows above my left side made a stripe of light in the wall opposite, disclosing two solid doors with some plumbing device between them. The wall to my right was stone, completely bare. At the end of the wall to my left a doorless opening to the outside admitted a slanting beam of light, and I assumed that it led outside. This assumption seemed portentous for no reason at all, so I stared witlessly at the door, hoping the reason would present itself.

Something important was hanging just at the edge of recall, begging to be remembered. I heard its flea voice, "Jewel, over here, over here, looky, remember me?" I acknowledged its presence grudgingly. "Give me a minute. I'm not awake yet. Let up, will you!" I couldn't identify it. A something strange. A something very strange, to do with the door or a door . . . Whatever it was, the shreds of cloudy stuff still in my head were hiding it from me.

Perhaps the answer was outside. I considered exploring the possibility of outsideness until a shadow fell through the opening, followed by a person, a bearded man of medium height whose dark hair fell smoothly over his shoulders and down the front of the long-sleeved, ankle-length sack he was wearing. He took a few steps inside, stopped as though surprised, mouth gulping like a fish, hands repeatedly clenching at his sides, breath issuing in dramatic sobs, once, twice, as prelude to his gasped, "Oh, God, Jewel."

I didn't know him, refused to know him, struggled to say go away, stranger, don't bother me. The words wouldn't come. Even his name took several tries. "Witt?"

He babbled at me. "How did you end up here? You didn't come looking for me, did you? Oh, I didn't want you to do that. I prayed you wouldn't do that . . ."

His voice was high, panicky, the same voice I'd heard the last time I had seen him. So many years trying to forget that particular voice! So many wakeful midnights spent imagining how I would feel if Witt ever returned, if he were ever found.

So much for years and imagining. I felt nothing at all. Here stood the person I had tried to re-create from scraps of memory, over and over, for years. Here he was, entire! Surely there was some proper response to make!

Whatever it might have been, it eluded me. He was still lamenting, plaints pouring from his lips like a fall of rain. I took a deep breath and determined to put an end to it. "I didn't come to Moss looking for you."

"Moss?" he cried. "Not Jungle?"

No, not Jungle. We were not on Jungle. Of course, we were not on Moss, either. I didn't know where we were, but I wanted him to stop talking and let me think my way around the emptiness inside myself. If I got any emptier, I would start to come apart like that earlier wall of mist. I would break into chunks and float away to be lost forever!

The only way to stop his talking was to talk myself. I babbled, "No, no, no, not Jungle. A . . . a spatial anomaly seems to . . . to intersect both planets, plus the moon. The moon, Treasure. Did you lose the photo album I gave you when you left?" That slipped out. I hadn't intended to mention it.

He cried despairingly, "On Jungle."

I said hastily, "Well, it was found on Moss. That's how we knew the places were interconnected somehow." There had to be something else I could say, some impersonal subject that would move us away from this whatever it was. All I could come up with was, "What are you doing here?"

"They sent me," he said, wearily, almost calmly. "One of us older ones always talks to the newer ones, to tell them there's no way to get out. To tell them we have to stay to take care of them. We're their best friends. We were born to take care of them, designed to take care of them. We've always looked after them."

With a sinking feeling, I asked, "Look after who?"

"The Simusi," he said. "The Simusi."

"The people who came out of the doors . . ." The memory was there, right there, in a moment I'd see it . . .

"The Simusi." He dropped his voice to a whisper. "You saw . . ."

"They were dogs!" I cried, as the scene came back in all its fantastic details. This was what my mind had been hiding from me. "What came out of the doors were huge dogs!"

He babbled, "No, no, no, they aren't that big, really. They can make themselves look bigger, that's all, very intelligent of them, too, other creatures do it, why not the Simusi . . ."

"Do they usually abduct people?"

He had some difficulty switching gears. "Ah, yes, abduct, well, yes, whenever they need some new ones. All of us here, we're all fixed, you know, so we can't breed. There are lots of us outside, though, so they harvest us from there . . ."

By that time, I was so confused that any further talk could scarcely add to it. There was no point in not finding out what I could, even if I couldn't put it together yet, so I crouched against the wall, leaned back, stretched out my legs, then crossed them and gripped both hands together to keep them from writhing. I forced myself to pay attention.

"What gives these Simusi the right to snatch us up and enslave us like this?"

He shrugged. "Well, it is their right, it really is, because when we're not being of service we're vermin, and the Orskimi are vermin, and the Derac are vermin . . ."

Vermin, yet again? Acceptable or unacceptable? The symbol on the pillar at the battleground had shown dogs and people. Not masters and dogs, as I'd assumed, but Simusi and their . . . servants, and in that case, what kind of creature had the servants actually been?

"When I was a child, Matty found that cavern on Mars, remember?" I waited for his grudging nod. "Were those pictures of human people and the Simusi?"

He made an impotent little gesture. "We only know what they tell us, and they don't tell us much, but it's obvious the Simusi have to have servants. They need creatures with hands or tentacles, creatures that can manipulate things, create things!"

"Could they have been on Mars?"

His face went blank. "They've never said anything about Mars. They tell stories about their history, but they do it in their language, and we can't understand them."

It was useless to go on questioning him when he obviously knew nothing and cared less. "Are you here in this room by accident, Witt? Or are you here because we know one another?"

"One of your . . . one of the new Simusi told someone you would be coming. The new Simusi said I should come to meet you."

"The new Simusi?"

"A female one. The one who brought you in."

Scramble. One of the Simusi? How and when had that happened? And how would she have known . . . ? Well, of course. I'd talked about Witt sometimes, when she was in the room. No doubt she . . . no doubt *all* of them had understood far more than they could express. I couldn't think of anything else to ask or say. Witt didn't move, didn't come toward me, didn't offer any words of comfort or encouragement. Finally, the silence became too burdensome to bear.

I said, "What's this thing you tell the new ones?"

"Just . . . what you mustn't do. You mustn't act untamed. They control you if you act untamed, and it'll hurt. Sometimes it can kill you."

"How?" I asked through a haze of disbelief. Though the essential reality of the situation was completely persuasive, I nonetheless kept trying to convince myself it was dream, or fantasy, or hallucination. "How, Witt?"

"Collar with a stinger in it. Cap with a knockdown in it. Tie you up for several days without water. If nothing works, they put you in the food pens or the hunting pens. Like all the bodies they get from the battles."

"Food pen?"

"They fill it up with dead people. Almost dead people. They dose them with zurflesh animators, and the young ones hunt them for practice. The dead ones don't last long, but the hunts don't last very long either. Animated ones can't run very fast." A long silence fell between us while I tried to catalog this singular horror. No doubt there were a thousand things I needed to know, but none of them were about Witt. I already knew how he felt, hopeless, and what he intended, nothing.

He must have seen the revulsion in my face. "Don't think about escaping," he whispered. "You can't. If the Simusi don't find you, the Phain do."

My head came up at that. The Phain! Something hopeful! I opened my mouth, but any questions I might have asked were derailed by a bark from outside. It was only a dog bark, but even I heard it as peremptory. So did Witt. He scurried back through the low door as fast as he could move, and I sat there for a long moment wondering at the persistence of this weird blankness where he was concerned. I had not wanted to touch him. I had not wanted to kiss him or call him by an old, intimate name. I had not actually wanted to remember Witt since . . . almost since the first day on Moss. No, since my first trip to the plateau. Since I met Gavi . . . Since . . .

Memory drifted. Since when. Well, since I'd bathed in the pool along the warmwall. Which Gavi had carefully prepared for me. A scent? Something she'd put into it. She'd asked me if Witt had been my first. She'd said something about imprinting. She must have done it. She had erased him. Just as she erased former fascinations from couples who got married, getting rid of prior attachments. Just like that! A bit of something marvelous in your bathwater and you were no longer possessed! I should have been outraged, but all I could feel was a faint indignation. There was no time even for that, however, not when there was something outside to be seen.

I stooped through the low door and came out into a fenced pen some fifteen paces either way, sweeping my eyes along the line of toilets against the fence to my left, the several open-air showers that were merely pipes over a hard surface with a drain in it, over the bowls lined up on a long counter across from me, a spigot above each one. On my right, Witt crouched inside the single gate. He faced a huge dog standing on the outside, half a dozen smaller creatures around it, one of them a Gixit, or perhaps *the* Gixit that had been with Scramble. Two of the other creatures were rather like four-armed lemurs. One of these opened the gate, which creaked with a peculiarly irritating screech, and Witt scuttled out, still crouching. The dog—Simusi— glanced at me incuriously, then turned away. Some of the smaller creatures rode on its back or scampered behind, others rode on Witt's shoulders as he walked quickly, just behind the dog's right shoulder, not looking back.

"Heel, Witt," I murmured to myself. "Heel. That's it. Good human." Again, I tried to find some feeling, like testing a griddle with a wet fingertip, but nothing hissed. Witt had been found, and so what? All I felt was a vague discomfort at being there in the open all by myself.

Back inside, the fixture between the two solid doors turned out to be a drinking fountain. I drank and splashed cold water on my face and neck before returning to the wall to sit with my back against it and sort through memories as though I were sorting out a closet, holding each incident up to the light, separating each recollection into an appropriate pile, everything I'd ever heard about the Phain, what Matty had said about the cavern, the Saik Sp'laintor story Paul had mentioned, things Gainor had heard from his ET friends about the Zhaar, about Zhaar technology. No one had ever admitted it to me, but I'd always suspected Zhaar technology had been used in breeding the big dogs, and I'd known damn well it had been used to adapt the trainers. There had been both dog shapes and Zhaar in that cavern on Mars, the bones of the one, the seals of the other. Had they ever been there simultaneously?

Delving into memory did nothing but make me so groggy that I fell asleep where I sat and didn't wake until I heard the peculiar screech of the gate outside, opening, shutting, opening and shutting again to the accompaniment of muttering voices. People seeped in from the pen, a few at a time. Some wore the same kind of sack that Witt had worn, but others were dressed in loose-fitting coveralls or trouser-tunic outfits. Some of the men had beards, others were close-shaven. The women, fewer of them than the men, had either shaved their heads or wore their hair tightly braided.

Several of the women came to me, extending their hands, greeting me in languages I did not recognize. I believe they named their planets of origin, for I recognized the names of several colony worlds I'd read of. I repeated them while pointing at those who had named them, then pointed to myself and said, Earth. They nodded and repeated it, patting my shoulders.

The last person to come in was an elderly man with a lame left leg. He limped over and greeted me, unintelligibly. When I said I couldn't

understand him, he smiled. "We'll use Earthtalk, then. My name is
Oskar. You are just come? Where did they get you from and what are
you called?"

"The planet Moss," I said. "My name is Jewel."

"A newly discovered planet? I don't remember it, and I'm fairly well
acquainted with most human worlds."

"Discovered twelve years ago," I said. "Maybe a year more than
that. The system is called Garr'ugh 290 by the Derac . . ."

"After my time," he said. "I've been captive almost twenty years."

"What do they want us for?" I asked. "What do we do for them?"

He thinned his lips in a sardonic smile. "Baby-sit. Clean out the
dens. Fetch things, especially things that need climbing to reach, like
fruit, or prey that can go up a tree. Even though they hunt and eat
their kills as a ritual commemoration of their ancestry, they prefer cuisine to corpses, so we cook and we work on the farms, growing crops
and livestock. If you have any choice about where you'll work, choose a
farm. That way you can eat some fresh stuff you'll never get here."

"Where is here?"

"This is a kennel. This particular one is called . . . woodsy-fungus-
smell interrupted by cold water smell."

"Does cold water have a smell?" I asked in dismay.

"Not that I've ever been able to detect, no. Nonetheless, that's what
it's called by the Simusi. We humans call this general area Nearforest
since it's mostly wooded. The Simusi don't live in buildings, of course,
though we 'friends' do, if we're lucky, and we build shelters for puppies
and new mothers."

"If that's what we do, what do they do?"

His brow pleated, becoming a solid bank of horizontal wrinkles.
"What do they do? Well. They sit around in the moonlight and do
group howl epics about their history and great achievements. They
spend a lot of time smelling things. They reanimate the almost dead
bodies that come in through the doors and let the puppies hunt them,
to learn . . ."

"Reanimate?" I asked. "How?"

"They dose them with something called zurflesh. They say they
got it from another race, ages ago."

That could well be true. We got it from another race. "Is that all
they hunt, reanimated dead people?"

"Oh, no. They bring through groups of strong, healthy warriors every now and then for their ritual hunts, sometimes human ones, though they prefer more challenging physical specimens, like Derac or Ocpurat. They have a whole penful of Derac. They came through soon after you did."

I remembered the willogs strangling the Derac. So. Someone had salvaged the bodies. Or, more likely, remembering what I had read about reptilian creatures, they hadn't really been dead. I rubbed my head fretfully.

"And why are we their servants?" I asked.

"It's a matter of pride with them. The taking of 'friends' to serve them."

"Like slave owners on old Earth," I said. "Too proud to dress or clean up after themselves."

"Oh, yes, they're proud, and it's wise to remember that. An alpha male demands complete surrender of individuality or personal thought from his 'friends,' as well as from other members of the pack." He made a face. "They use one race for fetching small things, another for under-water work, another for heavy lifting, and still another for sending information by air. And humans, as I've mentioned, for different things."

"And this is how we live?" I looked around the room with dismay.

"It's better than the hunting pens. Here, you get enough to eat, a warm place to sleep. You have a doctor to take care of illness or injuries. You're not allowed to breed, but you can sensualize, so long as you wash yourself afterward and don't do it where they can smell you at it. It makes a smell they don't like."

"No children."

"No. The Simusi consider us to be . . . a verminous life-form. They find us useful, but they keep us only so long as we are useful." He moved his lame leg, gritting his teeth as he rubbed at it. "When we get too old, they put us down."

"Do you know, did the Simusi ever live on a planet near Earth? One we call Mars?"

"If so, it would have been a long, long time ago. They don't talk to us about their history." He laughed. "They don't talk, period. Their own language is all in smells."

"Witt . . . the man who was here before, he said the Phain are near here."

"Ah, well, yes. It's mostly Simusi this side of the dike, but beyond it there's a big stretch of Phain country, with Guardian Houses all up and down it. If you could somehow get service with the Phain, that would be a good thing for you, but they say we don't have respect, so they don't take many of us."

I said, "When I saw into this space through the doors to the . . . outside, it looked like paradise. What's outside the pen, however, looks quite ordinary. A pleasantly warm, wooded sort of place, but nothing . . . splendid."

He looked slightly confused by this. "Well, through the door, you saw dazzle. The Simusi can do that, make you see dazzle, when you look at them, particularly. They dazzle you, make themselves looked bigger, stronger. This area here is a transitional way to Splendor, but it isn't actually part of Splendor. To the Simusi, however, this is Splendor enough. Their natural prey can live here, they can engage in the hunt here, there are no enemies to kill the pups. In order to get to Splendor, you'd have to go past where the Phain are."

"The Phain live both on regular planets and in here? I mean, they haven't gone extinct out there or anything?"

Again, he wrinkled his brow thoughtfully. "I get the impression they go back and forth from galactic worlds to the inner worlds . . ."

Worlds? Interesting. "More than one world, in here?"

"An infinite number, I'm told. All of them connected. You go in a door here, come out somewhere else, step through another door, and you're twenty light-years away from where you started."

That explained things being lost on Jungle and popping up on Moss, but it didn't explain the connection between Phain and the Simusi. "What are they, the Phain, to the Simusi, I mean? Relatives? Friends?"

He thought for some time. "I don't think they're anything except . . . neighbors. I know each of them despises the way the other race lives, so they leave one another alone. By the way, do you speak any of the languages of the other people here?"

I shook my head. No. "Just Earthian common speech, and a little Quondan and Phain-ildar. Is there any way I could send a message to the Phain?"

He gave me a long, weighing look. "Unlikely, unless you have access to a universal translator, which we are forbidden to use anywhere inside, even if we could lay hands on one. Neither the Simusi nor the Phain want us listening to their talk." He gave me a sympathetic look. "I know it's confusing. I'm by way of being overseer for a group of kennels . . . Think of them as housing units, it makes it easier. The first thing I'll do is try to transfer you to a kennel housing Earthers. Anyone you know special that you'd like to be with?"

"Gavi Norchis," I said. "If she came through with me, but I don't think she did." I laughed, ruefully. "The Simusi would like her. She . . . makes music with smells."

He gave me a peculiar look. "A woman. There was only one woman brought in with you, and I have no idea where she is."

Not long after he left, a bell summoned the people in the room, and they all went outside. I followed them to the feeding shelf. After everyone else had taken a bowl and filled it, I took one and turned the spigot above it to receive a quantity of warm mush. It was neither nasty nor palatable. About on a level with green algae crackers. You'd eat it if you were hungry, but you wouldn't salivate for it. I ate what I could and gave the rest away to three eager scroungers who smiled their thanks and split the remainder among themselves. When everyone had eaten, they prepared themselves for bed in one way or another. I waited until darkness provided some privacy to relieve myself outside and wash off the day's dust in the shower (cold water). I had a comb in the deep pocket of my jacket along with the wedding album and Matty's Seventh, so I sectioned off chunks of hair and braided my hair tight to my head as the other women wore theirs. There were no mirrors. The completed job felt uneven at best, but braided hair was either required or it made sense, so no point in testing to see if I could get away with letting it hang.

It all took far longer to accomplish than to tell of it, and I was thoroughly weary by the time I'd finished. Someone had opened a closet disclosing a pile of mats, and even the inadequacy of the one I lay down on didn't keep me from falling asleep almost at once. I did wake during the night, surprised to find I'd been dreaming about having a conversation with the Phaina, Sassanees, in her own language. The Phain-ildar words hung in the front of my mind like ripe fruit on a tree, succulent and fragrant words I hadn't thought of since learning them years ago. I found a bit of sharp rock on the floor and scratched the words on the wall so I wouldn't forget them. In the morning, when I woke, I read them over several times, repeating them.

Though I'm recording all this quite calmly, it would be false to give the impression that I was at all tranquil at the time. Often, between talking and eating and sleeping and thinking, my breath would catch in panic, I'd feel a fit of nausea, a shiver of mixed rage and fear and a strong urge either to throw up or throw a fit. Each time I gripped my hands together and made my nails bite my palms, concentrating on the pain until I could breathe easily once more. Paul's scornful tongue had managed me out of tantrums long ago, and it required no more composure here in Splendor than it had in Tower 29 of the Northwest Urb. I found myself actually being thankful to him for having given me an apprenticeship in self-control, and to Joram and Matty for whatever old-timey attributes I'd inherited from them. Spunk, Joram had called it. Grit, Matty used to say. "Buckle down and get at it." I was never sure what one buckled, but the sense of it was clear enough. Don't panic. Keep your eyes open, your mouth closed, and do the best you can. Be aware of tomooze. Think your way around flabbitz. The Simusi were certainly generators of tomooze, though no flabbitz had emerged as yet.

I was already awake when the morning bell woke the other sleepers. They rose, showered, used the toilets, shaved or braided, got dressed, all without seeming to notice the lack of privacy. They were all lean and well muscled, not at all overfed. We ate our morning mush. Oskar, my acquaintance of the previous day, arrived. He brought with him the pack I'd had on when Scramble pulled me through the door.

"Yours?"

I said, "Yes, it's mine. Will they let me keep it?"

He made a wry face. "The Simusi call our kind toolmakers. It's a contemptuous term they apply to several of their 'friends.' Any creature who needs any kind of accoutrement is considered inferior. Accoutrement includes shelter, clothing, devices, anything beyond one's own body and mind, because only vermin accumulate things. A pure creature, say the Simusi, should need nothing but itself. It does without clothing or shelter, it does without tools, without belongings." He gave me a wry smile. "A stupid, hypocritical idea, inasmuch as we provide all the things they lack, but then, we humans can be hypocritical, too. They profit from our building things, and they know we need tools, so we get to keep our property and even acquire new things if we need them. Some humans have moved out of the kennels and into private huts on the strength of their usefulness. It all depends on how well you get along."

I breathed deeply, determined to buckle down and absorb this.

He said, "I went through your pack to remove contraband. Didn't find any."

"What's contraband?"

"Food. Translation devices. Weapons. Let me see what's in your pockets."

I emptied them for him. My comb. A little kit with nail tools inside. The album of Matty's Seventh with her picture on the outside. The wedding album.

"Who?" he demanded of the album.

"My mother."

"She was a musician."

"Yes."

He picked up the album. "This is your liaison-mate."

"No," I said. "The liaison expired years ago."

"But you keep it."

"No," I said firmly. "I gave it away a long time ago. It showed up on Moss, that's all. Evidence of the spatial anomaly."

"The fewer things you ask to keep, the more likely you get to keep them," he said.

"Then throw that away," I told him.

I put my things back in my pockets, and he handed me my jacket. "So bring your pack along and come with me."

"Where are we going?" I asked.

"To meet some of your countrymen," he said, reaching forward in one fluid motion to fasten a collar around my neck. The attached leash was already in his hand. "Sorry about the collar, but I'm trusted, you're unknown. Just walk quietly, and we won't get into any trouble."

We went out through one of the heavy doors, which opened directly upon a path. Behemoth was sitting across from the door, with Scramble beside him. She whined. I started to go to her, only to be jerked hard by the collar. Before my head was jerked around, I saw Behemoth bare his teeth at her, and I smelled a very rapid exchange of odors. Before knowing Gavi and learning to sniff Mossen words, I wouldn't have detected them, they were so quickly dissipated, but I did smell them, clearly.

Oskar muttered at me. "You don't approach any of the Simusi, old or new. If they want you, they'll summon you with your bark-name. Until you have a bark-name, you don't look at them or go toward them or interact in any way. For the time being, I'm your owner."

"And I'm a slave," I said, abstractedly, my mind busy with the conversation I had just sniffed between Behemoth and Scramble, listing the odors and remembering them. Figuring them out could come later.

"Slavery," he mused. "Well, our race had dogs. Were they slaves?"

"We didn't think so," I replied. "The dogs didn't think so. They've voluntarily been with us since caveman days, forty or fifty thousand years ago."

"*Those* dogs, yes. Wolves. Jackals, Wild dogs. Canines. But the Simusi aren't canines. They are, however, the pure paradigm of all pack creatures."

"How did Behemoth get to be Simusi?" I asked.

"If any Zhaar genetics were used in breeding him, he'd have heard the call. Zhaar genetics had to have been used. I can't believe you didn't know that."

I said defensively, "I didn't *know* that. If true, I'm sure the people who did it were only intending to make them bigger, stronger, healthier, with longer life spans. I'm sure they didn't mean to hurt anything."

". . . said the child who'd played with matches, after the house burned down." He jiggled the leash. "Zhaar genetic matrices are like viruses. When they enter another system, they take it over and rebuild it in their own likeness, or some other likeness if they prefer. If enough of the matrix is used, the rebuild can be almost total."

He'd made a subtle emphasis on the word *almost.* I thought of the dognose I'd been given when I was sixteen. In the light of everything I'd seen here, it, too, had probably been Zhaar-modified. "And if not enough matrix was used?" It came out sounding almost as casual as I'd intended it to.

"You end up with a hybrid. The Simusi kill any of those they find, unless they can use them for something. The Orskimi use a lot of Zhaar tech, not to change themselves, though. They use it to change other creatures they can use as symbiotes."

"The Orskimi are trying to wipe out the human worlds."

He snorted. "The Simusi would approve of that."

We were strolling along a path through light-dappled woodlands.

On any other occasion, I'd have enjoyed such a walk. The day was warm, the air was sweet with slightly resinous odors; to either side I could see Simusi moving about, singly or in small groups, and they were gorgeous to look at. Graceful, gleaming, regal. Four very young pups were playing in a clearing. They were still a little wobbly on their legs, and they were being supervised by a human with a collar.

"Baby-sitter?" I asked.

Oskar glanced that way. "More like nanny. It's one way for us to gain a better life here. If the pups grow attached to their nanny, they'll be less likely to dispose of her, or him, over some small failing later on." His steps had slowed somewhat, and he was limping more heavily than before.

"How far are we going?" I said, glancing at his legs.

He grimaced. "A couple of miles. Don't worry about me. I'll make it."

We fell silent. I was still trying to correlate everything I knew or had heard about the Simusi. "If the Simusi would approve of wiping out the human race, out there in normal space, and if we're all non-breeders here in Splendor, what will the Simusi do for nannies and kennel-keepers when we're gone?"

He stopped, staring at the sky, his mouth twisted with anger or pain. "I don't know. The matter has never come up!" Angrily, he jerked me off-balance with the leash and stumped along with me running to keep up.

I gave him a while to settle down. "What's their real objection to us, aside from our being vermin?"

"We're not much worse than most other creatures. It's just that with Simusi, you're either more powerful, like the Phain or the Yizzang, or you're nothing. There's no category in between." He chewed his lips for a moment, thinking. "The Simusi do hate humans particularly, though."

"Why?"

"Because humans have dogs as . . . pets. Dogs share the holy shape. That makes humans guilty of blasphemy."

"Do you speak Simusi?" I asked.

He laughed. "No. I'm not a noser. The Simusi have odor-generating cells in their mouths and throats. They exhale their messages, except for the few bark-name words they use with us and the Gixit and the other creatures . . ."

"Who are also slaves?"

"Not the Gixit, no. They lived on some world that was damaged by humans, and only a few of them survived. They were brought here by the Phain to be safe, and a few of them seem to like being with the Simusi. It's the Phain who object to us most. If we all went to a sterile moon and drilled it out like an ant nest and populated the entire moon with human beings to the depth of miles, they wouldn't care. It's the terraforming they hate, because it involves killing the native plants and animals."

"I wonder if this is where Moss got its odor language from," I mused. "Through the spacial interface with the Simusi world."

"An odor language outside? Really!" He became animated. "That's interesting! I didn't know there were odor languages anywhere else . . ."

"There are odor languages on Earth," I said. "Or were. Toward the end of the twentieth century, scientists discovered that plants communicate with one another, and with other living things, through the exchange of odor molecules. If one plant gets eaten by a beetle, it sends a signal into the air, and similar plants downwind accelerate the manufacture of their natural insecticide. One plant gets invaded by a fungus, the ones around it increase production of fungicide."

"Rather primitive," he said.

"Nonetheless, it worked. A transmission and a response constitute a language, at least so my brother says. It's probably the way the odor language on Moss got started."

Either he could think of nothing else to say, or he was feeling too much pain to talk. His face was set in grim determination, and the farther we went, the more he limped. We came to the dike he'd mentioned, a heavily overgrown wall of stone that stretched across our trail as far as I could see on either side.

"Simusi territory on this side of the wall," Oskar said. "Guardian territory on the other."

Only a narrow defile led through the dike. Once we were past it, the woods thinned and gave way to grasslands. Oskar was dragging his leg by the time we came to a stretch of meadow that was being grazed by some large, six-legged, blue-skinned herbivores. The herd was between us and a structure across the grassland.

"Your friend is here, temporarily," Oskar said.

"Gavi?"

"Not the woman. The Simusi took her . . ."

"Took Gavi?" I cried.

"I don't know who the woman was. But this one is a man. Says he's your husband, from Earth."

I stopped short. "Oskar. Please. I'd rather be somewhere else . . ."

He looked me in the eye, really looked, then said sympathetically, "No, you wouldn't. If you don't want to have anything to do with him, then don't, but you don't want to pass up this chance. This is a Phain farm, you speak a little Phain-ildar, and the Sannasee has picked you from among the new ones. The Phain have first choice, you see, and the Simusi don't interfere with the Phain. They don't hunt here, because the Phain forbid it. This is the safest place you could be right now."

The idea of meeting Witt again was depressing, but I couldn't argue about the rest of it. We moved across the meadow, keeping well clear of the big, blue-skinned creatures. I had seen them before, on Tsaliphor, but only at a distance. As we came nearer to the building, Oskar stopped and drew in a shuddering breath. I followed his eyes and saw a pair of P'narg headed in our direction. Oskar's fingers grew lax on the leash. His face was ashen. I pulled the leash from his fingers and moved toward the P'narg. When I was within hearing distance, I bowed, and said in Phain-ildar, as I had said on Tsaliphor, "I greet you and wish you well."

The P'narg snuffled between themselves, then turned and shuffled toward a patch of woods at the top of a low hill. I turned, catching a glimpse of a Phaina standing in the door of a long, ramified structure. When I returned to Oskar and handed him my leash, he was still very pale.

"They're not supposed to be out loose," he rasped.

"When I knew them on Tsaliphor, they were always out loose."

"That's a Phain planet."

"I lived there for almost a year."

"And those things walked around loose?"

"They lived there," I said. "It was their home. I imagine this is also their home. The Phain don't cage animals."

"Maybe not, but when we're coming or going, they're supposed to get the dangerous ones out of our way, so we don't get killed. What did you say to them?"

"I just greeted them, that's all."

Now he looked angry, and I decided it wasn't the time to go into a discussion of whether or not the P'narg were dangerous or whether talking to them was inappropriate. He obviously thought so in both cases, and he was unlikely to be convinced otherwise. Besides, I had no real way of knowing that the P'narg wouldn't eat him. They might, for all I knew.

Oskar indicated the sprawling structure we were approaching. "That's the Guardian House."

We veered around one end of the building to enter a long, low annex at the back, going through a refectory with tables and chairs to a dormitory with rows of cots and storage units for clothes. Witt sat expectantly on one of the cots, obviously waiting for me. I gritted my teeth, introduced him to Oskar, and left the two of them talking to one another while I looked around.

Behind the dormitory were the doors to sanitary areas with toilets and showers, one for women, one for men. All in all, a considerable improvement over the kennel.

When I heard a third voice speaking, and then Oskar, saying, "She does not!" I returned to the dormitory. Oskar was very pale and obviously upset, staring after a man headed out the door.

Witt said, "The Phaina sent someone to tell you she wants you to work in the garden here. The house garden. And she says, you already know what to do."

Oskar challenged this angrily. "How could you possibly? I always have to tell the new ones what to do!"

I summoned up my Paul-soothing voice. "I worked on a garden on Tsaliphor. This Phaina may know of that, may actually have seen me there. I'm not an expert on Phain gardens, by any means, so what she probably means is that I can do the weeding without supervision."

Oskar took a deep breath, lips twisted in ... what? Defeat? Discouragement? "Oh, well, possibly that's it. Yes. Well then. If you don't need me for anything ... "

Then I caught on. The poor man wanted to stay here, at least for a while. He needed an excuse to rest somewhere before attempting the long walk back.

"Please, stay," I begged. "There will be other things I need to know before you leave."

He demurred without conviction, and I insisted. In the end, he lay down on one of the cots and promptly fell asleep.

I stretched out on another cot with every intention of resting, but Witt ignored the pillow I placed over my eyes and recited a long litany of complaint, ending with, "He said the P'narg were out. They're not supposed to be out when we're around. They eat us."

If I had hoped for a change in Witt, I was disappointed. He was still aggrieved and at a loss for a remedy, stuck where he had been for the last twelve years, I supposed. Rather than make me feel sympathetic, his whining annoyed me.

"They may well eat you," I said in a voice that sounded aggressive, even to me. "They won't eat me." I wasn't at all sure they wouldn't, but the P'narg, once greeted, hadn't made a move toward me, and I thought it very unlikely they ever would. Witt gave me a hurt look and went away. I didn't see him again until evening, when the dormitory filled up with workers, most of them able to communicate in common speech and a few able to translate for those who didn't. There were about thirty of us, soon joined by another eight or ten who came into the refectory bearing bowls and platters of food. It was all vegetable, no meat: something very like mild cheese, though the smell made me think it was probably a fungus; sections of an aromatic and sweet white root; greens, cooked and raw; fruits, cooked and raw; several dishes of mixed grain and legumes, cooked with various savory additives. Everything tasted better than Earth food, and there was plenty of it. Oskar sat near me, telling me the names of the foods and the plants they came from while eating more than I would have thought possible, another reason he had wanted to stay. The poor man was aging, tired, hungry, and in pain. At the moment, I was unable to be helpful, but I made a mental note to keep him in mind, to help if and when I could. He reminded me a great deal of Jon Point, with something of the same indomitability about him.

The people asked many questions about how I'd been caught, and where, and so forth, responding with their own stories. Six of the men had been among the eleven men "harvested" on Jungle. Since PPI operated under noninterference directives, it made sense that the six of them were here, for the Phaina no doubt approved of noninterference. They told me that the other five taken on Jungle had been new recruits to PPI. One of the five had been Witt, of course, though the others taken from Jungle rather ignored him during the meal. The others had gone crazy, Oskar whispered, so they'd been taken to the Simusi food pens.

Someone asked what I was going to be doing, and I said working in the Phaina's garden. That prompted a long silence.

"What?" I asked. "Is there something bad about that?"

"The Phaina doesn't let any of us in her garden."

Oskar spoke up, importantly. "Jewel was on a Phain planet once, where she worked on a Phain garden, and she'll only be doing the weeding."

They seemed to accept his explanation, but to avoid further problems I began asking questions of my own. Some had been harvested from spaceships, some from planets they were visiting, a few from Earth itself, or from Earth colony planets. When they had arrived, all those chosen had been questioned for many days by an agent of the Phaina.

I asked what they'd been questioned about.

One woman spoke up. "What were we doing on the planet, where were we going in the ship, why were we sending all our old people back to Earth, why were we having so many children, and why had we killed this bacteria or that weed, or that animal, or that insect?"

A man spoke. "They got me on a colony planet, they showed us a picture of this thing, and they asked how long we'd studied this kind of half animal half plant thing they called a fromfis. I told them we hadn't studied the things at all, we weren't supposed to, we were there to do research on a cure for Ban-Atkins Disease. So then this Phain told me this fromfis thing had a microbe growing in its gut that would have cured the Ban-Atkins Disease, so it was a pity we'd killed them all, and that really upset me. Maybe they were just jerking us around."

"No," I said firmly. "The Phain don't do that. If a Phain said that, it was the truth."

He turned even paler, if that were possible, and gave me a resentful look while I cautioned myself to keep my judgments to myself. Doubtless most of the captives had comforting ideas of victimhood and would become angry if contradicted.

The dormitory beds were far more comfortable than the pads in the kennel. Though we all wore collars, I had seen no one leashed thus far. From their talk, everyone knew what he or she was supposed to do, and everyone spent their days doing it. After supper, we had story-telling and dancing of a crude kind, and music also of a crude kind, though from the quality of some voices, they were capable of better. Everyone went to sleep early. Witt stayed away from me.

The following morning, after a quick meal, the people went off in different directions, and I was shown through a locked gate into the Phaina's garden. A stone-built toolshed contained everything I needed, and I worked up a considerable sweat (smell vocab: present tense. to work.) loosening the moist, loamy-smelling earth around trees (vocab: to dig), transplanting creepers into bare spots (vocab: no smell detected?), harvesting seeds (fragrant shells, various. vocab: to gather? or to ripen?), and putting aromatic seed (smell) in the ground (plus smell) (vocab: to plant). The creepers were obviously an edging plant, separating grasslike plants from decorative ones. The lack of smell . . . No. It came to me suddenly that wasn't lack. It was negation. Nons-mell. Separation. An undetectable odor eraser? Like the one Gavi had used on me?

I gradually worked my way along the side of the structure. At what felt like midmorning, I took a break and walked around the nearest corner of the rambling building to look across the garden. It was huge, and no one else was working in it, so the work would occupy me forever, which at that moment seemed a blessing. If there was no hope of being rescued, at least I would be employed in an enjoyable way. Also, once I had established what my hands should be doing, my mind was free to think things through, starting with yesterday's conversation between Behemoth and Scramble.

The first smell had been a milk smell. The "speaker" had to have been Scramble, and milk smell no doubt signified puppies. Next came the odor of Matty's perfume, one I wore from time to time. Scramble had never known Matty, so that smell had to be her word for me. Then there'd been a retreating smell, which meant, according to Gavi, going somewhere. And the last smell had been the milk smell and my smell combined.

No matter how I linked them, they came out to mean one thing. Jewel should go get the puppies or go be with the puppies.

Behemoth didn't agree. He had emitted the smell of the stuff Gainor used on his hair, then a nasty, "you must" smell. Then a coming forward smell of the hair stuff coupled with the puppy smell. Gainor has to bring the puppies or . . . blood smell and Matty's perfume again. Gainor bring the puppies or we'll kill Jewel.

I sat down with a shock. I don't faint, as some people are said to do, but I came close. How was Gainor supposed to get this threat? Some kind of ransom note, delivered how?

That hadn't been the end of the conversation. Scramble had said blood odor, plus dog odor. Which dog? I didn't know. Was she threatening to kill Behemoth if he injured me? Or threatening to kill me if I injured a puppy? Or telling Behemoth his way would get puppies killed? Or, kill herself? Behemoth considered himself mated for life. If Scramble was gone, he'd be a nonbreeder, a virtual eunuch, so Scramble's absence might have been a real threat to his primacy.

My stomach told me it was noon just moments before one of the kitchen people showed up with a bowl of food and a bottle of water. She told me to bring the bowl and bottle with me when I came back to the dormitory.

"When?" I asked her. "Is there a bell?"

"When the light starts to dim," she said. "This place has the same-length days all the time. Three meals a day. First light, middle light, when it's brightest, then when it starts to dim. Then's when you come in. Later, when it's dark, some really big predators wander around loose."

For the first time since I'd been in the place I realized the sky shone with an utterly sourceless light. No sun threw a shadow, though there was shade where the trees were dense and encircling. I sat down on a bench with my bottle and bowl, thinking my way through Scramble's conversation once more. Reconsideration yielded nothing new or fresh. Scramble wanted me to get the pups, Behemoth wanted Gainor to bring them, there was some bad consequence threatened on some-one by someone.

I was hunched over the bowl. The splatting of tears onto my spoon was the first inkling I had that I was crying. Over Scramble, of course. And Behemoth. All those years spent working for them, making a future for them. Had they been reached by the Simusi while we were still on Earth? Were they told then that they were Simusi? If not, when did they find out? Had the odor messages on Moss told them much, much more than the odors had told Gavi?

And what about Moss itself, the world of! Was it also Simusi? Owned by, managed by? Or was it just a nice little world trying to do its best for its inhabitants, rather in the same way Gainor and Shiela and I had tried to do the best for dogs and cats and any other life-form we could protect.

So I sat there, grieving over the loss of my lovely dogs, grieving over the fact that I couldn't care about Witt anymore, grieving over being separated from Mag, and from Gavi, and Gainor, of course. Even Drom and Sybil. What was going to happen to them? And Paul. Was he plowing along on the language? All these wonders, rages, and griefs had me astir when I heard a familiar sound, liquidly sweet, the music of a Phaina's voice, followed by the equally soft-toned translation by a lingui-pute.

"Why do you shed tears?"

"For the loss of my friends, the dogs," I said, without even thinking.

"But they are not wholly dogs," she said.

This was annoying. "Then I'm not crying for the part that isn't. I grieve for the idea of the dogs I believed they were. Not Simusi, but my friends." I dried my face with the backs of my hands. "And even if these dogs aren't wholly dogs, there are other whole dogs we are trying desperately to protect. I am ashamed to have wasted my time so misguidedly on these if they do not merit it."

"Ah," she said, sitting down beside me. It was the first time I had seen a Phaina seated. On Tsaliphor, we had always walked in open places where there were no seats. Her legs stretched a long way onto the path, and her head was far above mine.

"So you have real dogs you wish to protect. Why, then, were these not left to be merely real dogs?"

"Real dogs had short life spans, they had health problems. The arkists started out trying to breed them back to their ancestral form, their natural form, to get rid of the bone and breathing problems, but their life spans were still very short. The arkists thought ... think that longer life spans would allow more learning to be passed on to future generations, and that, in turn, would result in a better survival rate. Someone, I don't know who, must have decided to use Zhaar technology. I don't even know when or who or how they got hold of it! It must have been done in utero. I wish they hadn't."

She asked, "Is the pack leader hostile toward you."

"Behemoth? Now? I think so," I confessed. "He wasn't before, though, so why is he now?"

"He was told he was Simusi, that you knew and had kept it from him. Unfortunately, he will soon discover this is untrue. He is a superior dog, but far inferior to Simusi. He will not be pleased to learn of his true status. He can understand their odor language, he can even speak it, as a child speaks, but he will never be able to emit it eloquently. True Simusi have maraquar of experience in telling heroic tales about their past, reciting epics, and sniffing the stories and sagas of others. It is how they spend most of their time. Behemoth will never be able to do that well."

I thought of Walky's poems, "The Simusi must be like Walking Sunshine."

She asked me what I meant, and I told her about the willog who wrote poetry, and how delighted he was to have eyes and ears.

"On the planet?" she asked. Lingui-putes cannot convey tone of voice, but I could hear her tone before I heard what the words meant. She was astonished. "Where they brought you from?"

"Yes. I was just getting to know the place. It's very beautiful. If the willog is any indication, it has wonderful creatures on it. We must leave it, you know. It belongs to itself, not to us."

The great torso beside me tensed. "If a planet belongs to its own creatures, you let it alone?"

I thought about her question for a time, trying to frame an honest answer that wouldn't convict us in her eyes. "The Interstellar Confederation says if a planet is occupied by intelligent creatures, it belongs to those creatures. And usually, any creature with a language is considered to be intelligent. That's what was hard about Moss. The language is one of smells, like the Simusi, but we'd never encountered that before. We know about sign languages and vocal languages, but it may be there are many other languages that have missed being identified simply because they aren't spoken or visual."

"So you will leave the planet alone. And the Derac?"

"PPI is committed to noninterference, Earth will leave it alone. The Derac will be required by IC to leave it alone, though they have a history of cheating when they can get away with it. The humans who came there by accident, several hundred years ago, will be required to leave also, unless the World asks them to stay."

She was silent for a long moment. "The World?"

"I think it's all one being, the whole world. Everything is all tied together, with one mind running everything . . ."

She made a strange, high, tinkling sound. Laughter? Or pity? "But, that is always so."

I stared at her, knowing full well what she meant. "Yes, Sannasee, it is always so, as we know to our sorrow, but in most worlds the planetary mind is . . . or seems to be unconscious. My brother says transmission and response equals protolanguage, but in most worlds it takes years and years for response to occur. Because life spans are short, and the response is so late in arriving, the living things who detect it don't know it has anything to do with them."

"I do not understand."

"We are accustomed to conversations that are proximate in time. I say to you, you respond to me. Our World responds, but not for years or even centuries. When it does respond, we do not realize it is replying to something our grandfathers did; we do not recognize that it is speaking! On Moss, though the feedback is slow compared to any language we're familiar with, it's a lot quicker than we've ever known to occur at a planetary level, quick enough to tell us the Moss mind is obviously conscious. It feels what happens. It directs response. It actually speaks."

"I must go there," she said, making the high, tinkling sound once more. "I must go there soon. Will you go with me?"

"Of course," I said. "I would do anything to help you, Sannasee. You know that."

She regarded me again with that ring of eyes, fluttering open and closed, as though some looked at my skin and others at my heart. "Will you do it without telling anyone?"

Again, I heard the emotion in her voice before the machine translated it. It was a combination of eagerness and fear. As though she had been invited to meet God, personally, and was uncertain where she stood.

I said very softly, "Someone would not want you to go?"

Her great, oval head nodded, a very human-looking nod, and the eyes around her brow fluttered at me sequentially, like fingers waving hello or good-bye. "Our people are very conservative. They would not forbid, but they would . . . look askance. You will say of this . . ."

"I will say of this nothing," I told her. "What is there to say?"

We sat there a time longer. I asked about Splendor, and she told me a little of its discovery, of the determination of the elder races to keep it unspoiled, to keep the riffraff out of it. She said almost nothing about the place, or places, the people or peoples who lived there, if, indeed, anyone did. It could have been a marvelous vacancy for all the description she permitted herself, though she did speak of all living creatures doing well in Splendor.

When she finally departed, I went on with the garden. Gradually, as the day wore away, I grew a little achy, more than a little tired, but also relaxed and tranquil. My wanders on Moss had not been strenuous. This was the first real exercise I'd had in a very long time, and it was therapeutic.

When the light dimmed around me, I cleaned and put away my tools before returning to quarters. Witt was there. He came to sit beside me at the table and tell me he wanted to come sleep with me that night. I felt only a mild revulsion. I remarked that I had been doing hard, physical labor all day, which had made me too tired to want company.

His face wrinkled like a child who's been slapped. "But I only have tonight. My master only let me come for two days. I told him we were liaised . . ."

I gritted my teeth, reaching for the right tone. "It was very kind of your master to let you come, Witt. Be sure to tell him how grateful we are for his kindness, but our liaison expired more than seven years ago. We aren't liaised anymore, and I prefer to keep to Earth law, as I'm accustomed to that."

Besides, thought I, he may have been fixed, but I didn't know that for sure, and I did know I hadn't been. I did not want to make that mistake again.

He didn't argue, just dropped his head and looked pathetic. I wanted to say, "Now you need a good night's rest so you can be a good doggy tomorrow," but I took his hand instead, pressed it with a sad little smile that was intended to look regretful, and left him sitting there. I don't know where he went. Off, somewhere. All that charm, the poise, the knowledgeability that had made him seem so wonderful to me at eighteen had been only a well-practiced social facade. If I had not been so young, if I had had more experience of people, perhaps I would not have been so impressed by the veneer. Facing hardship, without the pedestal of money and family, he was lost.

Which did not mean I was not partly responsible. If I had not been so quick to liaise with him, his mother would not have sent him away. If she had not sent him away, he could be living still on his pleasant pedestal in an environment he had been reared to inhabit. The Phaina had said she would go to Moss and take me with her. Perhaps it would be possible for Witt to go as well. If I could restore him to his niche, somehow, my personal responsibility toward him would be met.

Only a thought. An attractive thought, nonetheless, one that remained with me.

ESCAPE

Deep in the night I wakened, thinking I'd heard something. I lay there, only half-alert, waiting for whatever it was to happen again. Around me the roomful of sleepers went on sleeping as the sound came again, a sharp *rrr-aroo*! And again. *Rrr-aroo*! Scramble's voice, my signal, perhaps a warning, definitely a summons.

The Phaina's doors had no locks, just like the ones on Tsaliphor. The door swung quietly closed as I slipped out beneath the pallid, shadowless sheen of an unlit sky, a gloaming with the glisten of polished steel. Halfway across the meadow that Oskar and I had crossed on arrival, I risked a reply, trying to make a convincingly doglike yelp. She came like the wind, a great gust of her, sound and scent and presence, thrusting her muzzle into my neck, breathing me in.

I threw my arms around her as she sat beside me, whispering to her, babbling at her. "Oh, Scramble, Scramble . . . Why doesn't Behemoth want me to get the puppies?"

She stood back, staring at me warily. "Ow u eer?" she asked.

"I didn't hear it. I smelled it. When you and Behemoth were outside that other place, that . . . kennel. Behemoth threatened to kill me? Or kill somebody else?"

She persisted. "Ow yu nnoh owr wrns?"

"I know your words because Gavi Norchis taught me to smell words, a little. Did you learn the language after you came to Moss?"

"Ess. On Moss. We lerhn we Simusi."

"You learned on Moss you were *Simusi*? Who told you that?"

"In nigh, woice sais, yu Simusi."

"A voice told you in the night?" That confused me for a moment. "Did that same voice tell to come to the gate? Is that why you took the puppies and headed to the battlefield?"

"Es." She stared at me, her head cocked, waiting for me to go on guessing. Our conversations were sometimes easier if I guessed and let her say yes or no.

"But you didn't believe the voice?"

"Ehemosh, es. He wery mush. Me, nuh noh. Nuh suhr."

She had not been sure, but Behemoth had believed very much, of course. Would his great pride have allowed him not to believe? If an angel stepped from heaven and told me I was kin to angels, would I doubt it? Well, yes, but then, I had a long history of doubting. Even Scramble had not been sure. "Do you believe the puppies are Simusi?"

"No," she said, half a growl. "No. Uhs nuh e'en Simusi, nuh mush. We nah ghoo Simusi. No ghan. Rr ghuh oghs."

She knew they weren't much Simusi, not good ones, couldn't be, and she was angry about it. Angry at not being? Or angry at being told a lie? She gathered herself, as for some great effort. "Ghewll, my ren, I shingh mohr ghuh we gho whar we uhs." She looked away from me, her ears drooping, tail tight around her feet.

"Jewel, my friend, I think more good we go where we us." She must have worked out that combination well in advance. The dogs couldn't pronounce B, D, F, hard G, J, K, P, T, Th, V, or Z. They used a throaty GH gargle for G J K sounds. Despite that constraint, she had made her wishes clearly known. Knowing what she said, she had called me friend.

I pulled her back into my arms, crouching beside her. "I think every creature is happiest where it can be itself. Do you want to go to Treasure as we planned? Where you can be just you, whatever you are?"

Tired of words, she breathed at me, a flowing line of scent notes, woods and mosses, forest and trees, water flowing, the attractive aroma of prey. Though they couldn't be Simusi, they had certainly picked up some of the scent language. Perhaps only enough to frustrate them as spoken language often did us. "Uhs ghuh oghs," she repeated softly, to herself.

They were good dogs, indeed. "And Behemoth?"

"Ehemosh hurs."

"He hurts."

"Es."

I should have realized that. Alpha dog, suddenly demoted to half-breed status, to nothingness, his puppies gone, his mate arguing with him, all in pursuit of a phantom glory. Hating me, hating everyone, probably, because the glory wasn't real. I leaned against her and she against me in mutual confusion and misery. Any urge to sleep had fled, and my mind was busy with possibilities.

"If I find a way to get out of here, do you want to come with me?"

She nodded, stopped, put her head down for a moment, then said, "Awl woman oghs."

All the woman dogs. That was new. "Veegee and Dapple?"

"Es." She threw her head back, sniffing, then said suddenly, "Mus gho." She turned and was gone, swiftly as she had come. Back, I supposed, to join her pack before she was missed. I walked slowly back across the meadow, not looking where I was going, almost running into a giant, furry wall of P'narg, who were busy browsing fruit from one of the Phaina's trees. I stepped back, bowed, and excused myself as the P'narg rumbled at me. When I got to the house, I was met by the Phaina herself, a Phaina who seemed only amused.

"Do you usually wander around at night, bumping into creatures?" her lingui-pute asked me.

"No, ma'am, but tonight I was summoned. Scramble came to talk to me."

"Scramble being . . . a dog? And what does Scramble have to say?"

"She says the female dogs don't want to stay here. They say they can't be real Simusi, and they want to go somewhere else, where they can be themselves."

"And the males?"

I rubbed my forehead in frustration. "It's as you suggested, San-nasee. They're... not happy with what they are. From Scramble's manner, I'd say she isn't sure what Behemoth and the others will do, but my hunch is they would follow the females, now or later, if they were allowed to go."

She was silent for a long, brooding moment. "Would you like to help them now?"

I spoke through gritted teeth, trying not to commit an un-Phainic impoliteness by yelling. "Helping them is what I've been trying to do for years, Sannasee. Of course I want to help them, but Scramble's gone back wherever they are. I'd have to get word to her..."

"Which we will try to do." She tilted her head back and turned deliberately around, the upper arc of her eyelids viewing the entire hemisphere, the whole of the sky from horizon to horizon. I don't know what she saw there. It was featureless, as far as I was concerned.

When she spoke it as to herself. "It is appropriate for me to do this. Dalongar is being diluted. The Simusi are overstepping them-selves..."

The lingui-pute whispered as she mused, half to herself, "When we were young races, the Zhaar made riot with shape and function, a vast usurpation of others' individuality, caring nothing for other peoples and worlds. Planets were burned, ancient civilizations were destroyed. We could not convince the Zhaar to accept our policy of noninterfer-ence, for they gloried in their power over others. At last, we declared them anathema and told them to depart or be destroyed, as they did, no one knew where or how, nor cared. We breathed with relief for a time, then we forgot them, considering them well gone.

"But it seems immutable law that there is always a pricking thorn on the flower, a bit of grit in the shellfish, a troublesome relative in the fam-ily. Some great time later, we met this new race, this Simusi. They told us they had adopted a simple primitivism as their way, the exaltation of aus-terity as their goal, but we soon realized their simplicity and austerity could be maintained only through the enslavement of a dozen other races." She snorted, a sound that was the same from her as from the machine.

"A simple, austere race would hunt or go hungry. The Simusi hunt and return expecting to find cooked food prepared for them. A primitive race would bathe or be dirty. The Simusi crawl through mire and return expecting others to bathe and groom them. A race of simplicity would mate for life, once only. The Simusi keep whole harems of various creatures, only to delight their senses. They are not simple. They have merely enslaved others to deal with their complexities!

"The Simusi tell us their accumulation of 'friends' is proof of their dalongar, their respectful regard for others, though in fact it proves otherwise, for it denies respect and courtesy. Slavery is against our law."

She made a high, keening sound that the machine made no attempt to translate, and was then silent for some time. I did not dare to interrupt her. I had assumed the Phain did not feel pain, but I had been mistaken. She felt pain, from a cause I would not perceive.

Finally, she said, "I will give you directions to the place the dogs are. Meantime, I will devise a path we may use without being prevented or followed, and you will bring them to meet me on the way . . ."

She followed this with explicit directions concerning where I was to go, and she had me repeat the whole business three times before she left me to return to her house.

I went into the dormitory, dressed myself more completely than I'd done to go night walking, packed all my belongings, went out the door and was halfway across the meadow on the first leg of the journey I'd been assigned before I was aware of being followed. I spun around and caught sight of him, ducking behind a bush.

"Come out, Witt."

He did so, his drag-footed reluctance bringing my previous thoughts to mind. If I wanted to erase my obligation to him by getting him out of here, there could be no better chance than this. The Sannasee might not allow it, of course, but if she didn't, he'd be no worse off than he was now.

When he came close, I said, "Follow me and keep quiet."

"But . . ." he began, in that whining tone that seemed to be the only one he had left.

I stopped, fighting down my anger at him. "Witt, if you will not follow me quietly, then you must go back to the Phaina's house. I will not risk my life for yours."

He looked shocked, but he followed me. At a trot, we traveled the path Oskar and I had used to get to the Guardian House. The Phaina had said to bring the dogs to the rendezvous by morning, so I concentrated on speed. The first landmark the Phaina had mentioned was the stone dike where the path ran through a narrow defile. I remembered the place from before and had no trouble finding it again. We didn't enter the passageway through it, however, but turned to our right along the wall, into the woods. Witt was panting, lagging behind, trying repeatedly to start a conversation. Each time I told him to save his breath for running as quietly as possible or we might be heard, sought, killed. Each time he responded with: "But, Jewel . . ."

Finally, I stopped in exasperation to whisper to him, "Tell you what, Witt. Since you're determined to get caught, why don't you concentrate on doing that by yourself. You can either sit out here and make noise, or you can find someplace to hide and just stay there until I return. Either way, you'll only risk yourself."

"But, Jewel . . ."

"The Phaina ordered this, Witt. Are you saying you won't obey her?"

Wringing his hands, he stood looking after me as I plunged on to the next landmark, a gravelly patch from which a half dozen rocky paths led in different directions. As I counted them off clockwise to choose the fourth one, I wondered what he would choose to do. He might sit tight, he might try to follow, or he might wander off and get himself lost, thereby losing any chance of returning home. I reproved myself for harshness but was able to care only slightly, one way or the other.

The new path was narrow as a game trail. This was another Joram expression which he had had to explain, for Tad and I had found the word *game* an odd one to describe trailing and killing something. The way led upward for some distance, over a wooded ridge, then down through the woods on the far side to emerge onto short grasses above a long, narrow dale with a chatty stream gossiping its way down the middle. Across the water, a like stretch of grass sloped up to an eroded bank dotted with dark tunnel openings. Dens, the Phaina had said, dug by the Simusi. After her description of the Simusi, however, I thought more likely they'd been dug by some burrowing creature adopted as a "friend," to save the Simusi the trouble of being primitive on their own.

I stepped well back into the shadow of the trees, turned to my left, downstream, and moved as quietly as possible parallel to the brook.

According to the Phaina, this stream and its grassy valley would meet another at the bottom of the slope, and from there the conjoined streams would flow to the right, down a steep combe where the dogs were digging their dens. I kept moving, without much anxiety, until a full-voiced howl stopped me in my tracks. It came from the right, ahead of me, out in the vale. More howls joined the first. I stayed, frozen. The noise got louder, but came no closer. Moving stealthily, I found a vantage point near the forest edge. On a flat area across the stream, a large fire was being tended by a few collared humans and some of the four-armed lemurish things. Inside the ring of rosy light sat a number of Simusi, shadow black and fire red, eyes glinting, muzzles toward the sky.

When the fire tenders threw more wood onto the fire, it leapt up, disclosing several cages near the stream. Firelight reflected from the stream onto the backs of the cages and onto a face pressed to the bars, eyes wide with frantic terror. Gavi.

I crept back into the trees again and sat down, head on knees, trying desperately to think what I could do, how I could free her. Alone, I could do nothing. Nothing. But . . . but if I had Scramble's help. And Veegee's, and Dapple's. If I had Behemoth's help . . .

Giving up caution, I ran, hoping the noise the Simusi were making would hide any I might make. Eventually, the dale widened and leveled in an almost flat delta, where it met the larger stream that ran from left to right before me. To follow the near bank of the conjoined stream, I had to cross both the talkative brook and the spread of grasses through which it ran. I told myself it was possible the Simusi had posted sentinels. I then tried to convince myself it was unlikely they had posted them so far from their gathering.

Joram came to mind, with all his tales of sneaking here and skulking there, which on occasion had forced him to wriggle like a snake. I wriggled, though imagining was easier than doing. People are not built like snakes, and they aren't waterproof, either. I reached the far stream side wet through and thoroughly chilled, while the Simusi howled on, uninterrupted.

The combe was narrower than the dale. The strip of stream bank between the water and the vertical high-water bank was also narrow, the upper edge of it overhung with arching grasses, roots, and branches that made a tunnel along the damp earth wall. I went slowly along inside it, right hand on the dirt, left hand pushing the branches and roots away from my face. The Phaina had said the dogs were digging dens into this bank, but if so, the overhang hid them completely. I was likely to stumble into a hole before I saw it. Behemoth would probably resent that.

I was dithering when a small breeze came toward me, heavy with the odor of dog, and through the masking branches, I saw the three males emerge suddenly onto the stream bank. They drank with quick laps, ears alert, then stood with their heads turned upstream, toward the cacophony that was still going on. In a moment they trotted upstream in single file, only a few arm's lengths below me, never noticing I was there.

I couldn't let them go. I stepped out onto the bank and called, "Behemoth. Titan. Wolf!"

They stopped and turned, unwillingly. The fur along Behemoth's spine rose into a ridge. His lips drew back from his teeth. He stalked toward me, tail down, ears down, and from behind me I heard Scramble say, "Noh. Yuh noh Simusi, ogh!"

She was beside me, with Veegee and Dapple behind her. Scramble went forward, mouth open, breathing words that floated away from me toward the dogs. I caught only fleeting scents. Milk scents as they spoke of puppies. Blood smell as they spoke of death. My perfume. The smell of the Simusi and one of those warning, keep-off smells I'd learned on Moss. The male dogs replied. Veegee joined in the conversation, then Dapple. I could only intuit what the females were saying. "You can stay and try to be Simusi, but we won't. We care about ourselves, our families, our dogness. You pretend you are like Simusi, but they know differently. You will be another of their slaves, like the pitiful humans, like the others . . ." A set of smells I didn't recognize flowed by, new vocabulary.

Then Scramble came back to me. It had taken very little time, actually, though it had felt like an age. "Wha, Shewel? We gho?"

"Will Behemoth go with us?"

"Me my sisrs gho. Ish he wans lil wons, he gho."

The sisters going was good enough for me. I told them to follow me, but instead of returning the way I'd come, I plunged straight away from the den openings, down the bank, through the icy, knee-deep water, up the far bank of the combe, and into the trees. There, well under cover, we turned left and kept going until we had passed the open end of the dale. The detour put us opposite the place I had left the woods, and required no wriggling to get there. I turned to see who was with us, and wonder of wonders, two of the males were close behind while Behemoth stalked after them, a considerable distance back and not hurrying.

We recrossed the chilly water, climbed one more bank, and were in the forest. Scramble cast about for my outward trail, finding it almost immediately. With the dogs smelling the way, we went more quickly than when I had been alone. As we approached the bonfire, the howls rose to an ear-piercing crescendo. I went slowly to the edge of the wood, pointed at the cage where Gavi still knelt, face pressed against the bars. "What will they do with her?" I asked.

Behemoth said, "Hunningh hoomans nigh."

"Their night for hunting humans?"

"Es."

"Will they . . . will they give them a head start?"

He gave me a long, calculating look. "Es."

I returned his look with one of my own. "Will you help me save her?"

He turned away, ignoring me, speaking with Wolf and Titan. Scramble pushed her way among them and growled. If I'd been doing the talking, I'd have been reminding him that Gavi had saved his life when the willog demon was choking him. Behemoth actually whined. I'd heard Joram speak to Matty in exactly that same tone: "I'm sorry, dear. I didn't mean . . ."

They returned to me. "Wha yu nee?" Scramble asked.

"I need one of you to sneak over there and tell Gavi . . . No!" I was being stupid! I could understand virtually everything the dogs said, but it was foolish to expect Gavi to understand them at all, much less under the circumstances. "No. Just wait here for me!"

Scramble came after me, taking my wrist in her mouth to tug me back, but I told her to let me go. I had to do it myself. I was already as wet as I could be, so another Joram-wriggle through the stream added little additional discomfort. The cage stood at the very edge of the firelight, not far from the stream, and Gavi was still pressed against the near side. Others in the cage simply sat with empty faces, reacting to nothing. They didn't even move when I spoke Gavi's name, very softly.

"Jewel," she whispered. "Oh, Jewel. Can you get me out of here . . . ?"

"Listen." I put a hand up to cover her mouth. "Listen carefully. They will release you and give you a head start. Cross the stream and run uphill, to your left, close to the trees. Close, Gavi, and uphill! Do you understand?"

She nodded. I looked curiously at her cage companions. She whispered, "These others in the cage with me, I think they're all dead people from the battleground on Moss. The ones in the other cage are mostly Derac, and they're alive. Tonight they hunt us, tomorrow the Derac, I think."

I couldn't take time to contemplate the risk if they hunted Derac tonight. I patted her hand and slithered backward through the water once more, away from the ring of firelight. When I gained the cover of the forest, the dogs were waiting. We went quickly uphill, upstream, staying close to the edge of the trees. When we came to the place my trail turned to go over the ridge, we stopped.

No one needed tell the dogs to be silent. We could see the fire down the slope, hear the howls building to the final climax and fading into silence. Though we had come a considerable distance, I could still make out the monumental forms of the Simusi sitting there, the firelight reflected from their eyes. I heard the creak of wood. A cage door, or doors. The Simusi sat, unmoving. Time went by. We heard panting breath first, then the thud of running feet coming toward us up the dale. Not many. Two or three people, perhaps. When I caught sight of Gavi, I stepped out to intercept her . . . and an unexpected companion. Oskar! The lame man running for his life, lame leg and all.

I pulled them into the trees, Scramble and the others began a mass urination out in the grass, Behemoth tore shreds of Gavi's clothing away in his teeth and ran out and up the meadow, dropping bits of the fabric as he went. They'd planned this while we had been waiting! We heard a great baying from the near the bonfire, as the Simusi went off in various directions, a few into the woods at either side, others downstream and away, yipping madly into the night, perhaps a few in our direction, though Gavi and Oskar had been the only ones to run uphill.

Oskar collapsed completely. Gavi was beside him immediately, saying, "He gave me chin leaves to chew, so they wouldn't smell us when we ran."

"He couldn't run," I said, stupidly. "He could barely walk."

She babbled, "He told me he'd been planning for a long time. He knew where they'd do it. He had some drugs to kill his pain and let him move fast; he had these chin leaves to hide his smell; and he'd found some secure places in the woods. He told me he'd lead them away while I went this way to the trail, then to the left, to the place the Phain live, but when I told him you were waiting . . ."

I said, "Gavi, listen! Have they turned Derac loose, to hunt?"

She shook her head. "No. Not yet."

"Then let's give Oskar a few moments to rest. Titan, Wolf, let's see if Behemoth needs help."

We ran, the big dogs and I, my hand on Titan's shoulder to keep myself balanced on the uneven ground. We had not gone far before we heard growls, snarls, harsh throaty coughs. We came through a fringe of trees to see Behemoth confronting a furious Simusi who was twice his size. Behemoth was not cowering. The fur on his neck and spine was up, his teeth were showing. Titan and Wolf slipped away from me, one right, one left. I caught a flicker from Behemoth's eyes and knew he had seen us, though the Simusi had not, for he was too busy demanding obedience and submission. The air was full of scent commands and sound defiance, most of the noise from Behemoth, who wasn't having it. When the two other dogs were in place, Behemoth waited no longer and attacked.

I thought he would be hurt at once, probably killed, but then, I had never seen him fight. More importantly, I had never seen him fight in company with other dogs. The three of them were like a well-engineered machine, each reading the others' intent, each moving in accord with the others' speed and direction. Their teeth slashed like sabers as they leapt forward and back on spring-steel legs, their thick coats baffled the Simusi's attempt to catch hold of them during the few early moments when he had a choice. Then both his rear legs went out from under him, the ligaments cut, and he no longer had any choice at all. He gave just one surprised yelp of pain before he fell, two huge jaws fastened in his throat, the third pair ripping out his belly.

The moment stretched. I let it go on, wanting them to relish their victory. They had measured themselves against the godlike Simusi and won. They could not envy an enemy they had conquered, and I wanted them to savor it, to remember it, though we could not take as long as it merited. They'd done well, three against one, but there were dozens of Simusi running the hills around and not that many of us.

"Come," I whispered. "Quickly. There are more of them out there."

The dogs slowly released their hold and stepped back. I started to turn away when a strangled sound from Behemoth made me look back. The body of the Simusi was changing. The huge paws were liquefying in a slow ooze that was not shapeless but reshaping. The legs, too, and the muzzle, becoming another shape, not the one we had seen before. I quickly pulled my recorder out of my pocket and focused it upon what was happening. The glossy fur melted like wax to be replaced by carbuncled, mucus-covered hide. The sleek muzzle became twisted bone, the narrow jaw and fangs melted into a lipless, gaping maw crammed with tentacled suckers, like tangled worms. What lay there at last was a creature of indescribable . . . I could find no word. Every animal I have ever seen pictured had a natural grace and elegance when in its own environment. Great wrinkle-nosed elephant seals, monstrous on the shore, became graceful in the sea. Clumsy albatross, tripping over their own feet on land, became glorious in the sky. Insects, monstrous on the hand, become elegant on the branch. I wondered in what hideous environment a creature like this one could be anything but a horror. I made myself go near it and look for some sign of life. Movement. Breath. A flow of fluid, anything.

Nothing moved. It stank. I prayed it was truly dead, but we could not stay to make sure. We raced back to the others. I pulled Oskar to his feet, put my arm around his waist, and told the dogs to lead on. It was Veegee who thrust her head between Oskar's legs from behind, heaving him onto her shoulders and moving along beside me to carry the old man's weight. We made the best time we could across the rocky area where the paths diverged. I scanned the area for Witt. If he had hidden nearby, he would see us, hear us.

Howls came from the ridge above us, no longer distant. They had picked up our trail, or Gavi's, or Oskar's, but at least they were coming from the side, not behind, which meant they had not yet found the body of their . . . packmate. We hastened along the rock outcropping, back toward the main path. Witt emerged from under a bush, about halfway along. He started to whimper about the howling, and I hissed at him to be quiet or I'd cut his tongue out. The threat sounded vicious even to me. I wondered if I meant to do it. Inasmuch as I had no knife with me, it was unlikely even though he went on whimpering.

At the main path, we turned right and fled down the defile between the two rocky banks, turning left at the far end, along the wall of stone, still under the cover of the woods. Scramble and Dapple stayed back, behind us. Over my shoulder I saw them urinating on the path, scratching it. I doubted, it would do any good. As I had understood what Oskar had said during our trip to the Phaina's, we had left Phain territory and had crossed into Simusi territory now. Nonetheless, we went on, following the directions the Phaina had given me.

"Where are we going?" Gavi whispered to me.

"Somewhere along here, there's an old stone hut. The Phaina is meeting us there."

"Ehr!" said Dapple, nose pointed ahead.

Almost invisible among the trees and against the piled rocks it had been made from, the hut was half-buried in vines. The plank door sagged, and the old shutters were splintered. At the moment, I didn't care what it looked like, I only wanted walls around us and a place to rest. We went in. The place smelled of moldy hay and mice. I reminded myself that Splendor, or its foyer, was not necessarily immune to mice, nor, possibly, to fleas, leeches, cold winds, and disappointment. Gavi and I thrust the shutters closed and yanked the sagging door shut. Oskar lay down on the hay with a gasp of pain, and the dogs fell panting beside him. Witt glared at them and started to say something, changing his mind after a glance at me. With a martyred expression, he sat down on the bare floor. There was no sign of the Phaina.

I crouched at the door, peering through a wide crack in the old boards. When nothing appeared, I put my pack down to use as a pillow and lay down with my eyes still next to the crack.

"Where are we going?" Witt asked.

"Wherever the Phaina takes us," I said. "If she'll take you at all."

Blessedly, he had nothing else to say, and I lay there in a mood of frantic resignation, a familiar state of mind. All het up, as Matty had used to say, and nowhere to take it, nobody to use it on. Whatever happened would happen. My only hope was that with the Phaina in charge, we might possibly get away alive. Though determined to keep watch, I was almost dozing when the howls began again, not far away.

"They're going to get us," grated Gavi, with a jarring laugh. "I thought when I escaped Belthos all those times, I wouldn't be prey any longer. Now here I am . . ."

We listened as the howls came closer, full of elation and wildness, interrupted by yaps and growls, almost playful. I smelled something, didn't know what it was, but saw Veegee's and Dapple's lips draw back from their teeth.

"What is it?" I asked.

"Nuh noh," said Scramble. "Monser."

She could mean a real monster or just something large. The howls came on, the smell intensified. The Simusi voices were only yards away when they broke off suddenly. I sensed their surprise and—was it possible?—shock. I put my eye back to the crack and saw a dozen Simusi among the trees at the edge of the woodland. They were glorious. Even afraid as I was, I had to admit they were glorious. Their fur gleamed in the steely light; their eyes shone; they stood like monuments of bronze and copper, graceful, potent, huge. Was this what Witt had called dazzle? Their stillness made them seem almost dreamlike . . . no. Theatrical. Posed. With falsity at the heart of it. I would never have thought so if I hadn't seen what had happened to the dead one.

Something very large moved in front of the crack; the strange smell became a familiar one. P'narg. The great beast crossed the front of the hut, followed by several more, all standing high on their hind legs, regarding the Simusi with huge, immobile P'narg faces that showed amusement? Satisfaction? Perhaps hunger?

Whatever the huge animals meant or thought, the Simusi didn't intend to leave. Instead they began a noisy dance, yipping as they leapt from side to side, half-charging, half-retreating, each time a little closer. The P'narg merely stood, the nearest one running his talons in and out, great curved blades as long as my forearm that made a snicking sound as they slipped in and out of their bony sheaths. The Simusi joined in a resentful howl, which broke off in the middle. In the quiet I heard the voice of the Phaina from somewhere close outside.

What followed was quite confusing. Evidently the Simusi under-stood Phain-ildar without translation, for they replied to the Phaina's words before her lingui-pute translated them into common speech. When the Simusi spoke, however, they spoke in smells, which I could detect but not decipher, and which the Phaina evidently did not under-stand either, for the 'pute used two separate voices to translate simul-taneously into Phain-ildar and Earth talk.

I sorted it out to go roughly like this.

The Simusi speaker: "You interfere with us again, Phain-being. Your smeller sniffs matters not your concern. Our prey is in that house. We want it. Our new dog-slaves are in that house, we want them!"

The Phaina: "I do not interfere, Simusi-beings. You are too hasty. What lies in this place is mine more than yours. You abide on the edge of our place by our let. What is mine I will go in and take out. What is yours, you may keep."

The Simusi: "On our land, stink-marked by us or our creatures, anything that moves is ours to hunt as we will!"

The Phaina: "In all the gateways to Splendor, from end to end of the affinitum, anything that lives is mine to protect as I will."

The Simusi: "We are the pure, the uncorrupted, whole in our skins, needing no protection and refusing protection for our prey . . ."

The Phaina, angrily: "You are puerile children, playing at being ancient, claiming to return to your primal state while living off the eyes, tongues, hands, shoulders, legs, and labor of others. You say you need no protection while a dozen other races provide protection for you!"

Silence, ending in a low growl that seemed to be coming from every Simusi out there. The P'narg still stood, still stropping their talons, a sound like knives against steel.

"I will go in," said the Phaina. "I will take what is mine."

The door swung inward. She stepped in. The P'narg came in behind her, filling the entire door and effectively preventing the Simusi from seeing inside.

"Come," said her lingui-pute. "We have only a few moments to get out of sight." Then she stopped at the sight of Witt, Gavi, and old Oskar.

I explained their presence in the fewest possible words.

The Phaina gave me a look of frank skepticism from her multiple eyes. "I cannot in good conscience leave them here to be eaten. Come now."

The last P'narg was inside, the hut was filled with flesh, fur, and a musty odor. Outside, the Simusi were becoming louder and angrier. The Phaina crossed the hut to the back wall, laid her hands upon it, and said something which the lingui-pute did not translate. The wall shimmered, the P'narg lumbered through the shimmer, and we followed. I was the last one through except for the Phaina herself, who turned and gestured the shimmer to be gone.

We stood in nowhere, looking into the room we had just left as though separated from it by a pane of dark, watery glass. The door burst open. Half a dozen Simusi leapt in, teeth bared, eyes blazing, only to halt, confused. Other heads and shoulders filled the door behind them. The Phaina's lingui-pute began translating. "Where the stinkshit did they go?" "I had my teeth set for that human woman!" "My slave was with them! The one I was going to hunt tonight!" With an exclamation of disgust, the Phaina turned its volume down.

They began sniffing the small room, digging into the hay, throwing it in all directions. One of them ran a large sliver of wood into his pads and yelped in pain. One group went out, another came in. Evidently, each separate Simusi wanted to see or smell for itself. Eventually, after a great deal of dispassionately translated invective, most of it directed at the Phaina, they gave up and went away. Still we stood there, waiting, more or less patiently, and I took the opportunity to whisper into the Phaina's 'pute that a Simusi had been killed by the dogs.

She shivered against me and whispered back, asking where the body was. I asked if she had ever seen a dead Simusi.

"I have not. Their folk are secretive about their dying."

"The dead one looks nothing like the live ones," I said, offering her the recording I had made.

She looked at it, reset it in order to see it again, then spoke over her shoulder to the P'narg, in a voice totally unlike any voice I had heard her use. It was full of iron and anger, and the 'pute did not translate it. She handed the recorder back to me as she said the words that dissolved the glass.

We were back in the hut again, shambling after the Phaina as she went out the door. Three of the P'narg turned to the right, to go back the way we had come, falling from their erect posture into a six-legged gallop. I assumed they were going after the dead body of the Simusi in order to . . . hide it, burn it, get rid of it. Or maybe not. Maybe the Phaina wanted to see it for herself.

The rest of us followed the Phaina as she turned left and continued along the dike. An occasional howl drifted faintly from various directions. Even I could tell they were saying, "Not here. Nowhere here."

"We will take a side street," said the Phaina, when we reached the end of the dike. "There is a door here." She once again used words that were not translated, and we went through a shimmer into somewhere else. We were on a mountaintop looking down into an enormously wide, mountain-encircled valley. Rivers crossed it; forests dotted it; dust rose from it, and as my eyes followed the billows to their origin I saw a great herd of fine, phantasmic elephants, marvelous elephants, hundreds of them, ears waving, trunks lifted, feet pounding the valley floor in a distant thunder. Beyond them I saw giraffe, and beyond the giraffe, herds of other creatures I could not make out except for their pooled darkness, flowing across the grasses like a tide.

∷ We turned on the mountaintop and took one step out onto a spectacular desert decked with mind-boggling rock forms and ranges of huge dunes in various colors. On a far dune I caught the silhouetted shapes of camels. A small, long-legged rodent burst from a thornbush and fled across my feet in a series of enormous leaps. A tortoise chewed reflectively on an ash gray leaf. We slogged through sand and around wind-sculpted stones until another shimmer led us into a garden full of ravishing colors and scents, and from that into a jungle, perhaps the jungle from which Witt had been taken, for he cried out, then another shimmer took us onto a meadow under a violet sky without a sun.

"Each of those shimmers . . . that would be seen by others as a flash of light, right?" I asked the Phaina.

The Phaina gave me an admonitory look and continued toward a stone cylinder standing in the meadow, slotted in the same way as the key pillar on the battleground of Moss. Again making the high, keening sound, the Phaina strolled around the cylinder several times before settling upon a particular place to thrust her hand. A door emerged, another shimmer yet, and when we stepped through that, we were back on Moss in the saucer of blue fire, the place from which we had been taken.

⋮ As the Phaina closed the door behind us I glanced at the sky. It was just before dawn, with sufficient light to silhouette the trees around the eastern rim, turning them into a pattern of black lace against the sky. At one place, the pattern was irregular. Telling the others I'd be back, I trotted tiredly off in that direction to determine if the irregularity was perhaps a familiar willog, Walky itself.

As it was. It greeted me as I neared. "Oh, and you have escaped from the creatures! I have been waiting these many days, sorrowing perhaps that you would not come. Is this not remarkable! What is that tall one with you? Who are those male persons?"

"Come on, Walky," I said. "I want you to meet the tall one, the Phaina. You will address her as Sassanees. You will be polite, won't you?"

"I will, oh yes, what great honor to meet a new peoples. Who are the hu-men?"

"Humans," I corrected.

"But plural of man is men," Walky said, sounding outraged.

I said, "It's not logical, but it's still humans. One of the men is someone I met on the other side, and I've known the other one for a long time."

Accompanied by a great flurry of strolling foliage, I returned to my companions, where I introduced Walky to the Sassanees, to Oskar, and to Witt. Witt seemed more horrified than pleased, but the Phaina conversed with Walky at some length while all six of the dogs sat patiently by. I thought they were being patient, at the time, though they probably were suffering from the same overload of anxiety that I was. I very much wanted to sit down next to them, doing and thinking nothing, but my flesh crawled at the proximity of that gate. The Phaina had opened it this time, but it had been opened by Simusi before, and they could probably open it again if they got onto our trail.

I walked out onto the mosses and tried my link. It hadn't worked in Splendor, but it worked here. I reached Gainor, who was so busy asking questions and being glad I had returned that it took some doing to convince him we needed picking up, soonest.

"Not floaters if you've got something faster, Gainor!"

He got hold of someone else, and by the time the sun was chinning itself over the tops of the trees, shuttles were setting down at the edge of the battleground. The first person off was Gainor himself, though it took a while to recognize him. His hair was down around his neck and he had a beard. He was holding a young dog. I met him halfway up the slope, as the others straggled toward the ship.

"What's happened to your head?" I cried. "And where did you get that pup?"

He just stood there looking at me. Finally, he asked, "How long have you been gone, Jewel?"

"Four or five days," I said.

"Try sixty or seventy," he replied. "This is one of Scramble's pups."

Scramble was at my side in that instant. Gainor put the puppy down, and she went to it, smelling it all over. Evidently both she and the puppy recognized the smells, though she looked up at me with an expression of terrible confusion. The Phaina came up beside me, speaking in that lovely, liquid language of hers. "I should have warned you all. In Splendor time can be either faster or slower, depending on where you are."

"Mine?" Scramble whined. "My ile?"

"Yes," I told her. "It's your child. All the puppies are well and healthy, I'm sure . . ."

"They are," interrupted Gainor.

". . . but more days have happened here," I continued. "Tell the others, Scramble, so they won't be surprised."

She turned with the big puppy at her heels and went down toward the other dogs, who were standing indecisively some distance away. I watched as the ritual of smelling and learning went on again. Veegee howled. Dapple answered. Behemoth growled. The Phaina went down toward them, and I heard her voice. I had not known her translator could create the smell language of the dogs, but evidently it could. The conversation went on for some time.

While the dogs talked, everyone else assembled at the ships, including Walky. The dogs came last, and as they went aboard, I went down the slope to the Phaina, so I could speak to her privately.

"Sassanees," I said. "All our peoples have heard of the Zhaar, the shape shifters, the bane of the galaxy. You believed they were gone. It seems likely they were never gone, that they took this new shape and lived in it."

She asked, "The thing you showed me, is it really true the three dogs killed it, unaided?"

"I saw the fight, and I saw it die, Sassanees. It did not seem well practiced at battle. Perhaps the so-called Simusi have not really had to fight for a long, long time."

"Indeed, the Simusi have not fought. They have lived among us for ages, just as they are. Even if they are of some other shape, however, one may not merely assume, as you have done, that they are therefore Zhaar. One must find the answers to many questions. Did the Simusi race come into being only when the Zhaar departed, or did they exist before? And if so, do any of them still live elsewhere? And if real Simusi live, do they all make this change at death? If not, is it possible that some, many, or a few Zhaar inhabit Simusi shapes?"

"Or are Simusi a pretense, another Zhaar game?" I said.

"It is true the Zhaar played such games," she acknowledged.

We were silent a moment. I asked "Why dog shape, Sassanees? That's what I can't figure out. It seems a bad choice to have no appendages for manipulation, no capability of oral language . . ."

Her voice was musing. "I have learned that in the long ago time of Earth, some of your subsets purposefully crippled themselves to show their power and wealth in having others serve them."

"In China," I said, having read of it. "Noblemen grew their fingernails so long that their hands were useless. Other people fed them, washed them, clothed them. The female nobility were crippled as children so they had to be carried everywhere they went."

"So. If a race were very . . . proud, it might choose to have slaves with hands, slaves with voices. If a race were very proud, perhaps it would take a form that requires having others provide these functions. However, there is a better reason, perhaps. If a race were very frightened, it might choose to take an unlikely shape *because* it was an unlikely one. The Zhaar were under sentence of death. They had been told to leave the galaxy, to go beyond the rim or to stay and face us all."

"All, Sannasee?"

"The elder races, who had had enough of them and their games. Then, too," she mused, "dogs are . . . can be very beautiful, and they are packish by nature, which would accord with what we know of Zhaar temperament. If we were only sure . . ."

The 'pute had translated the iron in her voice as well as the words. I murmured, "Well, if the Simusi are the Zhaar, they chose neither to go nor to die, obviously. Now that we know who they are . . ."

"May know," corrected the Sannasee.

"May know," I agreed. "But they don't know that we know. Not if your P'narg were successful in getting to the body first, which I presume you sent them to do. That body should be enough proof for anyone, shouldn't it?"

She stood very tall, placing her manipulators together and nodding in a slow, ritualistic way. "One body does not tell us that all Simusi are Zhaar. However, to protect you, both our peoples must act with the presumption they are Zhaar. Zhaar have ever been vengeful, and they will not forgive being bilked by humans of their prey and of their slaves and perhaps even of the Simusi masks behind which they have hidden."

I said, "But if they don't know we have seen through their masks, then we have some time to make our plans. Our race, yours, this planet of Moss, your home worlds are all at risk. If you could return to the plateau with us, your counsel would benefit us greatly."

She seemed lost in thought, her eye circle fluttering, the apertures on her neck quivering. The P'narg stood attentively around her, like a bodyguard.

"Jewel, what is it your people, not your race but your kind of people, those who believe as you believe, what is it they want most?"

I wanted to laugh and cry, both at once. "A return to Eden, Sannasee. A return to a world like Tsaliphor. A kinship with all of life. A place that welcomes all kinds of life among people who do not proliferate themselves at life's expense."

She nodded, slowly, three times. I had seen that same measured nod among the Phain who walked the streets of Tsaliphor, like a punctuation mark, ending one prayer, beginning another.

Eventually she said, "I will not stay just now, no. In matters of this kind, we are required to be sure, and it will not take long to be sure. Once we are sure, then I will return, not only for you, or us, or this place, but for all those who passed sentence long ago . . ." She sighed. The 'pute did not attempt to translate the sigh. "We, the Phain and our ancient allies, will confront this great threat. We must prevent greater damage than the Zhaar have already done to your race. We must not be unjust again . . ."

"What have the Zhaar done to our race?" I asked.

"Too much to take time for now. We will talk of it when I come again."

Suspicion reared its head. "Did they put concs on Earth?"

She gave me a long, long level look. "That is, perhaps, too subtle for the Zhaar to have done."

She headed back toward the pillar with her bodyguard of P'narg, and I went up the slope to the ship, where Gainor was waiting for me.

A MATTER
OF SCALE

﹒ When the G'tach G'gh'hagh of all the Derac received no word from the army that had been directed to attack the humans on Moss, a scout ship was dispatched to find out what had happened. It went, stayed a very short time, and returned to report.

"Ships there," said the scout. "Crews mostly there. Warriors not there. Tracers in warrior armor not work except one bellyplate I find by chunk of rock in middle of bowl. I not mean eating bowl, but like that. With things growing in it."

Successive questioning elicited, word by reluctant word, a slightly better description of the battleground at Moss.

"So our warriors and their armor are gone," said the Deracan Admiral.

"All gone except one bellyplate."

"But there's no blood or bones or scales lying around? Nothing like that?"

"No, no blood, no bones, lots of scales."

"As though there had been a struggle?"

"Or they were dancing," said the scout. "Sometimes when we dance on ship, many scales come loose."

The admiral frowned. Young Derac did dance, though he could not remember why at this stage of his life. "Where are the humans?"

"I go looking, find them on top of flat Mountain. Is force field place, like they have. Is spread-out place, like they have."

"How many of them are there?"

"Not grabbich. Brach, maybe, five eights, six eights. Lots of strange animals, like vlabbish. Hard shell with legs both sides."

"So basically, what you're saying is, a grabbich of our warriors have just vanished."

"No sir. I not say vanished. What I say is I not find Derac except few in camp, few in ships. Derac I find say our warriors go attack humans by lake, but humans not there. And I not say vanish, because maybe Derac still there, on planet somewhere, but if tracers not work, I not find."

The scout was waved away, to his pleasure. Scout ships were extremely small, cramped, and cold, and he desperately wanted a bloody, stinking meal and a long sprawl in a decently warmed sandbox.

"I do not believe," said the admiral, "that fewer than a brach of humans killed and disposed of a grabbich of Deracan without leaving any trace. In fact, even if they'd left a trace, I wouldn't believe it."

"Can we ask them?" suggested Gahcha, the representative from Gar G'tach.

"We can ask the IC, of course. It may take some time to receive an answer."

"What are we going to do in the meantime?" asked Gahcha.

"We are going to send two grabbichek of warriors to the third planet of Garr-290 to look for the one grabbich that disappeared," said the admiral. "And while we're at it, we're going to arm every ship that's available and send them to attack the Orskimi, wherever they're running to! We'll teach those twelve-legged bugs to fool with the Derac! Modify our females, they said. We'll modify them!"

⋮ On E'Sharmifant, ancestral home of the Orskimi, dawnlight disclosed the great mortuary temple empty except for a handful of Highnesses: the High Priest, the High Ritual Surgeon, the High Fire

Master, the High War Leader, and the High Council Leader. Outside the morning shrilling began, rising to its customary level and subsiding as it now did, into silence. There was no daytime sound of wings buzzing, feet scraping, voices murmuring, for the city was wrapped in profound gloom and uncertainty concerning its future. It was rumored among the common Orskim of the street that a plan laid by ancestors and burnished over a hundred generations had gone awry.

High above the gathered officials, on the dusty beam where it had rested for many seasons, the Tharstian observer recorded what was said, translating to itself.

The High Priest asked, "The immortals? Have they all been moved?"

The War Leader spoke. "They are on their way to the sanctuary world, Most High. The flight will be long, for it is far."

The High Priest made a ritual gesture of thanks. "We thank E'ikimi, All Most Holy, that the memory of that world was with us still!"

The High Ritual Surgeon murmured, "For one hundred thousand years the sanctuary world has been remembered, Most High."

"And no one knows of that world except those who are moving our immortals?" asked the High Priest over his shoulder as he moved down into the temple proper to collect holy relics from the walls.

Arms full of memorabilia, the High War Leader said, "No other race has set foot upon that world for half a million years, and of our people, only the immortal who remembered it will tell the captain of the ship, Most High. Owki are meeting that ship at a secret rendezvous, known only to the captains of the other two ships, the one carrying the breeding Orskim, and the ship that waits for our sacred objects and ourselves."

The High Council Leader spoke for the first time. "The city mourns. What will our people be told?"

The High Priest replied, "When owki leave, people will be told owki go on pilgrimage to E'Sharmirf, a holy place of owki's ancestors, and in time owki will return. That is not misleading, since it is possible owki may return, though unlikely." He walked back to the altar with the salvaged materials, feet clicking in triple time: whikalap-whikalap.

"All owki's worlds are to be told this," choked the High Council Leader. "Owki do this on all Orski worlds?"

"All are at risk," the High War Chief intoned. "Skitimor gerfmi. Sharmpifeskit kansa!"

From above, the observer recorded this as: "The long-laid plan is broken, i.e., not happening. The ancestral plan has failed."

The High Priest went on, "Owki do not despair. With racial memory safe from retaliation, with breeding stock safe, with owki-selves safe to lead the rebuilding of Orskim people, even if all these worlds are lost, owki's destiny continues. Now the warships may depart."

"Where do they go?" asked the High Fire Master, opening one of the packing cases that stood ready.

The High War Chief responded. "The first ships are going to the place where the Derac broke their oath to attack the humans!"

"How is it known the oath was broken?" asked the High Council Leader.

The High War Chief replied, "There is no war between Derac and Earthers. That is how it is known. So, the first ships go to the third planet of Garr'ugh 290. There they will attack the humans, making it appear the Derac did it, while other Orski ships go in all directions, to other Derac planets, which we will take for Orskimi.

"Is this necessary?" asked the High Council Leader. "Owki know the Derac will counterattack. Can owki not merely remain peacefully on all Orski worlds and here on E'Sharmifant? Must Orskimi retaliate against the Derac? Must there be war with the Earthers and Derac?"

The High Priest turned blazing eyes upon the leader. "High Council Leader, owki will pretend owki did not hear iki ask that question. Owki said Skitimor gerfmi! Owki said Sharmpifeskit kansa! An ancestral plan over one thousand ecres in the making has failed, has not come to fruition! *This does not happen unless owki have been betrayed or the E'Ilimi are punishing owki for laxity in owki's observances.* Both laxity and betrayal are mended by sacrifice! Having sent seed, memory, and rulers into safety, now warriors go to make that sacrifice while Orskim await sacrificial martyrdom."

"Of course," murmured the High Council Leader. "This one understands."

"It is well iki understands," said the High Priest. "Since there will be no council in the refuge for many years, while the population grows, it will be unnecessary for iki to go with the rest of us."

"But, Most High! All this one's family are already gone. One had expected to go . . ."

"Expectation is not always reality," said the High Priest, as he turned to take up the last of the ritual paraphernalia that had been set ready on the high altar. The scalpel. The retractor. The censer. From its post high above, the observer noted that the ritual censer was put into its carrying case without being inspected. It was as the observer had anticipated. While Orski high-ups had been collecting other items, the observer had placed a beacon in the censer. The Tharstians would be able to follow it with no difficulty at all, all the way to the secret planet of refuge.

A MEETING OF INTERESTED PARTIES

⫶ Even when I stood close in front of him, Gainor kept looking over my shoulder at the pillar in the center of the battleground, then reabsorbing its shimmering door. When the door had quite gone, he shook himself, turned his eyes on me, and said, "I see you found Witt."

"I think the best thing to do would be to send him back to his mother, Gainor."

"Your liaison . . . ?"

"Expired long ago. Expired before it expired, I suppose. There's nothing left there, we've both become other people. Besides, he'll be fully occupied being groomed to run the Hessing empire."

"He'll have to stop whining first," said Gainor. "He sounds like a two-year-old. What did they do to him over there?"

"He was a servant of the Simusi. They prefer lackeys, the more obsequious the better, and Witt had already been rather well schooled in groveling."

He gave me one of his "now, now" looks, and it made me angry.

"What the hell would you call it, Gainor? He was her possession. He made one attempt to do something on his own, and when she challenged him, he did as he was told. It was years ago, and I'm not involved anymore. Send him back. It would be politically inexpedient to do anything else."

He flushed and changed the subject. "Where did you pick up the Phaina?"

"From a place that seems to be upon the fringes of Splendor." I caught his raised eyebrow and reaffirmed what I'd said. "Splendor, Gainor. Truly. The Phaina may be the same one I knew on Tsaliphor, and she is deeply involved in our immediate crisis."

"Crisis?" He looked startled.

"It's possible something very nasty is going to pour out of that door to Splendor, and I'd be more comfortable if we put a little distance between ourselves and it!"

He took my word for it, and the shuttle flew us directly to our new location on Night Mountain. We were met by a few of the PPI staffers, including Duras Drom, who looked a lot better than when I had seen him last. He was a handsome man when his eyes weren't blurry and his cheeks sunken. I postponed his invitation to have coffee until after I'd reunited all the dogs, male and female, with their huge children, now housed in a recently built annex full of dog beds, puppy toys, and food bowls. Our older quarters wouldn't have held half this puppy pack, lolloping all over one another, making clumsy attacks and retreats, eager to be licked and welcomed by their sires and dams but no longer clamoring for their mother's milk.

"Tell me again how long we've been gone?" I asked Sybil.

"Sixty-four days," said Sybil. "Did it seem like more, or less?"

There had been days and nights where we had been, but no sun, no moon. I had thought we'd been gone only four or five days, if that. While Sybil measured out a diet supplement to make up for the hungry days the dogs had spent in Splendor, eating scraps left to them by the Simusi, the three male dogs continued a conversation they'd been having about the true shape of the Simusi. At least, so Scramble told me. There were a great many stinks involved, and Simusi envy, if it had ever existed, seemed to have waned, as had the Behemoth's antagonism toward me in particular or humans in general.

I had coffee with Drom, rejoicing at the taste. No matter how good the Phaina's food had been, there'd been nothing like coffee.

"You're looking a lot better," I commented, realizing the remark might not be a tactful one.

He said, matter-of-factly, "There's no temptation on the plateau, Jewel. It feels more humanish up here, not as warm, not as welcoming, but much more healthful."

After leaving Drom, I went to see Paul, who seemed surprised to learn I had been away.

He was, he crowed, making enormous strides with the odor language of Moss. Two prototype translation devices had already been tested and refined, the third version was being put together by the ESC technicians as we spoke. He looked excited and boyish, the way he does sometimes when he is almost likable. He actually gave me a copy of his extensive lexicon, so I could admire it, which I did, fulsomely—he was incapable of detecting irony if it was clad in acclamation. His lexicon was from human to code and from code to human, designed to be used with a translation device. It wasn't a system that would encourage intuitive leaps as to meanings, and I made a mental note to have Gavi spend some time with the ESC people. She could do things with odors that Paul hadn't even conceived of, she understood the associations and correlations of this world, and I had a hunch we were going to need all her capabilities.

Then I collapsed in my own bedroom in our quarters and actually napped until Gainor wakened me to say that Dame Cecelia and Witt's sister, Myra, were on the Hessing ship in orbit around Moss. They had arrived—in defiance of Gainor's orders—while I had been away.

"The Hessing-Hargess empire owns a mercenary starfleet," he remarked. "I haven't the authority to stop their going wherever they like in space, though I can keep them off this planet for the time being. Anyhow, Mama and Sister are up there, in case you care."

"Well, I care enough to be pleased that Witt is already in the bosom of his family," I said.

"He is, yes. The shuttle took him up to the Hessing ship before I knew he had family aboard. However, there seems to be a problem. A few moments ago, Dame Cecelia linked me wanting to come down to the surface to talk to her 'dear son's dear wife.' I took the liberty of telling her you were no longer his wife."

"Thank you, Gainor. I'm glad you have such a good grasp of the situation."

"She wants to meet with you, beg you to come back to him."

"Tell her . . . my affections are now directed elsewhere. I have learned I am oriented toward female lovers. Or nonhumans. Or I've taken a vow of eternal chastity or turned into a moss-demon."

"I'll think of something."

I yawned, struggled to my feet, and went to make coffee. "What's happened with the Orskim scheme using the Derac to start a war?"

He sat down, frowning. "A war hasn't started. Yet. Within a day or two after you got dragged away, we picked up some stiff little messages from the Derac base, wondering where their people were. Not long thereafter, a scout ship arrived to inspect the base and look for the missing warriors. They found a skeleton staff at the base, of course, and nothing else. Their high command, whatever it's called . . ."

"It's called the G'tach G'gh'hagh," I said. "According to Paul."

"Whatever. The G'whatsit asked the IC to find out where their warriors had gone. We told IC we didn't know where they were, which was true enough, since no one knew what was on the other side of that door. We tried to open it, by the way, and it wouldn't. All we could tell the Derac was that our people were mostly accounted for, and we weren't keeping track of theirs."

"That should have upset them."

"It did. Not long after, ships holding a couple of thousand Derac warriors came down on the previous site. They've had armed parties scouring the woods down there for days. We've not reacted at all except to increase security and put heavy weapons here and there on the plateau. Within the last couple of days almost all the Derac search parties have regrouped at the landing site. We've intercepted messages to their G'tach saying they found nothing, no body parts, nothing . . ."

"Gainor, when Scramble dragged me through the gate, I saw armed ships above us and the Derac were lying around the edge of the saucer. How in the devil did they get through the gate?"

"The ship was our shuttle, arriving a trifle late to pick you up. As for the Derac, the Day and Night warriors lugged them down, four men to a Derac, and pitched them through the gate. An hour later, when I asked them who told them to do that, they couldn't remember."

"So what are two thousand Derac doing now?"

"Settled down on the same place the others were, staying in camp. Listening devices tell us they're preoccupied by a new war they're waging against the Orskimi. It wouldn't surprise me if we were on the receiving end as well, at some point. They've got some new idea they need to change their breeding habits and occupy a lot of livable planets, which makes me very nervous. By the way, what did happen to the Derac that got hauled into Splendor?"

"The ones that weren't dead are being used as prey animals in there. And the Orskimi?"

"A couple of days ago the Orskimi advised the IC that several of their colonies have been wiped out."

I snarled, "I suppose everyone has been told the Zhaar did it?"

"Naturally. Isn't that usual?"

"Don't believe it, Gainor. The Zhaar didn't do it. There are no more Zhaar moving around out here. All the Zhaar are on the other side of that door, living on the fringes of Splendor, in the shape of big, big dogs calling themselves Simusi."

"You're joking." He stared at me as though I'd lost my mind.

"They've been living in there for a few tens of thousands of years, shaped like dogs. They haven't shifted shape at all. No one knew they were Zhaar. All the races that met them thought the Simusi were a previously unknown race."

"Why would the Zhaar have done that?"

"According to the Phaina, about a million years ago, the elder races put the Zhaar under sentence of death. They were told to get out of the galaxy or die. Everyone supposed they had left the galaxy; the last anyone had seen of them, they were headed for the edge. They didn't leave. They hid out, possibly on Mars, and decided to stay hidden until all the races that threatened them had died off."

Gainor gulped. "How many of them are there?"

"I don't know. I have absolutely no idea. Talk to Oskar! Find out what he knows. He's spent twenty years captive there, working mostly for the so-called Simusi. He should know a good deal about them, where they are and how many of them."

"And what do we do now?"

"I don't know what you'll choose to do, but I'm waiting until the Phaina satisfies herself that the Simusi are really Zhaar in dogs' clothing. Once she's sure of that, she might put together some help for us."

"When you say help, what do you mean?"

"I had no time to ask her. I assume she could ask for assistance from some of the elder races who sentenced the Zhaar to die in the first place."

"Some of which races may no longer exist."

It wasn't a thought either of us had the energy to discuss or the time to pursue. While I had been away, the IC had sent a Tharstian Marshal, along with a flock of translators, to convene a meeting among the interested parties on Moss: the Derac, the PPI, ESC, Day Mountain, Night Mountain, and the Hessing-Hargess legal contingent, (who had arrived in the Hessing ship). When Walking Sunshine arrived on the plateau, the willog was included as plenipotentiary to represent the planet itself. The Marshal asked Gainor to invite me to speak briefly about what I had seen in Splendor.

The meeting was supposed to start early but was delayed because the Derac claimed to believe that chairs, benches, or positions to the west of other positions had higher status than chairs placed in other relationships. (Later, Paul said, "I could have told them that!") The Marshal finally had everyone stand, sit, recline or float in a circle, and after every speaker, everyone rotated clockwise one position. Since there were many speakers, the rotation kept everyone awake as well as balanced, status-wise.

I spoke briefly, in spurts, to allow time for translation, telling them what I'd seen, personally. For the benefit of the Day and Night people, I explained what actually happened to their dead and wounded. There was an immediate outcry from both Mountains, some claiming I was a liar, others cursing the people, whoever they might be, of Splendor. Gainor and I had discussed mentioning the Simusi by name, or describing them by shape, and had decided against doing either. Let people get used to the idea that the door didn't lead into paradise before telling them the nearest section of it was run by dogs.

When Gainor asked me to speak briefly, he hadn't considered the Derac's great interest in prey animals and eating dead things. They had many questions about rotting times and kill rates, which I declined to answer and moved on to what I had been told by the Phaina. I used her words to describe Splendor, saying it was coiled up inside our own galaxy, touching it at many points, traversable through "wrinkles" or "folds." I said both the Derac and the ships from Forêt had accidentally flown through such wrinkles, as had ships of virtually every starfaring race many times before and since. Thousands of star systems had been discovered when ships went through wrinkles that skimmed the edges of Splendor.

According to the Phaina, energy constantly flowed back and forth between our galaxy and Splendor, pockets existed within both that had different time and space dimensions, the whole shebang constituting a self-regulating system that maintained this section of the universe, though occasionally all the matter in one area was drawn through to the other side and then exploded back in a big bang. It was, however, the Phaina had said, a system that could be upset if clever but not intelligent races started "flinging stars about."

"Meaning what?" asked the bubble-carried Tharstian from IC. His 'pute made the question sound rather anxious.

"Evidently at the time Splendor was discovered, the elder races had weapons of enormous destructive power. If used in or near Splendor, they could upset the balance. So, the elder races put a cordon around Splendor to avoid—what would one say—blowing out the fuses? The connectors . . . ? I don't know the right words, but the sense of it is that the balance between the two systems could possibly be destroyed, destroying the systems themselves."

The Marshal persisted: "Was this place populated when the elder races discovered it, or did everyone now in it come from out here?"

It took me a moment to think about this. "We don't know that it was populated before. The only creatures that I saw in areas that I believe might be part of Splendor were former Earth animals. However, those areas might have been planets in our galaxy to which former Earth animals had been transported. All we saw for any length of time was the edge, a kind of . . . buffer area."

"Who occupied the buffer area?" demanded the Marshal.

"The Guardians, including but not limited to the Phain, and farther out, the race that hunted and ate people."

There was another explosion of babble from Day and Night Mountains, and I said rather loudly that Gavi had been part of our group, that she had been caged to use as prey in the hunt, and that when she recovered from her injuries, she could verify most of what I'd said.

That was enough from me. Gainor introduced Walking Sunshine, who welcomed us all to Moss on behalf of the planet itself and restated the World's preference that all humans stay on the plateaus until such time as they had defined their wants and worked out their proper function with the World itself. Even with all the adjectives he had assembled for this, it took him very little time to say, but it started an argument that threatened to go on all day. Everyone had his own definition of "proper function," and everyone missed the point that it didn't matter how *they* defined it, the World would insist on its own definition. Quite frankly, I was surprised they could return to bickering over territory so quickly after learning what I'd told them. Perhaps they didn't take it seriously. Perhaps it hadn't sunk in!

Though I was interested in what would happen to Moss, I was not interested at all in the bickering, and since Gavi was resting in one of the nearby PPI housing units, I decided to go see how she was getting along. Aside from being tired, bruised, and hungry, she was in generally good spirits and curious about the meeting, so I brought her up to date. While we shared a pot of tea, I broached the subject I'd been cogitating over for some time.

"You do things with odors, Gavi. Not language things exactly."

"Ah, well." She waved it way.

I said firmly, "You changed my life by putting something in the bathwater, that time we first met. Don't deny it, because I know you did it."

She looked at me out of the corners of her eyes, pretending innocence. I stared her down.

"You were stifled," she finally said. "You were carrying around these mind-pictures made when you were first imprinted by those men . . ."

"Men!"

"Your brother and Witt. Many of us are having such imprintings. It is being necessary for many creatures. One is finding one's way in the pack or herd by knowing where one is ranking, who to be groveling to and who to be dominating. One is learning very young the smell or sound of the higher-up, the lower down. It is continuing for most or all of a life. Also, when we are mating, we are being imprinted, each by the other. No matter how unsuitable or disagreeable the mate is being, some people are staying imprinted all their lives."

I'm sure I looked doubtful. "We're talking about human beings, here."

"I am admitting humans are not being affected so much as animals not having language or not living so long. Our long lives are allowing much time for early imprinting to wear away. Also, we are not detecting the odors so much as animals are doing. But you . . . both brother and friend are imprinting on you when you are very young, and by time friend is imprinting, you are having very good sense of smell."

"And you removed it!"

"Person-to-person imprinting, I can remove it, yes. It is not being so easy when the imprinting is done between different species."

"But you can do it to anyone?" I persisted.

"Almost anyone. But what I do is not by chance, and imprinting is being the smaller part of it. Bigger part is convincing self to cast out much-used pathways that are no longer being useful. This increases possibility of making mesh! If you are being truly meshing with someone, if you are having similar opinions, same ways of dealing with difficulties . . ."

"I thought Witt and I did."

She shook her head in exasperation. "An imprinted one is always thinking so, even when it is not being true. Proof of this is easy to see: If you are truly meshing, wiping out imprint is not changing your feelings. One little bath and Jewel's feeling toward brother and friend are changing, so? Then Jewel was not being suited to that brother, to that husband."

I struggled for the best response to this, choosing between annoyance at her cavalier attitude and gratefulness for the result. "I suppose I must thank you, Gavi. It was kind of you, and I appreciate it. I wasn't thinking of that particular talent of yours, however. I was thinking more of how you might go about making peace. You say imprinting is the lesser part, the greater part being removal of ideas that get in the way. Whenever people try to make peace, there are ideas that get in the way. Can you remove them? From nonhumans?"

"Why don't you be telling me why you are wishing to know," she said.

I couldn't think of a reason not to, so I told her about the Derac and the Orskimi, and about the Phain and the putative Simusi. When I showed her the recording of the dead Simusi, she shuddered just as I had done on seeing the reality. It was an evil, horrible-looking thing.

I concluded, "We know that their dog form converses in smells . . ."

"Why are they being in dog form?" she queried.

"I'm not sure," I confessed. "There are several versions. One they told the dogs is that the Simusi shape is holy, so the dogs were also holy for sharing the shape. The Phaina thinks they probably saw the dogs first and adopted their shape because a form without hands or language would be the last one to be suspected. Also, the Simusi might have seen that dogs already had slaves, us."

"You are meaning other way around . . ."

"No. The dogs say they enslaved us, not the other way around. Who feeds whom? Who shelters whom? Which ones become veterinarians? Groomers? Anyhow, the Zhaar were also used to having slaves, so adopting dog shape would allow them to continue having slaves to serve them as manipulators and speakers and groomers and who knows what all."

"What are you wanting me to do?"

"The Simusi have an odor language, not unlike the one here on Moss. Our dogs picked it up from them, very quickly. The dogs can't emit all the range of odors the Simusi can, but they can do it somewhat . . ."

"How are they doing it at all?" she asked. "Dogs are not doing this, making smells on purpose."

The question stopped me. She was right, of course. Dogs couldn't make smells on purpose. Which meant the ability was part of their "special" breeding. Not an intentional part, just an unintended side effect of using Zhaarflesh in breeding them.

"Something that happened as a result of the breeding project," I said. "I overheard . . . no, oversmelled an aroma conversation between Behemoth and Scramble. I detected odors during conversations between the Phaina and the Simusi. I'm assuming it's the same language as Moss's, and I'm hoping you're able to understand it. In order to speak it fluently, we'll need Paul's prototype odor organ, the one that ESC is building now. If it's any good, we can speak directly to them . . ."

"But, if it's Paul's device, he can do that."

I waved this off. "Paul can't. He's great at languages, but he's rotten at communication."

"How would I learn to use the organ?"

"I get Gainor to give you a pass into the ESC enclosure."

She thought about it for some time. "I am always wondering the reason," she mused.

"What reason?"

"The reason I am being born as me. Why I am doing what I am doing. I am always wondering the reason for this. When I am growing up, I am thinking it is just so I am getting even with Belthos. Later I am thinking, well, I am making peace on Night Mountain. Making peace on Moss, among peoples, that is sounding even more important, very worthy."

"Making peace is extremely worthy!" I assured her before I went off to get a pass for her from Gainor.

Then I went to talk to the dogs. Halfway there, I met Walky, who said it had left the meeting because people were saying the same thing over and over. I asked Walky to come with me and translate the dogs' language.

The willog planted himself just outside the open door of the new doghouse. Adam and Frank were there. They'd been in human shape when I'd seen them on my way into Splendor, but they were in dog shape now. Clare had remained human. We all sat down together, even the puppies, though they were mainly interested in sprawling over their recumbent mothers and chasing one another. Twenty-eight dogs made a sizable sprawl.

With Walky translating their responses, I told them who the Zhaar had been, why they had been anathema to other races, and that the Phaina and I believed the Simusi might actually be what was left of the Zhaar. I picked up enough of the talk floating from dog to dog to believe the Zhaar had become anathema to Behemoth's pack as well. They really didn't like the fact that they'd been lied to.

Behemoth said something long and involved. Walky said something else, then I was out of the link among the overlapping waves of odor. When a lot of creatures talked at once, the no-smell borders between words tended to get lost in the confusion. I stepped away until the air cleared, and Walky beckoned to me.

"These Simusi. They spend evening times around the fire telling their histories, some in howling, some in odors. The dogs heard and smelled these histories, and they want you to know what they said."

Wonderful. "Tell away, Walky. I'd love to hear it."

"The Simusi say they came to your world, Earth, long ago. They found a young race of creatures who some of the time walked on two legs, an agile race with nimble hands, without much speech, but with intelligence enough to be useful without threatening the Simusi ..."

Where had I heard that before!

"They say this Earthian race had already been enslaved by a race of quadrupeds with good noses, a fast, clever race that had adopted the not-so-clever biped race in order to have help in the hunt, caves to live in, and fires to sleep by."

"So that is the way the Zhaar tell it," I said.

"Biped creatures were not yet man. They had only a little speech," said Walky. "The other creatures were not quite dogs, but according to the story, the Simusi saw the shape of the dog, and behold, it was the shape of the Simusi themselves! They accepted this as a sign."

"None of us believe that," I said. "It wasn't their shape until they made it their shape."

Walky rustled at me in irritation at being interrupted. "I am only repeating how the Simusi tell the story. The Simusi did not wish to stay on Earth, for Earth was included on many star-maps of inferior races, and the Simusi did not wish to associated with inferior races ..."

"That's not true, either."

"Nonetheless, it is their story," said Walky, much offended. "So, the Simusi went to the nearest other world, an old world, where one small sea still was, where air and water still lingered in many deep caverns and abysses, taking with them the bipeds and the ones in the shape of the Simusi themselves. Also they took small prey animals who could live in these deep caverns."

"That world was Mars," I said.

Walky nodded. "Mars. Yes. And there, they say, they taught both creatures to be good slaves of the Simusi, but the Earthers did not do well on Mars. Earthian creatures did not reproduce well; they did not live long. They were susceptible to a disease that the Simusi carried, one that caused the Earth creatures dreadful pain, then weakened them so they could not move ..."

I exclaimed in pain. Matty had died of a disease like that!

Walky patted me on the shoulder with a leafy twig. "Time after time, the Simusi returned to Earth to pick up more of both races, working on them to make them more ... durable?"

"Enduring," I offered. "Or tough, or hardy."

"Hardy, yes. Millennia went by. The last little sea on Mars dried away to dust, and suddenly, several ships of the elder races landed on that world! The Simusi had their own ships deeply buried in the caverns, but they heard the ships of the elder races when they approached, and they spied upon the elder races while they were there. Then, when the elder races went away, they left a beacon, and the Simusi knew that meant they would return.

"Since that world was dying anyway, they decided to leave it and go to a place they knew of long, long before, a place as remote as Mars itself, one very hard to find and to get into. On the way there, they returned most of their slaves to Earth, where they could breed well, for the Simusi planned to harvest them again, later on."

"But they left some behind on Mars, didn't they?" I cried, my throat thick with anger. "They went off seeking Splendor, but they left the old ones behind. And those old ones went down into a deep, deep cavern they'd shared with their dogs, and they painted and carved their sorrow at being abandoned . . ."

"Was it a poem?" Walky interrupted. "Oh, tell it to me."

I cleared my throat and quoted Matty's translation of the first words on the cavern wall.

"Our coats are thin as mist, our heels are horn,
beneath our eyes old sorrows build their nest
and peck at us where we are torn and tender,
reproaching us as shorebirds, lost and lorn,
rebuke the skies for what the sea has taken.
We here kept faith alive, but all the rest,
the wisest and the bravest we have borne,
left faith behind to go out, seeking splendor.
We are forsaken . . ."

"Oh, poor things," cried Walky. "Were there shorebirds on that planet then? Was it the humans who wrote that? Who were they speaking of?"

"They were speaking of themselves and of their friends, the old dogs who had been left behind, of their children, the strong young humans and dogs that had gone away. They painted and carved pictures of themselves and the dogs. I think probably the Simusi told them the young ones chose to go. That's the kind of thing a Zhaar would do, and they were Zhaar, all along. I don't think the Zhaar ever saw that cavern. If they had, they'd have destroyed it. I think the old humans put Zhaar seals on the wall as a kind of invocation, praying the Zhaar would return with their children."

"The Zhaar were supposed to be shape shifters," said Clare.

"Of course they were. And I don't believe for a minute their real shape was dog shape either, not until they saw real dogs on Earth and decided to take that shape and hide out with protohumans and real dogs on a dying planet."

Walky said, "According to your dogs, the Simusi said they gave many gifts to your ancestors, and your ancestors took those gifts back to Earth with them. They gave the gifts of language, and walking upright, and there were other gifts as well!"

"What other gifts?"

"I don't know," Walky said. "The Simusi did not include that in the story, or if they did, your dogs did not understand it."

"And that's the end of it?" I asked.

"Not quite. The Simusi (I will use that name for it is the name the story uses) decided to settle in that place, through the gate . . ."

"They decided that before they left Mars," I said. "Or the old humans wouldn't have known to put it on the wall. So much time had gone by since anyone had seen a Zhaar that no one was looking for Zhaar anymore. The Zhaar thought their disguise made them safe."

"Perhaps. The story does not say. The story does say that after many ages, the Simusi opened gates into other places, which they used now and then to harvest new slaves from among humans, which they had a right to do since they had invented humans in the first place."

"Invented?" I snarled.

"So the story says. Recently they opened gates onto Jungle and took slaves from there, and when you came to Moss, bringing dogs, they remembered the good slaves dogs had been in their old stories, and they determined to take dogs as slaves again."

I turned to the dogs. "You all heard this in Splendor, from the . . . Simusi?"

Scramble said "Ess." The others nodded, growled, or breathed assent.

Walky whispered to me, "When the Simusi called to the dogs, in the wind, Behemoth did not understand what a slave was. He thought it meant if the dogs went into Splendor, they would be like the Simusi. When he realized the truth, he felt angry and ashamed. He has told me when time comes for him to die, he will let me study him, his nose, his eyes, his type of body. He is most generous, Behemoth, as humans are."

I was trying to think of an appropriate reply, when we were all startled by a flash of light from outside. Walky shivered all over with a rattling of leaves. My first reaction was terror at the possibility the Zhaar had opened a door and come through to get us all, but no such thing happened. Instead, we heard the liquid burbling of Phain speech, and Walky's more exuberant reply as he moved aside to let the Phaina stoop through the door.

She spoke first to Walky, at length, then to the dogs before she turned to me to murmur through her 'pute, "It is true, Jewel. The Simusi are indeed Zhaar. There is no record of the Simusi until the time they came to our vicinity, fifty millennia ago, and the body is unmistakable. So, we shall do as we discussed, if the dogs are agreeable?"

"I haven't even had time to ask them, Sannasee. They have been telling me the history of the Simusi . . ."

"The story of the Simusi on the planet you call Mars?" she asked. "I have now heard that story. A small part of it is true."

She turned to the dogs and began talking, odors flowing from the lingui-pute. Behemoth growled softly, Scramble looked at me with a question in her eyes. I nodded to her, hands wide, silently saying, "Yes, I selfishly hate the idea, but if you all choose to do it, I will not object." The next thing I knew, they were all out the door, Behemoth and Titan dragging Frank and Adam along, the puppies in a long, waggling line, while Clare ran behind yelling, "What's going on, where are you going?" with Walky close behind her.

I didn't follow them. I slumped just outside the door, overcome by sadness. I hadn't even said good-bye. In very little time, Walky returned and settled beside me. "The Phaina found a good door not far away, and they have gone," it said.

"I know." I said, weeping.

"It is best," it said, firmly. You must not be sad that they have gone. If they did not go, all might become a disaster. There are so few of them, only six grown-ups and the children. One blow from the Simusi might end them all. Their race will be safer this way. You know."

"It's Scramble," I said. "She's like a sister, a dear friend. I miss her terribly." I went on wiping tears, while Walky hummed to itself, a kind of dirge that gradually changed into something more cheerful. When my eyes were dry, it suggested I go tell Gainor what had happened.

"Is he out of the meeting?"

"Gainor Brandt says the whole meeting is out. Every person is out, being very irritated and rude. No minds are meeting at all. I rejoice I was not there when it all came apart. Willogs cannot be blamed!"

"Where was Gainor?"

"He was walking to his office place looking angry, bothered, upset, exasperated, irritated . . ."

"All right, all right," I said. "I'll go tell him."

Which I did.

"All of the dogs are gone?" said Gainor, astonished.

"All," I said. "And the trainers, too."

"How long?" he asked.

I could only tell him I didn't know. For him, for me, the dogs including my Scramble might be gone forever, and I didn't want to think about that. I changed the subject. "I understand the meeting didn't go well."

"The meeting did not go at all. After we broke up, the Tharstian told me both the Derac and the Orskimi are behaving in strange ways. The Tharstians have never known the Orskimi to be as distraught or panicky as they seem to be at the moment. Some great plan laid by their ancestors has not fulfilled itself, evidently an apocalyptic event, and ships loaded with Orskim warriors are spreading in all directions into the galaxy. Meantime, Derac ships loaded with females are exploding in all directions away from their retirement planets. My friend thinks a war is about to start."

I stared out the window, wondering whether this had anything to do with us, whether it was something to worry about or something to ignore. I preferred ignoring it, but there were several thousand Derac not far away. They'd arrived in warships. Unfortunately, as targets went, we were as accessible where we were as we were where we'd been.

"Are any Orskimi headed here?" I asked.

"They could be," said Gainor. "Some of them are moving in this general direction."

"So we now have to worry about the Derac, the Zhaar . . ."

"The alleged Zhaar," he interrupted.

"The real Zhaar," I said. "The Phaina verified it. As I was saying, the Derac, the Zhaar, and the Orskimi."

Gainor snorted. "Plus the Houses of Hessing and Hargess, who are deploying their mercenary fleet. We should worry also about the willogs, the warriors of Day and Night Mountains, and Dame Cecelia Hessing."

"Gainor! Why?"

"Because there was no agreement at the meeting. The warriors of the two Mountains, backed by the mercenary fleet of the Hessing-Hargess empire, are blustering threats against the IC, whose Marshal has ruled that Moss may not be settled by outlanders unless formally invited to do so by the planet itself. This threat, when communicated to the plenipotentiary, was answered by the World, saying that it would invite people to stay when it had given the matter sufficient consideration, say a few hundred years. And before walking out, Walky indicated the willogs would be enforcing whatever the World wanted enforced."

I hated to ask. "And Dame Cecelia?"

"Demands to see you so you may be restored to your proper place beside her son. She is most upset that your liaison was not renewed . . ."

"Hell, Gainor. He was gone, and she was doing her utmost to get rid of me!"

"That's in the past. She wants to pay you a great deal of money to liaise with her son and have a grandchild or two for her. After which, you may do what you like."

"Why me!" I snarled, wondering if Witt had told her he had been "fixed."

"Seemingly Witt is unable even to consider liaising with anyone else."

I started to rave, when a thought hit me. I took a deep breath and considered it for a moment, then gave Gainor a dewy-eyed look I had never used in living memory, and said, "Tell her I will consider it, Gainor." After a moment, I said, "You forgot to include one of our perpetual worries on the list. What about the concs?"

"They've shown up on several colony planets for the first time. Now that we know for sure the Zhaar are still around, we can blame them for that."

I shook my head. "The Phaina thinks not, Gainor. She says it's far too subtle for the Zhaar."

⠿ Gavi used her ESC pass and spent every available hour working on the odor organ. When she came back from the first day, she wore the expression of someone who has just had an epiphany. "Wonderful," she murmured to me. "It is being wonderful. So many things I am saying all at once. But, I am needing Walking Sunshine. The saying is all very good, but what about the smelling? Is it working properly?"

Gainor was reluctant to let the willog into the ESC enclosure. "I've had experience with both honesty and duplicity from aliens. That walking dictionary could be a congenial copse or a vegetable villain. I have no way of knowing which." Also, there was the matter of spores, and seeds, and messages that might be scattered into the enclosure to ripen later. We compromised. From the room where Gavi was working, Sybil created an emitter that led outside, where Walky was invited to situate itself. This, coupled with a voice link, allowed the odors to get outside, where Walky could interpret them without breaching security.

"Do you think you can use it to make peace between all these people?" I asked her.

"Not all at once," she said. "No. Words are one thing, dear Jewel. They are being like currency, money, universal exchange, understood by all. This is what language is, also, meanings persons agree upon. But the odors that are moving a person may not have the status of a word. Most people are having particular scents that are meaning something to them while meaning little or nothing to others. One has to experiment to find these odors. If we make peace, it will have to be person by person, couple by couple, this tribe then that tribe, making it like a quilt, sewing them together."

I heard this with regret, for I confess to having had this marvelous daydream about being very useful to the Phaina, so useful that she would let me stay with her near Splendor, or, better yet, let me go to Tsaliphor, where there was not only a sun but also several moons. I had thought that making peace among groups of intransigent individuals might impress her in a way that few other things would.

"In the meantime, Gavi," I said, "can you do me a tremendous favor?"

When I told her what it was, she laughed, but she said she thought it was possible, she'd let me know the following morning.

The following day, at lunch, I asked Gainor to reach Dame Cecelia. "Give her this message," I said, handing him a onetime burn-book. "Precisely as it is written there."

He read it through curiously. "You're not really intending to . . ."

"Gainor, my intentions are my own. Just read her that message. If she and Witt are willing to comply, have Witt down here this evening."

He read: " 'Liaisons made or renewed on Moss should be done in accordance with Mossian custom and rite. Such a rite has been arranged for this evening, if Witt is interested.' "

"Exactly," I said. "Have him here this evening."

Evidently, either Witt or his mother or both were eager. They arrived at the installation about sundown. I was there to meet Witt, bathed, perfumed, and dressed as prettily as could be, considering the situation. Dame Cecelia had come to witness the event, so she said in an ingratiating tone so far from the manner I remembered that for a moment I thought she might be quite another person, a Zhaar, say, in the shape of a Hessing. Setting that thought aside as yet another example of my tendency toward overingenious extrapolation, I explained that no witnesses were allowed except those enacting the ritual, but newly joined couples were always available the following morning to receive gifts and congratulations. After some argument, she departed on Gainor's arm, and I led Witt by the hand to the cave Gavi and I had found the previous evening, one with a good warmwall and bathing pool. Since this area of the plateau was unoccupied, there were a good many vacant but quite livable caverns, and I confess that this one had appealed to me, as it was set about with fragrant trees and a number of colorful flowers.

Gainor had obtained some of the necessary materials from ESC stores, and Gavi had made a quick trip to Loam to fetch the others. Her assistant had been working in the cavern since morning, hanging the curtains, tuning the harp, and creating several of the things Gavi called burn-boards. Since there had been no time for the couple to provide the usual essences, Gavi had had to make adjustments to the ritual, which weren't complicated. She told Witt to go behind the curtains, disrobe, place his clothing outside, and get into the warm pool, submerging himself entirely. The descending material, whatever it was (Gavi had refused to say), was already in the water.

When splashing noises were heard, I slipped over to the curtain and took his underwear. We had borrowed the new odor organ from ESC, and it took Gavi less than a minute to analyze the smell and reproduce it. Gavi introduced me to the other person involved, and that person went behind the curtain and the splashing noises resumed, at which point I took the odor organ back to ESC before they found out it was gone.

I returned to witness the rest of the rite. There was a good deal of harping, singing, and odor squirting, as well as outcries of ecstasy from behind the curtain. Witt had never yelled like that with me, and I found myself in a bit of a snit over it. Then with a flash of intuition, I realized that Witt had been imprinted on concs. Of course he had. I had been a novice, he had been imprinted on another life-form, and we hadn't had Gavi to help. Finally, in the hour just before dawn, we packed up everything and departed, she and her assistant to the floater that was waiting to return her to Loam, I to my bed where I lay down and cried a few more tears, perhaps partly because I had long ago wanted someone to love and had thought Witt was that someone, but more likely because I was lonely and past the age where I could convince myself that just anyone would fill the void.

Came the morning, Witt and his bride were there to greet his mother and sister. The bride was veiled. Gainor told everyone that Mossian custom demanded a bride should be veiled the first few days of marriage. I was watching the whole thing from inside the nearest building. Though the bride was a good six inches shorter than I, Dame Cecelia didn't notice the difference. I did note Myra looking around, here and there, as though searching for someone. As I had thought, however, Dame Cecelia had never actually looked at me, and she would not have recognized me if she had seen me on the street.

While the group was sharing toasts, Myra sneaked away and made a beeline for the building I was in. Gainor let her go. He had probably told her where I was.

"All right, Jewel," she said, with some annoyance. "Who is she?"

"Her name is Gemma," I said. "Call her Jewel, she won't care. She is Witt's true love, and you may believe me when I say he will never love anyone else."

"*Who* is she!" demanded Myra again.

"A lovely young woman of Loam, one of the provinces here on Moss. Her people were originally from Forêt. She was a virgin at her marriage to Witt. She has a good reputation. She is a skilled tapestry designer. She is physically healthy and quite capable of producing several grandchildren for your mother if Witt is capable, which he may or may not be."

She waved my explanation aside. "And Witt loves her?"

"He does," I said firmly. "He will continue to do so even after they fix her face, back on Earth."

"Aha! So she's ugly?"

"She is quite plain, yes. Here on Moss, they were unable to do anything about that, but I'm sure any beauty surgeon on Earth will be delighted to help a Hessing."

"How will she put up with Witt?"

I sighed. "You don't understand, Myra. Witt was habituated to concs. That habituation has been erased and forgotten. They are both completely, absolutely in love with one another. Neither he nor she will ever love anyone else."

"Good Lord. That's possible? You arranged this?"

I said, "Yes. I 'arranged' it. Such things are often 'arranged' here on Moss."

"Mother will scream the ship down!"

"Let her scream. It won't affect Witt. Not after last night. He's been deprogrammed and reprogrammed." I had only my own example to make me sure it would work, but Gavi had told me she had never failed before and had no reason to think she would fail with Witt and Gemma.

Later that day, several Hessing ships left orbit for return to Earth, including the one Witt was on. I amused myself imagining various scenarios of what had taken place. The simplest was that Witt, thoroughly in love with his wife, had responded immediately to her request (which Gavi had schooled her to make at least twice during every waking hour) that she be taken to Earth where her appearance could be modified, making her more acceptable in her new position in life.

The whole business amused both Gainor and me greatly. We laughed about it. It was rather nice, in a way, to have such a humorous memory, since what was coming had nothing amusing about it.

⋮ The following day the Tharstian Marshal from IC recessed the meeting indefinitely and then he (she, it, or them) spoke privately with Gainor. Derac and Orskim peoples were at war, he said. Since there were several thousand Derac on Moss, we could probably expect an invasion of Orskimi, or at least a hit-and-run raid. He suggested very strongly that the Earther, together with all their force fields, shields, buildings, and weapons be moved into the nearest convenient cavern, inasmuch as there were no ships available to evacuate all of us.

I said, "What about the Hessing fleet?"

Gainor snorted. "They're not in a mood to be helpful, Jewel."

Moving the compound wasn't something that could be done in a few hours, but the ESC staff, together with crews and mechs from both the shuttles and the two small ESC ships in system, made a valiant effort. Luckily, there was a very large cavern nearby, into which mech crews could move the disassembled ESC installation while other crews took apart the PPI structures and moved them as well. None of the shifting about could be done, of course, without the Derac delegation seeing what was going on, and Gainor had to explain that we had "an intimation" we might be attacked and by whom.

That was enough to make the Derac delegation depart at once, in their own shuttle, and in an amazingly short time thereafter, their flotilla of warships soared up from the Derac camp below. As Gainor reminded me, ships don't fight well from the ground. The warriors and chiefs from Day Mountain spent the day finding their own cover and making it look as natural as possible. After several hundred years of practice, they were really very good at it. Walky observed everything that was going on, from start to finish, remarking from time to time that if he could just borrow a floater and bring up a few hundred willogs, the camouflage could be vastly improved. I think I was the only one listening to him, and it occurred to me that while he was right, it would be more useful to make false installations below, where they had been, rather than hide the ones we were moving. I talked to him about doing so, and he grew quite enthusiastic. When evening came, and everyone was too tired to be attentive, Sybil and I took a floater to transport Walky down to the site of our former encampment.

"Do we go back right now, or do we stay and see what Walky does?" Sybil asked me. "Is the attack theoretical or imminent?"

We decided to split the difference and stay for a while. There would be moonlight later on, and we would be able to see well enough to get the floater back to the cavern. Walky wasted no time. He had not been gone an hour before we began to see a ghost installation rising up where the real one had been. The headquarters building, constructed entirely from moss. The building we had occupied, the refectory, the workrooms and habitations, all rising up complete with windows and doors, even the ornamental mosses set as they had been when I first saw the place. Moss-demons, I thought, had no lock on similitude.

Walky came out to ask how we liked it, and we told him we liked it a great deal, but to remember that if an attack came, these structures might be set afire, or blown up.

"Oh, gracious, yes, Walky is not unintelligent! My, yes, it would not do to put delicate, rare things in the way of such a danger. These are ordinary mosses, easily regrown, and once the guides have put them in place, the guides themselves will go back into the forest. All that will be left will be the mosses, with no voice, no mind. Do not worry, Jewel. I would not commit an ethical misstep. No. Not for all the world!"

"Guides, Walky? What guides?"

Walky beckoned, and the mosses around our feet became alive with tiny creatures, like moving bits of vine, a twig with a leaf or two on its legs, many of them with crab eyes or insect eyes. When Walky called again, they swarmed away.

"Guides are needed to assure distribution of proper growth. Mosses have no minds. They must be pushed, directed, steered, pointed, focused . . ."

"Thank you, Walky. I think Sybil and I will go back up to the plateau now. Do you want to come with us, or will you stay here?"

"Ah, so kind of you to ask. I will stay. First we must make a simulacrum of the ESC installation, with something in it to make it sparkle, as the real one did. Also, I have been thinking greatly about the kindness of all your people to our World: eyes, ears, voices, wonderful gifts. Also I have been thinking that the Derac made no gifts. Those who opened the door in the battleground, they have made no gifts. If there is a war, then the willogs will want to fight in it. I am a shepherd of the willogs, and I will stay here to organize our resistance!"

We wished him farewell and went slowly and carefully back to the plateau, arriving there very early the following morning. Both the ESC bubble and the PPI installation were encaverned, and I fell into the bed in my rerelocated house like a single grain of rice into a nutshell, a tiny grain rattling in a vast emptiness. Only Paul was in the same building. I don't know where the concs were. I hadn't seen them since I'd returned.

We were all awakened shortly before dawn when the Orskim ships arrived in orbit and began bombarding the PPI and ESC installations that Walky had built the night before.

THE WILLOG WAR

⋮ Huddled together inside the cavern, we watched the bombardment as it was transmitted to us by the fish in the area. Walky had not only simulated the installation, he had also added simulation to its destruction. Great clouds of spores rose after each hit, red and orange and yellow, followed by billows of black and gray. When the weapons hit the sham ESC, out on the little island, it went up in a great cloud of energetic white and silver.

Duras Drom said, "Our installation would merely have burned, without any of those colorful clouds of smoke, but I must say it looks very dramatic."

"The Orskimi won't know the difference," I said. "They've never warred against humans before, have they?"

"An outpost here and there," said Gainor. "I doubt they'll pay much attention. Their real target is the Derac."

"Who have gone," I said.

"Except for warriors hidden back in the trees, ready to take on any landing parties," Gainor commented. "The Derac warships are hiding behind Treasure at the moment. I imagine they'll be along anytime."

He was quite right. They came along almost at once, red ships that glowed like embers, attacking silver Orski ships, beams of light flashing from one to the other. Before long, several ships on both sides had been damaged enough that they had to make emergency landings and continue the battle on the ground. During this early stage, we weren't involved, we weren't at risk, all the conflict was going on well south of and below us. Gainor maneuvered our fish-eyes to get the best possible view as though we had been at a sporting event. We wanted to be able to foresee the outcome, of course, in order to take appropriate action, but both sides had good body armor that limited fatalities, and neither side seemed to be winning.

There were signs of willog intervention from the beginning. When a warrior of either race bumped against the wrong tree, bush, or thicket, a mad thrashing occurred, and after a time the copse walked off, leaving the resultant corpse behind.

"No collateral damage," remarked Gainor, approvingly.

That wasn't true in the thick of the battle, which was catastrophic insofar as the landscape was concerned. I saw tree after tree go up in flame, while wooded areas on all sides erupted in showers of mosses, soil, and leaves. A hail of escape pods came from two badly damaged Orskim ships to land north of the battle. They were followed at once by a rain of Derac IMAVs—individual, mobile, armored vehicles—that hit the ground still farther north, establishing a battle line much closer to us than before, and several of us moved out to the edge of the plateau to get a better view.

From our vantage point, it looked as though half of Moss was burning, though the view transmitted by the ESC ships in near space showed fighting going on only in a narrow slice of country between the east side of the lake and an area south of Night Mountain. The slice grew wider and longer with every passing hour, but our plateau, which Gainor assured me looked completely uninhabited from space, remained unthreatened. I didn't care what happened to either the Derac or Orskimi, and the planet would renew itself very quickly, so I admit to feeling a kind of selfish optimism about the eventual outcome.

That mood soon passed when we heard the unmistakable scream of descending ships directly above us. We ran before we looked, kept running as the sound grew deafening, and stopped only when we were inside the cavern being stifled by a cloud of dust.

Gainor shouted, "By the tonsils of Twivus the Twelve-Throated. It's the Hargess-Hessing fleet!"

Only the first ship was down. The explosion of dust was renewed with each of the several others that landed. I had never seen Gainor move as quickly as he did in reaching the communication center of the ESC bubble, where he repeatedly hailed the captain or captains of the ships. Ignoring the hails, the other ships kept coming down, almost on top of us, the "almost" due solely to good fortune and not to any foresight on their part. Only then did the fleet captain of the Hessing ships respond to Gainor's hail.

The captain's protest that he had been sent to "Protect Hessing-Hargess interests," did nothing to assuage Gainor's fury, particularly inasmuch as the Derac had seen the ships and decided to attack them, an onslaught that began before the last ship had even landed. Hessing ships were far superior to Earthian military ships, a fact that resulted in recurrent congressional hearings on Earth. Earth's Navy was required to deal with Earthian manufacturers, but Hessing ships were known to have not only the latest armaments but also the newest technology from anywhere in the galaxy. They were so well shielded, that while the Derac bombardment could keep them on the surface, the ships themselves were undamaged. That no doubt annoyed the Derac, for in short order several larger ships showed up, and our "safe" plateau went up in flame. The only shelter was the cavern, where we had all moved into the ESC bubble, which had been designed as protection against indigenous and usually non- or low-tech hostiles on survey planets and was totally inadequate to the current circumstances.

The Hessing captain apologized profusely, saying he hadn't been informed there were any people where he had decided to land. His assertion was preposterous, as Gainor well knew. Not twelve hours before, Dame Cecelia herself had been on this same site, and we all knew her ships had her located down to the exact millimeter.

"Who ordered you to set down here?" Gainor asked.

The order had been given long before the battle started, and it had come from Dame Cecelia Hessing, who told them it was a perfect place to set down.

"I think your little jest with Witt and his mama has just backfired," Gainor told me through gritted teeth.

"Do you mean to tell me that she would . . ." And I stopped, because it was obvious she would. It had been obvious from the first moment I had set eyes on her in the University Tower that she would. What Dame Cecelia wanted, Dame Cecelia got, or she killed it so no one else could have it. What were fifty people, more or less? What were half a dozen Hessing ships and their crews if she could get even with me along with them?

It was too late to do anything about it. The Hessing ships couldn't take off without turning off the shields, they couldn't turn off the shields because the Derac had been joined by several Orski ships who figured any non-Orski ship was a target, no matter who it was.

In the space of a quarter hour we had moved from sensible safety to desperate danger and ended up doing what desperate people do. We ran, all of us but one. When Gainor and I went to get Paul, he insisted upon being left in the cavern to get on with his work. Gainor told him a direct hit would destroy him along with his work, but Paul was utterly oblivious to the risk. When he was working, nothing short of being actually blown apart could interrupt him.

The rest of us, Drom's people from PPI, Ornel's people from ESC, Gainor, and I gathered up whatever survival packs, weapons, and communication equipment we could pack on half a dozen tiny, two-man floaters that were guided by tethers as we went. In my own pack I had a lingui-pute and the prototype odor organ, which I had taken from the ESC dome moments after leaving Paul. No one knew I had it, and it certainly wasn't mine to take, but I was not going to leave it to be destroyed even though I knew the Phain already had a device that was probably its superior. The Phain were not known to be generous, and I felt we humans needed anything that would help us communicate with other races, including the two very nasty ones who were intent upon killing us at the moment.

"Do we try to reach Loam, or one of the other Night Mountain tribes?" I asked Gainor. "I have a map that shows where they are."

"Better we just get down into the forest, where it'll be warmer," he commented, breathlessly. "It wouldn't be quite fair to involve Night Mountain people by leading the enemy directly to them. We brought this on the world, they didn't."

"Don't say we brought this on the planet. The Derac did, if anyone."

"Whatever you say," he puffed. "I've already messaged IC for assistance as well as the ESC fleet. We'll have help eventually, but it may take a while."

We waited for a lull that gave us time to get into the slanting cleft used by ascending floaters. The rift was all that remained of a onetime waterfall. Though smoothed to some extent by the flow, it had been littered with boulders fallen from either side, and it made a continuous if somewhat tortuous route to the bottom. We scampered down, that is, some of us scampered. Others of us half dropped, half fell, crawled, and in difficult spots, hung by our fingers.

During a momentary halt to choose between a nasty climb to the left or a worse one to the right, I asked Gainor, "Where's the Tharstian Marshal from IC now that we need him?"

"Up there somewhere," Gainor jerked his head toward the sky. "Tharstians don't stay on planets any longer than they have to. As soon as he warned me, he left. I hope he remembers we're friends."

We clambered over ten thousand uncooperative stones, and then we rested before dropping and falling over another ten thousand. We stopped for lunch, then trotted along a fairly level path for a mile or so, counted noses to be sure we were all there, before another clamber. There's nothing interesting to say about it. We were bruised and cold, we were tired, by the time evening came we were wet with rain, and most of us were sharing a very bad mood. We had not, however, attracted attention from the combatants since our route was well hidden by the depth and narrowness of the cleft. We were forced into no adventurous detours; we had no reason to take cover; we simply followed the route all the way to the bottom, arriving there to find the battle much closer than we had expected or desired.

After a brief breather on the level, the time spent watching the nearest explosions through the trees, we began working our way eastward around the base of the cliffs, away from the fighting. Gainor was still keeping track of the overall situation, and he told us more and more warriors from both sides were now on the ground, fighting from hastily erected fortifications. I warmed up a little when my clothes began to dry, and I recall being momentarily and stupidly cheerful about the whole thing. I told myself the fighting would inevitably dwindle, and, at some point, the warriors would leave the planet.

We had not figured on encountering another set of warriors until a boyish voice cried, "Halt and be recognized!"

They hailers turned out to be half a dozen youngsters from Day and Night Mountains. We identified ourselves with some difficulty, since the boys, who were little more than children, had never heard of us. We were obviously human, however, so they invited us into their supply depot, nicely placed between a bulwark of fallen boulders in front and a sheltering overhang in the cliff behind. The lads had been set to guard a huge pile of supplies left there by a group of bellicose volunteers.

"Day or Night Mountain?" I asked one of the brighter-seeming lads.

"Oh, both, ma'am. We all want to get into it. A lot of the Day Mountain folk stayed here in the north after the fight with the Derac! Some had wounds to heal from or they found wives among the Night Mountain girls, and some of Night Mountain folk decided to go back with us and look for wives themselves. Today was the day we were to set out for home. When we got this far, they sent the women back up to the top and decided they weren't about to sit about while there was fighting going on!"

"They're fighting each other, not you," I said.

"They got in our way, they did. That's reason enough," said a slightly older youth who still regarded us with some suspicion. "And if it weren't, we've got reason enough for those lizards ambushing us near the battleground."

"So you're fighting on the side of the Orskimi?" cried Gainor.

"Is that who they are?" a guard asked. "Well, whoever they are, we'll help them get rid of the alligators."

Gainor said through his teeth, "The Orskimi are more dangerous than the Derac, and if your men get in among them, they'll come back dead."

The boys seemed to have difficulty comprehending that possibility and no idea at all what might be done to prevent it. The upshot of it was that Gainor and I decided that, since the warriors were on foot, we could probably catch up to them on a floater while the rest of our people went on around the plateau to a place of relative security.

Duras Drom offered to go with us. So did Sybil and Ornell, but Gainor thought the two of us would be quickest and quietest alone. While he and Drom unloaded the floater, I took a few moments to talk to Sybil.

"Unload a floater for yourself," I said. "Go on along the cliffs to the east, not very far, until you come to another deep cleft in the plateau. You'll know it's the right one if you see three falls close to the right of it, two low ones and a very high one in the middle that comes all the way down from the rimrock. Take the floater up to the top and yell for someone to get in touch with Gavi Norchis of the Tribe Loam. Give her this message from me. 'Jewel has the instrument you practiced on and she needs you to play it.' "

"What instrument is that?" Sybil asked.

"You don't need to know," I said. "What you do need to know is that getting to her with that message may save all our lives." I had no proof of that. In fact, it may have been one of my episodic incidents of self-dramatization that Gainor had so often deplored. It was only a feeling, perhaps one of those feelings Aunt Hatty had suggested I should pay more attention to. "Lend Gavi the floater to follow us. Better yet, you follow us and bring her. Gainor and I are both wearing locators."

She made note of the locator frequencies, and within moments Gainor and I were off. Riding was actually a rest from the climbing we'd been doing, and we spelled one another at the controls, following the easy trail left by, I said, several score intrepid and very stupid men. Gainor said "not stupid, but ill informed," and once again chided me for making judgments without sufficient evidence.

"In his heart, mankind has never been able to evolve past the tribal stage," Gainor said. "Civilization does not take the place of tribalism, but if it is well designed, it can control it. Here, on Moss, these men have their whole lives centered upon their tribes, the defense of territory, the shielding of honor. Any threat against tribe, territory, or honor is an acceptable excuse for battle. The women have children and caves and gardens to manage, but the men live only for what they think of as valor. When no fighting is imminent against a remote foe, they will fight one another, and whenever things get too peaceable, they may claim to have been deathly insulted if someone walks through their light."

I knew that. In the towers, back on Earth, sports teams from various locals or sections competed with one another for championships of a tier, or a section, or even a sector! They would crow or complain for days, depending upon the score of a game in which nothing had happened except that one team had scored one more point than the other team. The dogs were the same. Even among the six dogs we had brought to Moss, I had seen them defending their personal space, their relationship with their mates. I mentioned this to Gainor. "Perhaps it's why we get on with dogs so well. We and they have the same societies."

He gave me a surprised look and a grunt, whether of agreement or admonition, I had no idea.

The trail we were following was clear. I had already noticed that warriors in crab armor could not move without snapping twigs and crushing mosses. We drove the floater at its top speed, some good bit faster than a walk. The men ahead of us had one or two hours' head start, and we hoped to come up to them when they stopped for an evening meal. In fact, that is what happened. We came into a clearing at top speed, sliding to a halt when we saw thirty or forty warriors sitting stock-still around a small fire, plates on their laps, utensils halfway to their lips, frozen. Before we could realize what was happening, Derac poured out of the forest all around us.

The next few moments were too chaotic to make sense of. By the time things settled, we had been loosely shackled to good-sized trees, and the Derac were finishing the meal the warriors had started. They had not taken our packs, they had not tied our hands, they had simply chained us up out of the way in their hurry to get something to eat, and they were totally concentrated upon consuming it. I therefore opened my pack and took out the lingui-pute.

"You brought a 'pute?" Gainor whispered. "By all the tail joints of . . ."

"Never mind," I said. "You're the diplomat, some of the time, anyhow, what do you want to say to them?"

"Tell them we know the Orskimi have plotted against them."

Unfortunately, the 'pute wasn't an automatic model. We had automatic ones, but they were six times as heavy. Gainor couldn't remember the codes for common speech or Derac, so I had to look them up. I whispered them in, then said what Gainor had said, in my most ingratiating voice. Not that tone of voice mattered. The Derac responded with the most dreadful gagging, coughing, vomiting noises one might imagine. Nonetheless, the 'pute at top volume silenced them.

One of them stood, licking his jaws with an extremely long and sinuous tongue, and bellowed in my direction.

The 'pute bellowed at me on his behalf:

"You think we stupid? We not stupid. We know Orskis bad. We kill all them Orskis."

That response made me remember what Paul had had to say about Derac shipclan vocabulary and understanding, so I revised what I had been going to say next. Fewer, shorter words.

"We help you fight Orskis," I said, both mendaciously and telegraphically. "Why you take us prisoner?"

They talked among themselves, the 'pute translating bits and pieces, "Eat them, right? They meat? Not for eating? Why not for eating? Who said do it? We don't do what he says, he's not even our clan." This last by what looked like an elder among them, perhaps one who had reached midlife and was going through the morono-pause. Pinning a modest faith on that assessment, I directed the 'pute toward him.

"Orski long time keep female Derac from male Derac, tell lies to Derac, try to keep Derac weak. Humans find out. Humans want to help Derac. Humans fight Orski. Why you catch us?"

The 'pute translated a subsequent Derac conversation which was in all respects a duplicate of the former Derac conversation. Finally, the older one—I had become convinced he was an older one—told the others to leave us chained up but not to eat us. That decision resulted in an argument during which every Derac present asserted a pressing need to eat us, because they had been sent to Moss in such a hurry, no one had given them supplies.

One of the warriors chained quite close to me, whispered, "We've got food supplies back at the cliffs. Tell them we'll give them food."

I did. Another argument. Human food wasn't fit to eat. It wasn't bloody enough, we never let it rot enough, most of the smell was gone.

"If you're hungry now, you don't want to wait for us to rot, do you?" I said, with some anger. They were really just too stupid for words. "The human food will fill your bellies until you can dine on Orski flesh. Orski flesh rots very fast and smells very much."

Though it was obvious to me that the Orskim exoskeletons indicated both limited palatability and little likelihood of decomposition prior to desiccation, the Derac decided that what I said made sense. I suggested a few of them go with a few of the human warriors to get the food. When they had the food, they would bring it back to the others and let us humans go. My suggestion met with general approval after only another half hour's discussion in which not more than one hundred different words were used, jointly, by all the participants.

While the Derac wrangling continued, I turned off the translation speaker, though not the ear, long enough to tell the Mountain warriors that the rest of our party had gone on along the edge of the plateau and it might be a good idea to join up with them and stay clear until matters sorted themselves out.

A dozen Derac unchained a score of the prisoners, chivvied them back along the trail, and were immediately followed by every blessed Derac in the group. I asked the 'pute for a translation of the recent talk, and learned that none of them trusted any of the rest of them to bring the food back, so they all intended to stick together. After they had eaten, maybe they would come back and let us loose, or maybe they'd just go back to the battle.

So, there we were, a dozen or so warriors, Gainor and I, shackled to various trees. Gainor's weapons and those of the warriors were lying about, some of them within reach, but all of them were designed to affect flesh, in or out of armor, and none of them were designed to cut or melt steel. Gainor and I were still wearing our locators, and presumably, some of the people we had left with the boys back at the cliffs would eventually come looking for us, or Sybil would be bringing Gavi... right into the oncoming Derac. Oh, very fine, I told myself. Excellent.

As you can appreciate, our situation, while it had not yet become truly life-threatening, was continuing to deteriorate. The next thing we heard was a monstrous twittering, like a flock of enormous crickets, all sawing away. There were crickets in several of my Joram wall views, and these noises might have been made by giants of the species.

"Orski," said Gainor, through his teeth.

I looked up the translation code for Orski-speak and entered it in the 'pute, ready to talk when the next creatures arrived, which they did immediately, from above. One minute I was sitting there, rehearsing what I was going to say, and the next instant I was grabbed from above by six horny, segmented feet, and hauled into the air, an escalation which was stopped only by the length of my chain. All around the little clearing, people were being tugged between chains and feet, until finally a twittered order came. "Put them down."

"Yes," I cried. "Please put us down."

The 'pute twittered the request with my own panicky inflection, and we were, accordingly, dropped the last few feet. I rose unsteadily to my feet, saying:

"We welcome the Orskimi. We join with them in our abhorrence of the invidious Derac, who have gone in that direction, only a few moments ago." I tried desperately to remember if Orskim culture had a deity one could invoke.

Gainor saved me the trouble. "May we wish you success in your Great Work," he cried. "The invidious Derac have among them some of our people. We give great reward to those who free our people from bondage."

The 'pute burst into speech. "We, Orskim righteous followers of the plans laid by our ancestors, have come to take the preeminence formerly held by the Zhaar. That great people departed from this galaxy. Now, we, Orskim achievers of the Great Work, will rule in their stead."

"You will, indeed," cried Gainor. "But, as it is written by your own historians, in the interim you need allies, and we are your allies."

"Besides," I interrupted, "the Zhaar have returned, so it will be necessary to kill them first in order to rule the galaxy. You must report this at once to your officers!"

A brief confusion preceded the abrupt departure of the Orskim, half of them in pursuit of the Derac and the other half flying away through the forest at top speed, leaving us still shackled to our trees.

"How did you know that, about what was written?" I asked.

"I don't know what they've written," he said. "But neither do these guys. They're warriors, not priests."

"If you're both so clever," muttered one of the Day Mountain warriors, "maybe you can figure out how to get us out of here."

The suggestion received no reply, for from behind the chained warriors came a flash of light, followed at once by others, left and right, then by others still, as far as we could see into the trees. We heard a howl, then another, then a whole chorus of them, a cacophony of yelps, snarls, great chest-rumbling growls. I thought of Behemoth, first, but then I smelled them on the wind. Not dogs. Not dogs at all. Zhaar. Zhaar who didn't care what race they killed, or enslaved. Zhaar who had it in for me personally for bilking them of their prey in Splendor.

They came through us and past us at top speed, hides shining, plumed tails streaming. One or two of them made a quick reconnaissance around us, seeing that we were chained. Another one or two took a quick sniff, perhaps identifying us. When they came to me, they stopped, howled, as if in question, and received a delighted howl in reply. The 'pute didn't translate. Not that it needed to, as I could pretty well figure out the content. Unlike the Phaina's translator, this one had never been designed to decipher odors. I had the odor organ in my pack, but I couldn't play it. In any case, what would I say?

What would I say? Just because the Zhaar spoke in odors now didn't mean they didn't understand language!

"Gainor, the Orskimi lied when they said the Zhaar are finished," I screamed at the top of my lungs. "The Orskimi say they govern the galaxy, that the Zhaar grew weak and powerless and are no more, that the Zhaar are nothing, of no regard. Why did they say that if it isn't true?"

"That is what they said," Gainor bellowed. "The Orskimi told us they would kill all the Zhaar who may be left. . . ."

A look of pure astonishment went across the faces of the nearest Zhaar, then they streamed away from us, toward the thick of the battle. Through the trees more and more doors were glittering. They batted open and shut, like Earth eyes blinking. Somehow the Zhaar had managed to perforate the membrane between our worlds until it was permeable as a sponge, and I wished most fervently for the Phaina, or better yet, for her whole race. Surely, there would be something they could do.

Nothing miraculous happened, however, which gave me time to wonder which of our various enemies would come back for us first. Derac? Orskimi? Zhaar? Or maybe Dame Cecelia would think up something else.

As it turned out, it was none of the above. I felt the shackle on my leg seized by something, looked down, saw two woody roots growing through it, looked up into a spread of bright leaves that sparkled against the sun, and heard the shackle part with a shriek of tortured metal.

"Walky," I cried. "Oh, I'm so glad to see you!"

"I am glad to find you at this time," it crowed. "So many battles going on, such excitement, disturbance, and tumult. The World is quite overcome! Whole communities are fleeing all this fire and confusion. Luckily, I found you at first try!"

"How did you know to look?"

"When the great battle began this morning, I was already down from the height, where I thought it best to stay, rather than go where you were and be bombarded. I was waiting at foot of plateau for someone, anyone, and behold, there was Jewel coming down with a great many others, including Gainor Brandt—How are you, sir? Well, I hope.—and, thinking perhaps you would not want our acquaintance to be known to all these people, I went aside into the woods while you people went on to the little, what is it called, fortress? Where the children keep the supplies so well guarded?

"At that very time, I received a message from World, and that took a little time to take care of. When I returned, you had gone, so I waited, listening, and soon Gavi Norchis is there, talking to Sybil, and I learn you have followed after the warriors of the Mountains.

"Such adventuring! Such great turmoil, upheaval, and commotion! So, I set out to find you, and suddenly are Derac alligators here, there, and everywhere with warriors of the Mountains, so, I am pausing, quite still, and they go on by. I summon willogs from vicinity and tell them to go at once to protect warriors and your people, then I proceed on my way. No sooner have I moved than I see Orskim come flying, climbing, walking, great bugs, many legs, wings, many arms with weapons, very warlike ugly—though I long to send roots into a few dead ones to find out if there are useful parts! Again, I let them go by, summon more willogs, then I came on, and here you are.

"Excuse me, please, while I break the manacles, restraints, shackles, fetters, and chains that bind your fellow humans."

He did so, seeming to enjoy the task. The warriors, without even taking time to talk it over, gathered up their weapons and ran back along the trail after the Orskimi who were chasing the Derac who were looking for food. As Walky broke Gainor's bonds, he remarked, "Gavi Norchis is on her way. I gave her small, young willog to guide her along, off the trail, so as not to encounter anyone."

I thanked him, as did Gainor, and since we'd had nothing to eat since noon, and not much then, we dug out some rations and awaited Gavi's arrival. Walky settled itself beside me, remarking, "World is wanting to know who is cause of this battle?"

Gainor and I looked at each other. He shrugged.

"The battle began between the Derac and the Orskimi," I said.

"The cause of the fray was that the Orskimi tricked the Derac into attacking humans in order to start a Derac-human war so the Orskimi could take advantage of it to conquer the worlds of both peoples. The Derac tried to start the war at the battleground, as you know, but they were prevented from doing so by . . . willogs, mostly. The Orskimi don't know about willogs, so they blame the Derac."

All Walky's branches were nodding, up down, up down, as it processed the information.

It said, "Orskimi were doing a bad thing, this bad thing was the first bad thing even though other bad things followed, so Orskimi are to blame."

Gainor said, gravely, "No, that wouldn't be the first bad thing. The Orskimi became capable of doing this bad thing only because the Zhaar gave them the technology, long, long ago."

"Then that was the first bad thing."

"That would be the earliest bad thing anyone can remember," Gainor agreed.

"Both Zhaar and Orskimi are to blame," Walky said, firmly. "Then, World wants to know, who is responsible for ships coming down on top of Mountain if this is separate from the other bad thing."

I sighed. "It's a separate bad thing. The woman who . . . owns the ships wanted to hurt me, and she ordered the ships to set down there because I was underneath them."

I suppose in the last analysis, Dame Cecelia did own the ships, though there was undoubtedly a huge corporate structure of some kind between her and the responsibility for what "her" ships did.

"So this person is doing a bad thing not only to you and all the people there, but also to her own people on the ships?" Walky sounded thoroughly confused.

"This person does bad things all the time," I said, with some vehemence. "She is so powerful, no one can control her."

"What is this person's name?"

"Dame Cecelia Hessing. She is part of a powerful family, the Hessing-Hargess clan. They own many ships, they have a mercenary fleet, they have enormous businesses upon many worlds."

"Good," said Walky. "This is the very thing the World wants to know."

It stood beside me in companionable silence while Gainor and I finished our lunch. As we put things away, we heard the hum of a little floater. It came slowly through the trees, carrying Gavi and a vociferous sapling, who was soon introduced to me as Brightleaf.

Gavi hugged me and greeted Gainor, turning to Walky to declaim, "We have to stop this. The whole middle of the plateau is on fire! The ships in the sky won't let the ships on Night Mountain take off. They just keep firing at them."

"We have bigger trouble than that," I told her. "The Zhaar are loose on Moss."

She stiffened, and her face turned ashen. "How many?"

"Lots," I said. I thought hundreds at least, maybe thousands, with who knew how many more in the edge of Splendor, in reserve.

"I wish there were somewhere we could go to observe the fighting," Gainor said.

"Someplace high up?" asked Walky. "If so, we can have a high-up place not far from here. We will need to go carefully, quietly, not to get involved in this fracas, commotion, disturbance, uproar, or to-do."

I couldn't think of a height anywhere near the area of the fighting. I'd seen the area both from the ship and from the top of the plateau, and all I could remember was flatness broken by the occasional grove of tall trees. That's all we saw as we went, that's all we saw until we bumped into a low mound we hadn't even seen.

"Camouflage," said Walky. "I did not understand the concept until I learned the word. When the World extrudes its eyes, they are camouflaged not to be much noticed by others. This is one of the World's eyes which we will get on top of. The World will not mind."

I had no idea what it was made of. It was a quite substantial flat-topped mound, every inch of it clad in mosses that matched whatever one might be seeing from any conceivable angle. We were no sooner situated than the mound began to grow. It went upward at steady speed, at least as fast as tower lifts. As we rose, we saw that we were at the center of concentric circles of trees, circle after circle after circle, on and on past the limit of our sight. Once we could see the whole extent of the battle, the mound we were upon stopped rising. Gainor took some time setting up his tracking system and adjusting it, allowing us to see the battle through the fish-eyes.

Both Derac and Orskim were overmatched by the Zhaar, who were bigger, stronger, and faster. Derac and Orski weapons did not seem to touch them. The battleground, starting at the east side and working toward the west, was littered with the bodies of Orskim and Derac, but at most, half a dozen dead Zhaar.

"What will they do when they have killed all those two bad peoples," Walky asked.

"They'll come after us," I said. "Me particularly. And Gavi, and old Oskar. Where is Oskar? I haven't even thought of him since we've been back."

Gainor said, "We have him stashed on one of our ships, up there. Whatever information he may have about the Zhaar is too important to risk losing. Also, he was in a lot of pain, and we can give him better medical attention on the ship."

"I wish we had a power source," I said. "Gavi could be sending out soothing odors, right now. Something to calm them down. I wish we could broadcast the odor organ over a wide area."

Walky shivered all over. "But you can. The trees down there are relayers. From here to the first circle of trees is the distance of message, then it is copied and goes on to the next circle, and on, and on, the circles growing bigger and bigger, until they go around world like a belt, then smaller again to another place like this one."

I couldn't quite understand. "You mean that from this height, and I presume others like it, messages may be sent that are broadcast immediately? Then why in the name of all that's holy do we need all that business of growing words, and letting them ripen, and watching them dance?"

Walky rustled at me in indignation. "Because time spent is part of living," it said. "Slowness, ripening; slowness, dancing; happiness spent in doing, smelling, understanding. If everything is all the time instantaneous, prompt and sudden, then no one is having any time to enjoy! Life becomes a plethora, a glut, a surfeit of instantaneous amusements barely leavening the job, the task, the thing to get through somehow that life becomes. Who would live a do this, do that, right now, hurry up, finish, all the time finish? Such life has no peace. It is a disease! I will name it the human disease." It rustled again in indignation. "This is why World is insisting upon proper function before humans live on Moss. No more running about all the time."

I set that aside. "But you say that from here, we can send odor messages?"

"In case of an emergency, speed is sometimes needed," Walky said. "And World agrees, this is an emergency."

"And what do we say to the Zhaar?" said Gainor. "They don't care what the World says. The odor language probably isn't even their native tongue."

I shook my head at him. "It wasn't their native tongue, Gainor, but they've used it for a very long time. They may remember the former language, but I'd bet this is the one they will respond to emotionally."

"Respond how? What're you going to hit them with? Home, family, fireside? That might actually work with the Derac, but Zhaar never had home, family, or fireside. Conquest, victory, achievement? That might work with the Orskimi, but Zhaar never had to conquer, they ruled whatever they wanted to, just by taking it over."

"I wish there were some way I could hit them with remorse," I snarled. "Though that's a forlorn hope."

And while I thought, while Gavi set up the odor organ, the carnage below went on. Gradually, the Derac and the Orskim were learning how to kill Zhaar, and more Zhaar were added to the casualties. Gainor was trying to estimate Zhaar numbers from the screen, getting totals that varied between three and five thousand, each one a match for five to ten of the other races.

Our predicament was a round-robin kind of thing. If we could stop the bombardment of the Hessing ships, they could take off and knock down part of the armadas above us, but that really wouldn't affect the outcome on the ground. No matter who won on the ground, we were still at risk. Somehow, before that battle was finally won by the Zhaar, we needed a way to fight the Zhaar or a way to escape them. The only door we knew of was the one we had used, far to the west across a wide stretch of battleground and a lake. Walky could undoubtedly get there, but he had no way to open the door, which, in any case, led directly into Zhaar territory. I still had some hope for Phainic intervention, but both Gainor and I knew the Phain didn't make a habit of intervening on behalf of anyone.

As we sat there watching through fish-eyes and our own, the northernmost companies of Zhaar sent a skirmish line to the west, drawing a noose around both Orskimi and Derac. Then the line began to tighten, pressing the other races into a smaller compass, down toward the lake. They were rounding up the opposition. The end was certainly not far off.

Out of sheer desperation, I was about to suggest that we get our-selves back to the plateau, as it held the most defensible positions we were likely to find anywhere, when an errant sparkle at the foot of our giant tower drew my eyes downward. It was definitely there. Not the same flash of light that had presaged the Zhaar. Quite different from that, softer-looking. Moreover, as I looked out, I saw clusters of such glitter, all outside the area of conflict, a vast arc of them. I reached for the glasses and looked more closely. The arc was a circle that enclosed the entire area of battle.

I reached out to Gainor, but before I could touch him, the lovely liquid speech of the Phaina fell softly upon us, and I turned to see her standing at the top of a suddenly created stairway, almost beside us.

"What a mess," her 'pute murmured. "What a filthy mess."

"I know," I said, as guiltily as though I had personally created the situation below us. "Are all the Zhaar here, on Moss?"

"Virtually all. They left a few here and there in Splendor, but Phain and Yizzang have most of them rounded up by now. What are you doing here? I searched for you on Night Mountain."

I told her, as quickly as I could, concluding, ". . . and when they've killed all the Derac and Orskim, they'll come after us . . ."

"They would plan to, true," she said. "But I wish to speak to them first." She turned to Gavi. "You are a scent mistress of this world?"

Gavi bowed. "I have some small skill."

"You have a device there, to assist you?"

"It is quicker than the traditional way."

The Phaina turned to me. "Our people have analyzed the so-called epic history of the Simusi, as told by them, determining which parts of it are true and which are false. We had to find out the truth of their history in order to validate judgments we have made about others. Judgments based upon untruths are not worthy of us."

"Judgment," I said, lost. "Of what, of whom . . ."

She raised her hand, shutting me off. "No questions now. In Splen-dor, we gathered the Zhaar and spoke with them. Oh, very long we spoke with them. They had more versions of their history than a charb bush has roots. We elicited all known versions from our captives, who, though reluctant to howl for us, preferred storytelling to the alternative we offered.

"We then put all versions together, to see what truth had been left out, what lies had been inserted. Our labors gave us a slightly different story. In the story you were told of, it was said the Zhaar adopted as slaves dogs they had seen on Earth because dogs had Zhaar shape. The opposite was true as you thought, Jewel. The Zhaar took dog shape as camouflage. It was a way to hide.

"Once they took dog shape, however, they found great difficulty in maintaining the shape when frightened or angry. Such emotions made the Zhaar change instinctively, as one of your Earth gastropods could change color, to avoid discovery. Even simple hunger, irritation, or confusion made it difficult for them to keep the shape continually, without lapse. They feared greatly for their lives, however, and they needed to be sure their disguise would not give way. Can you guess what they did?"

I stared at her for a long moment before the bell rang far in the depths of my mind. Adam. Frank. They, too, changed like lightning when they were frightened, or angry. And they had been ... crossed.

I said, "They didn't use Zhaar genes on the dogs, they used dog genes on the Zhaar?"

"Quite right. They did. Proud of their flesh as they were, they used dog flesh because they had picked dogs for two reasons: dogs already had slaves with hands and speech; dogs were already Zhaarish in their ways. That is to say, dogs were packish. Dog family groups followed the most powerful leader, as did the Zhaar. The similarities between themselves and the dogs reduced their reluctance to play with the stuff of their own bodies. They crossed themselves with dog flesh and carried that shape within them.

"Only then could they cleave to it continuously, and they have bred themselves in that shape now for how many hundreds of thousand years? A million perhaps, back to the time your people strayed down from the trees because the Zhaar had changed you into bipeds. Back to the time your people began to speak sooner than they would otherwise have done, because the Zhaar had changed your minds and throats. And as a consequence ..."

Below us something went up in a thunderous roar. An ammunition store of one side or the other.

The Phaina said urgently, "You have with you music?" she asked. "Written by your mother? Concerning the old humans and dogs that were left behind on Mars?"

I nodded, wordlessly.

"Gavi has heard it? She has heard the words?"

Gavi said, yes. She'd not only heard the words, she'd translated them into Moss language, for fun.

The Phaina smiled. I know she had no mouth on her face, and I know there was no feature there to make a smile, but nonetheless, she smiled, and I felt it. "All that glitter down there," she whispered to us. "Doors. And outside the doors, the dogs of Earth become, for a time, the hounds of heaven."

It took me a moment. "Scramble? And Behemoth? Veegee and Titan? Wolf and Dapple?"

She barely whispered. "Oh, yes, Jewel. They and their children. I will loose the music, now. I will amplify it. Create the odors now, Scent Mistress, and the trees will spread them. Open the doors now, and the dogs will repay the Zhaar . . ."

Matty's Seventh had always been mixed up in my mind with the time she was sick and dying. It always made me cry, not only because of her death but because of the death she had read in that cavern, from the pitiful bones she found there. The Phaina took the album from my hand and started it at the second movement, that long, torturous climb into darkness, with death breathing up from the abyss, and the bridge as narrow as the beam of light that illuminated it for a single pair of feet to cross. It was all there in the music, all the horrid shadow, the pity, the sorrow, the need to know that kept her moving forward . . .

I heard the music through my skin, through my feet. I felt it flee away across the lands of Moss. Gavi, at the organ, pressed and pulled, touching this button, that lever, her hands leaping from side to side, playing it like the instrument it was. I have no idea how Matty's work was amplified, for it sounded no louder than usual where we were, but each tree it touched repeated it at that same volume, at the same scent, and the tree after that, over and over, so that it did not diminish with distance or fade into silence, and time was banished, for the note where we stood was simultaneous with the note miles to the north. All the embattled on Moss lay in the palm of the music: Zhaar, Orskimi, Derac, human, all of us surrounded by the sound, and the scent evoked visions that went with it. We could see no enemies but the darkness, we could invoke no help but the beams of light that reached out like the tentative touch of a spider's leg setting a web that would hold all this marvel together. I smelled the odor language, too, time suspended and simultaneous, so that odor and vision and music lay together, ply on ply on ply, each layer making the whole more potent.

Below us, the glittering doors opened to loose the hounds of heaven, as the Phaina had named them. I expected more than had left us, but what poured out was more than I could have dreamed.

The Phaina leaned down, and whispered to me, "I took them to a place where time slips by like a lightning stroke, Jewel. Here are the generations of Scramble's daughters, and granddaughters, and great-granddaughters. There are ten thousand of them. Ten thousand children and grandchildren and great-grandchildren."

The Zhaar below turned and hesitated, caught in the music and smells. I felt their hesitation on my skin. One here, one there stood high, mouths agape, ears twitching forward, searching for the source of what they saw, felt, smelled, heard. They threw back their heads and howled, to no avail. They could not hear their own voices. They could not smell their own odor. The only senses allowed in that place were those that Matty had woven as a requiem for the bones in that cavern, old people left in the chasm, old dogs left with them, to die there alone, their children far away . . .

The music reached the last cavern, and entered it. The light grew from a tiny stream to a great river that flowed over the old men and women working at the pictures on the wall, the old dogs lying beside them, their heads upon their paws, rousing sometimes to the sound of a dear voice, the touch of a familiar hand. We heard the sculptors' broken voices chanting each word of the story they were carving; we heard the dogs raise their voices in that same saga, a tale that stretched from generation to generation, from millenium to millenium, while oceans dried and wind scoured the bones of those who had fallen into darkness far from home. We saw and heard their creation of this memorial, a final monument to show that they had existed and waited here for those who had never returned.

The music ascended, fading notes, high and far as the call of a shorebird on a blue world they would never see again, higher and higher, beyond our hearing yet not beyond the hearing of the dogs then, or of the Zhaar now. The last note trembled into silence as we saw the carvers put down their tools and lie beside the dogs, their arms around their friends, both sinking into death in that last, dark place where no grass might cover them and no star shine upon them ever.

The sound faded. The odors were gone. The visions blinked out. Below us the Zhaar stood stunned, as if witless. I wondered if they had seen themselves in those old dogs, if they had felt their death and darkness and ultimate betrayal. Their very flesh had been shared with the dogs, their shape had been evolved by the dogs, and now that connection drew them in like a hook on an unbreakable line as the dogs circled them, herding them into an ever smaller compass. I could not turn my eyes from the spectacle below, but I heard low muttering growls behind me and felt a muzzle thrust into the hollow of my neck. Scramble and the others had come.

We crouched there together as the Zhaar moved like flotsam in an eddy, circling and circling, many of them trying desperately to change form, without success. They had used dog shape to escape their fate; only when they were dead would they take their own form again.

The circle slowed. The Zhaar were shoulder to shoulder below us, crowded tight, surrounded on all sides by dogs almost as large as they, and far more beautiful. I turned to Scramble and the others, dreading to find them old, but they were not yet aged, only mature, majestic in the way I had always dreamed they would be. They threw back their heads and joined the dogs below in howling a single question toward the place we sat.

"What shall be done with them, in return for what they did to our friends?"

The Phaina was no longer with us. We heard her voice above us. She stood on a higher ledge, where a group of the Phain were gathered, male and female, as a bench of judges might be gathered, to pass sentence after a trial.

"For all the crimes committed in ages gone, for which you had been already sentenced, you are expelled from the galaxy," said the Phain. Though the intention was clear enough in the tone of voice and the odors that floated down, my 'pute translated it for me.

"For the more recent crime of interfering in the development of other races, you are sentenced to lose all memory of the race you once were and to become, in actuality, the creatures you seem to be, as they once were, without the gift of words."

A few faint and plaintive voices were raised in protest, only to end, abruptly, as though cut off with a knife. At the center of the crowded mass of Zhaar, a door opened in the mosses they were treading, flat, barely shining, like the surface of a shallow pool or a sheen of rain on a hard surface. The surrounding dogs pressed in, the outer Zhaar pressed upon those at the center, and those at the center stepped onto the shining surface and vanished. Those at the outer edge could not see what was happening. Few of those at the center even looked down. They flowed around, like crowded ice chunks in a whirlpool, circling and draining away, bit after bit until all had gone.

The Phain above us conferred with one another. The polished circle that had swallowed the Zhaar became a well of green fire, and into it the dogs plunged, eagerly but orderly, without crowding or pushing, swiftly leaping forward and down, and away.

Scramble didn't move. "Where?" I whispered.

"Home," she said.

"In Splendor?"

"Ess. Hemosh an Sammle laish."

Behemoth and Scramble's place. "Can I visit you there?"

"Oh, Ewel. Ai nee you, now. Ai ash Ain."

She needed me now, and she would ask the Phain. And what would the Phain reply?

The prominence that had raised us above the world began to retract. Scramble kissed me. She did not want to go without me, but the others were around her, urging her away. I hugged her once again, but we were level with the mosses, and she was abruptly gone into the well of fire. We were left alone. The sky above us was empty of ships. As we watched, the Hessing fleet lifted from the plateau.

"We will eat together," said the Phaina's 'pute. "It is necessary."

A table appeared from somewhere, along with people of various kinds who set it and brought the food. Wine was brought and poured—I say wine for that is the closest approximation we have to what we drank, though even the best wine would not be comparable. The Phaina sat with us, and so did several other of the Phain, male and female. We ate, Gainor, Gavi, and I, and Walking Sunshine poured the drink on its roots and seemed to enjoy the taste. There were many courses, each a tiny serving of something variously wonderful. We ate slowly, but eventually the last taste was gone, and one of the Phain said something, which the Phaina translated.

"He wishes to know if you have any questions."

Gainor was looking at me. So was Gavi. Oh, I had so many questions!

"The Phaina told us the Zhaar used dog flesh upon themselves. Why then were they convicted of having interfered with them?"

The Phaina nodded. "You misheard, Jewel. It was the dogs' friends who were interfered with. It was your people the Zhaar changed."

"But you said, we humans were only speeded up in walking, speeded up in talking . . ."

"If that had been all, it would not have mattered greatly. But that was not all."

"What?" grunted Gainor. "What did they do?"

"Your ancestors were communal creatures, living in mutual support, possessing the dalongar all those born into a world owe to all others born in that world as kindred creatures—creatures of that world. We have a planet occupied by a race of ape creatures from your world. We rescued them long, long ago, for there were few of them left. We preserved them, as we have preserved many thousands of worlds and creatures. They have dalongar. We said, oh, it was a pity that race had it, and you had not. We judged you as not having had it, never having had it.

"But then we spoke to the Zhaar and learned it had been yours all along until the Zhaar took it from you. They took it from you and in its stead they gave you Zhaar virtues, dog virtues: pride and packishness. Those are not faults among dogs, who have no hands, who had no language, who needed pride of leadership and packish order in order to survive. This is a grievous harm to manipulating, speaking creatures, to allow the few to contend for pride of power while the many follow, packishly. You were made packish as the Zhaar themselves were packish.

"Though you did not thrive on Mars, the Zhaar continually took some back to Earth and brought others of you from Earth. Those who survived were the hardiest, the cleverest. Fifty thousand of your years ago, the Zhaar were almost discovered on Mars. They were afraid they might be found if they stayed where they were, so they left your system hastily, and on their way, they returned your changed ancestors of breeding age to Earth, along with all the younger dogs. This was not done out of kindness. The race of Zhaar had already lived for thousands of lifetimes. They foresaw a time they might enslave you again, both human and dog.

"From those returned to Earth, pride and packishness entered the genetic pool of humanity. You became followers of lead dogs, pack followers of power, and the small group of you spread across the face of the Earth. Over all those generations on Mars, the Zhaar had made you little copies of themselves.

"When the Zhaar abandoned the old on Mars, they committed a great cruelty. They abandoned those who had served them, left them behind on a moribund planet to suffer a slow death, and in this one instance, all the crimes of the Zhaar were exemplified. If they were to be punished as they merited, they could have been punished for this wrong alone. They were not moved to such cruelty by necessity. They did it simply because they did not care, and this is the great fault of packs. The pack is all. Those outside it are nothing but prey or impediments. The weak are nothing. The aged are nothing. Only the pack is important. Long ago I heard a human say, 'Me against my brothers. Me and my brothers against my cousins. Me and my brother and my cousins, against our tribe; our tribe against all other tribes; all our tribes against the world.' This is what Zhaar say, also.

"Packs do not care, and we dalongar-folk cannot get where we want to go in the company of those who do not care."

"You said . . . we're being rejudged?" I asked.

"On Earth, some of your people inherited the Zhaar characteristics; some of them have not. Even today, some of you have them, some of you do not. We have learned we cannot treat as one race a people who are, in fact, of at least two kinds."

I couldn't think. My mind was an absolute blank. One look at Gainor's face and I knew he was as adrift as I. Gavi was nodding slowly, as though she understood what had just happened, though I really understood only that the Zhaar were gone, banished, in the shape of the dogs they had wronged, and most of humanity was likely to follow them for crimes they had forced us to commit.

We were still a bit higher than the forest. We could see that the

Derac and Orskim had quit fighting both on the ground and in the sky. We could see that the Hessing ships had gone.

"How was all that stopped?" I asked, waving my hand to indicate the whole thing.

"The World did it," said Walking Sunshine. "So soon as the World knew who was to blame, the World fixed it. Pulled the warships down, sent the Hessing ships away. The World is following them now, to every place they go, for too much power is not good for creatures!"

"The World?" I said, stupidly.

"Walking Sunshine means Splendor," said the Phaina. "Moss is a part of Splendor. We have long had Guardian Houses on Tsaliphor, which sits at the edge of Splendor. We may walk through a door from Tsaliphor and enter here. We may walk through a door here, and enter my Guardian House on the other side. Many times over the last million years we have walked through a door in Splendor and set our feet upon an Earth prairie, or a jungle, or a savannah, and when we returned, we often brought creatures with us into Splendor that they might be saved. In Splendor we have:

> "*Elemental, monumental, fine phantasmic elephants;*
> *hairless hippopotami, snuggled close as spoons;*
> *riotous rhinoceri, roistering on grasslands;*
> *tiny, tender tarsiers, with eyes like moons . . .*"

She smiled again, that invisible smile. "Moreover, Splendor is aware of them, and they are aware of Splendor."

"But the Zhaar . . ." I cried. "They were there, but if Splendor is heaven, what were the Zhaar doing there?"

"Our Guardian Houses stand outside Splendor, on an edge, a boundary. There the Zhaar lived, along with others. From their place in that boundary, they were as far from Splendor as the next galaxy is to ours."

It was too much, I couldn't get my mind around it, and I wasn't alone. The Phaina saw our struggle. She said, "You're tired. You're unable to put your thoughts in order. Let it go for now. We will return you to Night Mountain. The World will remoss itself. Walking Sunshine will go among its willog constituency and assist in that renovation by slowly growing words to tell the World what has happened here. And when you are rested and ready to put all the pieces together, we will meet again."

"Just one question," I begged. "The Zhaar. They didn't fight. They just let themselves be rounded up. Why didn't they fight?"

"Because of what we said to them, what your mother said to them in music, what Gavi said in scent, what I said in words, what my people showed them in visions. Races can be judged in large part by their arts. We showed them what others thought of the way they had behaved, and they felt the emotion that depiction was designed to evoke. They had never felt it before, but now they felt shame. That was the last word, the last meaning they ever felt, the only one that will stay with them. All others have been taken from them."

She moved us, somehow, not just us, but all the people we'd started out with that morning, together with all our supplies and equipment, right back to where we'd started from that morning. We told one another it was an elder race thing. Probably something a Phaina could do without even thinking about it. I felt as though I'd spent at least ten days at hard labor since leaving. I felt as though the dogs had only been gone a few days, but I knew they might already have been gone for years.

Before falling into my bed I wondered briefly about Adam and Frank and Clare. I had not seen them. I wondered where and what they were. Then I thought of the Zhaar, facing an eternity with only one word left. To my amazement, I felt pity for them.

END OF A
DOG'S TALE

⦂ Out among the stars, upon planets, here and there in space, things happened:

On Earth, Evolun Moore held a meeting of several hundred of the major contributors and most dedicated workers of IGI-HFO. They were faced with a new challenge, a stir among the down-dwellers, who after several months of a petless world, were astir with resentment at having no more air or water than they had had previously.

"They say we misled them," cried Gabbern, who had been tireless in his work for IGI-HFO and had come to feel somewhat betrayed. "They're claiming we can't do what we promised. They say we have to get rid of some of these people coming in from off world, that there isn't room for all of them."

Evolun blanched. He was indebted to several members of the legislature for financing his organization. They did so in order to pay off outer worlds who depended on the continuance of the Law of Return. Any talk of limiting return would not go down well with any of them.

"Tell them to be patient," he said firmly. "Tell them to look at the average age of the people of Earth. It's gone well past seventy, and it's continuing to rise. The birthrate is way down; pretty soon people will start dying in droves. Besides, we're working on a scheme to open derelict towers to colonization by down-dwellers. Lots more air, more light, more everything . . ."

"Except power to run the lifts," cried another large donor. "They need . . . hell, WE need something more visible than mere promises. We need something dramatic, like knocking some of those exempt estate people off their high horses."

Evolun rose and strolled to the window. He had been saving this, just for such an occasion.

"There," he pointed. "The top three floors of that tower are owned by the Alred Family. Suppose we blow that away. Would that please you and your constituents?"

A moment's silence fell, while they looked at one another, then smiled, then laughed. Oh, yes, that would do it, for a while at least.

Smiling broadly, Evolun pressed the button on the detonator in his pocket.

⋮ Far out, toward the rim, three Orski ships fled toward an ancient redoubt, one seen by few ever, now known to none but those who were moving toward it. A pleasant enough world. Warm, with seas, with forests, with all the things that willing Orskim needed to build a new life, a new future. There a new temple would be built, and there the experience and memories of generations would once again begin to amass.

The captain of the lead ship was informed of a blip.

"Blip? What blip? There's nothing for light-years in any direction."

"The blip is a . . . well, it's kind of a squirm, sir. A wrinkle? Something odd. It started over there, you see, sir, on the screen, and it's propagating toward us. By the holy immortals, look at it come!"

The Orski ships were already moving at top speed. They were some distance from a nexus that would move them faster.

"What in the belly of a klonzi is that thing? And what is it doing?"

"It seems to be gulping, sir. Gulping space, like it's eating it. I've never seen anything like it."

"Evasive action. Can we avoid it by evasive action?"

It was the last question any of them asked. By the time the squirming brightness turned itself inside out and disappeared, the Orski ships were only dust, glinting in the light of distant stars. If one had wanted to obtain the Zhaar technology that had been carried on those Orski ships, it would have been necessary to reassemble it, atom by atom.

∴ On Earth, in the headquarters of the Hessing-Hargess empire, hundreds of district managers occupied the top several floors of the Great Tower of Industry. It was proving to be one of those mornings when nothing seemed to go right.

"What do you mean it burned?" cried a middle-aged manager into his far-link. "It couldn't burn. It was fireproof!"

"What do you mean it broke?" cried another. "They're indestructible!"

"Lost the contract!" boomed a third. "How in hell could you have lost the contract?"

"Send a ship," said another, in the tone of one who is never disobeyed. Then, "What do you mean, you don't have a ship? Grounded? On whose authority? Well, then, get one from Patfer IV, they have extras. Planet quake? I hadn't heard about a planet quake!"

Over lunch, this director talked to that director. After lunch, several directors went to see the general managers. Late in the afternoon, the general managers called upon the Vice President in Charge of Whatever.

As the VPCW read the documents placed before him, he turned very pale. "How could this have happened all at once?" he asked. "There's no power in the galaxy that could have done this all at once."

That night, at dinner, Dame Cecelia was surprised to see her husband look up from his sheaf of papers, and cry, "My God, Cece. We're ruined."

⋮ On Moss, the day after the battle, the PPI installation and the ESC bubble were moved out of the cavern, back onto the plateau, where they would be used as the official site of the IC inquiry into the future fate of Moss. Of course, such an inquiry was both useless and pretentious, as we all knew, including the IC, but the rules required everyone to go through the motions. The Tharstian Marshal had returned with several IC battleships, which were left circling in orbit, just in case some other race should start an unpleasantness. The Derac, who had suffered almost total losses during the fray, were now represented by a creature named Gahcha, who took some time to explain to the IC Marshal that females from any other race were of no interest to the Derac as females from his own race were now growing up with their brains intact. Gainor and I—and the Tharstians—believed we knew what this was about, but I don't think anyone else had a clue.

While the assembly waited for the members of the Hessing-Hargess delegation, who were unaccountably delayed, both the Day and Night Mountain tribes gave Walky a petition to be presented to the World. They asked to be allowed to remain upon the plateaus, except for an occasional journey between the plateaus for wife-seeking and a few trips a year into the forest to harvest thread, which they would do slowly and quietly, with care that human busyness would not disrupt the quiet enjoyment of the World by its parts. Walky told them they would receive an answer in due course. When I asked him how long due course was likely to be, he said a year or so, and the World said they could stay until the World made up its mind.

During all this, Paul continued to define all the ramifications and pontifications that linguists love and no one else pays any attention to. The actual language was by then well understood by those who needed to communicate in it, and the ESC techs had already combined a lingui-pute and an odor organ to get a translating device that worked quite well, though it was still far too bulky for personal use.

Recently I had seen Gavi in the constant company of Duras Drom, a completely healed Duras Drom who had lost all signs of having been addicted to redmoss. If the World let the humans stay, which it well might do, there was no reason PPI would not let Duras stay on Moss, and certainly there would always be much for a scent mistress to accomplish, beginning, perhaps, with assuring that she and Duras Drom would love one another forever.

Several days in succession, Gainor and I went for walks together, usually with Walky as our guide, while Gainor brought us up to date on the news from Earth and elsewhere. That was how we learned that the headquarters of IGI-HFO had blown up during a leadership meeting convened to consider what they were going to do next. Several prominent advocates of the Law of Return had been present at the time of the explosion, and a number of others had since died of mysterious diseases.

"Oh, and by the way," Gainor said. "The first concs have turned up on two more commercial planets of ours."

"You said they would, Gainor."

"I know. I should feel proud of being right. I'd rather have been wrong."

"I have met concs," said Walky. "When they were last being fed. They are very interesting for vegetables, though not very bright. Someone did not design them very well for conversation."

That made me envision Paul as he would no doubt be, living to a healthy old age on a world where there will soon be no children born at all; traveling to human worlds where children would soon be so scarce that every single one would be treasured, where no one could be spared to be returned anywhere. I thought of a world of derelict towers, slowly falling into ruin, grown over with vines and alive with birds. I thought of forty acres of trees shedding their seeds over a world that welcomed them.

I asked, "So, has anyone found out if the Orskimi . . ."

Gainor interrupted, "Oh, speaking of Orskimi, I forgot to tell you! A flotilla of Orski ships was destroyed in a remote area toward the rim. The ships were carrying their entire leadership and the only recorded history of their race."

"You mean . . . the memory people you told me about."

"That's right."

"The Derac destroyed them?" I asked.

Gainor looked puzzled. "As a matter of fact, no one knows who did it. Someone reported coming upon the wreckage, I don't know whom. The result has been, however, that the Orskimi have no people left who can remember anything farther back than their own childhood. What's left of the Orski race has retreated to E'Sharmifant and is said to be reexamining its racial purpose."

A day or two later, someone showed up from the Hessing-Hargess commercial empire, though only to say that the group had no further interest in the future of Moss. The Hessing-Hargesses were evidently in great trouble. On many planets, their businesses and warehouses had been burned. Elsewhere, properties had been condemned and offices searched to obtain proof that local officials had been bribed. Corrupt officials were under arrest and being asked to explain how vast sums of public moneys had ended up in Hessing-Hargess contracts, and how vast sums of HH money had ended up in the officials' pockets! Fleets of vehicles had been unaccountably wrecked, and all their mercenary starships were inoperable because of the destruction of various indestructible parts.

"Hessing-Hargess was one of the main supporters of the Law of Return," Gainor added.

"How could everything have happened at once, this way?" I asked, amazed. "All the threads unraveling, all at once. I can't understand it."

Walky commented, "It is perfectly understandable. The World wished to know who had committed the badness of the conflict, and you said it was the Orskimi. The World wanted to know who set the ships upon your head, and you said it was this Hessing agglomeration. The World suggested to all of Splendor that Orskimi be punished and Hessing be unagglomerated, so it was immediately done."

"Just like that?" asked Gainor with an expression of awe, snapping his fingers.

"Just like that," said Walky, snapping six sets of wooden fingers like a flock of castanets, all clicking off at once. "When a world speaks, smaller creatures do well to listen."

"But, how?" I asked. "I mean, it happened everywhere, Walky."

"Splendor touches everywhere," it said. "And I am now positive, absolutely sure, utterly convinced that Moss is indisputably, incontrovertibly, and beyond doubt part of Splendor. It was a revelation to me, a vision, a divination. I believe when Splendor warns a people, the people should listen. The Phaina believes she guards Splendor, and perhaps, in a sense, she does, but I sense Splendor has its own guardians as well. When they grow peevish, it is evident they can do large and final things."

After that, things went on for a few days quietly, without stress or anxiety. I confess to not thinking about anything much, just enjoying the tranquillity of each day while I waited for the thing that was going to happen. It would occur, I just didn't know when.

Then one night, while I was standing outside near the edge of the plateau, admiring the green moon, I felt a familiar warmth brush my fingers.

"Scramble," I whispered. "Oh, I've missed you."

"We know," said a lingui-pute.

The Phaina had returned. She murmured, "Now that the outstanding issues have been dealt with, we thought you might enjoy seeing . . . let us call it Tsaliphor II. You may enjoy a visit, a stay with your friends, going with them to see the fine phantasmic elephants and the wily alligators and all the other beasts in the worlds about them."

"Oh, I would," I cried. "But what about Adam and Frank and Clare . . ."

"Do not worry. They are quite content," she said. "They chose to stay, to be the same as those they had reared and trained."

It took, me a moment to understand her fully. "So," I said to Scramble, "it turned out they weren't just playing, after all."

"No," said Scramble, gazing at me from those deep, liquid eyes that seemed to see everything. There was gray around her muzzle. "An ai no you come. When ai nee you, you awwais come."

"You need me, Scramble? It seems to me you've done very well on your own."

"Na," she said. "Na frens lai Zhewel. Na frens na awais . . ." She sighed. "Na roo sisrs."

The Phaina whispered, "No friends who are not always jockeying for position in the pack. No true sisters. They miss humans, Jewel.

Scramble most of all. She is getting old, and she does not wish to die friendless."

I buried my face in Scramble's mane so she couldn't see I was crying. I hugged her. Oh, she was . . . a marvel. A wonder. A dear, dear otherness. An answer to the question of whether humans are any more important than any other creature. A rebuke to IGI-HFO, if any of them were left.

"You orghi' us?"

I didn't understand her. The lingui-pute murmured, "She wants to know if you forgive them."

"Forgive them for what?" I cried.

"For their having enslaved you, all those tens of thousands of years ago."

I laughed and cried and hugged my friend again. "It doesn't matter who enslaved whom, Scramble. What matters is we were together. What matters is all that time we kept one another from being entirely evil. So long as we cared for one another, we kept one another from turning into Zhaar."

With the Phaina as our guide, I knew I need take nothing with me, so I stood up, ready to go.

"One thing," said the Phaina. Her voice was rather remote, and even her 'pute sounded very slightly distant, as though reluctant to say the words. "Before you decide to make this journey, you may wish to know who placed the concs on Earth, and who is now seeing that they spread throughout all human planets . . ."

"Except the ark planets." I asked. "You do mean, except the ark planets.

I received her acknowledging nod in answer, and smiled to think of Mag safe with her cats, to think of all of them, safe with those they had loved and saved. The smile was a sincere one, for her, too.

"Never mind, Sannasee. I already know."